Wolves Of God

John Craig

Wolves Of God

© 2025 John Craig Burris

This novel is a work of fiction. Unless otherwise indicated, any names, persons, businesses, places, or organizations used in this book are either products of the author's imagination or are used fictitiously. Any resemblance to any business or organization or any person living or dead is therefore purely coincidental.

ISBN: 979-8-9993625-0-6

Cover Design & Layout by John Craig Burris

Printed In The United States

Published by Burrisaurus

www.johncraigauthor.com

Email: johncraigauthor@gmail.com

What is a lycanthrope in the eyes of God?

Robert R. McCammon

Chapter 1

October 2000
Stonelick, Ohio

The black wolf was too far from home. He had less than a mile to go, but that was too far. The forest glowed blue-white between the shadows, the light of the full moon still bright enough to paint the dying night in stark contrasts. Out of the forest, beyond the close-set branches that held the night beneath their boughs like clutching fingers, the first light of day broke the horizon.

Ian ran as fast as the forest allowed, stretching his powerful limbs to beat the dawn. As he hurtled a fallen log, he took no notice of the little possum huddled underneath. With daylight approaching, none of the woodland creatures concerned him. Getting home was all that mattered.

The forest thinned and leveled out for a stretch, allowing the wolf to accelerate, gaining momentum to climb the upgrade ahead. One more hill, then the going was level the rest of the way. He'd make it home if he kept up the pace. The forest ended at his back yard. He could change there and cross the yard with no fear of being seen. It wouldn't be the first time.

Idiot! You've been doing this for years now. You should never have to rush like this.

People had died in that time, some dear to him, some by his own hand, by his own teeth and claws, to put a finer point on it. That was the past. The guilt would always be with him. He accepted that, but he had a life again at last. He wasn't in control of the wolf. He *was* the wolf. Both his humanity and the wolf were 100% of who he was. He had love. He had a future. At least he dared to dream he had a future. To grow complacent now, to take everything for granted, was to risk it all.

Turner Jenkins grumbled under his breath as he stumbled through the brush to keep up with his brother-in-law. His mind was foggy from too many beers throughout the night, but his mouth was cottony from thirst and his back was stiff from a night spent in the blind. He had half a mind to kick Lester's ass right there.

"Say what, Turner?"

"I said if you weren't my brother-in-law I wouldn't be out here before dawn with a hangover."

"I ain't your momma, Turner. My job description don't include making sure you don't pass out drunk in the blind."

"That so? Hell, you have to *have* a job before you get a description."

"Don't start on me again. I told ya, Roger is getting me on down at the plant. All I gotta do is fill out an application. Nothin' but a formality. You think I like sleepin' on my sister's couch?"

"It's my couch too, Les."

"Whatever."

"Bow hunting. Fuck. You wouldn't know what to do with a bow if a ten point buck walked out of the brush with a bullseye on its ass."

"Like you're some expert. I keep tellin' ya-"

"Shush!" Turner held up a hand.

"I done told ya-"

"Quiet!"

"What?" Lester stood in an patch of moonlight at the crest of a rise, looking back at Turner.

"Oh, shit," Turner said. He dropped to one knee and slipped the bow and quiver off his shoulder. "It's heading this way, Les. Move."

"What?"

"Move! Get out of the way!" Turner didn't have time to explain. It was all he could do to nock an arrow into place with his shivering hands. He'd never trusted dogs, not since a vicious stray chased him up a tree when he was a fat little ten-year old. The thing he'd glimpsed bolting through the clearing at the bottom of the hill looked like the dog from Hell.

"What's gotten into-"

Lester turned.

The black wolf crested the hill then skidded to a halt, his claws digging through the thick layer of leaf litter into the black soil beneath.

Before him in the dim half-light were two men. The closest one was small, skinny, and smelled of sweat, beer, and pot. The other was a big man with a grey goatee. He also smelled of pot, and of cheap beer. He was holding a compound bow, his arms trembling.

No sooner did the wolf take in these sights and smells than the big man let the arrow fly. It struck him just below the collarbone, punching through his torso, dislodging a trough of tissue as the point erupted from his back. The force of the projectile at such close range drove him backward down the slope. Ian tumbled head over heels until he slammed against the base of a tree, where he lie panting, blinded by white hot pain. He nearly blacked out and his humanity receded before the superior survival instincts of the wolf. He rolled over, ignoring the terrible pain, dug his claws into the earth, and prepared to spring.

"Shit!," Les yelled. "Shit! What was that?"

Turner shook his head. "A wolf!"

"A wolf? Are you out of your mind?"

"A big fuckin' wolf, but I got it."

"A wolf. Right." Lester said, his voice as shaky as Turner's knees. "Next thing, you'll be telling me it's the monster."

"Les-"

"Well, I'm not scared." Lester gulped and drew an oversized Bowie knife from the sheath on his hip. "I want to see it."

"Brother, you should be scared. I sure as hell am."

"You're scared?"

"Shitless. Let's get the hell out of here. Leave it. "

Lester ignored him and started down the hill, gripping the big knife in his right hand.

"Maybe it's already dead, Les."

"I want to see it."

"I don't. I never want to see it again."

"You're losing your nerve."

"Fuckin' A. And I don't mind sayin' so."

They'd both grown up around Stonelick. They'd heard the stories. Now here was the proof. There really was a monster in these woods.

"Let's say it is the monster," Lester said. "Some mutated stray or something. I'm gonna get us a trophy. Something people will believe."

"Les!"

"An ear oughta do."

The black wolf crouched, watching as the skinny man approached with a huge knife in his hand and a wild look in his eyes. He could smell the little man's fear, but he was coming nonetheless.

The wolf considered running the other way down the hill, but a thunderous bolt of pain from the shaft impaling him stopped him. He was fading fast and he knew it. He gave thought to giving up right there, to let his life end rather than taking another, but that was his humanity talking. The wolf would not let that happen. The wolf intended to fight for his life.

Turner stood with the bow in one hand, another steel-tipped arrow in the other, and watched as the thing shot from the thicket, a bristling black missile of hair, teeth, and claws. Turner stumbled back and fell, his legs tangled in the gnarled roots of an old tree. He landed hard on his back and the bow bounced out of his grasp into the brush. He sat up and looked just as the beast tore the throat from Lester's body with one great jerk. Blood splashed over the foliage and the forest floor, arterial spray spattering Turner's boots and legs, but he couldn't look away as Lester convulsed twice then went still. The beast raised it's gory muzzle and glared at Turner.

He got to his feet still holding the arrow in one hand. He pointed it at the beast, holding the arrow in front of him as if it were a talisman that might ward off evil. The beast growled at him and he lost what remained of his nerve. Talisman or not, he dropped the arrow and ran. He had no idea which direction led back to his truck or what he would do when he got there besides drive the hell away as fast as possible. He was too scared to think beyond his next step. As he stumbled, fell, then found his feet to run again, there was one absurd detail he couldn't get out of his mind. It was early morning and the light wasn't good, but he knew what he'd seen: an earring. In the mottled shadows of the forest, he'd seen with crystal clarity the glint of a silver earring imbedded in the flesh of the beast's left ear.

The black wolf stood over the ruined body of the skinny man. He watched as the bigger man stumbled away, screaming. His instinct told him to run the man down and tear him to pieces, but he didn't have strength for the pursuit. The rush of adrenaline that saved his life passed and he was left with nothing but the agony of his terribly wounded body.

He stepped over the dead man and made the top of the hill before his front legs buckled under him and he pitched forward, his bloody muzzle plowing a wet furrow in the loam. The shaft of the arrow dug into his chest and twisted, sending a sizzling bolt of pain through his body. The wolf screamed and rolled onto his side, white bursts of light flashing before his eyes in synchrony with each tortured breath he managed.

As the morning light grew stronger, the wolf receded and Ian's human reasoning regained control. The wolf nature might have withdrawn, but the awful wound remained. Ian resisted the transformation that came wth the dawn. He knew his only chance to make it home was to remain a wolf, but what chance he had was fading fast.

Maybe this is how it ends.

He'd killed after all, with an efficient savagery that would make his would-be master proud. It would be a fitting end. Still, he staggered for another thirty feet before collapsing. He whined and closed his eyes. His sharp ears detected the trickle of his own blood as it left his body and soaked the crushed leaves and broken twigs beneath him.

People will come, Ian knew. The sun was rising. He didn't have the strength to resist the transformation any longer. They'll come for the body of his slaughtered victim and they'll find him. They'll see what he had done.

So be it. Let them.

"Hello?" Melinda Kearsey sighed. When the phone rang at this time of the morning it was always for Matthew.

"Hi, Mel," Ricky Thorogood said. "Can I speak with Matt?"

"Can it wait?" she said. "He's having his corn flakes. You know how he hates having his corn flakes interrupted." Her husband sat in the breakfast nook behind her. A carton of eggs and a pack of maple bacon sat on the counter. She meant to have a real breakfast today, even if all Matthew wanted was his traditional bowl of corn flakes. He was a creature of habit but that didn't mean she had to be.

"I'm afraid not. I need to speak with him."

"All right." Melinda sighed and handed the phone to her husband.

Matthew Kearsey wiped his mouth with the folded napkin next to his bowl. "Yeah, Ricky?"

"Mornin', Matt. I'm sorry. I know you had plans for today."

"What is it?"

"Lester Booth is dead."

"What?"

"Lester's dead. Turner Jenkins is here."

"How?" Matt kneaded his forehead with his free hand. It was too early for this.

Ricky cleared his throat. "Turner says it was a wolf."

Matt could hear Turner bellowing from behind Ricky. "Biggest fucking bastard you ever saw!"

"A wolf?"

"That's what he says."

Turner's slurred voice grew louder. "Just about took his head off!"

"Has he been drinking?" Matt said.

"Well, it is Turner," said Ricky.

"Shit," said Matt.

"A wolf," Ricky said again. "A goddamn wolf."

"Yeah." He didn't like where this was headed. "I'll be there in a few."

The sheriff hung up the phone and took a deep breath.

"I guess you won't be going with me to the antique mall this morning," Melinda said. She stood in the kitchen doorway.

"I guess not, Honey. You know how it is."

"Yes. I do."

A wolf, Matt thought. Of course that was crazy, but he hadn't told anyone about the beast he encountered in the cemetery last summer. No one would believe him anyway unless they'd been here ten, no, eleven years ago. Ricky was. The kid had come a long way since then. The man, he corrected himself again. The man had come a long way since those strange, dark days.

The sheriff opened the cabinet and got out one of the wide mouthed plastic tumblers. He upended the cereal, poured it in, then set the bowl and spoon in the sink. "I'm taking this on the road, dammit." He stopped on his way out of the room to give his wife a kiss. "I love you," he said.

"I love you, too. See you for lunch, maybe?"

"Probably shouldn't count on it."

"Bonnie?"

"Yes, Matt? I mean, Sheriff?" Her voice was small, quivering like a shy child on the first day of school. She clutched a soggy handkerchief.

"Matt is just fine," the sheriff said. "We've known each other since fourth grade, right?"

Bonnie Jenkins nodded. Her husband patted her shoulder.

"I need you to stay here with Deputy Thorogood."

"But Les is my brother."

"I know," he said. Her protest was weak, more out of obligation than anything else. Matt could tell she really didn't want to see what lie downhill. He couldn't blame her. He didn't want to see it either, but it was his job. "All the more reason." He gestured for Ricky then looked at Turner Jenkins. The big man looked like he was about to throw up. "Turner?"

"Yeah?"

"You need to show me where he is."

"Uh, all right." He let go of his wife and led the way. The sheriff followed. When they started downhill, Turner stopped and pointed. He gulped hard. "About twenty feet or so down. I ain't goin' no closer."

"OK. Go back up and wait with Bonnie. Send the deputy down."

Matt looked around at the forest while the shaking man trudged back uphill. It was quiet. Peaceful. Cool. Some might even say it was cold even though the sun was climbing higher in the sky by the minute. He always loved mornings like this, just before things turned toward winter. Halloween, Thanksgiving, Christmas, then this year was a wrap.

"You all right, Matt?" Ricky Thorogood approached the sheriff.

"Yeah. God, what a morning. Too beautiful to deal with this shit."

The deputy nodded.

"Ricky, what do you make of Turner's story? This wolf business?"

"There's an unpleasant ring to it." He put his hands in the pockets of his jacket and shrugged.

"Yeah. There is. Well, let's get this over with."

They took half a dozen short steps downhill before they saw the blood. It was spattered all over the undergrowth, dark red on green. For one absurd second, Sheriff Kearsey thought of Christmas again and felt his cornflakes rise in his throat. Turner's discarded arrow lay in the dirt.

A few more steps brought them to the body. Lester Booth lie with his face to the sky, eyes open but unseeing like the glass eyes in a mounted deer head. Most of the flesh, muscle, and tendons in his neck was gone, exposing his vertebrae to the air. They resembled nothing so much as a blood smeared string of oversized popcorn. The sheriff walked away from the body and said hello to his cornflakes.

"Matt?" Ricky said.

The sheriff waved at him. "Give me a minute," he croaked. *Christ, this is worse...worse than...* He stopped the thought right there. He didn't want to think it, much less say it in front of Ricky. While he stayed bent over, hands on knees, waiting for the nausea to pass, he was aware that the deputy was moving through the brush. A moment later, Ricky spoke.

"Matt? You need to see this."

The sheriff stood and wiped his mouth with the back of his hand. He avoided looking at the mangled body of Lester Booth, but it was there on the periphery of his vision and the blood was everywhere.

"Look," Deputy Thorogood said. There was a trail of blood, smears, and spatters leading away from the body. The two men followed the blood until almost stumbling over the pale shape slumped in the thick undergrowth.

"Oh, shit," the sheriff said.

The man was on his side, a bloody, steel-tipped arrow protruding from just below the shoulder blade. The chest still rose and fell, but the breathing was labored and unsteady.

I hit it dead nuts center! Turner Jenkins words shouted over the phone came back to him. "What did you do, Turner?" *I hit that monster dead nuts center!*

While the sheriff stood shaking his head, Ricky Thorogood walked around to get a look at the man's face. He knelt, got a good look, then punched the button on his radio to call for an ambulance. "Matt?" He looked back up at the sheriff. "It's Ian Murphy."

Chapter 2

June 1989

Stonelick, Ohio

"What's up, brother?" Chevy Patella sat behind the wheel of his Camaro in Ian's driveway, a cold bottle of Vernors in hand. He spun the dial of his car stereo with his free hand.

"If you wait a few seconds you might find a song you like." Ian Murphy folded his 6' 4" frame to fit into the front seat of the low slung car.

"Wait!" Chevy picked up the unopened bottle of Vernors on the passenger seat. "This one's for you. You almost sat on it."

"Thanks," Ian said. He took the bottle and leaned forward to use the door latch to pop the cap off the bottle. When he sat back he held up his long brown pony tail so it would fall over the back seat.

"I thought you were gonna ditch that hippie tail after graduation?"

"Blow me." Ian smiled out of the corner of his mouth.

"OK. What do I care if my best friend looks like a girl?"

"Brother, if I look like a girl to you, you've got problems."

"Hey, you wish you'd dated some of the babes I've been out with."

"Like who? Michelle Farquar?"

"I never dated her. She just, you know, had the hots for me."

"You went out with her."

"Twice. We never went past second base, anyway. Hey, are you gonna sit there with the door open or are we gonna hit the road?"

Ian shut the door. Chevy had settled for the moment on a station playing Skynyrd. Ronnie Van Zant was drawing out the word 'change' into a multisyllabic mutation, getting ready to let the Free Bird fly.

The wind ruffled Chevy's curly red hair as he backed onto Stonelick Road and accelerated.

Ian took a drink. He'd hung the nickname 'Chevy' on his new friend shortly after the Patellas took over the dairy farm across the road when both boys were in the fourth grade. Because he loved Chevrolets, the skinny boy took to the label immediately. He also hated his given name of Charles. To him, anything was an improvement and the nickname came with an instant identity. By the time they were in middle school, even his teachers called him Chevy. Now they were both freshly-minted graduates of Stonelick High School.

A mile down the road, Ian grew tired of hearing "Free Bird" for the nine-thousandth time and reached for the dial.

"Hey!" Chevy said, but he was sick of the song himself so he didn't protest further. "I have an idea." He reached behind the passenger seat without taking his eyes off the road and pulled out a case of cassettes. A moment later he popped in AC/DC. At the first chords of "Highway To Hell," he cranked the volume to near ear-bleed level.

"You gotta play that now?" Ian shouted. "We are going to church."

"You gotta sin to get saved, right?"

Ian laughed and took another swig from his bottle. He turned toward the window and smiled. The warm summer air felt good on his face.

"Are you nervous?" Chevy turned the music down to a level that allowed for conversation but still rocked. "About going back?"

"A little."

"It's been a long time."

"Six months."

"Kelly's going to be there. At least, that's what she told my sister."

"When?"

"A little while ago. She called to see if Jennie was coming."

"How's she doing? Your sister, that is."

"Still sick, I guess, but I think she just wanted to stay home and talk to some boy on the phone."

"And so it begins," Ian said.

Chevy shook his head. "I don't know what you see in Kelly, man. She's my cousin, but I'm not blind. Kell's a babe, for sure, but I don't know why you put up with her shit."

"I love her." Ian shrugged. "When she's ready, I'll be there for her. She knows that."

"Face it, brother, you've been friend-zoned. Once you're there, you're doomed."

It was Ian's turn to shake his head. They'd had this conversation before. Kelly Shepherd was the unrequited love of Ian's young life. She was going on seventeen, a petite, curvaceous brunette with big, dark eyes, a throaty purr of a voice, and a smile that could buckle a grown man's knees. She seemed to know the effect she had on men of any age and she wasn't above using that to her advantage, but Ian swore there was more to her than that. "You just don't know her like I do," he said.

"Brother, we were kids together. People have always felt sorry for her because her parents were killed when she was a baby. She uses that."

"That's a horrible thing to say. She's your family. Do you even remember your aunt and uncle?"

"No, I don't." Chevy sighed. "I just hate to see her stringing you along. How many guys has she been through while you've been waiting for your chance?"

"I don't care. She knows no one will ever love her like I do, and how many boyfriends she's had doesn't matter because I'll be the last one."

"You're a hopeless romantic, brother."

"Romantic, yes. Hopeless, no." Ian put the bottle of soda between his legs, took off his glasses, and used the tail of his shirt to wipe them. "Hope is all I've got left." He said the last part so low Chevy could barely hear him.

They reached the intersection in the middle of Stonelick, the small town that had seemed so large when they were younger. To their left was a hardware store, a grocery, and a coffee shop. On the other side of the street, a building that was once an old saw mill but now housed a bar and restaurant occupied half the block. The local rumor was that the building was haunted, a remnant of some nasty goings on in the early twentieth century when what was now Main Street had been the outskirts of town. Ian thought nothing of the local legend, but he reminded his heavy-footed friend to watch his speed through town. Everyone knew you didn't speed through Stonelick. Once you passed the diner on the other side of town you could open it up, but until then you risked a ticket if you exceeded the posted limit.

"Ian?" Chevy said when he passed the old Presbyterian church and turned left on Hutchison Road to head out of the town proper.

"Yeah?"

"Do you still believe in God?" The rest of the question-"after what happened to your mother"-hung in the air, unspoken.

Ian ran his tongue over his teeth as he looked out the window. "I want to," he said, "but it still doesn't make any sense."

"Cancer's a bitch, brother."

"It is, but...Mom still believed, right up to the end. It wasn't like it was a crutch or something. She was confident, Chev. She was sure."

"But you're not?"

Ian kept looking out the window. "No. I'm not."

"So why go back?"

"It's hard to explain. I feel like I have unfinished business there. Mom always insisted God had some kind of plan for my life."

"Hard to believe that when you don't believe in god."

"Yeah. I mean, I don't rule out the possibility, but..."

They topped a hill and drove past Stonelick High School. There, near the south end of the one floor building, Ian had experienced his first real kiss, even got yelled at by his uptight biology teacher. He smiled at the memory though he always wondered why the teacher yelled at him alone and not also at his girlfriend. There was comfort in the memory, in the warm nostalgia for a simpler time when he didn't have to wrestle with weighty issues such as the existence of god and his mother dying of cancer. His smile turned down at the thought that the latter might be directly related to the former.

"I guess I'm looking for some kind of closure. I don't want to still be trying to figure this out twenty years from now." He took a long swallow from his soda, draining the last of the Vernors, focusing on the pleasant, gingery tingle. "So how about you? Why do you still go?"

"Girls."

"Girls?" Ian chuckled.

"Yep. Some real hotties have come along these last six months."

"That's it?"

Chevy nodded. "I met Lisa Brandly there. That worked out nice."

"She dumped you after what? Two months?"

"Two months is better than nothing, pal."

"If you say so. But seriously, do you still believe like we did when we were kids?"

Chevy grinned and shook his head.

"Come on, man. You asked me. Now I'm asking you. Do you?"

"Maybe, but speaking in tongues, dancing in the spirit? All that holy roller stuff spooks me out. Can you see yourself doing that?"

"I suppose it depends," Ian said, "but these days I think if someone tried to 'lay hands' on me I'd feel like punching them in the mouth."

Owensville, Ohio

Lighthouse Pentecostal Church sat outside Owensville, a small town fifteen minutes from Stonelick. One four way intersection marked the middle of town, with two traffic lights and a smattering of Mom & Pop shops along the main route through the village. The county fairground was the only thing that made Owensville a destination, primarily for the annual fair but also for tractor pulls and a monthly demolition derby.

The church was an unadorned, whitewashed rectangle half a mile outside the town proper on US Route 50. In a good year when the spring rains were plentiful, the corn bordering the church on three sides grew higher than a tall man's head. The yard was seeded with Kentucky bluegrass, manicured and watered to maintain its lush appearance. Only the gravel parking lot broke up the carpet of green. It was revival week, though, and a canvas tent one-hundred feet long and fifty feet wide dominated the lawn.

Every summer the tent was erected for a week of meetings intended to stoke the fires of the faithful. The tradition dated back over a century. Elder members of the congregation still recalled revivals led by Billy Sunday, Oral Roberts, and others from the heyday of the itinerant evangelist.

Anachronistic as it now seemed to the younger members of the church, the tradition continued.

The gravel crunched and popped under the wheels of Chevy's Camaro as he eased it to a stop between a shiny new pickup and a red-primered El Camino. The parking lot was over half full and filling up, the fine dust stirred up by the influx of vehicles fogging the warm evening air.

It was Wednesday night, the third night of revival. The meeting was due to start in twenty minutes. Several men in sweat-dampened short sleeves were setting up rows of folding chairs outside the tent in anticipation of an overflow crowd.

"Ready, brother?" Chevy shut off the engine and checked his hair in the rear view mirror.

"Ready as I'll ever be."

Ian had hoped to slip into the tent without attracting attention. Every time he came to church he had to run a gauntlet of kindly older ladies who would take his hand and tell him how nice it was to see him. He felt it had more to do with their high regard for his mother than it did with him. He knew they meant well so he just smiled until he reached a seat.

When they slipped into a row of folding chairs, Chevy leaned toward him and grinned. "I see you're still a big hit with the ladies."

"Yeah. Cute."

"I mean it, brother. It's kinda creepy."

"Creepy?"

"Think about it, man. Most of 'em haven't had their ticket punched in decades, but if they can't have you, the next best thing is to score points for their granddaughters."

"What?"

"They're living vicariously, man. If they can't have you, maybe little Suzy can."

"You're sick!" Ian pushed Chevy but they both smiled.

"What else could it be, man? They dig you."

"Blow me, you trouser stain," Ian said out of the corner of his mouth.

"In your dreams."

"My nightmares, you big-"

Ian stopped when he felt a hand on his shoulder. He grimaced, expecting to be chided by one of those women, but when he turned around he found Kelly Shepherd standing in the row behind him.

"Wanna walk with me outside for a few minutes," she said.

"Sure, Kell." He turned to Chevy. "Hold my seat, will ya?"

"You got it, but if the girl of my dreams walks in, you're on your own. Hi, Cuz."

"How's the family, Chev?"

"Better. Mom stayed home with Jenny. And you know Dad. He hates these tent revivals."

"Tell them I said hello. Tell Jen I'll call her tomorrow."

Ian followed Kelly out of the tent. When they were outside, he fell into place beside her. "You've been hanging out with Jenny a lot, huh?"

"Yeah. She reminds me of myself when I was twelve. Lo, so many years ago." Kelly laughed, a husky giggle that always delighted Ian. " You're an only child. Do you ever wish you had a little brother?"

"Sure."

"She's like a little sister. I can be a kid again when I'm around her."

"Not like when you're with what's his face?"

"Ricky."

"Ricky. Rocky. Whatever. Your flavor of the month."

"Shut up!" Kelly punched Ian in the shoulder. She used just enough force for him to know she wasn't being entirely playful. "That's not what I mean. I just wish there was someone older around when I was her age, like an older sister. They could have put me wise to a few things."

It sounded to Ian like he was right on target with his sarcastic jibe about Ricky but he let it go and took another tack. "So how are things now?"

Kelly shook her head. "I can't talk about it."

"You brought it up."

"Now I'm dropping it. Can we just walk for a few minutes?"

"Sure."

Ian walked with her past the edge of the tent. The tall stalks of corn loomed in front of them like a wall. Kelly turned there and Ian turned with her. A minute later it was Kelly who broke the silence.

"How are you?" she said. "You told me you didn't know if you could ever come back here."

"I did, but here I am."

"And?"

"It's weird, but it's not so bad out here in the tent. Inside...I don't know if I could handle that. It is strange seeing all those faces again." Ian smiled. "I've seen Verna quite a bit. I've seen Pastor James a few times. Chuck Holmwood came by a while back. Dad helped him with his car, but I think it was just an excuse to check up on us."

Kelly nodded.

"People came over after Mom died, but it tailed off fast. I gotta admit, I was kind of relieved."

"How about your dad?"

"He was too. He didn't say so, but I could tell."

"What about Verna? Does she still come around?"

"Yeah, but it's different with her. She was Mom's best friend. She's like family."

Kelly kicked at an errant corn stalk in the grass. "I'm sorry I wasn't home when you called last night. I know I said I'd be there but-"

"Ricky."

"That's not-"

"Where is he? I thought you had him going to church, what with you two all hot and heavy."

Kelly shook her head. "I don't know about Ricky. He says he loves me and maybe he does, but things are kind of..." She trailed off and walked several steps ahead. "You don't want to hear this."

"Hey. I don't know about him, but you know about me. You know I love you, Kell."

"Don't say that, Ian. I know you mean it, but...not now."

"Well, it's true. I have for a long time."

"I know. You tell me all the time, and you send me cards and flowers and gifts."

"Do you want me to stop?"

"No. I don't."

"So what do I do? We're not just friends and you know it."

"I'm not sure what we are, Ian. We're..." She left the rest unsaid as she walked another few steps ahead. "I didn't want tonight to go like this."

"Neither did I," Ian said. He walked up behind her, started to put his hands on her shoulders but put them in his pockets instead.

"I'm going to stay out here a little while longer," Kelly said. She didn't turn around and she wiped her eyes and nose with the back of her hand. "You'd better go back in. They're about to start."

The worship band started into "Victory In Jesus." Ian slipped into the tent as the congregation rose to their feet. He glanced at Chevy then looked over his shoulder. Kelly was outside the tent, her arms folded, where he had left her close to the corn.

"Looks like that could have gone better," Chevy said.

"You might be right, Chev. Maybe I should give up on her. I can't take much more of this."

"You wanna go, brother? Maybe this wasn't a good idea."

Ian shook his head. "I've gotta deal with it sooner or later."

The air under the tent was warm and humid, the smell of fresh-cut grass giving way to the odor of perspiration. Two men in the first row left their seats to turn on oversized fans positioned in each of the front corners of the tent. The fans did little more than move the air around.

As the band played, Ian felt bitterness rising from the pit of his stomach to his chest. The memory of a circle of congregants gathering around his mother, hands held out to her, praying in tongues, was vivid. Their prayers were futile. Their faith was useless. Rose Murphy still died. "Maybe this *was* a bad idea," Ian grumbled. He was about to bolt when hands wrapped around him.

"Good to see ya, hon," Verna Cooper said in her musical Great Lakes accent. "I hate to be late but what are you gonna do?"

She was short and broad-she preferred the term 'sturdy'-and the top of her head fell well short of the neckline of Ian's black T-shirt. She had to crane her neck to smile up at him.

"Hi, Verna. I was about to leave." He shrugged. "I don't know if I'm ready for this."

She pulled him into a tighter hug. "I know it's hard, but you're here. Stay. Please."

Ian hugged Verna back. He bent one knee to rest his chin on top of her head. He could hear her praying for him, but both the music and her prayers seemed far away. He was drifting, the music fading into background noise, his mind conjuring images from his recent past; his mother smiling and healthy; Kelly walking away, her dark hair falling over her shoulders and almost reaching the small of her back; his mother in the hospital, pale and shrunken, her death only days away; Chevy snoring in one of the hammocks they'd strung up in the big tree by the creek; Kelly walking away again but this time with Ricky, looking at Ian over her shoulder, her sad eyes telling him not to give up hope; his mother's eyes hollow, closed forever.

"You're going to be OK, Ian." Verna's voice called him back. "You are." She let go and crossed the aisle, arranged her purse and her light jacket on a seat, then joined in with the singing.

Somehow Verna always made things better, Ian thought. He still had questions that wouldn't go away, but for the moment he didn't need answers.

The band played on through three more songs. Shouts of 'amen,' 'hallelujah,' and assorted other proclamations rang out from all corners of the tent. Across the aisle, Verna was hopping from foot to foot, her left arm waving in the air. From her mouth issued a stream of syllables for which there was no earthly translation. Throughout the congregation, dozens of others prayed aloud in their own version of Verna's ecstatic prayer language.

As the band tore into a rousing, honky tonk version of "Onward Christian Soldiers," Ian stood with his hands at his side, but he tapped his foot to the music and felt the bitterness that had plagued him before Verna's arrival recede. A coldness settled in its place. He glanced over at Verna, wishing she would work her magic again and pray this new dread away, but she was immersed in the worship experience.

Pastor Duncan James, a small man, stood on the raised wooden platform, hands in the air, eyes closed. Next to him stood a tall, silver-haired man in a pressed white suit. Ian couldn't take his eyes off the bigger man and after several seconds he realized the man was staring back at him with big, blue-gray eyes. A wave emanated from him, rolling over the audience and washing over Ian, forcing him to take a step back to keep from falling.

"Hey, big guy," Chevy said. "You all right?"

"Yeah." He forced himself to look at his friend. "I just, uh, lost my balance for a second."

"Pretty intense dude, huh?"

Ian looked back at the tall man. He was looking down now, eyes closed.

"Yeah. Intense."

Ian tried to tell himself it was just his imagination, but the wave, the power, was real. The look he'd seen in the man's eyes was real. He wondered if it was the same look a predator gave to cornered prey, and if in its final moments the prey yielded to their fate and accepted the inevitable. *Where did that thought come from?*

The band finished playing but the congregation continued to worship. Pastor James stepped to the microphone mounted on the podium. "What a beautiful night The Lord has made."

"Amen!"

"Praise Him!"

Beads of sweat dotted the pastor's broad forehead. He paused to wipe his face with a handkerchief. "Those of you who've been with us the last two nights have heard the story of when Brother Stubbs and I first met, but I failed to mention my amazement at how he has managed to stay so well preserved." He turned and looked at the tall man. "I've lost half my hair and gained fifty pounds. You've barely aged at all. How do you do it, brother?"

The tall man laughed and wagged a long finger at the pastor. "If you only knew the half of it. I'm no spring chicken." He was far from the microphone but his voice carried over the tent.

"I'll speak with Peter later about how he has managed to defy the calendar, but for now, I'll simply introduce you again to my friend and fellow servant of the Lord Jesus Christ, Peter Stubbs."

The congregation offered warm applause. Peter Stubbs smiled, took the diminutive pastor's hand in his massive right paw, and gave it a vigorous shake. When he stepped up to the podium, Ian was struck by the man's physical presence. He hadn't yet spoken a word to the crowd but it was clear he had their full attention. Ian looked around. All eyes were on the big man except for Kelly's. She'd joined her friends in the church youth group, but while the rest of them were standing at attention, she remained seated, one leg crossed over the other, her eyes down.

Stubbs motioned for the congregation to be seated and stood with one hand in the pocket of his smooth, white pants. With the other hand, he cupped his chin, his thick eyebrows crinkling where they almost met over his nose, then he brought the hand down on the podium. The span of his fingers seemed to cover half of the flat wooden surface.

"What a wonderful band you are blessed with. 'Onward Christian Soldiers,' indeed." Stubbs' voice was a deep, rich baritone. Amplified by the speakers mounted on poles to each side of the makeshift pulpit, there was no escaping it anywhere within the vicinity of the tent, much less inside it. "That song was written by a brother named Baring-Gould. As I understand it, he was a rather eccentric fellow, but I like to think of us as kindred spirits. His words have stood the test of time.

"Open your Bibles, please, to the book of Acts, chapter twenty." He produced a big, leather-bound Bible and waved it over his head. "You do have your Bibles, don't you? I fail to understand this new generation of churches were The Word Of God is treated as an accessory. I don't use slides. I have no need of commentaries. The Word itself is sufficient. Can I have an amen?"

A chorus of "amens" answered, followed by the rustling of pages.

"Verse 28," Stubbs recited from memory, the huge Bible still held in one hand. " 'Take heed unto yourselves, and to all the flock over which The Holy Ghost hath made you overseers, to feed the church of God, which He hath purchased with His own blood.' "

Stubbs walked away from the podium, beyond the reach of the microphone, and raised his voice to compensate. The wood creaked under his mass as he loomed over the crowd. " 'For I know this, that after my departing shall grievous wolves enter in among you, not sparing the flock. Also, of your own selves shall men arise, speaking perverse things, to draw away disciples after themselves.' "

Ian found it hard to look away from the man. Stubbs was a natural born speaker, with a resonant voice and crisp, clear diction. He had the slightest trace of a southern accent that hinted at origins south of the Mason/Dixon line but none of the country twang of Pastor James. It was more than the man's powers of speech that held Ian, though, more than his commanding physical presence, more even than his piercing eyes. It was as if Stubbs was composed of denser material than the average man. Ian could swear he felt the man's gravitational pull.

"Today there are many forces vying for your heart. Our children are surrounded by this iniquity every day. At school. On TV. On the radio. And friends, so are you."

Stubbs paused for a moment, then stalked from one end of the stage to the other, bounding back and forth like a caged animal. Over the next thirty minutes he led the congregation on a whirlwind tour of scriptures, alternating verses promising God's eternal favor on the faithful with those warning of judgement. Between words, his jaws ground together like a dog working over a bone.

Ian took it all in with a growing sense of unease. He'd grown up in Pentecostal churches. seen men and women pogo stick to exhaustion until they fell to the floor convulsing in ecstasy. He'd heard a thousand different people speak in a thousand different tongues. He'd never seen anyone exude the power emanating from Stubbs, never felt anything like the icy hand gripping his heart when Stubbs' eyes met his.

After long minutes of staring with unblinking eyes, Ian finally managed to look away. Chevy stood next to him, a grin on his face. He appeared to find Stubbs entertaining. There wasn't the slightest hint that he was anything other than amused.

Ian looked back to Kelly. She was still there, still looking down. The chair on one side of her was empty. The teens on her other side were in their own world, whispering and chuckling. She was usually at the center of things, but now, despite being in the middle of a crowd, she was alone, looking small and frightened. Ian wanted to go to her, but his attention was drawn back to the big man addressing the crowd, so he resolved to be next to Kelly as soon as the service was over.

"The Bible says to come out from among them and be separate, but what does that mean? Does it mean you don't go where they go, don't look like they do, don't act like them? It might, but it means so much more. It means you have accepted God's perfect will for your life, that you acknowledge that you have been set apart as a qualitatively different kind of creature. Amen?"

"Amen," a dozen people responded. "Yes, Lord," said others. "Hallelujah!"

"Tonight," said Stubbs then he paused for effect. "Tonight, God wants to change a life. He wants to impart a great gift.

"Amazing grace, how sweet the sound," Stubbs rumbled. "I'd like the band to come back up and play that blessed song. Softly. The Lord walks among us here tonight. Would you please rise."

The congregation stood while the band walked back to the stage. Ian stood with them as a lump rose in his throat. A rush of conflicting thoughts and emotions washed over him. He was tormented again by the memory of his mother wasting away during those awful final weeks, his father sinking into a morass of pain and despair while prayers went unanswered. Ian wished for something to hold onto, for someone beyond this mortal plane to give a damn. Then there was Kelly. Despite what he said to Chevy earlier, he knew that there was no giving up on winning her heart. If anyone brought that to an end, it would be her, no matter what it cost him.

"Friends," Stubbs said, "there are among you those who have been waiting for this very night. Come, won't you? Come and lay your burdens down before Him."

Stubbs stepped down from the stage onto the sawdust covered ground and beckoned for any who would to come forward.

Within seconds the aisles were filled. Ian took a breath and moved to join them.

"Brother, are you OK?" Chevy said, his hand on Ian's shoulder.

"This is it," said Ian."I think this is what Mom told me about. I'm going up there and-"

"Ian, don't." Kelly held onto his arm. For the second time tonight he hadn't been aware of her behind him. Over her shoulder, an exasperated woman sighed and went the other way into the aisle. "Please, don't."

"I have to, Kell. It's now or never."

"He scares me," she said. "I've seen the way he looks at you. Something isn't right about him."

"I have to, Kell," Ian repeated.

"Let's go somewhere. I need to tell you something."

"We'll talk after," Ian said. "I...I have to."

In the front of the tent, Stubbs was laying hands on those who made it forward. Left and right, they fell at his touch. Pastor James and the elders of the church caught those who were overcome and lowered them to the ground.

"Behold, I stand at the door and knock!" Stubbs voice reverberated throughout the tent. He was looking over the head of a small, gray-haired lady. His hands were on her shoulders, but his eyes were searching until they fixed on Ian. " 'If anyone hears my voice and opens the door, I will come in to him and dine with him and he with me.' "

The crowd parted before Stubbs like the Red Sea before Moses. Ian stood like a tree planted in the middle of the aisle. The band played softly from the stage, their voices just above a whisper.

Ian's eyes locked on Stubbs as the big man moved up the aisle until he stood directly in front of him. Stubbs' gaze was almost unbearable at such close range, but Ian couldn't have looked away if he'd wanted to.

"This is your night, son." He spoke in a lower voice, meant only for Ian's ears. "You are the reason I came here tonight."

Ian nodded but couldn't speak. He felt dizzy, as if he could pitch forward into the man's deep, blue-gray eyes. Ian saw things in those eyes. He saw snow and dark forests and mountains. He heard padded footsteps on heather and water flowing under ice. He saw secrets and power and life and death in those eyes, and he could taste blood in his mouth, feel the softness of something like flesh giving way for him. He was awed and frightened, unable to comprehend what it might mean, then Stubbs laid both huge hands on his head.

"Receive The Blessing."

A blast of cold energy flowed from Stubbs into Ian, pounding him with a force that took his breath away. He gasped and his eyes rolled back into his head. He was only dimly aware of the ground rushing up to meet his back. No one was there to catch him as he fell. By the time Ian landed, clouds of sawdust puffing out around him on impact, he was elsewhere.

He was standing in a field, surrounded by tall stalks of grain leaning in a cool breeze. The sun was low, orange and red spreading across the western sky, bleeding into a front of dark blue clouds. The air was different, not just the smell but the feel of the air on his face. It felt clean, but it was full of strange, earthy scents. Somewhere in the distance, dogs barked.

A sharp intake of breath came from behind Ian. He turned to see a girl, probably no more than fifteen, sprawled on the ground. She wore a simple dress of drab brown and dirty white. It was torn and soiled, her left breast exposed, the soft white skin gouged and scratched. She trembled as she pulled the ripped garment across her chest to cover herself. Dirt and plant material was matted in her tangled blond hair.

Disoriented but aware of the girl's distress, Ian bent to help her. The girl yelled and scrambled backward, her eyes wide and bloodshot. Tears traced through the dirt on her round cheeks. She shouted something, but he didn't understand a word. It wasn't gibberish, but neither was it English.

The barking dogs were closer now. Ian straightened up and looked around, searching for a clue to where he was. The ground sloped enough so that he could only see his immediate surroundings and the land in the distance. The field surrounded him on all sides. Weathered mountains loomed far away. He glimpsed what he thought might be a narrow dirt road with dark, deep ruts.

He turned back to the girl. She recoiled again, tried to stand, and fell on the trampled stalks underfoot. For a few seconds, her right leg was exposed to the hip, her inner thigh smeared with blood. She shouted at him then raised her head and shouted again, this time not at him. The dogs barked louder and men shouted a reply.

Ian started to speak but couldn't find any words. He stepped toward her, his palms up, but she scrambled backward again, aimed a string of what he took to be expletives at him, and spat in his face.

Ian wiped the bloody spittle away and realized she was now looking over his shoulder. He turned and saw a group of men charging through the stalks, two massive dogs straining at tethers in front of them. The men were dressed in drab clothes like the girl and many of them were waving things in the air. Most of them had hoes, shovels, and pitchforks, but some carried crudely made clubs. A couple of them carried stout planks of wood.

Ian ran, but the tall stalks and the soft, uneven ground made the going difficult. He made it only a short distance before one of the huge dogs bowled him over. The snarling animal was about to sink its teeth into his thigh when it was jerked back by a thick-set man with a reddish beard. Before Ian could regain his feet he was struck by something heavy. He wasn't sure what it was, but he dodged the blow at the last moment, taking it on the shoulder instead of the head. Something snapped there and Ian howled in pain. He opened his mouth to ask the men what he had done to deserve this, but he couldn't get any words out before they were upon him, punching him with hard fists and kicking him with heavy, booted feet. A thudding blow from something found his head and he blacked out.

Ian's shoulder hurt. The sharp pain where he had taken the blow earlier was the first thing he noticed when he came to, but his back hurt even worse and his head throbbed. A trickle of warm blood flowed from his nose into his mouth. He still had no idea where he was, only that every second brought fresh pain. His wrists stung and when he tried to move, every joint in his body flared into a white hot point of agony. He opened his swollen eyes and realized his predicament.

He was naked and bound to a large wooden wheel. The rough, heavy ropes that held him there dug into his skin. He coughed, pain wracking his body, and spat out a bloody, broken tooth. "Uh...hmmm." He tried to speak but couldn't form words yet. The wheel was propped on edge on a broad wooden platform, not unlike the makeshift pulpit in the tent but sturdier. He was in the center of what appeared to be a town square, the roads converging from each side, simple dirt paths with ruts full of muddy water. Men, women, and children crowded around the platform.

Ian tried to tell himself this was a dream, but the very real pain in his body told him otherwise. He could feel the breeze on his bare skin and smell the odors around him. The town stank of manure, garbage, and sweaty bodies.

"Why?" he tried to say but without success. "Why are you doing this?" His own voice sounded strange to his ears. They weren't the words he intended. It was speech to be sure, but like the girl in the fields, the words weren't English.

The girl? My god, he thought. What happened to the girl?

A loud voice from his right addressed the crowd. Ian turned his head to face the speaker even though the effort was painful. A man in dark, flowing robes was talking first to the crowd then to him, his voice lifting at the end, posing a question. Ian understood none of the words, but he understood the tone. He was being judged. The robed man spoke to him again, pointed an accusing finger, then paused to await a reply. Ian had no idea what to say or even how to say it. The man shook his head then walked to the edge of the platform. He looked back at Ian once more before descending a set of stairs and disappearing into the crowd.

Over his shoulder, Ian heard what sounded like the stirring of rocks and the clank of iron against iron. An intense heat moved closer, rippling across the bruised flesh of his back. In the crowd, some people turned and hurried away with their children. Some, though, hoisted their children onto their shoulders so they could have an unobstructed view.

A large man dressed in plain black clothes, a dark hood covering his head, walked around from behind Ian. He wore thick leather gloves and held a pair of enormous tongs that glowed red with heat.

"Whh, waa..." Ian sputtered when he realized the man was reaching toward him with the tongs. He barely had time to panic before the flesh of his chest started to sizzle. Ian screamed. He struggled against his bonds and screamed with everything left in him, thinking that somehow if he screamed long and loud enough he wouldn't feel the pain. He was wrong.

Chapter 3

Batavia, Ohio

Ian woke with a shudder. His breath caught in his throat as a fading ghost of pain throbbed in his side before burning out like a spent match. He opened his eyes but saw nothing but white.

"Ian? Son?" The words were unintelligible at first. Only when the speaker repeated themselves did they begin to make sense. "Son?"

A weathered, mustached face framed by thin strips of grey hair loomed over him. Wispy strands of red trailed across the lined dome of a high forehead. The white above the face resolved into a stuccoed ceiling.

"Dad?"

Henry Murphy's anxious grimace melted into a relieved smile. He ran a calloused hand over what remained of his hair.

"Where am I?" Ian said.

"Batavia. Clermont East."

"What?"

"Hospital. You have a couple of friends here, too."

Henry straightened up. He was a tall man, nearly as tall as his son, with the same long-limbed build. He wiped his eyes, took an old Cincinnati Reds ball cap out of his back pocket, and pulled it onto his balding head.

Chevy stood beside Ian's father. "Glad you're with us again, man."

Ian looked at the IV stand next to his bed, smelled antiseptic and...something else. "Hospital? How did-" He stopped short. He recognized the other smell and turned his head to his right.

Kelly was in a chair in front of the window. The sky behind her was a dark rectangle in the wall. She got up, walked to the bed, and wrapped her arms around him. "You scared us," she said.

"What happened?"

"Dude, you freaked," Chevy said.

"I what?"

"When that Stubbs guy touched you, you went down like you'd been shot. You were out."

"For how long?"

"Too long," said Kelly. She sat on the bed and rested her head on his chest.

"You got up and ran out," Chevy said. "Straight into the corn field. We couldn't catch you."

"The preacher found you," his father said.

"Pastor James?" Ian put his arm around Kelly.

"No," said Chevy. "Stubbs. We were looking all around. Me, Kell, Verna, and Pastor James. That Stubbs guy walked right up to you. Pastor James called for an ambulance. It took them forever to get there."

"You were saying things." Kelly's voice resonated in his chest.

"What was I saying?"

"Don't know, man," Chevy said. "When Stubbs said he found you, we came running. Me and Kell were the first ones there. Stubbs was kneeling beside you. You were babbling but you wouldn't come around."

"You screamed," whispered Kelly.

"I screamed?"

Chevy nodded. "Scared the shit out of us!" He looked at Ian's father. "Pardon my French."

Henry Murphy waved his hand. "Don't worry about it."

"You were quiet after that," Chevy continued. "Like you were asleep."

"Really?"

"Do you remember anything?" Chevy said.

"I remember Stubbs looking at me. His eyes... He put his hands on me. It doesn't make any sense after that." He recalled everything, but he didn't want to tell them, especially with his father there. "I saw things but it was all jumbled together, like..."

"Like a dream?" Kelly said.

"Kind of, but not... It felt real."

"They said it was about 9:30 when you went down," said his father.

"Dude, you were still out an hour later," Chevy said. "Kelly tried to wake you. So did I. Verna did, too. Stubbs just smiled. He said God wasn't done with you yet. That's when you got up and ran out. It was almost 11:00 by the time the ambulance got there."

"I don't like that man Stubbs," said Kelly. "I lifted your eyelid and it was like you weren't in there at all, like your body was just a shell and you were somewhere else. It scared me to death."

"We started wondering if you hit your head," Chevy said.

There were no IV tubes in Ian's arm, but he had a bandage in the crook of his left elbow. "It's still dark outside," he said. "Have you guys been here all night?"

His father and his friends looked at each other.

"Ian?" Kelly said. "It's Thursday night."

"What?"

"It's Thursday, Son," said his father. "After 9:30. You've been out for a good twenty-four hours."

"No."

"Yes." His father pushed the ball cap further back on his head. "I'm gonna find a nurse. Tell 'em you're awake." He patted Ian on the shoulder, paused for a moment, then left the room.

"You guys have been here all this time?" Ian said.

"I was here for a long time" said Chevy. "I was on the nods in the waiting room. My folks were here, too. They insisted on taking me home so I could get some sleep. I've been in and out. Verna was here for hours, and Pastor James, too. Kelly, though...we couldn't get her to leave."

Ian looked down at the petite girl. "What about your job?"

Kelly sat up and shrugged. "Gram and Grandpa know where I am. " She yawned. Her big eyes were bloodshot.

"What about, uh..." Ian didn't have to finish.

"Ricky? We had a bit of a fight. I suppose I should give him a call. I need to call my folks, too. They'll want to know how you're doing." She gave his hand a gentle squeeze and stood.

"Tell them I'm fine. And tell them thanks." Ian watched her go. He was perturbed that she felt the need to check in with Ricky, but he knew it wasn't the time to go there. After all, she'd been at his bedside for an entire day. "Hey, isn't it past visiting hours?"

"Yeah," Chevy said. "They cut us a little slack."

"What about Video Monster? Weren't you supposed to work today?"

"Ah, Old Man Jenkins knows we're buds. He understands. It's just a video store. No biggie."

"It's your job, Chev."

"What's he gonna do? Fire me?" Chevy smirked. "And Kelly, well, you know her grandmother thinks you're the greatest thing since sliced bread. She'd be thrilled if Kelly dumped Ricky for you."

"I know. Sometimes I'm not sure that helps."

Chevy stepped closer to the bed and lowered his voice even though no one else was in the room. "Brother, it's just us now. What happened? What did you see?"

"Ahhh, Chev." Ian rubbed his eyes. "Where's my specs?"

"Next to your bed." Chevy handed him his glasses.

Ian put them on. The room swam around him. He took them off, tried them again, then sat them back down on the nightstand. "That's weird."

"What do you mean?"

"I've been wearing glasses since I was eight. You know how nearsighted I am."

"Yeah?"

"It's better with them off," Ian said.

"OK." Chevy shrugged and appeared confused but smiled nonetheless. "Leave 'em off for now. You said you saw things. What did you see? God? Angels? What?"

"No, I didn't see God. Or the other guy." Ian remembered everything. The girl. The mob. The pain. He trembled at the memory of the red hot tongs. He felt like he was going to be sick so he swung his feet around to sit on the edge of the bed, ready to make a run for the bathroom.

A nurse came into the room, followed by Henry Murphy and a short, balding man with glasses. When the man took the chart from the nurse, Ian guessed he must be the doctor. The nausea passed and he laid back in the bed while the doctor looked over his chart, nodding and muttering to himself.

"Ian, you appear to be completely healthy." The man introduced himself as Doctor Loyd and shook Ian's hand. "What we can't figure out is why you passed out. Your blood sugar was a little low but not enough to be a concern. You were dehydrated and sweating profusely, but you were fine after we gave you some liquids and glucose."

"Tell him about the glasses," said Chevy.

"The glasses?" the doctor said.

Ian looked at his father. "Dad, I don't need my glasses anymore."

Ian's father looked confused. "I don't get it. What do you mean you don't need them?"

"When I put them on, things look weird. When I take them off, everything looks great."

"All right," Henry said. He shook his head. "Let's not worry about that right now."

"When was your last eye exam?" The doctor said. "Maybe it's time for a new pair."

Ian knew the doctor was grasping at straws. He didn't want to belabor the point so he let it go. He didn't need a new prescription. He didn't need glasses at all.

"Be that as it may," said Doctor Loyd, "what I'm looking for is a physical reason for your feinting, but I can't find any yet. It seems we may need to consider other causes."

"Such as?" Henry Murphy said.

"Mrs. Murphy passed away recently. I can't imagine the stress both of you have been under. How long has it been?"

"Six months," Ian said before his father could answer.

"How are you coping? Are you sleeping well? Both of you?"

"I never needed much sleep," Ian's father said.

"I guess I am," said Ian. "As well as can be expected."

"There is no expectation. Processing loss is different for everyone. Do you have any other stresses in your life?"

"Kelly," Chevy said. Ian scowled. "Dude, it's true. You've been pretty wound up over her."

"Girlfriend?" Doctor Loyd looked at Ian then at Ian's father.

"You could say that," Henry said. "She was here."

"Oh, the girl who wouldn't leave. Pretty." He jotted down something on Ian's chart.

"What does she have to do with this?" Ian sat up a little more.

"Maybe nothing at all," said the doctor. "Ian, you're in a tough period of life under the best of circumstances. Just out of high school. Your mother passed away. Girlfriend troubles. I think we tend to underestimate how hard it can be for young people to transition to adulthood."

"Come on, Doc. Give me some credit. I'm not a kid anymore."

"That's my point, Ian. You're not." He looked over the chart again and handed it to the nurse. She took the chart and left.

"So when can he come home?" Henry cut in. He was fidgeting, impatient, all sighs and shrugs.

"To be on the safe side, I'd like you to stay another night, Ian. Just for observation." He turned to Ian's father. "There's no evidence of head trauma, nothing that indicates an epileptic seizure-"

"Seizure?" Ian said.

"I don't think so." Doctor Loyd shrugged this time. "I can't find anything out of the ordinary."

"Passing out for twenty four hours is pretty out of the ordinary," Henry said.

"It is. That's why I want him to stay another night. At this point, though, my guess is that it is stress related. I can prescribe some anxiety medication, but I'd like both of you to see a good therapist."

"A therapist?" said Henry.

"Yes. Believe me. I'll leave some names at the desk."

"Well, OK," Henry said. "Anything that might help."

"I think it will," said the doctor. He shook Henry's hand then turned to Ian. "Get some rest. We'll talk tomorrow." With that, he smiled and left the room.

Henry approached the bed and put a hand on his son's shoulder. "I'm not too sure about this. I wish I could just fix this." He shrugged again. "I guess we'll take the doctor's advice for now. I'll stop by the front desk on my way out and call one of those shrinks tomorrow."

"What are you going to do now, Mr. M?" said Chevy.

"Go to work, I guess. Nothing else I can do."

"Shouldn't you take the night off," Chevy said. "Maybe go home and get some sleep?"

"I only needed sleep when I was your age."

"Dad, you look tired. I can see it in your eyes."

"Feeling better by the minute. I need to head to work."

Ian knew his father had to be feeling relieved if he was going to work. Henry was a night shift supervisor at the Ford plant a few miles from the hospital. If he left now, he'd be early. Ian knew the earlier his father left for work, the better he felt. "Well, don't work too hard, Dad."

"No such thing. I love you, Son."

"I love you too, Dad."

Henry patted Chevy on the shoulder and left.

"Hey, man," Chevy said when Ian's father was out of sight. "Talk to Kell. Something's up with her and that asshole Ricky. The time might be as right as it's ever going to be."

"Chev, I don't want to use this-"

Kelly came back then. She looked more composed and less puffy around the eyes. "Chev, can you give me a lift home?"

"Sure, Cuz. Do you want me to wait in the Z? I can catch a few winks in the parking lot if you want to stay a while."

"Thanks, but it won't be long. I think they're about to kick us out, anyway. If you want to wait in the car, though, that would be great. I'll be down in a few minutes."

"OK. No hurry. Ian, brother? I'll see you later."

Ian smiled and gave his best friend a thumbs up then looked at Kelly. "You said you had something to tell me? Is now a good time?"

"Let's talk tomorrow." Kelly took his hand but avoided his gaze. "I'm beat right now."

"It means a lot to me that you were here when I woke up."

"I wouldn't be anywhere else," she said. She looked at him then and leaned over the bed to kiss him on the lips, lingering for a second kiss. She put a hand to his cheek and opened her lips as if to speak, but she seemed to lose the words. A sad, sweet smile crossed Kelly's face. She dropped her hand from his cheek and in a husky voice whispered "I'll see you tomorrow."

Ian watched her go. He hoped that somehow he finally was on the verge of winning her heart. It certainly felt like it. Something *was* up with her. Her smell lingered after she was out of sight. Ian laid his head back against the pillows and luxuriated in her scent.

"That is a striking girlfriend you have there."

Ian opened his eyes. Peter Stubbs stood in the doorway, his broad shouldered physique occupying most of the frame.

"Please don't misunderstand," Stubbs said. "I meant nothing salacious. She's a beautiful girl. That is all." Stubbs smiled. He was wearing a suit identical to the one from the night before. His white hair was combed smooth against his head, glistening and in place.

When he stepped into the room, Ian felt a change in the air pressure and felt the same wave of energy roll over him that he'd felt at the revival. For a few seconds he thought his ears might pop.

"I know visiting hours are over, but I explained that I was the minister present when you went under so they were gracious enough to allow me to look in on you."

Ian couldn't say anything yet. He could only stare.

"How are you feeling, Ian?"

"I...uh, I'm all right," he sputtered.

"I left the meeting tonight as soon as I could. I wanted to see you. The remainder of the service is in the pastor's capable hands."

"OK. Uh, please, have a seat."

"Thank you, but I won't be staying long. You need your rest."

"I actually feel pretty good," Ian said. The words came easier now. "When you touched me-"

"God touched you. I am nothing more than the conduit through which His power flowed."

"I scared some people. My dad. My friends."

"It is an awesome thing," Peter said. "I've seen very few go under the way you did."

"Last night..," Ian cleared his throat and swallowed. He spoke louder, aware of how timid he sounded at first. "You said I was the reason you came. What did you mean?"

"Ian, the ways of The Father are mysterious. I know that sounds like a cliché, but it's true. I have been entrusted with the task of furthering His kingdom. Every so often, I am made aware that there is a special work to be done. Sometimes I have no idea what that is until I find myself in the midst of His will, then it becomes clear to me. When I saw you, I knew."

"I saw things." When Ian closed his eyes, the images were there. The girl. The tongs. "I saw things I don't understand." He opened them again and looked at Stubbs.

"God has a special plan for everyone, Ian. Some of us, though, are truly special. Some are set apart for a glorious purpose beyond their imagining." He pointed an extraordinarily long finger at Ian. "You are one such person. Wait upon The Lord, Ian. 'They that wait upon the Lord shall renew their strength.' That's a promise. The work God has begun in you will become clear in time."

"Mom used to tell me God had something for me." Ian's voice trembled as he spoke. He hadn't cried in a long time. He shut his eyes tight to contain the tears. The images were still there. He opened his eyes and wiped the tears away with the back of his hand.

Stubbs handed him a tissue from the box on the night stand.

"I'm sorry," Ian said.

"No apology necessary," Stubbs said. "You have a good heart. Your mother would be proud." The preacher sighed. "I'm afraid I must be going."

"I'd like to make it tomorrow. If they let me go home, that is."

"I'd like to see you there," Stubbs said. He nodded and looked at Ian, unblinking. "Goodnight, Ian. Sleep well."

"Thank you," Ian said. "I appreciate you coming."

When Stubbs left, he had the sense that some unquantifiable measure of energy left with him, trailing after him like a cloud. Ian recalled a word from his Sunday School classes: Shekinah. It was a Hebrew word that translated roughly as 'The Glory Of God.'

The full moon was high in the clear indigo sky. An even blanket of white lay over everything, the top inch of snow a brittle crust. The creek before Ian was frozen, the shallow watercourse now a smooth, level path through the forest. Along one bank, gnarled roots protruded from the exposed soil ten feet above the ice. Ian walked on the ice with no destination in mind, only the knowledge that each step took him deeper into the forest, farther away from the warmth and safety of home.

The higher bank sloped down to meet the creek, the intersection of soil and ice obscured by the snow. Ian paused to look around, peering through the cloud of his breath as it condensed in the frigid air. The night forest was silent. The brilliant white of the full moon and the snow contrasted with the starless indigo sky. The shadows were the continuum of shades between the extremes.

Twin points of light emerged from the darkness on the high bank to Ian's right. He stared, fascinated, and a shape behind the lights resolved into the form of a huge, white wolf. As he looked at the creature, his fascination was replaced by the first stirrings of fear but it was outweighed by awe and wonder at the beauty of the magnificent beast.

Two by two, more lights appeared in the darkness, more wolves in a variety of shades, from mottled black and white to gray to brown, until the higher bank was lined by dozens of the sleek, powerful animals. All of them were beautiful, awesome in their own right, but none was a match for the shimmering colossus looming over the creek.

Across the ice where the bank was low, more wolves stepped forward from the gloom. They stared at him and ran their tongues around grinning, black-lipped muzzles, then sat back on their haunches. Ian turned to see that the wolves on the higher bank had done likewise with the exception of their huge, white leader. Instead of sitting down, the shining giant leaped from his perch, landing with silent grace on the thin strip of earth along the creek. He walked beside the creek, his huge feet leaving deep indentations in the crust of snow, but he didn't venture onto the ice.

As fear began to overtake his awe, Ian looked around for any avenue of escape, but there was none save for the frozen waterway. He didn't dare take his eyes off the great beast, opting to walk backwards while the white wolf kept pace with him.

After a moment, the white wolf stopped, settled onto its haunches, and watched Ian. Its eyes were blue/gray and intelligent, its head misshapen, disproportionate in a way that Ian could make no sense of. Ian blinked, rubbed his eyes, looked again, and this time the head looked correct.

For the better part of a minute, the great beast stared as Ian took slow backward steps. He could see the wolves on either side of the creek but only at the periphery of his vision. They sat on their haunches, patient, unmoving except for their wagging tongues.

When Ian had put a hundred feet or more between himself and the white wolf, the beast raised its head and howled. It was joined by the rest of the pack. Their rising song grew in volume until the sound filled Ian's head and overwhelmed his senses, driving out all rational thought. Ian ran. Within seconds he was sprinting down the corridor of the creek at a speed he never thought possible. He chanced a glance over his shoulder and saw that the white wolf was loping after him with the other wolves behind, none of them daring to pass or challenge its position.

His pulse a hot throb in his ears, Ian pushed harder. His side ached, his arms and legs felt more like lead with each step, and his lungs burned for more oxygen. He threw another glance over his shoulder. The white wolf was gaining on him with long, easy strides. At any second the powerful claws, the gleaming canines, and most of all those piercing, inescapable eyes would overtake him. The creek stretched ahead of him and around it the cold, dark forest. There was no sanctuary in sight. There would be no escape. Still, Ian ran and realized he was now running on all fours.

Ian opened his eyes and blinked against the blinding sunlight filling his room. He shielded his eyes with his hand and looked through the tall window in one wall. The landscape outside was clothed in green. Leafy trees swayed in the breeze. The sky was blue and cloudless. The scent of honeysuckle seeped into the room through the minute spaces between glass and windowsill. The gray ribbon of Ohio State Route 32 wound from east to west, disappearing behind gentle, rolling hills.

Ian reached for his glasses from force of habit, but when he put them on the world melted into wavy, funhouse shapes that made his head hurt. He took them off, bewildered.

He got up from his bed and stretched. It felt glorious after being on his back for so long. Despite the bright sky outside, he thought of the creek and the wolves. "Had to be a dream," Ian said aloud. He shrugged off the memory as best he could and went to the window. After a second of looking through the glass he lifted the latch and slid the window open.

Outside, the day was as warm as it looked. Ian breathed deep of the smells of summer: fresh cut grass; wild onions; honeysuckle; the sweet air itself. He was amazed and delighted at the number of scents, things he recognized but couldn't remember ever smelling before. There was tree sap, feathers, the fur of forest animals large and small, even the smell of the soil. There were a multitude of other smells, many of them not so pleasant. From somewhere around the corner of the building came the smell of rotting garbage, perhaps a dumpster. There was manure, more pungent then the garbage but somehow less offensive. He smelled livestock from a farm at least a mile away, carried to his high vantage point by a light but steady breeze. From much closer came the smells of grease, motor oil, and automotive exhaust. After a minute at the window, the overlapping smells became too much to bear. He slid the glass shut. The barrier muffled the smells but they were still there. With the window closed, the smells inside the hospital dominated; antiseptic; perspiration; mucous. Blood.

Through the glass, Ian could see the facade of a restaurant next to the highway more than half a mile away. Black plastic letters on the marquee beneath the logo spelled out the words FRESH STRAWBERRY PIE. He glanced at his glasses on the nightstand then back at the sign. Even with them on, he doubted he could have made out the words from this distance before...before what?

He listened. He could hear conversations up and down the hall, on the floor beneath, and a couple talking in the parking lot outside. Even through the glass he heard birds in the forest beyond the lot, the chatter of insects, and if he listened closely, the light, deliberate tread of a doe and her fawn stepping through the underbrush. Like the multitude of scents, the cacophony of sounds were soon too much for him. He was too distracted to hear the tread of soft-soled feet in the hall outside his room.

"Ahem!"

He turned and saw the nurse who had accompanied the doctor yesterday standing in the doorway. She smiled and gestured. Ian smiled back out of reflex before he felt the cold air on his exposed rear. "Oh, boy!" he said. "Sorry. I'm not used to these hospital gowns."

"That's all right," she said. "In my time I've seen things I never wanted to see. It figures that when we get someone in here with some tone to their backside, they'd be the shy one."

"Uh," Ian sputtered. He started to thank her for the compliment but wasn't sure it was appropriate. He decided he didn't really mind, though. "So, uh, Rebecca? When can I go home?"

She tapped the name tag on her chest. "Good eyes. Call me Becky." She chuckled. "The doctor will have to answer that question. He'll be around in a bit. Now have a seat so I can check your vitals."

Ian sat on the bed and she wrapped a pressure cuff around his arm. "When do they serve breakfast around here? I could eat a horse."

"You missed breakfast. It's almost 2:00. I came by with a tray, but you looked so peaceful I let you sleep. The doctor said to check in on you, but as long as everything looked fine there was no reason to wake you. I figured you'll eat when you're ready."

"I'm ready."

"Good." She finished her casual examination and marked his chart. "Your father stopped by on his way home from work. He said he'll be expecting you to call and not to worry about waking him."

"Thanks."

"Your friend? Shekky or whatever? He stopped by. He said he'd be back later with Kelly."

Ian's eyes brightened at the mention of Kelly.

The nurse smiled again."I take it she's that cute little thing that was here yesterday. Got it bad for her, huh?"

"You have no idea."

"I might. I was young once, too. She called and left a message. She wants you to call her at the shop. Says you know the number."

"Thanks."

"I'll be back with a tray. Don't hold your breath for the doctor. He has a full plate today. It'll be a while."

Ian reached for the phone before she was out of the room.

It was after four o'clock before Kelly arrived. Chevy was stuck at work until nine, filling in for someone who decided that their job at Video Monster wasn't so important after all.

"Ready to blow this joint?" she said as she bounced into the room.

"Soon as I get the OK."

Kelly gave him a light kiss.

"What was that for?"

"Just because," she said.

Ian smiled. Something was up with her, but he wasn't about to question what at the moment.

She read something pained in his smile. "Are you OK? You look like you've seen a ghost?"

"It's just...nothing." While waiting to be released, he'd wolfed down two full trays of hospital food and gotten dressed. Before Kelly arrived, he sat on the windowsill and tried to make sense of his dreams. He wasn't even sure dreams was the right word.

When Ian was thirteen years old, his mother showed him her tattered copy of *Fox's Book Of Martyrs*. It was a gruesome tome, but she told him it was important that he understood what others had suffered for their faith. Could he have been given a taste of their trials? Was he for a few moments in their place? There was something wrong with that idea, though. The girl in the field had been assaulted, probably raped. She was terrified of him. He couldn't escape the conclusion that he'd done the deed himself despite the fact that it went against everything he'd been taught. "A man who hits a woman isn't a man," his father had told him. Rape was far beyond that. If he had for those moments walked in another's shoes, they'd done a terrible thing. The men who caught him certainly seemed convinced of his guilt. And the man with the red hot tongs-

"Ian?" Kelly said. "Are you sure you're all right?"

"Sorry. Yeah. I'm fine. I just want to leave. You smell wonderful," he said, eager to change the subject. She did smell wonderful and not just because of her perfume. She looked wonderful, too, in her snug jeans and black t-shirt, her chestnut hair pulled back into a ponytail. "You are beautiful."

"Thank you." Kelly took a step back, a curious look on her face.

"What?" he said.

"You're not wearing your glasses."

"I don't need them."

"What do you mean you don't need them?"

"I just don't need them anymore."

"Knock, knock." Doctor Loyd rapped on the door as he spoke then walked into the room. "Ian, everything looks good. You're fine as far as I can tell, better than fine. You're perfect."

"You still think it was just stress?"

"I'm at a loss. I don't know what else it could be." The doctor sat on the bed, Ian's chart on his lap. "I was raised much the same as you were. My parents took us to church. People look to God for answers, but they look to people like myself for answers to the everyday questions, for medical guidance. We don't have all those answers. There are many things we just don't know. You're eighteen, just out of high school, and your mother passed away. That's a lot to handle. Those church services can be emotionally charged. Maybe you were caught up in that and your body needed a break. I gave your father some references to people who might be able to help you with the emotional side of these things. All I can say is that I'm satisfied that there's nothing wrong with you physically. I would like to have you back for some tests but I don't see any reason to keep you another night."

"Doc, something happened to me." Ian left the windowsill and picked up his glasses. "I don't need these anymore. I've been nearsighted since I was eight years old, but all of a sudden I'm seeing 20/20 or better. I can hear better, too, and I can smell things you wouldn't believe."

Doctor Loyd shrugged. "I can't explain any of that. I'll have to take your word, but I wouldn't throw the glasses away yet." The doctor stood up. "Ian, these things you're describing are great and I'm not saying they aren't real. I'm just saying I can't explain them. Hell, I'm envious. I'd love to ditch these damn glasses of mine. Whatever it is that got into you, if you can figure out a way to pass it along, come and see me. In the meantime, take your pretty little friend out and celebrate your good health."

"I would have been here sooner, but I had to take care of some things first." Kelly was still holding his hand as they walked across the parking lot. She hadn't let go since they left his room.

"Ricky?" Ian had to ask.

"Yes. Ricky. Let's not talk about him right now. I've got some things to figure out, but I'm here now. That has to mean something, doesn't it?"

"It does." Ian nodded. There was no point in going there. Things did seem to be heading in the right direction. That was good enough for now.

She let go of his hand when they reached her Volkswagen Cabriolet. It was even warmer than the day before and the top of the little convertible was down. While Kelly went around to the drivers side, Ian tucked himself into the passenger seat. Even with the seat back as far as it would go he didn't have much leg room, but he didn't care. He loved the fresh air and was beginning to get a handle on the myriad of new scents he had to manage.

"Seatbelt," Kelly said when she got in. "Remember the other night at the revival meeting? You said something about us not being just friends?"

"Yeah. I remember. You said you had something to tell me."

"I do. You were right. We aren't just friends."

"Is that what you wanted to tell me?"

"For now," she said.

Kelly started the ignition. She didn't say anything more, but she smiled at Ian. Another minute later, she pulled onto Route 32.

Ian undid his ponytail and shook out his hair. He inhaled through his nose and recalled reading that dogs hang their heads out of car windows because the air forced up their nostrils gives them a huge olfactory rush. He held the air in for several seconds then let it out and breathed in again, taking even longer this time before he exhaled. Yesterday he found the myriad of smells overwhelming, Today he found it delightful.

"Are you OK?" Kelly chuckled.

"What do you mean?"

"Your eyes are open wide and you keep taking the deepest breaths."

"Yeah. I'm not sure how to explain it."

"What was all that stuff about your glasses?"

"Uh...I don't need them." He pointed over his shoulder at the overnight bag his father brought him the night before. He'd stuffed his dirty clothes into the bag and tossed his glasses in at the last minute. "Something happened to me, Kell. It's like I told the Doc. I can see perfectly, I can hear things I couldn't hear before, and the smells...Do I look different?"

"You do. You're still you, but something is different."

"Do you like it?"

Kelly giggled, shook her head, and looked at Ian out of the corner of her eye. "Yeah. I do."

Stonelick, Ohio

Ian's father fixed his specialty for dinner; beef stew. He had always liked Kelly and insisted she stay to eat with them. "Tis the same recipe me ol' grandpappy brought over from the Emerald Isle," he said in a thick parody of an Irish accent. She brought something out in his father that Ian rarely saw anymore. He was Henry Murphy again, the same lighthearted, quick to smile man he was before his wife became ill and life ground him down.

The three of them talked about one thing after another though nothing of any importance. The closest the conversation came to getting weighty was when Ian tried to explain why he didn't need his glasses. His father shrugged after a few minutes, said they would talk about it later, then continued with the corny Dad jokes.

By 6:30, Ian realized he wasn't going to make that night's revival meeting. He felt a twinge of regret. He really did want to see Peter Stubbs again, but he wasn't about to interrupt his father's enjoyment of the evening. Truth be told, he was having a nice time himself, the best time he'd had around the dinner table in a long time.

"You still camping out with Chevy tomorrow night?" his father said.

"Yeah," said Ian. With all that had happened the last few days he'd almost forgotten. Chevy had pulled teeth to get a Saturday night off from Video Monster so rescheduling was out of the question. He would still have Sunday, though. If they rose early enough, he could make the Sunday morning service. Morning or evening, he wanted to see Peter Stubbs one more time.

After dinner they enjoyed a dessert of cherry pie and ice cream. The pie was Verna Cooper's own, delivered the previous evening while Ian was still in the hospital. By the time they finished and pushed away from the table, it was after 8:00. Ian walked Kelly outside to her car.

"Any messages for your cousin?" Ian said. "We're going out for a pop when he gets off work."

"You're not driving, are you? The doctor said-"

"I know what he said. Chevy's picking me up."

"Tell him he'd better not forget my birthday."

"That's right. Big seventeen in three weeks. I almost forgot."

"Yeah. Right. Like you'd forget."

Ian shrugged. He already had a present for her.

"Are you going back to work tomorrow?"

"I guess so," Working as a farmhand for Chevy's father certainly wasn't his dream job, but it was fine for now. College beckoned, but he didn't want to head off in the fall without a good idea of where things stood with Kelly. He'd already decided to give it a year.

"Well, don't stay out too late. Give me a call tomorrow night."

Kelly hopped behind the steering wheel and started the engine but didn't leave. She sat in the car with the engine idling, looking up at Ian.

"Are you waiting for something?"

Kelly nodded. "I am. What you always say."

"What is that?" It was unlike him to be less than direct when it came to her, but playing it coy felt right at the moment.

"I love you?" she said.

"I love you, too!" He grinned and leaned over to kiss her.

"Very clever." She reached up to cup his cheek with her palm. Her kiss was warm and vigorous. "You need a shave," she said before putting the car in reverse and backing out of the driveway.

Ian ran his hand over his cheek as he watched her go. She was right.

Chapter 4

"So let me get this straight," Chevy said. "When God healed your eyes he also gave you five o'clock shadow?"

Ian shrugged. "I take after Dad's side. Nobody in his family can grow a decent beard."

"What about your mom's side?"

"Why would it show up all at once?"

"Maybe you just didn't notice it before."

Ian shook his head. "I couldn't grow a mustache a month ago but I had to shave the last two days in a row. Last night Kelly touched my face-"

"Did she touch anything else?"

"Touch this, will ya?"

They were walking along the bank of Stonelick Creek, a shallow waterway that cut through the woods a mile behind Ian's house. The creek served as the baseline for their excursions into the surrounding forest. If they got lost but found the creek, they could find their way back home again. At 7:45 the sun still shone bright through gaps in the forest canopy, but the air was cooler than in the middle of the day. The moon was rising in the east, a pale circle low in the light blue sky.

Ian stopped walking. He lowered the pack from his shoulder and stared at the creek.

"What is it?" said Chevy

"I feel like I've been here before."

"Sure you have. Lots of times."

"I know, but not like that."

"What do you mean?"

"Never mind." Ian shook his head but couldn't shake the feeling. He hadn't told anyone about the wolves in his dream, about his run down the frozen creek. He knew this part of the woods like the back of his hand. This was the creek in his dream. Of course it was, he thought, and he chalked it up to nothing more than his subconscious.

"So you can grow a beard now?"

"Look at this." Ian pulled the sleeve of his T-shirt over his left shoulder. It was covered in fine dark hairs. "It's all over. My chest. My legs. Everywhere."

"Hmm." Chevy took a close look at Ian's back. "So our little boy has become a man. Is your Johnson bigger, too?"

"I'm serious." Ian rolled his sleeve back down. "Mom always said God had something special for me. Something happened when that preacher laid his hands on me. Something *is* happening to me."

"Man, I don't know what to make of it. I joke around, but that's just how I deal with shit. You know I'm on your side."

"Yeah. I know, Chev."

"You wanna stop by the cabin?" Chevy said.

"I don't think we have time. I just want to get to the tree. We can do the cabin another time."

Ian loved the old husk of a building they called their 'cabin.' Between them, he was the first to see the old structure peeking through the brush on one of their jaunts two years before. He normally took advantage of any chance they had to spend some time there. He felt both anxious and tired at the same time, though, and hoped that getting settled in for the night at the tree would calm him. It was still early, but they always talked for a long time before dropping off. He shouldered his pack again and they went on their way, joking and sniping in the good-natured manner of best friends.

"Dad said you worked like a dog on the farm this morning," said Chevy. "You didn't have to be there. He would have understood."

"I know. I just had so much energy. I think the pace of the last few days is getting to me, though. I'm sore all over."

When they reached the enormous oak they called the sleeping tree, Ian sat his pack on the ground and pulled on the two by fours nailed into the tree. He always tested their makeshift ladder as well as the eye hooks they strung their hammocks from twenty feet above the ground.

"Still strong, man," Chevy said.

"Hey, are you guys ever going to replace that old milker?" Ian said. "I swear, your dad spends half his time keeping that thing going."

"It's our bread and butter. Well, butter, anyway. Dad's looked into upgrading, getting all-new equipment, but he hasn't pulled the trigger yet."

"I can't believe the two of you used to milk all those cows by hand."

"We only had four of them then. Now we have two dozen. It was the happiest day of my life when we got that thing. Saved my wrists a lot of wear and tear."

"I'm sure you figured out other ways to keep your wrists in shape."

"Hah hah. Speaking of wanking, how are things between you and Kelly? Did you talk to her?"

"A little. I get the impression she has more to tell me."

"She was shaken up by what happened at the revival. I think it got her to thinking."

"You think? I'm still not sure what's happening between her and that asshole Ricky."

"Not to get your hopes up, brother, but I think she's slipping away from him. He's bad news."

Ian nodded then started climbing the tree. True to habit, he pulled hard on the eye hooks before getting the canvas hammock out of his backpack and trusting it to the hooks.

By the time Ian got into his hammock it was well past 8:00. He took off his shoes and hung them from one of the hooks, then laid back in his sleeping bag and and looked up through a gap in the branches at the sky, more purple than blue now.

"So what did you see that night at the revival," Chevy said when he was settled in.

Ian sighed. "I'm still trying to figure that out. It didn't make any sense." A shiver ran through his body from head to toe. He breathed in deep through his nose and a thousand different smells flooded his senses. He was aware of his mind recognizing and categorizing each one of them, but he felt as if he was at a distance from that part of his brain.

"Tell me," Chevy said. "Maybe we can figure it out together."

Maybe, Ian thought. For the last three days he'd felt fine when he was awake, but getting up early to work on the farm was harder than he let Chevy's father know. He was a creature of habit, anxious to get back to his normal routine. He didn't feel normal. Nothing felt normal. He wasn't exaggerating when he told Chevy he was sore all over. He didn't know what was going on in his body.

"Hey!" Chevy said.

"What?"

"You went somewhere else on me. You didn't say anything for the last five minutes."

"Has it been that long? Did I miss something?"

"Nothing all that important. You sure you're OK, man?"

"Yeah. I'm fine. Just..."

"Just what?"

"Where were we?"

"You were about to tell me what happened at the revival."

"OK." Ian took a deep breath. "I was in a field, kind of like the cornfields around the church but different. Some kind of grain. Maybe wheat. I don't know, but it was tall. There was a girl there with me. Her clothes were...well...she was exposed. Let's put it that way."

"OK. Sounds all right to me. Was she hot?"

Ian shook his head. "There was nothing sexy about it." Ian paused and ground his teeth together. His jaws hurt. Every joint in his body ached. "She'd been assaulted. I tried to help her, but she was terrified of me. Chev, I think I was the one who did it. I was the one who assaulted her."

"What? That's not you. You wouldn't do that."

"It was different in the field. I was different."

"It was a dream. Some kind of nightmare."

"It didn't feel like a dream." Ian shuddered. The pain in his jaws and his joints flared stronger. "I was chased by a bunch of men. They had dogs, and you're going to laugh at this, but they were carrying farm tools and stuff like the villagers in those old Frankenstein movies."

"Dude, that's..."

"I ran, but they caught up and they beat the hell out of me. I blacked out and when I opened my eyes I was tied to a wheel."

"A wheel?"

"Like a big wagon wheel."

"You got knocked out," Chevy said, "while you were unconscious?"

"That's just it. I didn't feel like I was unconscious, not until I got clobbered with something. And when I woke up, I was tied to this big, wooden wheel. I can still feel the ropes. They were so tight they dug into my wrists."

"Go on."

"I was in a town square, I think, and I'm not sure, but I think everyone was speaking German."

"German?"

"Or something like that. I tried to talk. When the words came out, I sounded just like they did."

"You were speaking German?"

"I told you it doesn't make any sense." Ian's breath hitched and he looked up at the sky. It was darker now. He'd never seen the moon look so bright. He gripped the sides of his hammock and tried to go on with the account, but he couldn't. The red hot tongs were reaching for him. The pain. "I...I can't, Chev."

"It's all right, brother. Hey, maybe we should go back to your place."

"I....I..." Ian found it hard to speak. He tried to tell Chevy that was a good idea, that he should call his Dad or even an ambulance. He tried, but the words wouldn't come. He heard Chevy say something but he had no idea what it was. The words were gibberish. Ian arched his back and spasmed as a tide of pain rippled through him. He gasped and looked up through the gap in the branches again. It was getting darker and the moon was higher in the sky, high and bright and round. The glow from the orb seemed to flow toward him, iridescent tendrils of silver light reaching out to him. His joints popped, and his muscles rippled. He convulsed as a chill ran through him then relaxed as it flowed way, taking his consciousness with it.

The black wolf found his voice and cried his first cry into the night sky. He had no idea where he was, of what came before this moment. He simply was, his consciousness blinking on.

Everything felt strange: the ghosts of shapes crossing the pupils of eyes he was afraid to open; the multitude of smells and sounds surrounding him; even the feel of his own fur-covered skin as it folded and wrinkled when he shifted his weight. He ceased crying and sat panting, his long tongue lolling over sharp teeth. His ears twitched, his nose burned, and his closed eyes watered. He was a newborn creature trying to make sense of the world he found himself in. He opened his eyes and things took shape before him. He could perceive depth, his inner ear found balance, and both his hearing and sense of smell found their bearings. He lifted a foot to take a tentative step and almost pitched forward. The surface under his feet was not stable. It swayed as he shifted from foot to foot so he dug his paws into the thick material to find purchase.

He wasn't alone. The black wolf froze at the sound of another creature a few feet below him. The creature gasped, took in a breath, and muttered something. The wolf turned his head toward the noise and the hair on his shoulders rose as he fixed his eyes on his shadowy companion.

"No, no, no," the pale thing muttered. The sounds meant nothing to the wolf though he took them as some attempt at communication. The creature reached backward toward the rough bark behind him-the wolf realizing that they were suspended in a tree though he had no word for the thing-and its hand slipped off the bark. The creature almost fell and cried out. The shout startled the wolf and he reared back. The surface under his feet shifted again and began to twist so he jumped, landing on the creature below. The surface there was no more stable and it began to twist as well. Desperate now, the wolf clutched at the creature, digging his claws in, and they both flipped over and hung suspended for a brief second before their scrabbling grips were lost and they fell together to the forest floor below.

The wolf was stunned but never lost consciousness while he lie on top of the creature at the base of the tree. He untangled himself and rose onto his two back legs. His upper appendages waved in the air before him as he pondered; two feet or four? Either seemed possible, but four seemed more stable so he dropped down onto hands and feet.

The creature that had been in the tree with him did not move. The wolf nudged it with his snout and he felt the slackness in its muscles. His claws had shredded the thing's flesh in several places, blood oozing from its body. Its head was turned back at a severe angle and its chest did not rise and fall. The wolf's sharp ears detected no pulse. There was no life in the thing. Perhaps, the wolf thought, it had gone where he came from.

The black wolf looked up from the body. He was still confused, still frightened, but the ground under his feet was firm. It didn't move, didn't swing back and forth with each shift of his weight. He was hungry. The wolf considered the creature at his feet but knew somehow that it wasn't food. He stepped back and almost fell, his feet tangled in some kind of fabric that covered half of his body. He tore at it as he stumbled away, freeing himself step by step, leaving a trail of tattered material..

Gaining confidence with each step now that he was loose from the constricting garments, he was managing an awkward lope by the time he reached the bank overlooking the creek. The trees were thinner there and the bright circle of the moon bathed him in silver light. Where are the others? he thought. There must be others of his own kind. The black wolf raised his head and let instinct guide his voice into the night sky.

Chapter 5

Batavia, Ohio

"...how we...going to tell..."

The voices faded in and out like weak radio stations.

"...understand...better time..."

"...something like this...no good..."

Ian felt a dull pain in his left shoulder. He felt like a marathon runner after crossing the finish line; exhausted but invigorated. He could tell that it was dark in the room, but he listened with his eyes closed, the words clear now that he was awake.

"I have to tell him."

His father sounded weary, his voice catching. Ian had only heard his father sound so anguished once before. Six months ago. "What's causing this, doctor?" He knew his father's voice but found that his smell was somehow even more familiar.

"I wish I knew. The EMTs said he was somewhat dehydrated when they arrived. There were no signs of shock. That's a good thing."

"What about those scratches?"

"They're superficial. My guess is that he picked them up on his way out of the woods."

Ian recognized the doctor's voice, but more even more so he recognized his scent, masked though it was by a heavy layer of cologne.

Ian opened his eyes. The room was darkened by heavy shades over the windows but stripes of bright daylight glowed around the edges. He sniffed. Antiseptic. Perspiration. Blood. Urine. It was a different room but it was the same hospital he'd awakened in before. His father's aftershave, familiar to Ian from his earliest years, competed with the doctor's cologne.

"I want to run another round of tests," Doctor Loyd said. "Another CT scan. MRI. Blood work. Perhaps we missed something the first time."

"Epilepsy?" Henry Murphy swallowed hard. "I told you about my uncle."

"You did." The doctor sighed. "I have to admit, I don't think we can rule that out now that it's happened twice. I still don't think it fits the profile, but I could be wrong. Honestly, I just don't know."

Ian's father scratched his head and grimaced. His work shirt was untucked and wrinkled, his sparse hair mussed. Even his gray mustache seemed to droop. "I just don't know," he said, shaking his head. "I don't know how to tell him."

"Tell me what?" Ian said. He had to force the words from his mouth and hoped he said what he meant. Speaking didn't come easy.

"Son." His father stepped around the bed and took Ian's hand in his. "You're OK. You're in-"

"The hospital," Ian croaked. He got the words out but it was still difficult to speak.

"Hello again, Ian." Doctor Loyd looked tired but not as careworn as his father. His smile was practiced, professional. "How are you feeling?"

"Good. A little..." He tried to say disoriented, but couldn't manage the word yet. "Good."

The last thing Ian remembered was the moon. So big. So bright. Vague impressions came to him, brief images, unclear and disjointed. He remembered the awful pain in his joints. He remembered falling and running, the earth soft beneath his feet. And his hands.

"Son, do you remember anything?" His father spoke slowly. "Do you remember last night?"

"Uh, we were in...our sleeping bags...hammocks. The tree. We were talking. It's...pretty fuzzy. My body hurt all over."

"Does it hurt now?" the doctor said.

"My shoulder hurts a little." Speech was becoming easier. "I'm hungry."

"Can you tell us anything else, Son?"

"I...I think we fell." Ian looked at the moisture in his father's red eyes. "Dad, how did I get here?" His heart beat faster. "Where's Chevy?"

"Ian? Are you awake?"

Kelly's voice in the doorway was soft, almost a whisper.

Ian heard her coming, smelled her perfume and her scent beneath while she was still halfway down the hall. For once his heart didn't beat faster at her approach. He'd been staring out the window for the last hour. The death of his mother, terrible though it was, had been expected. It was awful beyond words, but he'd had time to prepare, at least as much as possible. Neither he nor his father were blindsided by the tragedy. This was different. He didn't have the tools to deal with this. Yesterday his best friend, his brother by every definition but birth, was alive and well. Today he was dead.

Ian turned away from the window. "Hi," he said.

Kelly's eyes were puffy and red. She was clutching a wad of tissue, her red t-shirt spotted with errant teardrops. Her hair was windblown and tangled. Without a word, she crossed the room, shaking with every step, climbed into the hospital bed with Ian, and laid her head on his chest.

"Dad found me," Ian said. "I was in the yard when he came home, in the grass. He thought I was dead at first."

"Where is your dad?"

"He went to the Patella's." Ian knew Kelly had come from there. He didn't ask how they were. What was the point?

"They're having a hard time right now," she said. "Gram and Grandpa are with them."

"Dad said Leon found Chevy. It took him a while, but he found the tree."

Ian held her close. They lie there staring together out the window at a beautiful summer day.

Ian awoke with Kelly's scent filling his nostrils. He'd never felt closer to her, but guilt followed hard on that thought and he closed his eyes tighter, squeezing the tears from under his eyelids, a slow stream trickling down each cheek.

There was someone else in the room. They'd slipped in without his noticing, but his sharp sense of smell left no doubt who he would see when he opened his eyes. "How long have you been here?"

"Hello, Ian," Peter Stubbs said. "I'm so sorry about your friend." He was sitting in the chair next to the bed, one leg crossed over the other, his white suit crisp, his hair impeccable.

"How long have you been sitting there?"

"Your father left a message for you." Stubbs handed Ian the note pad from the nightstand.

Ian took the pad. The note informed Ian that his father and Verna had left to see the Patellas and would return soon. He set the note on the bedside table and looked out the window. The sky outside was a dull purple. "What time is it?" he said.

Stubbs turned the digital clock on the nightstand toward Ian. "Quarter till eight," he said.

Ian stroked Kelly's dark auburn hair. He looked down at the smooth curve of her hip, the rise and fall of her chest. He wanted to retreat back into sleep with her but he knew there would be no more sleep for now.

" 'The Lord is nigh unto them that are of a broken heart and saveth such as be of a contrite spirit,' said Stubbs. "Psalm 34:18. The Word is a great comfort in difficult times."

"No offense, Reverend, but right now I'm not finding much comfort in anything."

Kelly stirred after he spoke.

Stubbs smiled. "It appears the young lady brought you at least some measure of comfort."

Ian didn't like the way Stubbs referred to Kelly. The words themselves weren't the problem, but there was something predatory in his tone. He couldn't suppress a scowl as he looked at Stubbs and for a second he thought the man's canine teeth looked abnormally long. Ian blinked and focused his attention on that mouth again. They were no longer than his own. "Reverend, Kelly is one of the two people left that I love," he said. "What's your point?"

"Please. Call me Peter. I disdain titles such as Reverend. The only one worthy of reverence is The Lord Himself."

"Well, I'm not feeling too reverent of anyone right now, God included." Ian realized he was sneering at the preacher. Chevy's death had torn something loose. Despite the desire he felt the day before to see Stubbs again, he just wanted the preacher to leave now.

"I understand, Ian."

"You do? How?"

"I lost a son years ago. I was angry. Hurt. Like Job, I raged against the injustice of it all, but I came to understand that the purposes of God were grander than my limited scope allowed me to understand."

"Are you trying to tell me that Chevy's death was part of some grand plan?" Ian wanted to sit up, but with Kelly resting against his chest he was unable. He couldn't keep from raising his voice, though. "That it will make sense some day?" She stirred again and this time she opened her eyes.

"Ian? Are you..." When she turned over and saw Stubbs, she jerked backward and sat up.

"Hello, Kelly," Stubbs said. "I'm sorry if I startled you."

She yawned, rubbed her eyes, and cast a wary glance at Stubbs. "I should call Gran," she said to Ian. Her voice was hoarse and thin. "She's been worried about you," she said as she slid off the bed.

Ian started to say she could call from his room, but he could tell she didn't want to be in the same room with Stubbs. "Tell her I said hello."

"I will. I'll call Aunt Faith first in case Gran is still there." Kelly kissed Ian and left the room.

After a moment of awkward silence, Stubbs continued their conversation. "Romans, chapter eight, verse eighteen says that our present sufferings are not worth comparing with the glory that will be revealed in us." Stubbs slid open the top drawer of the nightstand to reveal a hardcover of the King James Bible. "The Gideons placed this here for your benefit, Ian. Read it."

"I'm sure you mean well, Peter." Ian closed the drawer. "I just don't see what I'm supposed to take from that."

"For you, it means that the sufferings you endure will pale in comparison to the glory God will manifest in you. You are marked, Ian. Chosen. Despite how you may feel at the moment, your future in Christ is magnificent."

"What about Chevy's future?" Ian snarled.

"Your friend is in God's hands now."

Stubbs smiled at him, a warm, compassionate smile that made Ian's skin crawl. "Shouldn't you be somewhere right now?" he said to the preacher.

"My work is here. You truly are the reason I came this week. That is clearer than ever to me now. In time, you will understand the wondrous work God has begun in you."

Ian bit his bottom lip and looked at the ceiling.

"I would like to pray with you before I leave," Stubbs said. "I fly home to Minnesota tomorrow. I feel God has placed you in my care. I don't want to leave you like this."

Ian felt the urge to spit at the man and tell him to get out, but he couldn't bring himself to do that. Instead, he lie back against his pillow, his eyes watering, and chose his words carefully. "No thank you. It's not a good time." He didn't know what else to say.

"I respect that," said Stubbs. "Let me leave you wth this." He leaned forward and placed a large hand on Ian's arm. A mild ripple of electricity passed from the man at his touch. "The Word of God tells us that in all things God works for the good of those who love him, to all who are called according to his purpose. You are called, Ian, make no mistake of that. In time, you will understand the nature of that call. Hold on to that, Ian."

Another familiar scent entered the hallway, accompanied by welcome, savory smells that made Ian's mouth water; his father's aftershave and the smells of grilled meat and warm onion rings. A moment later his father strolled into the room carrying a white bag in one hand.

"You must be Ian's father. You have a remarkable son, sir." Stubbs stood and offered his hand. "I feel very privileged to have made his acquaintance, even under such tragic circumstances."

"I'm proud of him," Henry Murphy said. He set the bag on the chair, took Stubbs' hand, and gave it a shake. "Are you the minister from the tent revival?"

"Peter Stubbs, sir. It's a pleasure to meet you."

Stubbs took a card from the inside pocket of his suit jacket and handed it to Ian. "If I can be of any assistance, please call, even if you just want to talk. I travel a lot, but you can reach my answering service at that number. I check my messages at least twice a day. I look forward to seeing you again." Stubbs nodded at Ian's father than started to leave the room but stopped. "Please give my regards to your lovely friend Kelly," he said before he left.

Henry Murphy picked up the bag and sat in the chair next to Ian's bed. "I thought you were anxious to see him again."

"I was." Ian said.

"What changed?"

"Everything."

Stonelick, Ohio

"Matthew, you can't believe my son had anything to do with Chevy's death."

"No, Henry, I'm not saying any such thing."

It was a little past noon on Monday, two days before Chevy's funeral. Ian had been released from the hospital two hours before. They'd run the battery of tests and again found nothing unusual. There was simply no discernible cause for his blackouts. The doctor strongly advised Ian not to drive until they had reason to believe he'd have no further episodes. It was even possible that his drivers license would be suspended for the time being, but that hadn't been determined. In the meantime, he asked Ian to make an appointment for a complete physical. They would go over the results in a couple of weeks.

Ian's father explained on the way home that he was taking the next week off from work, an easy thing given his accumulation of unused vacation days. They'd been home for less than an hour when Sheriff Kearsey arrived on their porch, hat in hand, looking too tired for that hour of the day.

They sat at the table, the sheriff's coffee growing cold. "Henry, Ian was the last person to see the Patella boy alive," he said, "and his own circumstances the morning after were pretty unusual. I need to get a better idea of what went on that night."

Henry Murphy sipped his coffee and studied his old friend's face. They had known each other for over thirty years, going back to the days when they warmed the bench together as second stringers on their high school varsity football squad. They saw little of each other now, but the ties forged years ago on hot August days pounding the sleds were still strong enough to warrant a measure of loyalty. He could see how pained the sheriff was to pursue the matter.

"Sheriff, exactly how did he die?" Ian said. His tone was flat, matter of fact, his emotions shut down for the moment. "No one seems clear on that. If they are, they're not saying."

"I'm sorry, Ian. Are you sure you want to hear this?"

"Yes. I...I think I need to."

"The fall, it seems." The sheriff sipped his coffee and grimaced. "His neck was broken and he had a fractured skull."

"Leon said he was all torn up," Henry Murphy said.

"He had deep wounds in his chest and throat. According to the ME, one or two of them in particular might have been fatal without medical attention. It seems they occurred prior to the injuries from the fall. The ME said they looked like claw marks."

"Claw marks?" Ian and his father said almost in unison.

"Rubin Paulson-he's the county Medical Examiner-has been around. He's seen about everything you could think of and some you wouldn't want to see. He says the wounds remind him of a little girl that had been mauled by a German Shepherd. The poor little girl was all torn up, mostly by the teeth, but she had gouges on her abdomen and legs from where she was trying to scramble away."

The sheriff paused and took a deep swallow of the room temperature coffee. He studied the mug for a moment then set it down. "The wounds on your friend were like those gouges but worse, much deeper. Rube thinks the only reason he didn't bleed to death was because the fall killed him first."

Ian leaned forward in his chair, his face in his hands.

"There were also hairs," the sheriff said.

"Hairs?" said Henry.

"Black hairs, coarse, long. Canine, probably. They were in the gouges and on the boy's clothes."

"Dog hairs?" asked Ian through his fingers.

The sheriff nodded. "We found your clothes, too, Ian. Some of them, anyway. They had the same hairs all over them."

"Anything else?" Henry said. The words came out in a hoarse semi-whisper.

"No."

Ian looked over the sheriff's shoulder at the sky visible through the window. The bluish-purple clouds rolling in from the northeast promised an end to the unseasonal dry spell. Just in time for Chevy's funeral, he thought.

"All I have right now is what I've told you," Sheriff Kearsey said. "Charles Patella fell out of his hammock. Broke his neck, bashed his head in. Died pretty much instantly. Before that, though, he was apparently attacked. By one hell of a big dog." He shook his head. "In a tree. Twenty feet off the ground. As if that makes any sense."

Milford, Ohio

The line of cars crossing the intersection of State Route 131 and Wolfpen Pleasant Hill Road stretched for almost half a mile. A uniform blanket of dark gray clouds hung low in the sky from horizon to horizon. A steady drizzle pattered off the vehicles and splashed on the grey asphalt before running off the road into the overflowing ditches.

Ian stared out the window of his mother's red T-bird, through the rivulets of water running down the glass. He was sitting in the back seat, his gaze fixed on the little black flag on the roof of the car. From his vantage point with his face pressed to the cool glass, he could see the flag as it was alternately rippled by the wind blowing from the northeast and jinked up and down by the falling rain, the forces of nature running counter to each other to play with the small destiny of the little vinyl rectangle.

Kelly nestled up close to him, her head resting on his shoulder. Just a few days ago he would have been in heaven to be with her like this. For the last two years, any displays of affection had taken place where no one could see, most of all whatever boyfriend she had at the time. He'd hated the clandestine nature of their relationship. He wanted to be able to walk with her hand in hand around Stonelick, through the mall, or anywhere for that matter. He took what crumbs he could get, though, biding his time for the day when it would be possible.

That day had arrived. She'd broken up with Ricky, but Ian was sure the punk hadn't accepted that yet. Kelly was spending nearly all her free time with Ian or Chevy's little sister Jennie, but Ricky still called her, no matter how many times she hung up on him. That would have to be sorted out soon, but not today. Today, Kelly was all his. All it had cost was the life of his best friend.

"The sheriff came by," Ian said.

"What? What did he say?"

"He told us how Chevy died. He wanted to know what I remembered."

"Chevy fell, right? You were traumatized. That's all. He doesn't think you had anything..."

"No. I don't think so. He's just trying to figure things out."

Ian couldn't help but be troubled as much by the things the sheriff left out as by what he did say. He didn't think the sheriff suspected him, but there were wheels turning in the man's head. Ian was sure of that. There were wheels turning in his own, too.

Kelly took Ian's hand in hers and turned it over once, twice, before placing it palm down on her leg with her hand over his. "I never noticed that before," she said. Her voice was low, flat, and tired.

"What?"

"Your index and middle fingers are the same length."

Stonelick, Ohio

Ian went back to work on the farm Monday. There was more work than ever to be done, but he tried not to think about why.

The Patellas were living in a haze, going through the motions, doing little besides eating and sleeping. Ian exchanged greetings with them each morning, but that was the extent of their interactions. Leon told him what needed to be done each day then the grief-stricken man disappeared for hours at a time. Ian saw him a few times standing at a fence, staring into the distance, but he had no idea what Leon was doing with his days. Twice during the week he asked Leon how he was but got not so much as a twitch in response.

Kelly kept close tabs on Jennie. When she wasn't with Ian, she was with her young cousin. She told Ian how helpless she felt at being able to do little but be with her. Ian drew upon the experience of losing his mother to tell Kelly that sometimes that was all you could do. He meant it as much for himself as well and he made it through those first days after the funeral by leaning as hard on Kelly as she did on him. They spent most evenings together, sometimes at his home and sometimes at hers, watching old movies with her grandparents.

Late at night when he was alone, Ian was dogged by an awful guilt he couldn't understand.

On Thursday morning, Ian stood outside the barn, work gloves in his back pocket, waiting for Leon to emerge from the house. It was early, the sun just breaking over the treetops to the east. Ian raised a hand to knock on the kitchen door when a voice from the milk house doorway stopped him.

"I miss him, Ian," said Leon.

"I know. So do I."

"I know Charles was like a brother to you."

Ian swallowed hard. "How are you, Leon? You look like you haven't been sleeping."

"You were like a brother to him, too. Somewhere out there, there's an animal that killed him. A big...dog or something."

"Leon..."

Chevy's father was looking past him with the thousand yard stare Ian had seen too many times that week. "I'm selling the farm," he said.

"What?"

"I don't have the heart for it anymore."

Ian started to say something about how Leon shouldn't make any rash decisions right now, how time heals or some such thing, but he knew how vapid and inadequate such platitudes were so he kept his mouth shut.

"There are just too many reminders of Charles around here," Leon said. "I don't need the money and I sure don't need the reminders." He walked out of the doorway, over to the fence that separated the barnyard from the pasture, and stood looking past the clueless cows milling about in the field.

Ian followed, still searching for something to say.

"I think I'll take the day off," Leon said.

"Leon, there's, uh, there's so much to do. That fence in the south pasture-"

"The fence will be fine." Leon clapped a hand on Ian's shoulder. "I know this has been hard on you, too. You look like you haven't been sleeping much yourself."

It was true. Ian hadn't been sleeping well. It took him hours to drop off now. "I guess I am pretty beat."

"We all are. Go home and get some sleep."

"But-"

"Go on now." He patted Ian on the shoulder then turned and headed for the barn.

Ian sat on his bed and bent to take his shoes off when he heard the shots. Living in the country, it wasn't unusual to hear gunfire now and then. There were a number of homes in the vicinity occupying large tracts of land. Ian thought of his own father teaching him how to handle a gun, of Leon teaching Chevy how to shoot tin cans off a post back in the...

He stopped unlacing his shoes and sat up. The echo made it difficult to pinpoint where the sound came from, but he thought he knew. Two shotgun blasts.

The Mantle's house was less than half a mile down the road. Their big rottweiler Mickey...

Ian ran for the phone and dialed the Patella's number. Faith Patella answered on the third ring.

"Faith, is Leon-"

"I tried to stop him!" She sounded frantic. "I tried to call the Mantle's, but I couldn't find their number. We weren't friends, really, just neighbors so... Leon got it in his head that their dog-"

"Call the sheriff," Ian said.

"The sheriff? What's he going to-"

"Call him! I'm going over there."

"Be careful, Ian. Ever since Charles...I don't think Leon's in his right mind."

"I'll be careful. Call Matthew. Now!"

He hung up, retied his shoes, and was two steps from the door when his father walked in, lunchbox in hand. "What's happening? You look-"

"I think Leon just shot Mickey Mantle."

The scene at the Mantle's house was awful. The dog was dead and Leon was kneeling in their driveway, crying, his shotgun on the black asphalt beside him. Regina Mantle was crying, too, afraid to approach either the mangled body of their dog or the sobbing man in the driveway.

"That dog," Leon mumbled to Ian and his father, "it had at my boy. What kind of father am I if I don't do anything?"

Ian almost threw up at the sight of the dog's corpse. Mickey was big but harmless, an imposing but playful animal he and Chevy had found rambling in the woods on two occasions when the dog escaped the Mantle's yard. Both times they'd led the playful giant home and let him slobber affectionately over them before they returned to the woods. He wanted to tell Leon there was no chance the rottweiler had harmed Chevy, much less killed him, but he knew it was pointless at the moment. Leon was too distraught for reason.

A few minutes later, Sheriff Kearsey arrived and shortly after that Elwin Mantle. After that, things got even worse.

Chapter 6

July 1989

Owensville, Ohio

"Good to see you, hon," said Verna Cooper. Her meaty hands engulfed Ian's. She wrapped her arms around him then let go and repeated the gesture with Kelly. "It's good to see you. I've been praying for both of you." She stepped back and looked them each in the eye. "If I can do anything for either of you just let me know."

"You've done plenty already," said Ian. "You always do." Verna's wide hips nearly spanned the width of the aisle as she walked to the front of the church. She had been his mother's best friend and now that Rose Murphy was gone, Verna seemed to take it upon herself to look after Ian and his father.

"She's the heartbeat of this place, isn't she?" Kelly said.

"Yeah," Ian said. "If not for her, I wouldn't have much reason to believe there is a God."

"She keeps you thinking there is?"

"She makes me wonder if there might be, at least."

With a meal here, a dessert there, and her simple, loving presence, Verna let Ian and his father know they weren't forgotten. While it took little time for them both to grow tired of the people who stopped by after his mother's death, Verna was always welcome. Those people meant well, but they were doing it as much for themselves as for Ian and his father. It was different with Verna.

It had been three weeks now since Ian had gone to church. It felt longer. So much had changed in that time. Of course, it was only the second time he'd been there in the last six months and the last time had left him with more questions than answers.

The pew creaked when they took a seat and it felt harder against Ian's back than he remembered. He put his arm around Kelly as she nestled against him.

Ian grew more uneasy by the moment. He mouthed the words to the songs as the band played but he was going through the motions. After half an hour he couldn't take it any more.

"Let's get out of here," he said.

"Are you sure?" Kelly answered.

"I can't do this."

When Pastor James invited the congregation to stand, Ian took the opportunity to exit the church with a minimum of attention.

Kelly followed. "I don't think running is the answer," she said when they were outside.

"I know," Ian grumbled. "I...just can't. Not yet. I'm sorry."

"Don't be sorry. When you're ready, I'll be there for you."

"Yeah, but who's there for you?"

"You, silly. Let's wait for Jennie out here. I hope Gram didn't see me duck out."

"I'm sorry."

"Stop saying that!" She stood with him under the awning and watched the rain fall around them.

Ian hadn't told Kelly what he'd seen that night or about his recurring visions of wolves. Dream wasn't the right word. The visions felt real, as real as anything he experienced in his day to day life. They haunted him, but he didn't want to tell her. He didn't want to add to her burden. She loved Chevy too. Besides, it was her birthday. He'd wanted to take her to the cabin, to share that special place with her, but the all-day rain scuttled that plan. They settled on a matinee at the theater in Eastgate and invited Jennie Patella to join them. The girl was in desperate need of a pleasant day out. They all were.

"You want pizza before the movie, birthday girl?"

Kelly smirked. "You'd live on pizza if you could."

"It's your birthday. You pick. Besides, you're driving."

"I don't mind. You know what the doctor said."

"I know. I just don't like being driven everywhere."

"You're a control freak."

"Am not."

"Are too."

Kelly gave him a playful punch in the arm, but he knew there was truth in her jest. He felt lucky that his license hadn't been suspended. Yet.

They waited for Jennie to come out with her parents. Gram was with them. Kelly's grandfather had feigned a headache, but they all knew he was getting an early start on sports for the day. Ever since they got ESPN, it was hard to drag him away on weekends.

Leon looked more worn each day. Faith didn't look much better. The legal mess over the Mantle's dog was far from over. Leon was fortunate he hadn't spent more than a night in jail, but by the time this all played out his luck might not hold on that count. The Mantle's knew the Patellas had lost a son and Leon was in need of some serious help, but there were limits to their forbearance. Elwin Mantle loved that dog. The matter wouldn't be legally settled for some time.

Jennie brightened when she saw Kelly and Ian. Ian had a hard time looking her in the eye at first, but her twelve-year old smile warmed him. He was encouraged that he might be able to put his guilt aside for a while and enjoy their afternoon together.

"Happy Birthday, Sweetheart," Faith Patella said. She handed Kelly an envelope. "It's not much but I don't want you to think we forgot about you."

"Thank you," Kelly said. She opened the envelope while they waited, the congregants from inside the church passing them. The envelope contained a birthday card and a twenty dollar bill. "Thank you!" Kelly said again and she hugged them both.

"We have a cake for you later," Gram said. "You're already wearing your birthday presents."

"But..," Kelly sputtered. She had insisted on wearing the stylish jacket she'd had her eye on for months despite the weather.

"But nothing. You three have a good time."

Batavia, Ohio

"Wake up, knucklehead."

Warm breath made the sensitive skin in Ian's ear tingle. He grinned, half awake, but didn't stir.

"I'm naked," she purred.

His eyes sprang open. His head was resting against the edge of Kelly's seat. Her face was inches from his, her eyes sparkling, her lips spread into *that* smile, the one that turned guys into human filets.

The theater was empty and the lights were up, the screen blank.

Ian stretched and smacked his lips. "I could get used to waking up next to you."

"I'm sure you could."

Ian stretched again, longer this time, and sat up. "Sorry I fell asleep. Must have been the big lunch. How was the movie?"

"Great. You would have loved it."

"Hey, where's Jennie?"

"Probably waiting in the lobby by now. She went to the restroom."

"Did I snore?" Ian said as they walked toward the hallway.

"A little. If you plan on waking up next to me you'll have to do something about that."

Stonelick, Ohio

Gram had gotten the birthday cake from Verna's bakery. The angel food was soft and sweet. Ian preferred devil's food or German chocolate, but he had a big slice anyway and washed it down with a tall glass of cold milk.

Kelly blew out all seventeen candles at one go. Her grandfather offered to take Jennie home when they were finished with the cake. The rain had stopped for the moment so Ian and Kelly decided to chance going for a walk. The evening was warm and muggy, steam rising from the sidewalks. The clouds were dark, promising more rain, but the evening sun was visible, tinting the western sky orange. They held hands and dodged puddles as they walked.

Ian still hurt for Chevy. Regardless of how good things were at the moment, the loss of his best friend cast a shadow over the day. He tried to keep it from showing, but when Kelly spoke he knew he hadn't succeeded.

"You miss him," said Kelly. "I do, too, but I think he'd be happy for us."

"Yeah. I think he would." Chevy's death still made no sense. He wished he could remember what happened that night, but it was a blank. There was nothing left of that evening but the guilt he didn't know how to put down.

"Ian?" Kelly said. "You never told me what happened that night at the revival."

"What does that have to do with anything?"

"I don't know," Kelly said, "but I know you don't like to talk about it. Maybe that's a sign that you should."

"You're right. I don't like to talk about it. It doesn't make any sense. Like what happened to Mom."

"What if you're not supposed to make any sense of it right now. Maybe it's not over yet and there's another side. Maybe nothing will make sense until you get there."

"Kell, I know you mean well, but that sounds too much like there really is some kind of plan that involves the people I love dying. I just think that's a, well, a pretty shitty way to run the universe."

"I've asked myself the same questions. I love Gram and Grandpa with all my heart, but growing up without knowing my parents has been hard. All I have of them are photos and home movies, and the stories Gram and Grandpa told me. I don't have any memories of them."

"I forget that sometimes," said Ian. "I know that sounds terrible but I never knew your parents. It's always been you, Gram, and Grandpa. They're pretty terrific, too."

"They are. Sometimes I forget, too, but not for long." Kelly shook her head as a raindrop landed on her shoulder. Another one landed on her head a few seconds later.

Ian bent down, brushed a strand of hair out of her eyes, and kissed her. They turned a corner and walked along the sidewalk in silence. The streetlights came on with an audible buzz. He heard the sound of children playing in and around mud puddles before he saw them and he could smell them even sooner. The town was alive with smells and sounds.

"Ricky was the first," Kelly said.

"Huh?"

"He was the first. I know what some people say about me. Some of the kids at school." She looked down at the wet sidewalk and sighed. "Do you even want to hear this?"

"If you need to say it, I need to hear it."

"I just don't want you to think I was going around giving it away."

"I don't."

They walked on for another block before the rain began to fall in earnest. They headed back to Kelly's house, but they were soaked by the time they got there. They went around to the back door and started to go inside, but Ian stopped.

"What?" Kelly said.

"Your present. I left it in your car. In the glove compartment."

"It can wait. It's pouring."

Ian shook his head and smiled. "I don't think I can get any wetter. I'll be back in a jiff."

Half a minute later he was back at the door with a small wrapped package in a plastic bag. Kelly was standing at the door with a big towel. She took the bag and handed him the towel.

"You know where the bathroom is. Take your wet clothes off. Put on Grandpa's old bath robe."

Ian went straight to the bathroom. Roy Martin's blue and white checked bathrobe was hanging on the back of the door. He was a broad man but much shorter than Ian, 5' 8" at the most. The robe would be short on him, but it would do.

"Throw your wet stuff out here" Kelly said through the door. "I'll toss them into the dryer."

"Uh, what about my underwear?"

"Can't help you there." She giggled. "Throw them out here too, unless you want wet britches."

A few minutes later, Ian was in the living room standing by the fireplace. The big TV was off, the set getting a rest while Roy took Jennie home. Ian was right about the robe. It stopped just short of his calves, but it was wide enough that he felt covered, though he was still conscious of wearing nothing underneath. He felt no more at ease when Kelly came down the stairs in sweats and a t-shirt, her hair wet but combed. She carried a small, unwrapped box in one hand and sat it on the coffee table next to the present Ian had retrieved from her car.

Gram peaked into the living room. "Go ahead with your presents. Roy called. He'll be a bit yet."

"Are you sure?" Kelly said.

"I'm sure. Don't mind me, either. You two need your privacy."

When Gram went back into the kitchen, Ian sat down on the couch and removed Kelly's present from the plastic bag. "You always gave me grief about showering you with gifts," he said, "so this time I thought I'd keep it simple."

Kelly sat next to him and handed Ian the little box. "You go first."

"Aren't you the one who's supposed to get the presents today?"

"I wanted to get you something. It's just a little thing. Open it."

Ian smiled and opened the box. It contained an even smaller box with a hinged cover. He lifted it to reveal a single hoop earring.

"Sterling silver," she said.

"I love it, but...I don't have a pierced ear."

"We can fix that. I think it'll look good on you."

"Thank you."

"You're welcome."

"Your turn."

Kelly picked up her box and turned it over in her hands. It was covered in shiny, silver wrapping paper. "Did you wrap this?"

"Yeah. I did. Open it."

Inside the box was an old gold watch that Ian had attached to a chain.

"It belonged to my mother," he said.

"Your mother? Ian, I can't. What would your father say?"

"It was his idea. I was stumped. I wanted to get you something special, but I didn't know what. He gave it to me. Mom used to carry it in her purse because it's a little big for a wrist watch. It'll make a dandy pocket watch, though, and it looks good on the chain."

"You should have this," Kelly held the watch up so that it caught the light and sparkled.

"I want you to have it," Ian said.

"Thank you. It's beautiful. And special."

"There's one more thing." Ian kissed her forehead. "Something I've wanted to share with you for a long time. It'll have to wait till next weekend, though."

"What is it?"

"I want to take you somewhere."

Stonelick, Ohio

"The He Man Woman Hater's Club, eh?" said Kelly.

"Huh?"

"Grandpa used to watch this old show all the time whenever it was on. It was in syndication for years. Spanky And Our Gang. An old serial from the 40s."

"Don't know it."

"They had this clubhouse. No girls were allowed in."

"You're allowed in."

Most of the week was so wet that Ian wondered if he'd have to postpone their trek out to the cabin for another week. When Friday dawned clear and the forecast for Saturday was the same, he breathed a sigh of relief. The rains were due to return with a vengeance on Sunday so Saturday it was.

"You guys never brought any girls here?" said Kelly.

"No. It wouldn't have seemed right. I was afraid you'd think this place was kind of silly."

"It's not," Kelly said. "I wish I had a special place. I can't believe no one else knows about this. You'd think someone would stumble across it."

"I'm sure they have. The woods are full of these old buildings."

Ian and Chevy had put a lot of work into making the little shack semi-habitable, but they'd taken just as much care to preserve a dilapidated look on the outside. The holes in the roof were patched, but the patches were concealed with debris that appeared to be natural. The roof sagged, but it was reinforced on the inside. The single window was broken, the remaining half-pane of glass coated with grime, but plexiglass covered the window on the inside. The floor of the little shack had been swept clean and the water damaged floorboards replaced with rough but clean lumber. Roach motels and bug spray kept it as pest free as possible for a structure in the middle of the woods, and a padlock on the door discouraged anyone who did find the place from entering.

"What did you guys do out here?" said Kelly. She was sitting on the raised platform under the window, a thick sleeping bag beneath her. She patted the spot next to her. "Sit down. Talk to me."

Ian was still standing in the doorway. When he'd come out of the house carrying the sleeping bag, Kelly grinned and made a joke, grinning even more as he floundered through a guileless explanation that she might want to sit down, trying not to give away the secret of the cabin.

"Come on," she said. "Tell me what you guys did out here."

Ian left the doorway and sat beside her. "We talked," he said. "About the three Gs."

"The three Gs?"

"Girls, God, and Grades."

"In order of importance?"

"Pretty much," Ian chuckled. "Chevy was smart, more than most people knew. He got better grades than I did and he could talk about almost anything and know what he was talking about."

Kelly threaded her left arm around Ian's right but said nothing.

"I feel...God, I don't even know how to say this." Ian looked at her and couldn't ignore her appearance. She wore jeans and hiking boots as he suggested, and a long sleeve shirt to protect her from thistles, but it was warm and muggy. As soon as they made it to the cabin, she rolled up her sleeves and undid the top two buttons on her shirt. Sweat beaded on her skin and ran under her silver necklace into the cleavage revealed by her open shirt.

Ian sighed. "You're beautiful, you know that?"

"Thank you," she said with a crooked grin. "Now tell me what you were about to say."

Ian looked away through the open door at the green forest outside. "I feel guilty."

"Guilty?"

"Yeah. I can't seem to shake it. I feel like I had something to do with Chevy's death."

"You know that's nonsense, don't you?"

"Is it? I can't remember much about that night. Nothing important, anyway, but I was there. I should know something, but all I have is this gut feeling that says I'm responsible."

"Hey." Kelly reached up and turned his head to face her, her fingertip on his chin. "You are not responsible. You loved Chevy. Everyone knows that." She kissed him on the lips and rested her head against his chest.

The sun edged lower in the west, the sky streaked with gold, red, and purple. Daylight clung, resisting the advance of night with the vigor of midsummer, but the shadows deepened with each minute as the light lost strength. Small things that hid in the daytime began to stir. The noises coming from within the cabin were nothing to them. A single possum, bent-backed and lame, paused outside the closed door and listened for a few seconds before limping away into the growing darkness.

Inside, Kelly's breath was coming in short, rapid gasps. She gulped air and ran her hands across Ian's shoulders, down to the small of his back.

It started with her head against Ian's chest. By slow, wordless degrees their shared experience of tenderness gave way to a release of long-repressed passion. Over the previous two years there had always been someone else in the way. Now there was no one, but even so, Ian was gripped by conflicting emotions. Authority figures from the past crowded into his memory, a jumble of voices clamoring for his attention, preachers and teachers from youth group conventions where middle-aged men with beautiful wives proclaimed the virtues of abstinence to masses of hormonally charged teens. He wondered if they really had any idea what they were talking about.

Ian had dreamed of this moment countless times, but before the last few weeks he'd wondered if it would remain a fantasy. When they were both naked and he felt awkward and unsure, he'd experienced a sort of paralysis, the eye of God looming over his shoulder, but he thought of Chevy, wondered where God had been for his friend, and the paralysis passed. He hadn't been sure of anything since that night and it seemed that any answers forthcoming would be of his own making. He was sure of only one thing; he loved Kelly more than he loved life itself and desiring her in the way he did was the purest emotion he'd ever experienced. If he would be condemned for that, he told himself, it would surely not be by a God that could ever claim to truly love him.

"Ian?" Kelly breathed into his ear.

"Yeah?"

"Be here. With me. Right now."

He bent down and kissed her. He was more than a foot taller than her and as closely entwined as they were, he had to arch his back to reach her lips, but he managed. She kissed him back, hard, and pulled him even closer.

They moved together, finding a rhythm in the motion that grew more intense with each moment. Ian was astounded at first by her energy and then by his own. Time passed without meaning. Seconds? Minutes? Hours? There was no way for him to know, no marking of the passage of time. There was only now. He felt an electricity ripple through his body, felt stronger than he'd ever felt before. He bore down and Kelly matched him, grinding her teeth when she wasn't gnawing on his shoulder. Finally, she cried out and he followed as they reached the end of their resources and slumped onto the sleeping bag, drained.

"Fuck," Kelly whispered. "Fuck..."

Ian looked her in the eye, his forehead against hers, and smiled. Kelly rarely cursed. They lie with their limbs wrapped around each other's sweat-slicked bodies, without a care in the world.

"Jesus," she said. "Wanna go again?"

"Yeah. In a little while." It was all Ian could say. He raised a hand and brushed a wet, stringy strand of dark hair from her face. *She is so beautiful* was his last thought before they both fell into an exhausted sleep.

An owl hooted its greeting to the night. The moon was a bright disc in the blackening sky.

Ian woke with a start. He was being chased by wolves again, this time down the center aisle of the revival tent. He stumbled and fell just before he woke, almost scooting off the edge of the platform and onto the floor before Kelly reached out a hand to steady him. He opened his eyes and saw her lying beside him. Her naked body glistened with sweat. He ran his hand over the curve of her hip and up her inner thigh. He forgot all about the wolves. Ian kissed her until she opened her eyes.

"We should be going," he said.

She shook her head.

"But your folks-"

"They're in Cleveland. At my aunt's wedding."

"I know but-"

"But nothing. Can you find our way home in the dark?"

"Yeah. No problem," Ian said. There would be time to explain his night vision later.

"I love you," she said.

"I love you, too."

"Now come here," she said as she pulled him to her.

Ian trembled as another wave of electricity coursed through him. He ground his teeth and felt his bones moving as Kelly put her hand on his shoulder and pushed herself up. Following her lead, he rolled over onto his back.

"God, when did you get so hairy," she said when she braced herself with one hand on his chest. With the other, she reached between his legs and guided him.

Ian didn't answer her question. He knew he'd grown hairier, especially of late. His chest was covered in fine dark hair when he woke up that morning and his arms and legs were as well. He figured that his back was covered in similar fine hair. None of that mattered at the moment. He recalled Kelly's request earlier that he "be here" right now and he gave himself over to the moment. Another tremor passed through him and he arched his back into it. Kelly moaned and bucked harder. The feeling was exquisite and excruciating at the same time. His bones ground together and popped. He arched his back again and this time heard himself snarl. He convulsed beneath Kelly and the cabin grew less distinct around him. He tried to focus on her. Her eyes were closed and she was biting her lower lip, a high-pitched whine issuing from her throat. She twisted back and forth, bucking toward a climax when she opened her eyes. And screamed.

The black wolf awoke to find himself pinned beneath a writhing, whining creature. They were joined and he felt himself exploding into the strange beast that straddled him.

He opened his mouth to snarl, to give voice to his terror, when the thing above him whipped its head down, sweat from its long, drenched hair showering the dark fur on his chest. It opened its large, round eyes, paused for a second, then pulled full lips back from white teeth and screamed. The sound was a knife that spiked the wolf's sensitive ears. He screamed himself to drown out the piercing shriek, and his right forearm and paw drove upward to ward off the strange creature. His black claws tore across its throat and cheek, snapping the creature's head violently to the side. A geyser of hot blood sprayed across the cabin, spattering the nearest wall in a wide arc. The creature swayed for a moment, clutching at its ruined throat, then listed to the right and fell. Its head banged off the floor and the rest of it followed, tumbling off the platform, limp. The eyes were wide open but unseeing as the life of the creature pumped out through the rend in its neck, slicking the boards with a pool that shone black in the rectangle of moonlight illuminating the rough, wooden floor.

The black wolf turned and scrambled to a sitting position. He trembled, head low and ears flattened against his head. He looked left and right then at the single window. It was far too small to allow an escape even if it wasn't covered by a rectangle of transparent material.

A memory, an impression, struck him, and he reared up on his hind legs. He felt more comfortable on all fours, but standing on his back legs was easy enough and it freed his forelimbs. He stepped over the fallen creature, careful not to slip in the pool of its blood, and gripped the doorknob in something that resembled both a hand and a paw. He turned the knob, and the door clicked and swung open. He stuck his head out and scanned the forest around him before leaping out into the muggy night.

He sniffed the air, searching for some clue that would tell him what to do next, where to go. How to live. He smelled animals with blood running warm in their veins. He sensed other creatures that were cooler or wetter. They moved through the underbrush, pursuing prey even smaller than themselves, creatures with many legs that took shelter inside pungent, rotten logs. There was water not far away, a slow current laden with silt, and a larger body of water farther off. The water there was almost still. The smell of rain hung in the air though the sky was still clear. It wouldn't be clear for long, he knew, less than a day at the most. The wolf smelled carrion, too rancid for consumption unless he was desperate. There were other smells, potent odors with none of the sweetness of life about them. They were oily, off-putting smells accompanied by noises that approached then receded. Traces of the odor remained, hanging in the air in unpleasant clouds.

The black wolf turned a full circle, sniffing the air, until his eyes fell on the twisted body on the floor of the shack. He took a step toward the body and his legs trembled beneath him. He swayed and almost fell as a grief beyond comprehension overwhelmed him. He didn't understand at all why he should feel such agony but he did feel it. This creature was important, or at least she had been. She? Yes. She. The creature was a female and even though he was hungry, the black wolf knew she was not food. He whined, unsure of what to do, but he couldn't leave her there. With no clear idea why and no destination in mind, he stepped into the cabin and took one of the creature's upper arms into his jaws and lifted to test her weight. She was perhaps half his own weight. He shifted his grip, being careful not to break her skin, and carried her out of the cabin.

He paused to adjust his grip and blood from the massive wound in her neck trickled down his throat. The wolf's hunger flared again, but he would not eat her. He regretted killing her even though he was by nature a predator. She shouldn't have died, he was sure of that.

The water, he thought, not the stream but the larger body. He would take her there and...what? Hide her? Release her into the water? He wasn't sure yet what he would do when he got there, but it was a direction at least. He sniffed the air for the scent, found it, and headed in that direction.

After carrying the girl's body for a while, the wolf came to a wide, curving path of some dark, unyielding substance. The strange path interrupted the forest. On the other side of the path, the forest resumed. The water was over there, beyond the trees.

The black wolf placed first one paw then another on the path without putting down the burden he carried in his jaws. He tested the surface with both paws then stepped onto the path with all fours. This was the place that stank of strange, unnatural smells. The oily smell was embedded into the path, a part of the rough surface itself. Beneath his feet he could feel the vibration of something moving to his left. He could hear it, too, but it was still some ways off so he started to cross the path with slow, deliberate steps, holding the body in his jaws as high as possible from the offensive surface.

He was half way across the path when the vibrations grew stronger and the noise grew in volume much faster than he expected. Whatever it was, it would be upon him in seconds. A bright light swept around the bend to his left, heralding the big, rumbling object behind. As the wolf watched, the light seemed to divide as it rounded the curve until there was not one but two bright lights blinding him, casting everything around him into high contrast shapes of black and harsh, stark white.

The wolf stood still, transfixed as the lights swept over him. There were other lights, but they were swamped by the two large lights in front, each so similar to the white disc in the night sky. It was as if the moon had doubled and descended upon him, accompanied by a great, roaring beast. The roar was in turn accompanied by higher, wheezing exhalations of noxious gasses that made the black wolf's wide-open eyes water. Before he could move from his spot in the middle of the path, a high-pitched squeal came from several places at once behind the lights. There was a new smell, acrid and burning. Warm, white smoke jetted from behind the lights, visible for a few seconds until it wafted away into the dark. The wolf dropped the body and reared up. He stood easily on two legs as the enormous beast fishtailed back and forth before skidding to a stop less than twenty feet away.

After several seconds, the wolf was sure the beast's forward motion had ceased, but he stayed upright, listening to the rumble, the pops, and the liquid sounds emanating from the stationary monster. He snarled and snapped from apprehension and more than a little fear before he looked down at the soft, small body sprawled across the strange, broken line that ran down the middle of the path. Feeling the need to protect her still, the wolf dropped back down to all fours, stepped forward, and straddled the body. He stood there, head low, and growled a warning.

The wolf faced the rumbling beast for several seconds before he decided he'd seen enough. He was about to lift the small creature again in his jaws and go on his way when the enormous beast opened on one side and a smaller shape emerged. It was not entirely unlike the female at his feet, but it was more like the being he'd encountered in the tree on the first night of his life. With the bright lights still dominating his vision, the wolf couldn't make out any details, but he could see that the creature was large, with broad, rounded shoulders and a heavy beard of hair that spread across its chest. The wolf bunched his muscles to spring forward, if not to outright attack the thing, to at least impose his will upon it so that it would give ground and perhaps retreat inside the larger beast. If it failed to do so, attack would follow. He saw no sharp claws, nothing the creature could defend itself with. It was large and soft, and might well supply more than enough meat to satisfy his hunger for the moment.

The wolf growled again and stepped over the prostrate female, but the large shape behind the lights did not give ground. Instead, it raised a hand, a bright light flashed, and a deafening roar split the air. The wolf jumped and froze, head low, and came no closer. He didn't like that noise. The man-the wolf grasped the concept in the same wordless way he understood that the smaller body he'd carried was a female-repeated the gesture. He raised his hand again and there was another flash of light, another thunderclap. The wolf stumbled back over the body behind him. Before he was aware of it, he had one foot off the path itself onto the narrow strip of dirt between the path and the grass. He kept his eyes on the man behind the lights. The big man said something in a loud, trembling voice. His fear was palpable but he still refused to yield. Instead, he pointed both hands at the wolf, holding an object the wolf now understood had produced the flash and the thunderclap. The man hesitated, though, and the object didn't roar again.

The black wolf was confused. He was not sure at all that the man could resist him, much less harm him, but the object he held in both hands might have that power. On another night when he was more comfortable, more sure in his own skin, he might have attacked and discovered for himself if the man could harm him, but for now it seemed more of a risk than he was ready to take. The female would have to stay here. She was lost to him. Perhaps she would mean something to the male. She was more like him, anyway, then she was like the wolf. Still, he regretted having to leave her there even as he turned and trotted off the path into the forest. The wolf picked up speed after entering the comfort of the dark under the trees and ran, hurtling fallen logs and tangled roots to put distance between himself and the path, the rumbling beast, and its shadowy companion.

A half mile later, the wolf slowed to a trot. His heart, which had been beating steady but faster, slowed its pace. His breathing returned to normal and his long tongue lolled over his black lips. He was more aware than ever of his immense hunger and he pushed the memory of the dead female from his mind. He sniffed the air, the ground, for a scent that would lead to acceptable prey. It was time to feed.

Chapter 7

"What the hell is going on, Matthew?"

Sheriff Matthew Kearsey heard Deputy Farrell's question, but he had no answer to give.

The road flares were distributed along the curve of the shoulder, choking off the southbound lane, leaving enough room along the narrow shoulder for traffic to pass. Traffic was light even in the middle of the day. It would be even lighter at 1:30 AM.

The rear driver's side door of the deputy's cruiser was open. Buddy Hargiss sat sideways in the seat, sipping coffee from a thermos, his size fifteen shoes on the road.

The sheriff looked over his shoulder at the truck driver and shook his head. "A wolf?"

Rollie Farrell shrugged. "That's what he said."

"I guess I should have a word with him." The sheriff looked down at the small shape under the tarp. By the time he got to the scene, Deputy Farrell had covered the body with a yellow tarp and weighed it down with wrenches, tire tools, and other objects from the cruiser's trunk. Not that there was any chance of the tarp blowing away. The warm, muggy air wasn't moving at all. The sheriff was just glad he didn't have to take another look at the girl's ravaged body. One look under the tarp was enough. He mopped the sweat off his neck with an old handkerchief as he walked to the deputy's cruiser.

"Who is she, sheriff?" the truck driver asked without looking up.

"Can't say," he said. He knew, but protocol dictated that the girl's family be the first to know. That was going to be rough. He knew the family, at least a little. The girl was the cute little teenager who worked part-time at her grandmother's floral shop. The girl's parents were both killed years ago and she'd been raised by her grandparents. Those poor folks had already lost their daughter and son-in-law. Now their granddaughter was gone, too.

"I know what I saw," Buddy Hargiss said when the sheriff approached.

"No one said you didn't."

"Yeah, but who's going to believe me? I done told that deputy. He tried to tell me it was a stray dog or something, that it just found the body." He shook his head. "I know what I saw."

"So tell me."

"It was a wolf. Had to be. And it was carrying the girl."

"A wolf?"

"That's right. A wolf. Except..."

"Except what?"

"I don't know what else to call it. It looked like a wolf, but it stood up."

"What do you mean?"

"It stood up like a man on two legs. It stood up, and I'm telling you the damn thing looked right at me. It was lucky I was able to stop in time, but if I'd plowed the thing it would have served it right. It was just instinct, I guess."

"Instinct? I don't follow you."

"I'm talking about myself! I was tired, but my reflexes are fast. You see something big in the road, you stop. If I'd been pulling a trailer there was no way I could have stopped. I'd have jack-knifed trying. As it was, I was only able to stop in time because the road was dry for once. That thing got lucky."

"OK." Sheriff Kearsey nodded. "Back up to the beginning. Tell me what happened."

"Not much to tell about that part. I was coming down 727, rounding the bend, ya know, then I seen it. It was carrying that little girl across the road."

"Carrying her?"

"In its jaws. It was big. Big as a bear. Big enough to carry that girl like she was nothing."

"Go on."

"When it saw my lights it stopped, like a deer caught in the headlights. It dropped her and stood up. I got down from my truck. I was scared to death so I...I got my gun out of my glove compartment."

"I'm not worried about the gun right now. Go on."

"Hell, I'm glad I had it. Fine me. I don't give a fuck. My headlights were all over that thing. I saw its eyes. It growled at me, was gonna kill me for sure. I got off a couple of shots, just in the air, to scare it. It flinched and when I pointed the gun at it, the thing took off. I musta scared it away, but I don't mind telling ya, I think I was more scared than it was. The thing was a monster."

"I thought it was a wolf?"

"It was, but...look, I know there ain't no wolves in Ohio. Not supposed to be, anyway. I don't care. I know what I saw. It was a wolf but...but something wasn't right about it."

"How?"

"I don't know. Well, other than it being so fuckin' big and standin' up like a man."

"OK." The sheriff sighed and crossed his arms. "What happened then?"

"Well, like I said, it ran off. When I was sure it was gone, I went over to check on the girl, to make sure she was dead. I was pretty sure she was but I wanted to make...oh, god! I'm gonna throw up again if I think about it too much."

"I understand."

Buddy Hargiss took another sip of coffee, swished it around in his mouth, and spat it out. "I need some water. Or some whiskey. That would be better."

"Is that it, Buddy?"

The truck driver shook his head. Drops of coffee and spittle clung to his gray beard. "Helluva body, I gotta say. A damn shame that such a good lookin' little thing had to-"

"Buddy? Try to show a little respect."

"I know. I'm sorry. It's just something else to think about besides...besides..."

Buddy got up, trotted to the edge of the road, and threw up.

"ME's on his way, Matt," said Rollie Farrell from behind the sheriff.

"OK," Sheriff Kearsey grunted. The wheels in his head were turning and he didn't like where they were going. He was pretty sure the girl had been seeing Ian Murphy of late. He'd seen them together around town, at least. First the Patella boy, Ian's best friend. Now his girl. No, he didn't like where this was going at all.

Chapter 8

Ian stumbled through the growth to the edge of the forest. His bare feet weren't accustomed to the rough forest floor, but it didn't hurt as much as it should have. His disoriented mind registered this curious fact at the same time that it dawned upon him that he was naked. He had no idea what time it was, only that it was early. He looked through the trees at his back yard. The sky was dim, the sun still close to the horizon, and the green grass of the yard sparkled with morning dew.

Dad's not home yet. From where he stood he could see that his father's pickup was still gone. That meant it must be earlier than 8:30 AM, much earlier from the look of the sky. He had no idea how or why he woke up in the woods let alone how he could explain it to his father.

Before he started across the yard he ran his tongue over his teeth. He had an odd taste in his mouth, metallic and sour. He looked up at the sky again. Despite the morning sun, clouds were rolling in fast from the west and the smell of rain hung heavy in the air. It was going to be a wet day.

The back yard was bordered on one side by the forest and by a line of trees on the other. They had only one close neighbor, the view from their house blocked by the trees and the garage. Taking a deep breath, Ian sprinted across the back yard and up the porch steps. He had a brief moment of panic when he considered that the door might be locked. His breath caught in his throat and he covered his crotch as best he could with one hand while reaching for the doorknob with the other. The knob turned. "Thank you!" he said. He wasn't sure who he had to thank, but saying it made him feel a little better as he ducked inside. He closed the door and leaned against it, waiting for his heart to stop pounding.

He was dirty all over and damp from spending the night outside. He had no memory whatsoever of his father finding him in the middle of the yard the morning after Chevy's death, but he imagined he must have looked much like this. *Again? What's happening to me?*

"First things first," he said aloud. He looked at the clock on the dining room wall. 6:14 AM. The time gave him something to grasp, to center himself on. He looked down at his feet and saw the wet, dirty tracks he was leaving on the polished hardwood floor-*gotta do something about that*-but first he had to get cleaned up.

Ian ran to the bathroom, where he flipped on the light and looked at himself in the mirror. He had to grip the porcelain sink to keep from falling when he saw the nightmare visage that stared back. His long hair was a mass of tangles, mud, and leaves. His body was scratched and filthy but leaner, more muscular than he had ever known himself to be. For a moment, he felt as if he was looking at a portrait of a wild man stolen from some primordial forest instead of an eighteen year old country boy, but when he gasped the wild man gasped as well. When he shook his head, the wild man did the same. Despite the fog he had yet to shake, he felt strong, as strong as the wild man in the mirror looked. When he grimaced, the wild man grimaced too, and there was dark red between his teeth. It was then that Ian placed the strange taste he'd awakened with in his mouth. Blood.

He looked at his hands. There was blood under his fingernails, thick, almost black, and half dried. The fog in his head began to lift and dim memories of the night before assembled themselves. He looked deep into the bloodshot eyes of the wild man in the mirror and watched as the lips formed a single word into a whisper.

"Kelly."

Sheriff Kearsey rang the doorbell again. He heard someone moving inside the house, but it was almost a minute before the door opened. Ian Murphy stood on the other side of the screen, soaking wet, his long hair hanging in ringlets over the towel on his broad shoulders. "Mornin', Ian. I'm sorry to bother you so early but I figured you might be up, what with working on the farm."

"It's Sunday, Sheriff."

"So it is. So it is. We need to talk. May I come in?"

"Sure." Ian opened the door and gestured for the sheriff to enter. "I don't work on the farm anymore. Leon is selling the place."

"That so?" Sheriff Kearsey stepped inside and took off his hat. He didn't mention the incident with the Mantle's rottweiler, but he couldn't help but wonder if that played a part in Leon selling the farm if he was indeed doing that. He made a mental note to drop in on Leon. "That's a shame."

"He said he doesn't have the heart for it. You want some coffee?"

"It shows, huh?" The sheriff mustered a weary grin and followed Ian into the kitchen, hat in hand. "It's been a pretty rough morning. You look a little rough yourself."

"I was in the shower when the doorbell rang. I was up early doing yard work. Trying to get ahead of the rain." Ian got two mugs out of the cabinet next to the sink. "It's not Mo's, I'm afraid."

"I'm sure it'll do." The sheriff glanced at the clock on the wall over the sink. It was still only 7:30 AM. He knew the time, but his eye for detail compelled him to look around. To the left of the counter bisecting the kitchen was a small cherrywood table with four matching chairs. The pantry door and the floor to ceiling shelf on the adjacent wall matched the table. On the shelf were various knickknacks that must have belonged to Ian's mother; Precious Moments figurines, praying hands, polished geodes on stands, plaques with homey sayings printed in feminine scripts. It had been the better part of a year since Rose Murphy's death, but it was still very much her room. He'd only glanced into the kitchen on his previous visit. This visit figured to be even less pleasant.

"Dad will be home in another hour or so," Ian said. "He still takes all the overtime he can get."

"We can wait till he gets here if you prefer."

"That's all right."

Ian dropped the towel on the counter next to the sink. His navy T-shirt was spotted with water.

"Cream and sugar?"

"Black is fine," the sheriff said. While Ian poured coffee into each mug, the sheriff had the distinct impression that the boy was taking pains to seem casual, but there was a furtive, clipped nature to his speech and gestures.

He sipped at his coffee. Ian was right. It wasn't Mo's. He swallowed and sat the mug on the counter, leaning forward to better observe the kid. His eye was drawn to the beads of water clinging to the boy's jawline. He followed the line of water along the sweep of Ian's cheek to the small, silver earring in his left earlobe. The flesh around the earring was bright pink. A recent addition. The sheriff was no small man himself, but he couldn't help but notice Ian's physical stature. *When the hell did he get so damn big?* He was too young to have filled out yet, but his arms looked toned and powerful. He might have been working out a lot, but he'd seen Ian a month before and he didn't look so imposing then. Maybe it was the clothes.

"What can I do for you, Sheriff?" Ian was pouring creamer into his own mug, half turned away.

"Ian, when was the last time you saw Kelly Shepherd?"

Ian nearly dropped the creamer into the sink. He turned and looked at the sheriff. "What?"

"I need to know the last time you saw her."

"Uh...last night. I tried to call her before I got into the shower. There was no answer."

"You two have been dating, right?"

"Yeah. We...we are."

"Sit down, son. Maybe you'd better put that coffee down first, though."

"Why? What's..."

"How about her folks? Any idea where they are? I haven't been able to reach them."

"They're in Cleveland. They went to a wedding. Kelly didn't go. They'll be home tomorrow."

Sheriff Kearsey sipped at his coffee and paused. He knew the girl's family should be the first to know about her death. He knew Henry Murphy pretty well. He'd never had any cause to believe his old teammate wasn't the same decent person he'd been in high school. His son's reputation was just as solid. If anything, Ian was known for being downright shy, some might even say timid. He was the last person one might expect of being involved in something awful, but there was definitely something here. The sheriff didn't outright suspect him, but he decided to brush protocol aside on the chance that he might learn something from the boy's reaction. "I'm sorry to have to tell you this, Ian, but she's dead."

The young man's face fell. "Wha...what?"

"I'm sorry, Ian. She's dead."

"There must...must be some kind of mistake," Ian said. "That can't be true."

"It is, I'm afraid. There's no mistake." Sheriff Kearsey took a breath. The pain and disbelief on the boy's face was genuine. "There hasn't been an official identification, but I saw her at her grandmother's floral shop a few days ago. It's her."

"I...oh, god." Ian turned and threw up into the sink. He leaned on his elbows heaving into the basin until it seemed there was nothing more to come up. He ran the water, his back still turned.

"I'm sorry," the sheriff said.

Ian turned off the water but stayed at the sink, his head down, his body trembling. "I can't...what...what happened?"

"We're not sure yet. The county ME is examining her body. I need to speak with her grandparents. Do you have a number where I can reach them?"

Ian shook his head. "The Patella's might. Chevy and her...they're cousins. Leon and Faith are Kelly's aunt and uncle. They didn't go the wedding, either. They're...they're not going much of anywhere right now." He filled a glass with water and took a long, slow drink. When he was done, he wiped his mouth on a hand towel but still didn't turn around. "What happened?" he asked again.

"A trucker found her body in the road out on 727 near the lake. I can't go into the details, but she didn't die there."

"I don't understand. You...you found her in the road?" His voice quivered.

"A trucker did. You saw her last night?"

"She was here," Ian said. "We didn't go much of anywhere."

Ian straightened up, his voice stronger, but he sounded to the sheriff like he was trying to swallow something too big for his throat. Sheriff Kearsey noted Ian flinching when he said Kelly had been there, as if he'd said something he shouldn't have. Still, he thought the boy was telling the truth, or at least part of it.

"I don't see another car in your driveway. I take it she left?"

"I picked her up. We hung out for a while. Wound up back here. When you're in love you don't really need to do much. Being together is...enough. We grabbed a bite at the Micky D's then I took her home." Ian barely got out the words before he put his head into his hands and sobbed.

"You're driving?"

Ian nodded but didn't look up.

"I thought they might suspend your license."

"So did I." He still didn't look up.

Sheriff Kearsey waited while Ian composed himself. "Which Micky D's, Ian?"

"Does it matter?" Ian lifted his head but looked away. Tears ran down his cheeks and a bubble of snot hung from his nose. He wiped the mucus away with the back of his hand.

"Everything matters," the sheriff said. Unless the boy was a world class actor or a total sociopath, his shock and grief were real. "I need to establish a timeline for last night. I need to know everything I can about where she was, who she was with, who she might have seen."

"The one in Milford. The Micky D's. We went back to her place after that. I left early."

"What time?"

"Around 9:30 or so, I think."

"That's pretty early on a Saturday night. Especially with the house all to yourselves."

"Sheriff, am I a suspect? I'm getting that feeling."

"No. You're not." *I wouldn't tell you if you were, but I am interrogating you without a lawyer present.* The sheriff knew he was coming very close to violating the boy's rights, but there was something here even if he wasn't sure what. "The medical examiner will have the final say, but it looks like she was killed by some kind of animal."

"An animal? Like Chevy?"

The sheriff nodded. The Patella boy's cause of death was listed as the result of head trauma from the fall, but his wounds were similar to the girl's and there were black hairs on both bodies. Then there was the trucker and his story about the giant wolf. "Is there someone you can call, Ian? Being alone right now might not be the best thing for you."

"Dad will be home soon." His lips still trembled and fresh tears ran down his cheeks. "I love her, you know? Loved...her."

Sheriff Kearsey stood and sat his mug on the counter. He took a long look at Ian. The boy was pale, his hair still wet and tangled. His entire body seemed to sag under the weight of grief. He was much bigger than the sheriff, but he looked like a boy in need of comfort despite his bulk. "I wish to God I could say or do something that could help. I'm so sorry, Ian."

"Would you like some coffee to go," Ian whispered.

"No thanks. I hate to leave you this way. If there's anything I can do, anything at all, or if you think of anything else, no matter how trivial it seems, don't hesitate to call or stop by the station."

Ian nodded but said nothing.

The sheriff was almost out of the house when Ian stepped away from the sink, followed him to the door, and spoke up.

"She broke up with Ricky Thorogood a few weeks ago. You know him don't you?"

"Yes, I do." Sheriff Kearsey wasn't about to let on that he was well acquainted with Ricky. Ricky was a punk, a troublemaker, but the sheriff had always sensed there was more to him than that. Potentially, at least. He even thought Ricky had the makings of a good cop in him somewhere if he could get his shit together and grow up. He also knew the Shepherd girl had gone out with Ricky for a while. His next stop after speaking with the girl's grandparents would have to be the Thorogood's. He wasn't looking forward to that. At least the punk's asshole of a father wouldn't be there. His mother was no better, even worse in her own way, but she wasn't as belligerent. "I'll have a talk with him."

Ian wouldn't meet his eyes and the sheriff thought he looked rather sheepish, even ashamed. Was he attempting to throw Ricky under the bus to protect himself? That seemed out of character, another odd thing to file away. No, he didn't believe Ian was guilty but he didn't think the boy was coming clean about everything, either. "If you think of anything else," the sheriff said again, "please let me know. Anything at all." He patted the young man on his shoulder. "I'm sorry, Ian. I truly am."

"Thank you, Sheriff. I appreciate you stopping by."

Ian loped along the creek bank, running as fast as he could. He hurtled a log without breaking stride and only stopped to duck through a hole in the rusty fence that ran along the high side of the bank. Fat rain drops broke the skin of the creek below. The drops were coming closer together now but the morning mist still clung to the underbrush and shrouded the forest floor.

"God, what's happening to me?" Ian said through gritted teeth. He'd lied to the sheriff as his fractured memories fell into place. He wasn't sure the sheriff believed him. He knew his account of the evening sounded flimsy, but it at least bought him a little time. "Please let it be some kind of bizarre nightmare," he said as he ran. He knew better. The memories were hitting him now and they were terrible. The experience of making love with Kelly was everything he had hoped it could be. He could still feel her bare skin against his, remembered waking up with her, their passion igniting in an instant. Then the horror began.

Her face, her lovely, perfect face frozen in a rictus of terror, a scream rising in her throat; her eyes bulging, straining against their sockets, the blood vessels bursting, a spiderweb of red spreading outward from each pupil as if just seeing him was enough to kill her. It was the final image of Kelly, his love, and he knew he would carry it forever.

The memories were harder to make sense of after that awful moment. They didn't feel like they were his but how could that be? There was an otherness to them he couldn't understand. The perspective was different, lower. There was a great rumbling beast and an earsplitting sound. A gunshot?

Ian turned to follow the curve of the creek then headed away from the water up the bank. Passing landmarks burned into his gray matter, he neared the cabin. A tiny tributary trickled downhill, but it was obscured by the mist. He knew it was there without looking so he cleared the running water without breaking stride. The land leveled out and the brush grew thicker, but he plowed through the brambles without flinching or caring as they tore at his bare arms and snagged his jeans.

He approached from the back where the forest ran up to the cabin. He put one hand against the weathered wood and took a deep breath. He'd run full out for over a mile, most of it through dense forest. He bent over and put both hands on his knees. The rain was steadier now, the drops closer together. The forest canopy caught some but on the other side of the cabin where he and Chevy had cleared the brush there would be no cover. He didn't want to face what he feared was in the cabin, but he had to know for sure if the terrible memories were as real as they felt, so he forced himself to move, taking slow, careful steps like a man walking barefoot over sharp gravel. He swallowed hard to force down the lump rising in his throat. Water poured down his forehead into his eyes, mingled with his tears, and ran down his cheeks to drip from his chin. He walked past the single window, rounded the corner, and looked inside.

Clothes lay crumpled on the floor in two piles. The chain from the pocket watch that had belonged to his mother peaked out from under the pile of Kelly's clothes. When he reached to pick it up he saw the blood. A dark red puddle was soaking into the boards beside the low platform. The sleeping bag was torn, balled up under the window, and blood spattered the wall in a wide arc.

Ian doubled over, his head close to the floor. He began to sob, full body shudders that jerked him up and down. The sobs ran together into a tortured scream that exhausted his remaining breath, and he slumped on the stoop, half in and half out of the cabin, his face inches from the puddle of Kelly's blood. He rose to stagger a few feet away and throw up what remained in his stomach. It wasn't much. He didn't know where to go or what to do, so he returned to the doorway and collapsed in a heap. The rain soaked him to the skin, but he didn't care. Nothing mattered now that Kelly was dead, but Ian forced himself to think about the implications of the scene inside. It was a forgotten cabin in the woods, nothing more than an old shack that only he knew about. The only others who had known about it were both dead. He still rebelled against the idea that he was guilty of their deaths, but seeing was believing. He'd been with Kelly at the cabin and judging from the amount of blood, she hadn't left it alive.

He could go to the sheriff, tell him everything he remembered, even bring him out here so they could sample the blood and confirm what he knew. It was a tempting thought. It was the right thing to do yet he couldn't bring himself to do it. He needed to know what was happening to him. How could he know? Who could possibly help him?

The evangelist? Stubbs? Things had grown stranger for Ian ever since that night at the tent revival. In some ways things had been better for a short time. His dreams of Kelly had come to pass, but had that come at the cost of Chevy's life? None of it made any sense, but it all seemed to trace back to that one night. What could he do about it, though? He didn't know where Stubbs was now.

Ian's stomach still churned when he struggled to his feet. He pulled the pocket watch out by its chain and looked at the face, thinking of his mother. The watch still ticked, the second hand sweeping around the face. What would she have him do? What would his father have him do? It was after 8:00. His father would be home soon. *I'll tell him, tell him everything. Even if he won't believe any of it.*

Minutes later, Ian slogged home through the downpour, the sleeping bag over one shoulder, the watch in his pocket. The bag was torn but intact. Inside, the two bundles of clothes were rolled into a soggy ball. If his father was there he would tell him everything, whether he believed it or not, and if his father decided they should go to the sheriff, he would do it.

Ian crossed the back yard unconcerned with whether his neighbor saw him or not, as unlikely as that was. As he walked to the back porch, he could see that his father wasn't home yet. "Dad never turns down overtime," he said aloud. He felt relief, but it was mixed with the weight of responsibility. There would be no one to take this horror off his shoulders. The responsibility was his alone. Ian sighed, hesitated for a moment, then carried the sleeping bag into the garage. He put it in a large, plastic garbage bag then shoved that bundle into another bag. His father's tool rack dominated the wall over the work bench, as orderly as the display in any hardware store. A large ball peen hammer lay on the bench to one side. Ian thought for a moment then picked up the hammer. He paused outside the garage long enough to stuff the garbage bag into one of their two big cans then took off for the woods.

Twenty minutes later he burst through the trees with a howl and slammed the hammer into the side of the cabin. The old wood gave with a dull crack. Half an hour after that, Ian stood gasping for breath, the structure reduced to little more than a pile of rubble. Only the floor remained. The steady rain was washing the last of the blood through the splintered boards but a wide stain remained. Raising the hammer one more time, Ian pounded it through the middle of the stain and left it there, the handle sticking up through the shattered boards like a makeshift grave marker.

After destroying the cabin, Ian wandered in the woods, exhausted, without a conscious thought of where he should go. His feet seemed to move with a mind of their own and he realized he was heading across country to the Patella's house. To get there, he had looped around his own yard and his neighbor's, and crossed Stonelick Road. By the time he was conscious of his destination he was standing in front of their long gravel driveway. A few minutes later he stood on the Patella's doorstep, soaked from head to toe.

The door opened slowly but Faith Patella's eyes went wide when she saw Ian. "Oh, Lord!" She threw the door open wide. "Oh, my poor boy. Leon, it's Ian!"

She embraced him and pulled him inside. "What in the world..." She left the question hanging.

"I walked..," Ian mumbled. He made it into the house without collapsing and Leon arrived just as Ian's knees buckled. With their help, he made it into the living room and leaned against the back of a chair, Leon supporting him while Chevy's mother spread two towels on the couch. She draped one over his shoulders, handed him another, and helped him to the couch. Ian sat down and wiped at his face.

Leon Patella turned the big chair in their living room around to face Ian. "What's going on? The sheriff was here. He wanted to know if there was a number where we could reach Eve and Roy."

Ian looked down at the carpet.

Jennie Patella came downstairs. She sat next to Ian.

"Jennie," her mother said, "Ian's soaked."

"I don't care," the girl said.

The phone rang and they all startled. Leon got up to answer.

"Hello. Yeah, Roy," Leon said. "No...you need to give Matt Kearsey a call...Yeah, the sheriff...I don't know. He didn't say..." He took the cordless phone into another room.

Ian could make out every word if he focused on the conversation, but he didn't want to hear it. He held Jennie's hand instead and said nothing. Chevy's mother asked him if he wanted some hot chocolate. He shook his head.

Leon came back into the room. He was still holding the cordless phone. "They called from their hotel. No one answered at their house. They're worried about Kelly." He turned to Ian. "They called your house, too. Talked to your father. He'd just gotten in. You should probably-"

The phone rang in Leon's hand, startling them again.

"Hello...Henry...Yes, he's here." He held the phone out to Ian. "It's your dad."

Matthew Kearsey yawned and rubbed his eyes with the heels of both hands. He lit another cigarette and stared through the windshield, past the rain running down the glass, at the people going in and out of Mighty Mo's Coffee Shop on the other side of the street. Some of them made a dash for their cars. Others stood under the wide awning, sipping. Half of the tables inside were occupied by folks who sat there waiting for the rain to stop. It was going to be a long wait. It was looking like an all-day soaker, Matt thought, but he had more important things on his mind than the weather.

"Shit." He loved being sheriff. He loved being respected by an entire town, even if it was a small town of only a couple thousand people. He was looked up to around Stonelick, admired, and he did his best to repay that admiration by being a good sheriff, standing on principle and doing the right thing. Most of the time, he loved being sheriff.

Not today. Today was not just the worst day of his career, but the worst day of his life. He'd managed to grab a couple hours of fitful sleep after reaching the Shepherd girl's grandparents. They were four hours away when they called and he wasn't about to break the news to them over the phone. That meant he had to meet them at their home, had to look into their tired, road-weary faces and break the terrible news about their granddaughter.

Before that, he'd stood in the ME's office and took in as much as he could. According to Rube, the girl died well before midnight, possibly as early as 10:00 PM or so. Where she died was impossible to say, but there was no doubt how. Her throat was torn open, her carotid artery not just severed but destroyed. She'd bled out fast. The scratches all over body were post-mortem, likely from being dragged naked through the woods. She had black hairs in her hair similar to those on the Patella boy.

There was something else, too; semen. It didn't appear to be rape as there were no bruises or signs of rough treatment, but she'd had sex with someone shortly before her death. If that someone was Ian Murphy, there would be another issue to address since he was eighteen and she was still a minor, but unless her grandparents wanted to press the issue, he wasn't prepared to either. Sexually active teens weren't unusual these days and there was only a year between the two of them. Of course, if it had been one of his own girls...

The sheriff took a long drag from his cigarette then crushed what was left into the overflowing ashtray of his truck. The damn thing had been empty a few days ago. His attention shifted from the bright lights inside Mighty Mo's to the neon lights in the window of Bingo Bob's across the street. It was still too early to drink, especially the amount he had in mind, but the place was calling to him. No disrespect to Mighty Mo's, but coffee wasn't going to do the job.

"Damn," he said aloud. He almost said *damn wolf,* but he wasn't ready to go there yet, regardless of the trucker's story. This was Ohio, after all, but something was out there, something with dark hair and it was a danger to the people of his town. He wasn't happy with the scenario because it raised as many questions as it answered. What was this animal? Where and how had Kelly Shepherd encountered it? And why was Ian Murphy not telling him the whole truth about last night?

He kept as much of that to himself as he could when he told the Martin's of their granddaughter's death. They lived in the nicest neighborhood in Stonelick. When he pulled into their wide driveway he couldn't help but think of how their expansive house made even his none-too-shabby home look humble by comparison. Roy Martin was a retired investment banker and he'd done well for himself. Eve Martin's floral shop was a hobby, a fun little bauble that kept her busy even as it became an institution in the town. None of that affluence, though, could save their daughter or their granddaughter. He'd brought grim news to two very nice people who deserved better. It was the worst possible reminder of what he already knew: it might be the nicest neighborhood around but there was as much tragedy behind those doors as there was anywhere.

Eve Martin, still an attractive little slip of a woman, answered the door. Within minutes she nearly passed out. Roy Martin looked as if he'd been lobotomized. The Patellas arrived while he was still there, with Ian Murphy and his father along. The sheriff had to repeat the news to them a second time. A third time, counting his conversation with Ian that morning.

"The hell with it." Matt tossed the empty pack of cigarettes onto the floorboard of his truck. He decided to take the rest of the day off. His sanity demanded it. He got out and headed for Bingo Bob's. It had already been the longest day of his life and it was barely noon. Bob had just opened. *Thank God for Melinda.* His long-suffering wife knew when he needed to get away from things for a while. She would also be good for a ride if he was too far gone to drive. The truck would be fine where it was parked. He'd call her when he got inside. Right now, he intended to get drunk.

Chapter 9

Milford, Ohio

The rain began to slack off on Tuesday. By Wednesday morning, patches of blue sky were visible in the east. The barest trace of a rainbow shimmered. Ian saw the rainbow before the road curved to the right. He strained to make it out but it faded like the empty promises of a benevolent deity he could no longer believe in.

"Dad?"

"Yeah, Son?"

"When did you stop believing in God?"

Henry Murphy sighed. "I didn't, exactly. I can't tell you the moment, is what I mean. It just stopped making sense. Your mother was a good Christian woman. She never hurt anyone. She lived out what she believed. For her to die like that, wasting away, in pain all the time...I know bad things happen to good people. Hell, there have been books written about that. I would like to believe in God, but I don't see much reason other than just wanting to. That's not enough for me."

Ian saw firsthand how much his father had suffered. He'd suffered himself. Though his father understood the loss of a loved one, there was no way he could understand the guilt Ian carried on top of that grief. It was almost too much to bear. He'd given serious thought to taking his own life to end the pain, but he couldn't bring himself to go through with that, at least not while their deaths made no sense. Unlike his mother, he couldn't escape the feeling that there were answers to their deaths. There were reasons to be found and he didn't want to give up until he found them.

"Son," his father continued, "I'll tell you how I see it, or I'll try. Sometimes I'd swear it's all a lie. The 'God said it, I believe it, that settles it for me' crap doesn't cut it for me. That kind of bumper sticker theology is bullshit. On the other hand, there are folks who think they have it all figured out in the opposite direction. They're sure there is no God. Maybe they're right. Maybe they're wrong. I don't know. If I had a reason to believe I would. I just don't have any. That sums it up."

Ian looked hard into his father's face as the older man steered his pickup around the last bend before the straightaway that would take them to Milford for Kelly's funeral.

"I guess that doesn't help much, Son. I don't know what else to say other than I love you. I know that for sure."

"I love you too, Dad." He meant it, but when he looked out the window and winced it was because of the lingering question that wouldn't leave him alone. "Mom used to talk about God having some kind of plan for our lives, a destiny, I guess you'd say. What if this is part of the plan?" He didn't believe it himself but he needed to say it anyway.

Henry grimaced and brought the truck to a stop at a red light. He drummed his thumbs on the steering wheel and looked in the direction of the convenience store on the corner. "I think a man makes his own destiny, his own meaning. No one makes it for him. I'd rather choose my own, wouldn't you?"

"Yeah. Yeah, I would."

Stonelick, Ohio

Sheriff Kearsey stood near the back of the crowd gathered at the cemetery outside of Stonelick. The funeral home in Milford had been packed with people and at least half of them made the thirteen mile trek to the cemetery. The sheriff felt it was the right and proper thing to attend both. Still, he had no plans to stick around for long so instead of filing through the gates, he pulled the cruiser onto the shoulder and parked there.

Buddy Hargiss was on the fringes as well. The sheriff approached the trucker. "You come down from Wilmington?" he said in a low voice. "I didn't see you at the funeral home."

"It was the least I could do," said Buddy.

"You sent flowers, didn't you? There was an arrangement delivered that no one knew anything about. I guessed it was from you. Anyone here know who you are?"

"No. I'd like to keep it that way. Too many questions. Too many bad memories. These folks don't need to remember her like that. Besides, there are enough people thinking I'm crazy."

"I don't think you're crazy."

The trucker muttered something that might have been a thank you. "Who's the big kid?" he said. "The one with the long hair?"

"The girl's boyfriend."

"Looks like it hit him pretty hard. How about that other fellow over there?" Buddy didn't point. He just nodded. "The tough looking guy in the leather jacket?"

"Name is Ricky. He dated the girl before the big kid."

"I'm a helluva lot bigger than he is, but I wouldn't want to mess with him. He's a mean one. I can tell."

"He's a tough kid, all right, but..."

"But what?"

"Never mind."

"He still has it bad for the girl," Buddy said. "I'm glad neither one saw what I saw."

"The wolf?"

"Whatever it was. I told you and your deputy about it, but I know you didn't believe me. I saw what I saw, though. That thing was as much man as it was wolf."

"So now it's a wolf man?"

"It always was. I see it every time I close my eyes. I see it in my dreams, when I get some sleep. I've been drinking every night since then. Hell, my old lady's about to throw me out."

"Buddy, if you hadn't been there we may have never gotten the girl's body. At least this way her folks can have some closure."

"What do they know, Sheriff? I mean really, how much?"

"They know where she is. They can lay her to rest."

"Closure is overrated," he grumbled. "That the boy's mom?" He pointed at a short, wide woman with graying hair standing next to the big kid, her arms around his midsection.

"No. She's a friend of the family. The tall man next to the boy is his father. The boy's mother died a while back. Cancer."

"Those the girl's folks?" The trucker indicated the slumped shapes of Eve and Roy Martin on the chairs nearest the grave.

"Grandparents. They raised her. Kelly Shepherd's parents died when she was a toddler."

"Shit. This is just one tragedy after another here."

You don't know the rest of it, the sheriff thought but didn't say. The trucker meant well. He seemed like a decent guy. There was no need to make it even worse by telling him about her cousin. Charles Patella's folks were there, too, sitting next to the Martin's. Their remaining child, a girl no older than twelve or thirteen, sat with them. All three looked exhausted and shell-shocked.

"Well, I've had enough," Buddy Hargiss said. "If you need me, you know where to find me."

"Take care, Buddy." The sheriff watched the trucker go to his car at the end of the procession just inside the massive gates. His Chrysler was the only car in the line without the magnetic flag. When he started backing out, Sheriff Kearsey took that as his own cue to leave as well.

"Just come right out and say it, Matt," said Henry. "You suspect him."

The sheriff ran his hand though his short, gray hair. He liked to project strength and confidence, but the face that stared back at him in the mirror looked weary and unsure. He didn't need the mirror to tell him that. He felt as haggard as he looked. It had been a week since Kelly Shepherd was found dead in the road and five since the Patella boy's death. There were no leads, no satisfactory explanation, and contrary to Henry Murphy's fears, no suspects. He still believed Ian wasn't telling him everything but the boy had a lawyer now-at his father's insistence-and the minute things got tense the lawyer pulled the plug.

"Sheriff," the lawyer said, "We all know there is no evidence implicating Ian in either death." He was a pudgy man named Shuler with a receding hairline and a Napoleon complex. Though everyone in the room was a foot taller than him, he seemed intent on leaving the biggest impression.

"You're not hearing me." Sheriff Kearsey sighed and shook his head.

"It's time to end this constant questioning," Shuler said.

Sheriff Kearsey turned his attention to Ian's father. "Henry, tell me again why he's here? As far as I can tell, he's only here to earn his retainer and his hourly. That has to be costing you a fortune."

"I'm here to protect my client's rights," Shuler said. "I'm here-"

"All right!" Sheriff Kearsey held up his hand. "I don't believe Ian killed those kids. I can't make that any clearer. Henry, we've known each other for thirty years. We played football together in high school, for God's sake."

"That's all very well and good-" the lawyer started, but it was Henry who stopped him this time.

"Mr. Shuler, it's all right. Let him have his say."

"I know what kind of people you are," the sheriff continued. "Ian is not a suspect. How many times do I have to say that?" He scooted forward in his chair, both arms resting on the dining room table. Rose Murphy smiled down at him from a framed picture on the wall behind. "I'm just trying to connect the dots, to piece together what happened. In both cases, your son was the last person to see them alive. You know how that has to look."

"I don't care how it looks," Henry said. "My son loved Kelly. He loved Chevy. He was closer to them than he is to anyone, including me."

"Dad, that's..." Ian sat forward but made no serious effort to correct his father. "I've been sitting here, listening to you three talk about me like I'm not even in the room."

"I'm sorry, Son."

Ian opened his mouth to speak again, but Shuler beat him to it, seemingly intent upon earning that hefty wage. "Sheriff, it seems to me you should have a word with this Ricky Thorogood, the disgruntled ex-boyfriend. He has the motivation in Kelly Shepherd's case, and a history of violence."

"Juvenile nonsense," The sheriff said. "Nothing since he's turned eighteen."

"Why are you defending him now?" said Henry.

"I'm not defending Ricky. And I already told you, she was killed by an animal."

"Yes," Shuler said, ignoring his own comment pointing the finger at Ricky Thorogood. "That's beyond dispute. And the same animal, or something like it, tore up Charles Patella. I suggest you leave my client out of this and give him space to move on from these terrible events. He's lost his mother, his best friend, and the girl he loved. Isn't that enough?"

Sheriff Kearsey sat back in his chair. "It's more than enough." He looked across the table at Ian. "I'm sorry, Ian. You know I am."

"I know," Ian said.

"That's enough for now, I'd say." Shuler wore the satisfied expression of someone who had just scored a major victory.

Sheriff Kearsey stood and put his hat on. "I should be leaving. This is going nowhere." He ignored the lawyer again and looked at Ian's father. "Henry, I really would like to talk without this...this guy. He's not necessary."

"Maybe not," Henry said. "I'm just covering my son's butt."

"I understand. Ian? If you ever want to talk-"

"I wouldn't advise that," the lawyer said.

"Shut! Up! For once!" the sheriff shouted.

Shuler turned red and started to rise, for what good that would do him. He was scarcely taller on his feet than he was seated.

"It's OK, Mr. Shuler," Ian said. "Thank you. All of you. I appreciate your efforts." He got up and left the room, leaving the others at the table.

Over the next two weeks, the nightmarish visions that had plagued Ian since the night of the tent revival became a little less disturbing, but he wasn't sure if that was only because he'd grown used to them. The girl in the field, the wolves along the riverbank, even the torture wheel...their impact was duller now. Not that he welcomed them. Far from it. On any given night he didn't know which it would be, but one or more would be there, stealing his sleep, leaving him exhausted for the next day, but he was no longer blindsided and confused.

He couldn't go back to the farm, not even to visit. Looking into the worn faces of the Patellas was too much to bear. There were reminders of Chevy everywhere he looked. His best friend's death had driven a wedge between Ian and Chevy's family, despite their good hearts and good intentions. They needed to heal if such a thing was possible, and his presence was a constant reminder of their son. Perhaps some day they could rebuild a relationship, but not now.

The second Saturday after Kelly's death, Ian awakened feeling stronger than he had since then. His first session with the therapist was not encouraging, but the prescribed sleeping pills, which he feared would only trap him in his nightmares, turned out to have a positive effect. His sleep was deep, refreshing, and devoid of the terrible nightmares.

After showering, Ian stood in front of the mirror, his face half-covered by shaving cream. "What the?" His eyebrows were heavier and wider, almost meeting over the bridge of his nose. He'd already noticed that Kelly's off-hand comment about the length of his fingers was correct, but she hadn't said anything about his palms, each of which now showed fine, dark hair. There was stiffer dark hair on his shoulders, heavier than it was when he showed his shoulder to Chevy. His chest and arms were hairier than ever. After shaving his beard, he turned his attention to the bridge of his nose, then his chest, and as much of his shoulders as he could reach. After that, he shaved the fine hairs from his palms and took a good look at himself in the mirror. He had always been lanky, long-limbed, and stronger than he looked, but not especially muscular. The person who looked back at him was more toned, with a larger chest, muscled arms, and a tight abdomen. Farm work was hard physical labor, but he'd done none the last two weeks. Had this change been occurring for some time now without him noticing? He stepped onto the digital scale next to the bathroom sink. Not that he'd monitored his weight closely, but he was pretty sure that just a few months ago he was around two-hundred and ten pounds. The digital scale put his weight at two-hundred twenty-six pounds and change.

"Son, are you about done?" his father said from the hallway.

"Yeah, Dad. I'll be out in a minute."

"That Jeff fellow from school called again."

Jeff Boudreaux was a friend from high school he and Chevy sometimes had hung out with. He was a rail-thin fellow from a wealthy family who still preferred tattered jeans and old t-shirts. Jeff was making the rounds to see his friends from school one last time before heading out of state in the fall for a college on the west coast. "I'll call him back when I'm done," Ian said through the door. "We're going to a movie tonight."

"About time you got out," his father said.

"Yeah. It is." Ian knew his father was worried about him. He'd barely set foot outside the house since Kelly's funeral. He was worried, not just about the rapid changes occurring in his body, but about his future. His heart hurt for his friends and he didn't expect that to stop for some time, if ever. There was also the awful guilt, the suspicion that he really had played a part in their deaths. And that horrible memory of Kelly's face. His mother's belief that God had a plan for him seemed like nothing more than an empty platitude, but his father's statement that a man makes his own destiny had the ring of truth.

After touching base with Jeff, he had lunch with his father. It was nothing special, just sandwiches at the diner on 131, but they lingered there for almost two hours without bringing up Ian's mother, Kelly, or Chevy. His father needed that almost as much as he did, Ian sensed. It was the best time they'd enjoyed together in months.

When they got home, Ian showered, shaved again, and joined his father in the kitchen. Mutual Of Omaha's Wild Kingdom was on the little black and white TV at the end of the counter.

"Some shows are just better on the small screen," Henry said, sipping coffee while Marlin Perkins and his stalwart sidekick Jim wrestled an alligator on the ten inch monitor. He already had his lunch for work packed, his steel lunch box at his elbow.

"Working tonight again, Dad?"

"Yep. They asked. I said OK."

"It wouldn't hurt you to have a Saturday night off every now and then."

"No. Wouldn't help, though."

Ian knew his father would have turned down the Saturday night shift if Rose was still alive. He was sure his father knew it too, but in keeping with the upbeat tone of the day, neither was about to say so.

"I'm gonna go," Ian said. He clapped a hand on his father's shoulder. The prominent bones underneath the work shirt gave Ian a start, but he didn't let it show. On the TV, Marlin and Jim had wrestled the gator to a standstill, a muddy burlap bag over the big reptile's head. "Don't work too hard, Dad."

"No such thing."

"You always say that."

"I'm not too keen on you driving. The doctor advised against it."

"I know, but they haven't suspended my license. Besides, I'm only going to Jeff's house in Owensville. He's driving after that."

"I still don't like it."

"I know, Dad. I'm all right, though. Really."

Henry sighed. "Call me if you don't feel well. Call me at work if you need to. I'll be gone by the time you get back."

"Goin' in early?" Early meant 10:00 instead of midnight, so his father would be gone by 9:00.

"Yep. You have a good time, son."

Ian did have a good time. Jeff was good company. They split a pizza that Ian knew he could have made short work of by himself and caught a 7:30 show at the theater in Milford. It was after 11:00 by the time Ian left for home.

As he neared his house, Ian glanced at the headlights behind him. The car had been following him for several miles now, taking every turn with him on the drive home. When he pulled into his driveway, the headlights followed him in.

Ian turned off his car and swallowed hard before he opened his door. "Hey, can I do something for you?" He tried to sound braver than he felt.

The drivers side door of the car opened. The driver left his headlights on, the bright white rendering him nothing more than a silhouette as he approached.

Ian was about to speak again when the silhouette took two quick steps forward and slammed a roundhouse right against his cheek. The force of the blow buckled Ian's knees and he blacked out for a second. When he opened his eyes again, he was on his back, his head throbbing.

"Get up, fucker!"

The voice was raspy and slurred, but Ian knew who it was. His head cleared faster than he would have thought possible. Ricky Thorogood stood over him. He smelled of Old Milwaukee and pot. His face was twisted into a mask of wild-eyed rage.

"I said get up!"

Ricky kicked out with a pointy leather boot, but Ian twisted to the side, eluding the blow.

"She's dead, motherfucker! Dead! If she hadn't been with you she'd still be alive!"

Rolling over to crouch on all fours, Ian pulled his lips back into a snarl. He took a deep breath and rose to his feet. Blood from his nose trickled over his lip into his mouth. "Ricky, you don't know what you're talking about." His voice trembled. He was afraid but he also felt a rage rising within.

"The hell I don't! She dropped me like a hot rock and took up with you. A couple of weeks later, she's dead. Just like her cousin! And you were there, too!"

"You..." Ian shook his head, at a loss for words. Everything Ricky said was true.

"And who does Kearsey come after? Me!"

"He talked to me, too, Ricky." Ian was struggling to maintain his composure. There was more than a little sense to what the punk was saying. *Still,* Ian thought, *if he hits me again...*

"He should fuckin' arrest your ass!" Ricky punctuated his statement with a hard shove intended to knock Ian off balance, but the thug only bounced off him instead.

"Get in your car and leave before something bad happens," Ian said.

"Oh, yeah? Well, maybe I want something bad to happen."

Ian saw a flash of fear in the smaller man's eyes, but he also saw anger overtake the fear. He noticed the twitch of a shoulder, the shift in weight that told him what to expect, and this time he was ready. Ricky threw another punch, this one shorter and straight at Ian's chin, but he stopped the punch cold with his open right hand. At the same time, his left hand darted up and caught Ricky by the throat. Ricky gasped as his stocky one-hundred and eighty pounds was lifted off the ground and slammed against the siding of Ian's house with bone-shaking force. Ian held him there, Ricky's feet dangling six inches off the ground, the grip around his throat like a vice.

"Listen, you stupid prick!" Ian locked eyes with the man, amazed at himself, at his own speed, at his strength. Ricky felt like a child in his hand. He could hold him there for as long as he wanted. "I loved her more than a piece of shit like you ever could. She was nothing but a trophy to you!"

"You're...wrong," Ricky managed to choke out. His eyes were bulging. He was clearly afraid but still defiant. He hammered at Ian's arm with both hands and kicked out, but it did him no good.

Ian opened his mouth to speak again but stopped cold when he noticed his hand around Ricky's throat. The headlights illuminated it in harsh white light. Before his own eyes, coarse, dark hairs emerged from the back of his hand and his nails lengthened into blackened talons that dug into the flesh of Ricky's neck. Blood welled up and flowed over his hand onto Ricky's shirt. Ian ran his tongue over his teeth, feeling the pointed tips of too-long canines. He looked from his hand into Ricky's eyes, saw the horror there, and wondered what he looked like to the man. Ian knew it would be easy to tear Ricky's throat out. He thought of Kelly, of his last memory of her face, and he let go. Ricky dropped to the ground, gasping and choking.

"Get out of here," Ian said. "Get out of here before something bad really does happen."

Shaking and holding a hand to his bloody throat, Ricky got to his feet and stumbled to his car. Once inside, he jammed the gearshift into reverse and the dark car shot backward up the driveway, tires spinning, throwing gravel across the yard. When he reached the road, he spun the wheel to straighten out and took off in a cloud of white smoke as if the devil himself was after him.

Ian watched the tail lights fade into the distance then ran inside. In the bathroom, he flipped on the light and looked at himself. He saw the tips of sharp teeth receding as dark, black hairs disappeared under rippling skin. He looked down at his hands just as the dark hairs there receded as well.

"What's...what's happening to me?" A terrible thought occurred to him and he pulled his wallet from his pocket. There behind the single credit card, the blue corner of a thin business card was visible. He pulled out the card and stared. The pale blue in the left corner of the card transitioned to dark, midnight blue on the right. An irregular, jagged line bisected the card at an angle. Behind the line, a white circle was half visible. Below the line, against the deep indigo, the words "Peter Stubbs Ministries" were printed in bright yellow. "The wolf and the lamb shall feed together. Isaiah 65:25" was printed beneath in bold red. A phone number was printed in white beneath that.

He'd looked at the card several times, almost thrown it away at least twice, but it was only then that the image struck him not as the morning sun he'd taken it to be, but as a moon on the rise.

Chapter 10

August 1989

St. Louis, Missouri

"So that's the famous Gateway Arch?"

Ian was six hours from home, talking to himself as he drove across the Poplar Street Bridge. St. Louis reminded him of Cincinnati in many respects. Busch Stadium was virtually identical to Riverfront Stadium. The Missouri River was twice the width of The Ohio River, but the water was the same muddy brown. The landscape was different, though, with none of the rolling hills that presaged the Appalachians to the south and east back home, and there was nothing like The Arch in Cincinnati.

He glanced at the digital clock on the dashboard of his old Maverick. 4:10 PM. That was Eastern Time, of course. He was now in the Central Time Zone. He was making good time, but he had at least three hours to go, perhaps closer to four, before he reached his destination.

No one picked up the phone when Ian called Stubbs the night before. "God Bless you," Stubbs' baritone voice said on the prerecorded message. "You have reached Peter Stubbs Ministries. I am currently in Springfield, Missouri for a conference. I will return on Monday, August 14th. Please leave a message after the beep and I will return your call as soon as possible. May the boundless love of Our Lord Jesus Christ be with you always."

Ian hung up without leaving a message. After the disturbing encounter with Ricky, he was too keyed up to sleep so he popped one of his father's tapes into the VCR and stared at old episodes of Bonanza until he dropped off sometime after 3:00 AM.

"Son?"

Ian awoke to his father shaking his shoulder.

"Ian?"

"Wha?" he mumbled.

"You fell asleep in the chair. I turned off the TV. It was nothing but static."

Ian yawned. "Did Little Joe wear that green jacket in every episode?"

"Yeah, I think he did. Did you have fun last night?"

Last night. Ricky. Ian didn't answer his father's question. "What time is it?"

"Almost 9:00. Are you OK?"

Ian rubbed his eyes with the palms of his hands. The hairy palms of his hands. "I gotta grab a quick shower."

"Go ahead. I'm done in there."

Ian headed for the bathroom before his father said anything about his eyebrows. He was pretty sure they were meeting in the middle again.

Twenty-five minutes later he emerged from the bathroom, still wet but freshly shaved. His father was in the kitchen sipping on a cup of coffee, looking ready for bed. "I'm glad you made it back from your friend's house last night," his father said. "I've been thinking about that. It was pretty foolish, to be honest. You'd be best not to drive for now."

"You're right, Dad." He had no idea how he could explain his plan to speak with Stubbs even if that meant driving across country when he shouldn't be driving at all. He wanted answers and Peter Stubbs was only the person he knew of who might have them.

"OK," Henry said. "I'm hittin' the sack." He got up from the counter but stopped in the kitchen doorway. "You sure you're all right, Son?"

"I'm sure, Dad. That coffee gonna keep you up?"

"One cup?" His father smirked. "I'll be up around four. We can talk then."

"OK. Get some sleep."

Ian waited to let his father get settled into bed then grabbed the cordless phone. His first call was to the office of Lighthouse Pentecostal Church. Verna would be there printing out the programs for the Sunday Morning Service that was due to start soon. She wasn't on staff but she might as well be. She always answered the phone when she was there, volunteer or not. He had a hunch she could confirm. Verna answered on the third ring.

"Verna, it's Ian."

"Well, hiya, Honey. How are you?"

"Uh, fine. Hey, is Pastor James around?"

"I'm afraid not. He's out of town."

"Were is he?"

"He's in Missouri at some big conference."

"Springfield?"

"It's some big to-do evangelical event out there."

"Do you know where it is in Springfield?"

"I do. Are you sure you're OK? Is this an emergency?"

"I'm all right, Verna. I just need to know where he's staying."

Verna sighed. "The Ramada. On Glenstone. I booked the room for him myself."

"I just need to...speak with him."

"I can call him, tell him you need to talk. You know him. He'll call you when he can."

"That's OK. It can wait." He didn't know what else to say. He didn't like lying to her, but just as with his father, he knew it wouldn't make any sense to Verna. He only knew the pastor and Peter Stubbs traveled in the same circles and he'd played a wild card, hoping his hunch paid off.

"I'll be bringing dinner over this evening," Verna said. "I'm looking forward to it. I haven't seen either of you all week. If you want, you can tell me about it then."

"Sounds good," Ian said, glad that she couldn't see him cringe.

After he got off the phone, he packed a change of clothes and was out the door. A quick check of his oil and tire pressure, a stop to gas up, and a visit to the ATM was all that stood between him and the highway. He'd go through a drive-thru somewhere along the way for a bite, something with lots of meat. Just before he left, Ian scrawled a hasty note to his father. He didn't say much other than to tell him not to worry. That was pointless, of course. His father would worry, but at least he wouldn't be completely in the dark. He left the note on the kitchen counter, and left.

Springfield, Missouri

Three and a half hours after passing through St. Louis, Ian rolled into Springfield, Missouri on Interstate 44. The scenery had been virtually identical for much of the way: soybean, corn, grass, and endless fields interrupted now and then by low hills. The low floodplains around St. Louis were interesting by comparison. When he was halfway to Springfield, the land began to dip and roll as it did close to Cincinnati, foreshadowing the Ozarks to the south, topographic cousins to the Appalachians that skirted his southern Ohio home.

He was hungry, running on gas station hotdogs and chips, wolfed down on the go while behind the wheel, but the first order of business was to locate Stubbs.

Route 44 became Glenstone Ave, the main route through Springfield. Less than a mile inside the city limits, he passed an expanse of old barracks-style buildings to his right. The whitewashed wood structures sat next to much newer red brick buildings. An enormous auditorium dominated the lawn beyond a freshly paved parking lot. A big sign in the grass at the corner of the campus read South Central University Of The Temple of Christ.

The Temple Of Christ was the largest Pentecostal denomination in the country. During his preadolescent years, Ian's family had attended a Temple church for a time. Speaking in tongues, prophecy, the laying on of hands-all were common practices there, just as they were at Lighthouse Pentecostal. He had no idea why his parents stopped attending that church, but he was glad they did. He met Chevy at Lighthouse and Kelly, as well. The little church soon felt like home. After his last few experiences there, however, Ian wasn't sure if he'd ever feel comfortable there again.

The thoughts of Lighthouse Pentecostal brought him full circle to Peter Stubbs and the tent revival. The memory of the man's touch, of the power that seemed to flow from his fingertips, caused Ian's breath to catch in his throat. It had been the most powerful moment of his young life up to that point until it was surpassed by...

Kelly. Ian looked at his two hands gripping the steering wheel so tightly now that his knuckles were white. He relaxed his grip, let go with one hand, and studied his open palm. The fine dark hairs he'd shaved off that morning were there again. He stopped for a red light. While he waited for it to change, he looked at himself in the rearview mirror. His eyebrows didn't yet meet in the middle but they were heavy and reaching. He raised his lip to appraise his teeth. Were his canines a bit longer than usual? He wasn't sure, but he thought he felt subtle movements beneath the gum line.

"What did you do to me?" Ian wasn't sure who his question was directed to; Stubbs or God?

The Ramada Inn was located just past the intersection of Glenstone Avenue and Battlefield Road on the south end of town. Ian ignored the beckoning neon restaurant signs on either side of the road and pulled into the lot. The marquee under the sign welcomed the conference attendees. The conference must be near.

Ian parked, shut off the car, and took a deep breath. This time he ignored the digital display on his dash and pulled the old watch out of his pocket. He ran his thumb over the embossed design on the case before flipping it open and checking the time. It read 8:42 PM, but he knew it was an hour earlier here. He fingered the silver hoop in his left ear. The piercing was still tender but the sting was nothing compared to the pain that still throbbed in his broken heart. "Time for some answers," he said. He started to get out of the car but checked himself. He wasn't even sure if Stubbs was staying here and even if he was, he would still be at the conference. Ian had been to enough church conventions over the years to know that they always ended with a big Sunday night service. He guessed this conference would as well. That meant he would have some time to kill before Stubbs returned to his room, but what if Stubbs wasn't staying here? He would have driven six hundred miles for nothing.

A thought occurred to Ian. He got out of his car and shoved the watch back into the pocket of his jeans. The chain bounced off his hip as he walked into the lobby. In less than a minute he found what he was after. There it was, the scent trail of Stubbs leading right up to the desk. From there it led into the hallway. Ian was amazed. His brain had cataloged Stubbs' scent from the hospital and recognized it at once. He could even tell that the man had been here hours ago but he was gone now.

"Can I help you?" A blond woman in a pressed uniform stood behind the polished counter. She was smiling, but there was a hint of dismay in her eyes.

"Oh, no. That's all right." He wondered what he must look like, a large young man sniffing at the air. He made a mental note to be less obvious in the future. "I was thinking about staying here sometime." He winced. It was lame and he knew it. The woman's eyes followed him out the door.

Well, at least I know he is staying here. He'll be back.

Henry Murphy answered before the second ring. Distraught, angry, and relieved all at the same time, he gave Ian a tongue lashing before calming down.

"I'm sorry, Dad, but sometimes a man has to do what he has to do. You told me that yourself."

"Yes, but taking off across country without telling anyone? Driving six-hundred miles in an old car without anyone knowing where you're headed? And when you aren't even supposed to be driving? If I'd known what you were up to-"

"You would have tried to stop me. You have good reason to be upset. I really am sorry, Dad, but I am eighteen and the car is mine. And my license hasn't been suspended."

"You wanna talk about legalities? What about the sheriff? How would this look? This mess is a long way from over, you know."

"He only suggested I stick around. I'm not legally required to, and he doesn't have to know. I'll be back and he'll never know I was gone."

"I just don't want anything to happen to you, Ian." His father's tone changed now from rebuke to concern. "When I found your note I thought all this terrible stuff that's happened got to be too much for you. I was afraid you'd, well, do something. I don't want to lose you, son."

Ian heard his father's voice catch and he was reminded that he wasn't the only one with something at stake here. He'd been so caught up in his own needs that he hadn't considered that his stoic father was also in serious pain. He wasn't working all that overtime because he liked it.

"I'm sorry, Dad. I'm all right. I'm with that preacher from the revival. Peter Stubbs. The man who came to see me in the hospital?" He wasn't with Stubbs yet, but he hoped that would calm his father's fears. "I just need answers."

"And you think he has them?"

"I don't know. I hope so. Please try not to worry. I'm at a hotel in Springfield. I haven't even checked in yet. I'll call you tomorrow when I start for home."

"What about money? Do you have enough?"

"I do. I'm fine. I'll try to explain when I get home but I can't promise it will make sense to you."

"No. I don't expect it will." His father sighed. "I pulled some damn fool stunts myself when I was young. Call me when you get settled in there. Tonight. I want to know the hotel, the room number, everything. And call collect next time. It'll save you money."

"I will, Dad."

"I love you, Son. You be careful."

After several more reassurances, Ian was finally able to get off the phone. He hung up and stepped through the inner door into the lobby of the Bob Evans next to the Ramada. Fifteen minutes later he was walking back to his car, two pot roast sandwiches and a side of green beans and ham in the bag in his left hand, a large Coke in his right. For reasons he didn't bother to ponder, he paused for a moment and looked up at the darkening sky. It was almost 8:30 Central Time and the moon was on the rise. He was transfixed for a moment, staring at the almost full orb before getting into his car.

Two empty boxes sat on the Maverick's front passenger seat. The container of green beans was still half-full, but every piece of ham was gone. The soda cup held nothing but melting ice. Ian sat in his car with a paperback novel. The book wasn't great, but it was something to do. Still, his attention was divided. He looked up whenever a car pulled in, only to look back down at his book when the car parked, the door opened, and a man in a business suit or a weary family got out. Sometimes he just stared at the glowing moon, his mind gone blank. As a result, he'd covered only ten pages before Stubbs arrived. Ian had no idea what to expect, perhaps a Mercedes or Cadillac, so it took him a moment to react when the white Ford Explorer pulled in fifty feet away and Stubbs got out.

If the car was a surprise, there was no mistaking Stubbs for anyone else. He walked across the parking lot as if he owned the ground under his feet, his head held high, shoulders back. He wore a white suit like the one he'd worn at the tent revival and carried a big, leather-bound Bible in one hand.

When Ian got out of his car, there was the slightest falter in Stubbs' stride. *Does he know I'm here?* When Stubbs stopped at the door and turned, the question was answered.

"Hello, Ian," Stubbs said. "I didn't expect to see you here. I intended to call you before I left for home in the morning, but that won't be necessary now. Come." He waved his hand and smiled.

"How did you know I was here?"

Stubbs tapped the side of his nose.

Ian followed him across the lobby to the stairs, the eyes of the blond woman behind the counter following them all the way. He was about to ask why they weren't taking the elevator when Stubbs answered the unspoken question. "I find elevators claustrophobic. They're too much like a cage. I prefer driving to flying. I've been on planes when it couldn't be avoided but they're too confining."

"You drove here?"

"All the way from Minnesota. The Explorer is not a rental. It's mine."

Stubbs jogged up the stairs to the fourth floor. Ian followed. He was tired from the long drive, but the stairs were easy. Still, he thought he would sleep well tonight.

Stubbs' room was at the end of the hall. "Here we are," he said. "417." Inside the room, the window was wide open and the curtains pulled back. "I like the fresh air," he said. "My home in Minnesota has huge windows. I keep them open in all but the coldest weather."

The room was small but tidy, the beige walls decorated with prints of adequate if generic landscape paintings. On a round table near the open window were a briefcase and a notebook. Stubbs sat the leather-bound Bible on the table, the initials P.S. embossed in gold on the cover. He took off his suit jacket and hung it on a steel hanger in the closet then loosened his tie.

"Have you been watching the calendar?"

"What?" Ian wasn't sure what he expected Stubbs to say, but the comment seemed irrelevant.

"The calendar," Stubbs said. "For the rest of your life you will need to pay special attention to the cycles of the moon."

"What are you talking about?"

"The Blessing. God has given you a rare gift, but it is one that comes with certain responsibilities, as all gifts do."

"I have no idea what you are talking about. Cycles of the moon? What does that even mean?"

"Over time, the cycles will be less important." Stubbs hung his tie next to his suit jacket and pulled out the chair next to the desk. He sat down and motioned for Ian to do the same. "You will always answer the call of the lesser light, but in time you will be able to exercise your gift at will."

Ian remained standing. He crossed the room to the window and felt the cool night air on his face. "I don't know what you're talking about. I came to you for answers. Ever since that night..." He looked out at the night sky. It was full dark and clear, almost black beyond the city lights. A soft halo ringed the glowing orb of the moon. Ian felt a painful tingle. He shuddered. "My best friend is dead. The girl I love...loved...is dead, too, and I can't shake the feeling I had something to do with their deaths. I see things, nightmares..." The shudder gave way to an involuntary sob. "I have memories that don't feel like mine. Am I losing my mind?"

Stubbs stood and walked over to Ian, placing a large hand on his shoulder. "God's Word says that He gives order to the steps of a good man. He will not lead you astray no matter what it may feel like. Give yourself over to His purposes and you will find the peace you seek."

The words barely registered, but when Stubbs put his arms around him, Ian responded by burying his face into the man's shoulder. He gave himself over to the pain, the sobs buckling his knees, but Stubbs held him up with ease. He heard the preacher mumbling under his breath then realized Stubbs was praying for him. It sounded much like Verna, like what she called her prayer language. A great, good weariness settled over Ian and he wanted nothing more than sleep.

Stubbs led Ian to the bed and settled him there. "Does your father know you're here? I'd be glad to call him and put him at ease."

Ian mumbled his phone number. In another minute, he was deep in a blessed, dreamless sleep.

Ian heard whistling before he opened his eyes, the old hymn "Onward Christian Soldiers." The smells of coffee and soap filled the room. He opened his eyes and saw slender rays of sunlight slanting in through the half-open vertical blinds. He swung his feet onto the floor and sat up.

The whistling paused. "Good morning" Stubbs said from the bathroom around the corner.

Ian rubbed his eyes and looked at the clock next to the bed. 12:10 PM. The king sized bed was half-made, the bedspread on the opposite side smoothed down and tucked in. Stubbs' scent was strong on the bedclothes. He had slept next to Ian last night.

On the table next to the window, steam from an open thermos of coffee rose toward the ceiling. The window was open and Ian smelled a myriad of scents from outside; a dumpster; the oily smell of traffic; the enticing scent of multiple restaurants mingling together, a miasma of bacon, garlic, and smoked meats that caused Ian's stomach to rumble.

"You should shower," Stubbs said. "We have a full day ahead of us."

"A full day?"

Stubbs stepped around the corner, smiling. He was wearing jeans and a short sleeved shirt, the unbuttoned shirt revealing a torso befitting an Olympic athlete. His white hair was loose, more casually styled, and longer than Ian had realized. "There are towels in the bathroom. Feel free to use my razor if you like. The beard does get heavy at this time of the month."

"What?" Ian was confused by everything but most of all by Stubbs' attitude. The man was giddy as a boy on his first day of summer vacation. Ian reached for the phone to call his father.

"I spoke with your father last night," Stubbs said. "He was relieved that you're with me. He's a good man. I take it he has fallen from the faith but the grace of God is great."

"Mom was a believer. Dad has struggled with believing since she passed away." Ian rubbed his eyes again and looked at his wrinkled clothes. He'd slept in them all night.

"I'm sorry about your mother."

"Uterine cancer. She died nine months ago." Ian reached for his socks and shoes. Stubbs had taken them off sometime after Ian fell asleep.

"She must have been quite a woman to raise such a remarkable son."

"What's so remarkable about me?" Ian grumbled. "Dad was there, too."

"God really does have an extraordinary plan for you. In fact, you've already begun the journey."

"Did his plan include the girl I love and my best friend dying? Because if it did, I don't want any part of it." The bitterness rose in him like bile. He finished pulling on and tying his shoes then looked up at Stubbs. "I don't know what I expected from you. Maybe this was a bad idea."

Stubbs sat on the bed next to him. "It's not easy to walk the road you are on. I don't blame you for feeling the way you do. Others have felt the same."

"Others?"

Stubbs ignored the question. "It will all make sense when you begin to understand what you've been entrusted with. Did you bring a change of clothes?"

"Yeah. I did." Ian stood. "In my car. I'm getting into some clean clothes then I'm going home."

Stubbs stood as well and shook his head. "You can't do that."

"Why not?"

"Not today," Stubbs said. "That would be disastrous."

"Really? Why?"

"I will explain, but let's get something to eat first. Take a shower and get dressed." Stubbs poured a cup of coffee from the thermos. He took a sip and smiled. "You are hungry, aren't you?"

Ian didn't give a damn anymore about Stubbs' explanation, but he was hungry. More than hungry. He was ravenous.

Ian sat back from the table and sighed. "I don't think I've ever eaten so much."

"I love coming here when I'm in town," Stubbs said. "Springfield doesn't have much to offer, to be honest, but if there is a better barbecue restaurant anywhere, I'd like to know."

Behind Stubbs, Ian could see an extensive salad bar with all manner of green, red, and yellow delights. Time was when he would have loaded a plate with the vegetables, but they were of no interest to him now. Meat was what he'd wanted and it was only after his third rack of ribs that he felt sated.

"When I was your age I could have eaten as much as you, but the appetite decreases as one grows older." Stubbs smiled and patted his midsection. He'd settled for a mere two slabs. He was as trim as anyone Ian had ever seen, young or old. The short sleeve shirt did nothing to conceal his muscled arms and broad, powerful chest. Ian had already seen the man's hard, flat abdomen. Stubbs didn't appear to have an ounce of fat on his body.

"How old are you?" Ian wiped sauce from his lips with a napkin. Now that his stomach was full, his impatience was returning, but he was curious about the man.

"You'd be surprised," Stubbs said. "Still, time does leave its mark."

"I came to you for answers," Ian said, "but you talk in riddles and quote scripture. That night at the revival," Ian said then took a drink from his glass of iced tea. "What did you do to me?"

"I did nothing. I am only the vessel through which God chose to work."

"More riddles. This is pointless."

"You have been chosen, Ian, to do His work on earth. You are His hand, as am I."

Ian smirked and slammed his hand on the table. "I've had enough of your spiritual double talk!" Several diners turned their heads. Some glared at him. He lowered his voice but couldn't keep from snarling. "I want to know what's happening to me. I want to know why Kelly and Chevy are dead. And I...I need to know if I had anything to do with it. If you can't tell me, I'll be on my way."

Stubbs spoke softly. "I can answer all of your questions, Ian. Just be patient a little while longer. You cannot go anywhere today. I told your father I would see you home safely and I intend to do so, but if you leave now, you won't make it home. You must wait until tomorrow."

"Why?"

"Please, Ian. You must stay here tonight. I promise all of your questions will be answered."

"OK. Answer them, then."

"That requires your patience for just a bit longer. A few hours. And a short road trip."

"A road trip?"

Mark Twain National Forest
Missouri

The parking lot gravel crunched under the tires of the Ford Explorer as it rolled to a stop. They'd entered Mark Twain National Forest two miles back.

"Peter, this little drive into the Ozarks has been pleasant, but you promised me answers." Ian was at the end of his patience. "You said it would all make sense. We're here. Start talking."

Stubbs looked at him, smiled, and turned off the ignition. "You'll understand. In time."

Ian stepped out and slammed the door. "In time? I'm out of time."

Stubbs ignored Ian's protest. "I hate what they've done to Branson." He was already lifting the hatch in the back of the car.

They'd passed through the garish tourist trap that had once been a city half an hour earlier. Ian had been there with his parents years ago, before Bobby Vinton's Blue Velvet Theater, Presley's Country Jubilee, and the Hollywood Wax Museum. The tacky lights and signs provided a few moments of mild distraction, but his irritation returned full force as soon as they left Branson behind.

"A den of iniquity, to be sure," said Stubbs, "but there is a life to the place I find intriguing."

"I don't care."

"How do you feel?" Stubbs pulled a large but empty backpack from the car and shut the hatch.

"How do I feel? Frustrated. Angry."

"Your agitation is part of your gift. You just don't recognize it yet. I feel it, too, but I've learned to manage it." Stubbs pointed to the mirror on the door of the Explorer. "Take a look at yourself."

Ian shook his head but looked into the mirror. The face staring back at him was still his own but altered. His eyebrows were thick and dark, a single brow now running across the bridge of his nose without interruption. His beard was dark and heavy, a week's worth of growth for most men.

"I shaved this morning," Stubbs said, "Now look at me." He smiled again and Ian noticed that Stubbs' eyebrows were as thick as his own and the man's cheeks and chin were heavy with stubble. The hair was white, though, so not as immediately noticeable as his own. What chilled him, though, was Stubbs teeth. The canines were long and pointed.

Ian looked into the mirror again but opened his mouth. His own canines were long and sharp. He raised a hand to nudge his lip back further and saw that his nails were longer and darker. He looked at his hands. Dark hair covered the backs of both. He'd felt a dull ache in his joints but passed it off as the effect of spending so much of his time in cars the last two days. *My god. What did Ricky see?*

"We must hurry, Ian." Stubbs shouldered the pack and started walking across the lot toward the woods. "The moon is rising."

Ian jogged to catch up, along the way passing several people leaving the forest. Some stole wary glances at him and walked a little faster toward their cars.

"Before you awoke today," Stubbs said, "I made arrangements to procure a camp site."

"A camp site?"

"I needed an excuse to park for the night. The modern world is full of complications. Time was when we could just head for the nearest forest, but sometimes that isn't an option. You are fortunate to have a fairly extensive wood at your disposal at home."

Confused and more than a little frightened, Ian had no choice but to follow Peter. If it got too weird, he told himself, he could always walk back to Branson and catch a bus there. *Who am I kidding? This has already gotten weird. I should bail. Now.*

He didn't. They passed a small ranger station at the edge of the lot before entering the forest on a clearly defined path. A few yards in, several other paths branched off in various directions. Stubbs kept a course straight ahead. The sun was low in the western sky now but still strong enough to cast shadows across the path where the gaps in the branches allowed.

"A mile or so that way is Table Rock Lake," Stubbs said, pointing to the west. "We'll want to steer clear of that area. Too many campers. There's no sense risking unnecessary exposure. We must choose when and where to be seen. Rather, we must let The Lord choose for us."

"Look, Peter, I'm not going any farther until you tell me what we're doing out here." Ian grabbed Stubbs by the arm, intending to stop him in his tracks.

In one swift motion, Stubbs wheeled, clamped first one hand then the other on Ian's shoulders, and pulled the younger man close so that they stood face to face. He looked Ian in the eye and spoke in measured but firm tones. "I know all this seems strange to you. You're frightened. You don't understand. I told you I would answer all of your questions and I will, but right now we must put more distance between ourselves and the station back there." He relaxed his grip on Ian's shoulders but didn't release him just yet. "Bear with me just a little longer. Please."

Ian considered his situation. He was in a forest, nearing nightfall, over six-hundred miles from home, with a man whose behavior was becoming stranger by the minute. He was frightened, but his desire for answers was stronger than his fear. Whatever happens, it couldn't be worse than what has already happened. He'd come this far. He wouldn't turn back now.

"This way." Stubbs said.

Ian followed as they moved deeper into the shadows of the unbroken forest. Somehow, he felt better, at least emotionally. Physically, he itched all over and his bones ached, but it felt better to be among the trees. It felt right to leave the well-worn paths of men.

"I said God had chosen you."

Stubbs' voice was low but resonant in the quiet forest. Ian's sensitive ears picked up other noises, creatures scurrying for cover underfoot, the breathing of some who stayed where they were, keeping still in the hope of avoiding detection. He smelled them along with the rich scent of decades of loam accumulating on the the forest floor, of rotting leaves and pungent decay, of trees felled by age or lightning becoming one with the soil. Daylight was fading fast yet Ian's vision was undiminished. He saw everything as if it were bright daylight, but the colors grew dimmer as the outlines grew more stark.

"In the past, those with our gift were subject to persecution. Hundreds, thousands were put to death under the mere suspicion that they were as we are. The vast majority were not, but they were executed anyway, such was the fear of the ungodly. As it was with the original apostles of

Christ, there is a price to be paid by those of us who are marked to walk in such fellowship with our Lord."

"Marked? You keep saying that."

"Did you think your mother was speaking in Sunday school platitudes when she told you that God had a plan for your life?"

The forest began to thin, a glade opening ahead. The sky was dark, the moon visible through the branches.

Ian was offended by the mere mention of his mother coming from Stubbs. He wanted to tell him so but the pain in his joints was distracting.

"She was right, Ian." Stubbs stopped short of the clearing, leaning against a fallen hickory marking the edge. He removed his shoes and socks, and began to unbutton his shirt. "You need to experience the truth of who you are."

Ian was terrified and speechless. He could only watch as Stubbs put his shoes, socks, and shirt into the backpack then undid his belt and unbuttoned his pants.

Stubbs must have seen the look on Ian's face. "Oh, come now," he said. "I didn't bring you here to indulge in any prurient activities. You feel it, too, don't you, the quickening in your flesh? There is no stopping The Lord's work. His Spirit is coming upon you. It would be a shame to ruin your clothes."

"My clothes?" Ian took two steps back but stopped. There was nowhere to go. "I don't...I don't understand." Even as he said it, though, he heard his own teeth clack together and his voice turn rough.

"You've been through it twice, Ian. Your body remembers. Many do not survive those first few times. That you have testifies to your strength."

Ian felt a ripple that was painful but at the same time not unpleasant spread through his body, from his arms and legs to his fingertips. The pain passed, leaving in its wake the sensation of the most glorious full-body stretch, then came again, his joints popping and shifting. His clothes felt constricting, limiting. Unbearable. He couldn't get them off fast enough. His heart pounded in his chest and his breathing became rapid and shallow. He was panting.

"Step into the glorious moonlight with me," Stubbs said. His voice was clear and strong, but it was as much growl as human speech. " 'And God made the two great lights; the greater light to rule the day and the lesser light to rule the night.' The lesser light is the symbol of our purpose in God. The lesser light to serve His Greater Light. It calls to us, and once marked we must answer. Come with me, Ian. Step into the blessed plan that God has for your life!"

Stubbs turned and bounded over the log into the moonlit glade. As he did so, his form shifted in midair so that when one foot hit the ground he was no longer a man but some kind of furred, bipedal beast. His other foot hit the ground and his body altered again as he dropped to all fours and assumed the shape of an enormous white wolf.

Ian's first impulse was to cry out in horror, but he realized he was changing himself. He saw his hands morph into something between a human hand and a paw, the dark hairs there growing longer, and he closed his eyes. His spine contorted and his hips flared, the bones there rearranging. He felt as he were being forced into a container of a different shape, a contortion he found bearable if he stopped resisting. When he relaxed, the pain lessened. He felt himself slipping away as his jaws extended, his brow lowered, and he dropped to the ground on all fours.

A few seconds later the black wolf opened his eyes. He had a dim memory of another life, of being something other than this. That creature had a way of expressing itself that eluded the wolf. He had no words at his disposal. They'd been traded for heightened senses, greater strength, and a deeper awareness of the world around him. As he stood at the edge of the glade, his memory of existing as anything other than a wolf came to resemble nothing more than a dream. He was a wolf, imperfect, awkward, but a wolf, a wolf who dreamed he had once been a man.

A soft chuff cut through the cool night air and a short howl silenced the drone and cheap of a thousand insects. The black wolf's head swiveled on instinct toward the sound of his own kind. An enormous white wolf stood in the glade beckoning him.

The black wolf hesitated for a moment then hurtled the log. The great white wolf greeted him with a lick on the muzzle then turned away. The black wolf didn't hesitate this time. He trotted across the glade into the trees beyond and followed.

The white wolf moved through the forest with ease, gliding through the trees and undergrowth without making a sound. The black wolf had to move fast to keep up. He had no idea where they were heading, but it was clear that they weren't wandering aimlessly. Seconds after this realization he picked up a scent. It was similar to the scent of the female he'd killed before, similar enough to bring with it the feelings of grief and sorrow. The emotions were so strong that his steps faltered and he began to fall behind. An involuntary whine escaped his throat. His head and tail drooped and he stopped.

Where was the white wolf? He was nowhere to be seen now, but his scent was strong so the black wolf followed this time by smell, not sight. The smell of the white wolf mingled with the female scent, growing stronger with each step. The black wolf blundered through a thicket, not skirting it with the grace of the white, but crashing through it like some great, feral beast returning to the ways of the wild. He found that if he moved too fast, his back legs overtook his front legs. He felt insecure and uncoordinated. The white wolf was sleek, beautiful, and moved with grace. The black wolf knew he was powerful, but he stumbled where the white wolf glided. He lurched where the white seemed to float. Now he was alone. He could smell the other but couldn't see him, and he whined again.

The white wolf emerged from the underbrush a few feet ahead were he had been all the time. The beast approached and licked his muzzle again. Something like love swelled in the black wolf's chest. This great white wolf understood him, accepted him. In return he knew would follow wherever he was led.

For the better part of a mile the female scent grew stronger until the white wolf stopped. The black wolf stopped beside him and appraised his leader again. The white wolf was no larger than he was, but it wasn't the other's size that mattered. It was his bearing. He was sure of himself, confident, everything the black wolf could aspire to be.

Beyond them in a clearing sat a small domed structure. On the ground outside was a ring of stones surrounding a shallow pit, still radiating heat long after the flames that reduced the wood in the center to carbonized ash had died. The black wolf sniffed at the ground, at the air. The entire area smelled of the creatures that reminded him so much of the one whose memory filled him with sorrow and regret, but these creatures bore no relationship to that one. He had nothing to fear here, nothing to regret. There was a faint memory of one he had left lifeless at the base of a tree. In the wordless way of the wolf, he wondered if that was as much dream as memory, but he still recalled the scent. The scent did not lie. That one had been real, too. Then there was the the big one that had emerged from the rumbling beast. His senses lumped them all together and labeled them as human.

The white wolf nudged him out of his musings. It was time for action. He followed his leader to the dome, a flimsy fabric that rippled when the wind blew. Unlike the white, he was still too clumsy to approach in silence. They were several feet from the dome when he stepped on a dry branch levered over a small stone. The branch snapped, the sound loud and sharp in the quiet night. A few seconds later, a head emerged through a flap in the dome. It was a female, larger than the special one he'd encountered before but still much smaller than either himself or his companion.

The female opened her mouth, but before she could make a sound, the white wolf clamped his jaws around her head and dragged her out. She came out naked, writhing, and sweaty. She tried to cry out, but the most she could utter was a guttural moan, her mouth clamped shut by the pressure of the white's jaws. She pummeled him with her hands, but her blows had no noticeable effect. The white wolf put an end to her struggles with a crunch of his jaws, cracking her skull with practiced ease. She slumped, her blood soaking the grass as her body hung lifeless in his grip. He let the body fall to the ground, and looked at the black wolf.

He was so fascinated by the white wolf's actions that he had all but forgotten that there was still another female inside the dome, a second scent distinct from the dead one at his leader's feet. The female inside was cowering against the far side of the structure, her form a bulging outline against the fabric. He could hear her gibbering cries.

The white wolf nodded at him, the gesture making his intention clear. *Your turn.*

The black wolf approached the dome and stuck his head through the flap. The inside was darker, but he had no trouble seeing the figure inside.

Like the one who now lay lifeless outside, she was also naked but attempting to cover herself with a thick, padded material that smelled of both of them. A thin cloud of smoke hung in the air, his eyes watering from the pungent vapor. The female screamed, a high, piercing cry that annoyed him but offered no threat. She had no claws, no sharp teeth, and no device in her hand to produce the thunderous noise that had unnerved him before.

He hesitated, reluctant to do what he knew was expected of him. He was about to turn and look to the white wolf for assurance when his leader nudged him from behind. The black wolf approached the female. He felt no animosity toward her but likewise no fondness. She might be important to others of her kind, but unlike the one he'd killed out of fear and confusion, she meant nothing to him. Still, he hesitated again until the white wolf nipped at his rump. The cowering female pressed herself even harder against the thin barrier behind her and waved her hands in a futile attempt to ward him off. The black wolf shrugged and closed on her. She screamed, first in terror then in pain as he tore her flesh in a clumsy, inelegant manner. He knew what he had to do, but it took him some time to figure out the quickest way to do it. When he did, she was still fighting, kicking and screaming. He took a step back to appraise her position then lunged forward and seized her throat. Once he had a grip, he bit down, bringing his teeth together, and pulled. She convulsed once than struggled no more.

The black wolf let go and stepped back, his mouth full of her flesh and blood. The blood excited him and her flesh awakened the hollow feeling in his stomach. He was about to swallow when the white wolf burst through the flap and batted at his muzzle. He understood then; this is not food. He was hungry, but despite the wonderful taste of the female's flesh and blood, he wasn't about to defy his leader. He coughed, hacking a wad of flesh, blood, and saliva onto the soft, yielding floor of the dome. The white wolf backed out through the flap and called. The black wolf took a last look at the twisted body at his feet then followed.

"Ian? We must be going."

Ian opened his eyes in the dim morning light. At first he had no idea where he was or what was happening, but after a moment he remembered and drew back from the man crouching before him. He was naked. Again.

"No need for modesty," Stubbs said. He stood and walked back to the fallen hickory.

Ian's clothes were folded and stacked on the ground beside him. He snatched at the damp clothes and began to dress. His hands trembled.

"I know you would like to sleep. I would, too, but we've been here too long as it is."

Stubbs stepped over the fallen log and stood in the clearing. He was dressed, his jeans and shirt wrinkled but looking better than Ian's clothes. He smiled and ran a comb through his silver hair.

Ian got up and leaned against the log as he pulled on his socks and shoes. His memories of the night before were fuzzy.

"Their first few times," Stubbs said, "some have lost their minds and with it their souls. I used to wonder why God would bestow His gift upon them. It seemed a waste, but one day it became clear."

Ian had his back to the man. The dreams and memories were merging as he tied one shoe.

"Free will," said Stubbs. "It is the Father's greatest gift. We can choose to accept his gracious blessing or reject it. Those who reject it step outside His grace. 'To whom much is given, much is required.' That is the maxim. Spurning the will of God is a serious thing, my young friend."

"Oh, my god." Ian sat upright, the laces of one shoe still loose. "That was no dream."

"No. It was real."

"I...we...," Ian stuttered.

"We did."

"We killed those girls." Ian felt nauseous. "You had me...I wouldn't have..."

"You followed your instincts, Ian, and did as The Lord led."

"As the lord led?" Ian shook his head in disbelief but couldn't dislodge the knowledge. He remembered killing the girl. He recalled her flesh in his mouth, the taste of her blood. His stomach lurched and he almost threw up. "They weren't hurting anyone," he muttered.

"Come now," Stubbs said. "Surely you know what they were. You could smell their unnatural essence. They were abominations. It was God's judgement that they die. It was His will."

"Is it his will that I become a killer like you?" Ian wanted to yell, but he could only grit his teeth and snarl the words. He closed his eyes, his long hair hanging across his face.

"You already are a killer. Surely you know that."

"No!" He stumbled away from Stubbs. "Don't you tell me that! Don't you try to make me believe that I killed...I don't know what happened to Kelly...or Chevy."

"Yes, you do." Stubbs followed Ian, speaking in calm, soothing tones. "God judged them and found them wanting. He used you to carry out that judgement."

"No!" Ian found that he could yell at last. "No!" He turned and ran, one shoe still untied, stumbling over roots, tripping and rising only to fall again. After falling for the third time, Ian lie face down, sobbing into the blackened soil. "What am I? God, what am I?"

"A werewolf?" Ian mumbled the words into the cool glass of Stubbs' passenger side window. It was preposterous. Impossible. Any word he could think of seemed inadequate. There simply were no such things outside of books and movies.

"An unfortunate term," Stubbs said. "I've always considered it rather pejorative."

"Would you prefer monster?"

"I prefer to think of our kind as blessed."

"How can you call this a blessing?" Ian had long since exhausted his tears, but his stomach still rebelled against the notion. He wanted to be as far from Stubbs as possible. He considered walking to Springfield, but that would take all day. He doubted Stubbs would allow it either, and he was too deep into his despair to muster the energy to oppose him. He settled for huddling against the door with his shoulder turned. He'd endure the ride back to Springfield and leave for home as soon as he got there.

"You have received a great gift, Ian. You will live a long life. Much longer than you would have?"

"What?"

"You asked me how old I am. Let's just say I was already well into middle age by your reckoning when the Civil War was fought."

"What are you, immortal?" Ian looked at him then.

"Hardly. And neither are you, but barring some unfortunate circumstances, you will live well past the 22nd century. You may well even see the 23rd."

"I suppose I should thank you, then?" Ian snorted his disgust and turned away from Stubbs.

"Thank The Lord," Stubbs said. "You must be hungry. The transformation burns an enormous amount of calories. The feral hog we brought down last night satisfied our immediate needs, but the change left us famished again. If you'd like, we could stop for something to tide us over."

"No." Ian left it at that. He remembered the hog. The nasty beast put up quite a fight, but it had no chance against the two of them.

"My illustrious namesake was the first of our line."

"I don't care."

Stubbs ignored him and continued. "Peter Stubbe. Stubbe Peter in many sources. Or Stumpf. Many tales were spread about him, how he struck a deal with the devil. To discredit the gift of God with such nonsense is blasphemy. You've heard of the Hugenots?"

"No."

"Religious refugees. My ancestors aligned themselves with the Hugenots. They left Germany, then France, and ultimately Europe to escape persecution."

Ian heard little of what Stubbs said, something about Stubbs' ancestor's immigration, their life in Georgia, but he didn't care. After five minutes of listening to the history lesson, Ian snapped. "Enough! I don't...just don't talk to me anymore."

Ian looked out the window at the morning sun. An orange/yellow glow spread across the horizon. *I'll kill myself before I do this again. I will. Do I need silver?* He wanted to know what it would take to do the job, but he wasn't about to ask Stubbs. The lunatic would try to stop him. *Lunatic?* Ian smirked at the word. If that wasn't irony, it would do.

Half an hour later Stubbs turned into the Ramada Inn parking lot. He pulled the Explorer into a spot, but before he removed the key, Ian bolted from the vehicle and headed for his own car.

"Ian!" Stubbs hurried after him. "Ian, wait! I told your father I would see you home safely."

Ian didn't listen. There was no way he could endure the ten hour drive home with Stubbs. He was reaching for the drivers side door when Stubbs caught up and clamped a hand on his arm.

"You must come to terms with what you are, Ian, what you are called to be."

"And what is that Peter? A monster like you?"

"An angel would be closer to the truth. An angel of death to some but an angel nonetheless, an agent of God. Few have been blessed as you are. Don't spurn the gift you've been given."

"Or something worse could happen?" Ian jerked his arm from Stubbs' grip. "According to you, I've already killed two people I love. I killed that poor girl last night. How could it get any worse?"

"You have no idea. You could become the monster you fear you are. I told you many don't survive. They go mad. They lose themselves to the destroyer of souls, to Satan. Do your homework, Ian. Research your heritage. In the past, many like us became savage, ruthless killers. They met their end on the rack or at the stake. In the process, they brought persecution upon those of us who would follow the narrow road to do the will of our Lord."

"How...how many are there?" Ian almost said how many of *us* are there but caught himself.

"The Blessing has been bestowed only upon those to whom The Lord has directed me."

Ian turned away and opened his car door.

"Be wise, Ian. Follow the cycles of the moon. Live by them. I can't stress it enough. Soon you will not need the moon to change, but for the rest of your life you will have no choice when it is full."

Ian recalled his black-haired hand around Ricky's neck, his claws digging into Ricky's throat. He shook off the memory and climbed into his car.

Stubbs held the door open. "If you don't come to terms with your gift, it will mean your destruction. Even those who serve Our Lord will not understand. There is no room in their theology for those like us. Guard yourself. Pray. When you are ready, I will be there for you."

Ian jerked the car door from his grasp, closed it, and started the car. "Go to hell," he snarled at his would-be mentor then pulled out of the lot and headed for home.

Part 2

Chapter 11

September 1992

Batavia, Ohio

Ricky Thorogood sat on his bed with his back to the wall. The breeze coming through the window felt good against his skin. His mother liked air conditioning in the summer and heat in the winter. He liked fresh air. As long as he shut the vent and kept his door closed, she didn't mind. Tonight, the evening was a comfortable 59°, just fine with Ricky.

The view was nothing special, just a cracked asphalt parking lot full of old cars. Beyond that was Bingham Road and a line of humble houses. If they lived on the other side of the building, he'd have a view of the woods. He'd just as soon look at the parking lot.

His stepfather came home drunk again last night. The creep had a problem. Why his mother stood by Travis was beyond him. As far as Ricky and his sister knew, he had never hit their mother. Ricky was certain he could lay the man out and he was pretty sure Travis knew it too. If the asshole ever lost control and did hit her there would be hell to pay. Jamie-Lynn would want to get in her licks, too. She was well on her way to being the toughest of them all. Heaven help that poor bastard if he ever put a hand on her. Ricky would kick the guy's ass for his mother. He'd fuckin' kill him to protect Jamie, whether she needed the protection or not.

His father's offer still stood. His dad was a roughneck, an asshole many people didn't care for, but he wasn't abusive. The end of his parents' marriage wasn't all their father's fault as Ricky and Jamie had once assumed.

Living with their mother for the last three years had made that clear. He loved his mother, but he knew it was only a matter of time before Travis was gone and there would be some other creep in his place, someone who might well be abusive instead of just an alcoholic. Ricky decided he wasn't going to be there when that happened. He wasn't going to see his future go up in flames because some motherfucker with a chip on his shoulder charmed his way into his mom's pants. It was up to Ricky to break the cycle his family seemed trapped in, so his dad's offer was looking better all the time. It would get him out of here and Jamie soon after. He'd talked to people at the academy and he had a surprising ally in Sheriff Kearsey. No one besides Kelly, his little sister, and the sheriff had ever seen anything worth a damn in him. Because of them, he believed he had a future. It was time to act like it.

Without thinking about it, Ricky touched his hand to his neck. The wounds had healed long ago but the scars remained. They might always be there. Even if they did fade on the outside, he'd always remember that night, and he couldn't think of that night and not think of Kelly.

He still loved her. He'd been a real dick to her. He was ashamed of that now. The more he'd felt her slipping away, the more he'd fucked things up trying to hold on. He had no idea how he could have fixed things. She was gone now. He couldn't change that, but he could make himself into a better person, someone Kelly would be proud of. He wasn't stupid, though. He knew that only went so far. Eventually, he'd have to do it for himself. Not for Kelly. Not for Jamie. For himself.

Ricky took a sip from his lukewarm can of off-brand soda. It was a poor substitute for a good beer, but it would do. He hadn't had a drop of alcohol in months. He felt pretty good about his sobriety.

His hand still to his neck, he thought about Ian Murphy again. No one would believe him. Sometimes he didn't want to believe it himself. He'd tried to write it off as the alcohol, as the weed, as his despair, as all three working together with his imagination. He didn't have that much imagination. It was the nightmares that finally convinced him. They weren't nightmares at all. They were memories, crystal clear memories of a black-haired hand, of claws digging into his neck, and teeth growing long before his eyes. They were memories of a monster.

May 1993
Cincinnati Zoo And Biological Gardens

The wolf sniffed the ground at its feet, its full attention on the scent marking the trampled path. The animal was so focused on the scent that it almost ran into another of its own kind, a larger wolf with a thick ruff of shoulder fur. The larger wolf lowered its head and the smaller one deferred, raising its own head to expose the throat. The larger wolf sniffed then licked the other's face, and the pair trotted together around a stand of bushes.

"I thought they were bigger, Daddy." Amber Kearsey's ten year old face wore a bemused frown. Her comment failed to draw a response from her father. Matthew Kearsey's mind was far from the Mexican Wolf enclosure at the Cincinnati Zoo, wandering back to the woods surrounding his hometown of Stonelick thirty miles away.

Melinda Kearsey crouched next to their youngest daughter and smoothed the unruly hair that hung over the child's face in strawberry blond ringlets. "Maybe they aren't full grown," she said.

"Are they babies, Daddy?"

Matthew stared into the distance then blinked and looked down at his little girl. "I'm sorry, Punkin. Did you say something?"

"Where are the big wolves?" Amber said. "Toby is bigger than these."

"Well, Toby is a pretty big dog."

"Wolves are always bigger in the movies." Amber sighed, her frown relaxing as she accepted the reality before her. She shook her head and sighed again as if she had apprehended some great truth.

"She's right, Dad," said fourteen year old Megan. The teenager stood several paces away from the family, looking bored and tired. Her dark hair and lanky frame mirrored her father's.

"Maybe they're juveniles," Melinda offered. "They might still have some growing to do."

"Let's see what this says." Matthew pointed to a placard. Amber and Melinda followed him over to read the signage. Megan stayed where she was, leaning against a faux-weathered, split rail fence.

"Mexican wolf. *Canis lupis baileyi*," Matthew read aloud. "It says here they can get up to eighty pounds. That's as big as Toby. These look closer to forty, maybe fifty. That big one might be sixty."

"Do they have bigger wolves here?" Amber sighed again. She was clearly disappointed.

"Well, sweetie," her mother said, "the Mexican wolf is an endangered species. They might not be as big as a timber wolf but we're fortunate to see them. Besides, they're kind of cute. The big ones are scary." She twirled a strand of Amber's curls around one finger. "Don't you think they're cute?"

"Jess Warner said he saw a wolf," Megan said.

"That boy and his tall tales." Melinda waved a dismissive hand. "He also said his uncle caught a fifty pound catfish in Stonelick Lake. Remember that?"

"Yeah, he exaggerates sometimes, I guess, but his dad said the same thing. About the wolf, I mean. They were out hunting-"

"Hunting? When?" the sheriff said.

"Well, huh, I think they were just target shooting." Megan scrambled to recover. "I don't really know. But they saw a wolf. A really big one."

"Sweetheart, there are no wolves in Ohio," her mother said.

"Go on, Megan honey," Matthew said. "What did they see?"

"Jess said they were out one morning a few weeks ago and they saw a wolf running across a field. It looked at them, but it kept going. Jess's father got so scared they went back home and haven't been out since. His dad says they may never go hunt..uh...they may never go out there again."

"How big was it?" Amber said.

"A lot bigger than any of these wolves. They weren't close, but Jess said it was twice the size of any dog he's ever seen."

"Wow!" Amber's eyes went wide and she smiled at her big sister.

"That's silly," Melinda said. "You need to stop listening to that boy. Isn't that right, Matthew?"

Matthew nodded but said nothing. He ran his hand over his stubbled chin and thought of Kelly Shepherd, the trucker, and the Patella boy. That was four years ago, but he could never get it out of his mind for long. He made a mental note to pay a visit to Carl Warner tomorrow. Just to talk.

September 1993

Eldon, Minnesota

The North American Wolf Studies Center

"One hundred percent." Tim Montford sipped his coffee and leaned back in his chair. "It's way too big to be one of ours. This thing is huge."

"Don't even think about putting your feet on this desk," April White growled without looking up from the spreadsheet on her monitor. She thought the kid was too cocky, too aware that he was handsome, but he was also a first-rate research assistant, as good in the field as he was in the lab. She had the impression that he'd like to show her he was even better in bed.

"I wouldn't think of it, April," he said.

She did look up this time.

"Sorry. Doctor White."

"Leave the cast out," she said. "I'll take a look at it."

"There are more, but that's the best one. The measurements are in the database."

"I want to see the actual specimen."

"Old fashioned, eh?"

"That's the way I roll."

"Speaking of rolling, I have tickets for-"

April stopped him with an upraised hand. It was her turn to lean back in her chair. "That was the worst segue I've ever heard. You aren't going to ask me out again, are you?"

"Well...uh..," he stuttered, "I know there's a bit of an age difference between us, but-"

"How much?"

"How much...what?"

"Age difference."

"Well, uh, you...you're a Ph D. You've been at this for a while so you must be older than I am."

"How old do you think I am?" He was squirming. April loved it when she made men squirm.

"Um...I..."

"It's the white streak, right? You see the white in my hair and you think 'old woman.' "

"Well, uh, 'hot old woman,' maybe." Tim winced at his own words. He seemed to know he'd screwed this up badly. "Older woman, I mean. Older than me, I mean."

"Have you ever heard of Wardenburg Syndrome?"

"No," Tim said, his face as red as the cord of the lanyard hanging from his neck.

"I've had this streak ever since I was a child. Younger than you, even." April smiled at that last shot. It was a pretty good one, though she'd developed the streak a decade before she was Tim's age.

"Doctor, I'm sorry. I didn't mean to-"

"Tim, I'm not blind. You're a good looking guy but you're my subordinate." She noticed him wincing. Having a woman superior was a problem for his ego. "That's one thing. I'll give you another; you're too cocky.There's a difference between being confident and being cocky. One of the two is sexy. The other is a big turn-off in my book. Not that you should worry about my book, but you get the point. Don't you?"

"I, uh, yeah. I think I do." Tim sat up and nodded. "I apologize, Doctor White. I didn't mean to be a dick."

"You're not a dick, Tim. You just try too hard sometimes. You're going to fit in here just fine. You're smart. You're observant. I like you. If I didn't, you'd be gone already. Do what you're good at. You're what, twenty-three?"

"Twenty-two."

"Your whole career is ahead of you. It can be a good one. Now go have a good weekend."

"Thank you, Doctor."

Tim nodded. He got up to leave the office and was almost out the door when April stopped him.

"Tim?"

"Yes?"

"Don't ask me out again or I will have to let you go."

"Yes, Doctor."

"That new docent, Jan."

"Jan Williams? What about her?"

"She has eyes for you. You want to ask someone out, how about her?"

Tim smiled. "I noticed that, too."

"Good. Go on. Get out of here. I'll be here for a while yet."

Twenty minutes later April White stood in the lab looking at the cast Tim had taken from the forest to the north. There were two others much like it in the drawer next to the bench. He'd collected some scat, too, and some hairs. She hadn't had time to match those to the database yet, but they kept a close watch on the local population. Tim was right. It wasn't one of their wolves.

April tucked the long lock of white hair behind her right ear and reached for the phone.

Chapter 12

Dec 1994

Clermont Community College

Batavia, Ohio

Ian walked across the parking lot to his car, a backpack slung over his shoulder. One more day and he could take a break from the books for a couple of weeks. When he reached his aging Maverick he dropped his backpack into the car and sat behind the wheel.

The fall semester was over, the campus emptying. Many students were done with finals. It was a warm day for the season, the temperature topping 60°. Some of the remaining students were taking advantage of the weather, sprawled across benches, basking in the afternoon sun or tossing footballs. Couples strolled together. One in particular caught his eye, a tall guy with long, wavy hair and a short, curvaceous girl. They reminded Ian of himself and Kelly. He sighed and turned away.

He fingered the silver hoop in his ear. His mother's watch was in his pocket, secured to his belt by a chain. They were reminders of the two women who had meant the most to him in his life.

Ian had spent the last two years with his nose to the grindstone. For over a year before that he'd shuffled from one dead-end job to another, mired in a deep depression. Eventually, he came to realize that he needed to work toward something. He needed a goal, no matter how modest, if he was going to make something of himself. So far, he'd been able to keep his condition, his "blessing" as Stubbs called it, a secret. His father knew something was up with him. Verna suspected as well. Neither of them had the slightest idea of the truth.

May 1990
Stonelick, Ohio

For months after returning from Springfield, Ian led the barest of lives. He spent much of his time either in bed or alone in the woods. His father tried to get him to open up, but Ian had no idea what to say so he said nothing. There was no way to explain himself so he didn't try. He was seldom out of bed before noon, ate like a condemned man at every meal, and retreated to his room well before his father left for work. Not that he slept. Sleep never came before 3:00 AM or later.

Verna Cooper dropped by often, cheerful and laden with food. She was a good woman, a walking, talking example of the unconditional love that preachers liked to talk about but too often failed to practice. Ian liked Verna but he didn't know what to say to her any more than he knew what to say to his father. Once, she remarked about the calendars Ian had hung around the house, one day each month highlighted by a red X. "You aren't falling into some sort of astrology hooey, are you, Hon?" she asked. Ian shook his head. His father took Verna aside and told her he was pretty sure it had something to do with Kelly's death. "I traced it back," he told her, "and the night she died was a full moon. Every day marked with an 'X' is a full moon. I'm not sure this is healthy, but I don't know what to do about it." They spoke in whispers from another room but Ian heard every word.

Sheriff Kearsey came by several times. The last time he was there, he informed them cooly that the cases of Charles Patella and Kelly Shepherd were officially closed. " 'Animal Attack' is the final verdict," he said. He sighed and ran his fingers around the rim of his hat. "I've already told the families of the deceased. They're not happy about that, especially the Patella's, but we've hit a wall and there are other matters to deal with. Unless something else comes up, it'll stay that way." Ian could tell the sheriff wasn't happy but that he had no other choice. "I'm telling you this as a courtesy," the sheriff said, "considering that you were close to both of them."

After the sheriff left, Ian went to his room, locked the door, and cried. He accepted that he had killed both Chevy and Kelly and he had nightmares about the campers. He still couldn't remember anything about that night with Chevy and he remembered little about the night with Kelly after they'd made love except for her horrified face. She'd seen him change. She'd seen the monster. He considered going to the station and telling the sheriff everything, but he knew that was out of the question. He'd be thought delusional at best, a mad man at worst. Even if he was put away, be it in a prison or a mental institution, what would happen when the moon was full? How many more would die?

His father left him alone in his room, apparently reasoning that Ian wanted to be by himself to process the sheriff's news, but he knocked before leaving for work.

"I love you, Son," Henry said. "If you want to talk, just say so. Anytime."

"I love you, too, Dad," Ian replied, but he didn't open the door.

He listened to the soft rumble of his father's truck recede into the distance. A few minutes later, he opened the door and stepped into the hall. The hall light was off but the light over the kitchen sink cast a soft glow around the corner. He didn't need it to see where his father's bedroom door was. He entered the room and went to the old roll top desk near the window, opened the top drawer, and took out the key to the locked drawer on the right side of the desk. He opened the drawer and removed the compact, heavy object within.

Ian sat on the bed and looked at the Smith And Wesson Model 29 Mountain Gun. The hand gun was older than he was and the only weapon in the house. When he turned twelve, his father and Leon took him to a far corner of the Patella's property. "Son, it's time you learned how to handle a gun," his father said. The gun bucked hard. Ian missed everything set up as targets and took nothing away from the experience but a ringing in his ears and the knowledge that guns held no interest for him. He wasn't sure if it had been fired since but his father kept the gun clean and in good working condition. Ian thumbed the latch and swung the empty cylinder open. The shells were in a box in the same drawer.

"Do I need silver?" he said aloud then touched the silver hoop in his ear. "Am I really going to do this?" He looked straight ahead. "Where? Not here but where?"

As he wondered, his eyes fell on the framed photo on the dresser. Even in the dark he could see it clearly. His mother sat in a wheelchair, flanked by her husband on one side and her son on the other. She'd lost her hair due to chemotherapy and was wearing a multicolored bandana around her bald head. Her cheeks were sunken and her eyes bulged from their sockets, but her smile radiated warmth and optimism. Ian had the same photo in his room. He knew the inscription on the back by heart;

To my two men.
As you love each other you'll be keeping a part of me alive in both of you.
"As I have loved you, so you must love one another." John 13:34
Rose

"Shit!" Ian hissed. How could he do this? How could he take this way out? His father would never understand what he was, but Ian still loved him. He'd suffered terribly before and after his wife's death. He'd just begun to regain his strength when the deaths of Chevy and Kelly stunned him again. To lose his only son now would be too much.

As genuine as Ian's concern for his father was, though, he knew there was more than that staying his hand. Staring at his mother's gaunt but smiling face, he knew he couldn't go through with killing himself. She had endured chemotherapy, the loss of her hair and her health, and spent the last several months of her life bedridden, in excruciating pain. Through it all, her dignity remained intact. For him to put a gun to his head and pull the trigger would be an insult to her memory.

Tears ran down Ian's cheeks as he returned the gun to its place and locked the drawer. No matter what his mother had said and certainly regardless of what Peter Stubbs claimed, Ian no longer believed there was any god-ordained plan for his life. His father was right. We make our own meaning, our own destiny. Ian resolved to create that meaning, no matter what form it would take. And the guilt? He would have to deal with that and take steps to make sure he never killed anyone again.

On his first full moon after Missouri, he left the house well before dark, while his father was in the early stages of preparing for work. As soon as Henry turned on the shower, Ian was out the door.

The days were still long. He wasn't looking forward to the time change and the early sundown. He'd also have to deal with hunting season, when there were more people in the woods. He wished he had more control over the black wolf's actions. According to Stubbs, that would come in time.

The black wolf. Me. We are one. Despite the fact that he'd abandoned any belief that there was a god who watched out for him, Ian prayed anyway. *Please, please, don't let me kill anyone.*

By the time he was deep enough into the forest to feel there was little chance he'd come across anyone, his joints were aching. He undressed before they began to pop and shift, shoving his clothes into a large plastic bag. He stashed the bag and his shoes in the cleft of a tree well above the ground, trusting that the wolf would return here when the night was almost over. It was one bit of useful knowledge he'd brought from his otherwise horrible experience in Missouri. Seconds after securing his clothes, the transformation came over him. *Will it always hurt like this? Will I ever get used to it?*

The pain passed, Ian faded, and the black wolf was there in his place. The wolf remembered his other existence, his humanity, but it felt like a dream he couldn't quite recall. It was there, as much a part of him as anything, but to the wolf it had no further significance. All that mattered was now. He had no words with which to express himself and no memory of the conversations his human self had had earlier that day, but emotions passed through the veil unhindered. If anything, they were enhanced.

His first order of business, even more urgent than the gnawing hunger he'd awakened to, was to find others of his own kind. He spent half that night searching for a scent, a trail, droppings, anything that would lead him to others. He looked for the great white wolf, the beautiful one who accompanied him before, but he was nowhere to be found. He sniffed the ground, the air, and paused several times to howl, advertising his presence to any who might hear. Nothing.

He whined, despairing at this unexpected loneliness. He thought he would see the white wolf again, but when it became clear that he wouldn't, that he was truly alone, he turned to his other great need: hunger. Sometime during the night he'd passed a dark, hard path much like the one where he encountered the strange, rumbling beast and left the small female's lifeless body. He paced the edge of the path, unsure of what to do.

There were other scents, and they led him to structures that were larger than the flimsy domes he'd encountered before. One in particular stood out. It sat close to several others, surrounded on three sides by open fields full of deep footprints and the fading smell of large herbivores. Their drying scat littered the field, full of plant matter. The black wolf followed the scents, but the closer he got to the large structure, the more he was gripped by an unexpected sorrow. One scent in particular stood out, the scent of the creature he'd encountered in the tree, and it filled him with such an overpowering grief that his legs almost folded beneath him. He didn't like this place, whatever its significance might be, so in the mental map of the area he was constructing, he marked it with a firm "Do not go here." He left and determined that he would never go there again.

As the night progressed, the black wolf found food here and there, mostly small animals he ran down and devoured. It wasn't enough, but it was something. Before the sun rose, he headed back to the place where his evening began. Reaching the tree, he settled down with his head resting on his paws. Within minutes he was lulled to sleep by the sounds of the night forest.

April 1995

Stonelick, Ohio

Ian finished his two year program with no fanfare. He knew a 2 year degree wasn't terribly impressive, but it was a major accomplishment to him.

On his first day, he was sure someone attending their first class at Yale or Harvard couldn't feel any better. After all, to go from holding a gun to your own head and contemplating suicide to starting work toward a degree, any degree, felt like a major accomplishment.

He made a few friends in college but none he considered close. More to the point, there were none he allowed to get close. There were a few girls he found attractive and at least two he was sure saw him the same way, but he couldn't imagine making a relationship work and he wasn't interested in casual hookups. How could he let someone in when he still wasn't sure how to manage his dual nature? He was learning but the learning was slow. So far he'd been able to manage it, but letting anyone get close was bound to complicate matters. He had no guide, no mentor, and the world was perilous for himself as it was. He had enough blood on his hands already.

He hadn't seen Peter Stubbs since Missouri. It troubled him that Stubbs was out there killing as "the Lord led him," but he felt powerless to do anything about it. He'd considered trying to stop Stubbs, that ending the man's mad mission could be his purpose, a way of creating his own meaning. Upon reflection, though, that seemed like nothing so much as a death wish. As the months turned into years, he simply avoided thinking about the man as much as possible. That would have been easier if Stubbs didn't send him a monthly newsletter detailing his evangelistic activities and an occasional postcard. They went straight into the trash can, but the day Ian received them was a ruined day.

August 1995

"That was some awesome pie, Verna." Ian leaned back in his chair, eyes toward the ceiling but closed. His stomach was full of pot roast and dessert. He'd left the vegetables untouched but managed a serving of mashed potatoes drenched in brown gravy and several rolls that dripped melted butter.

"Thank you, Ian. I love to see a boy enjoy his food."

"The boy's right," Henry said.

"What's with all this 'boy' stuff?" Ian smiled, but still reclined in his chair.

"Oh, you know what I mean." Verna wiped her mouth with a napkin. "To me, you'll always be that little boy who showed up in Sunday school."

"That was years ago," Ian said.

"He has a point, Verna," Henry said. "He's the biggest person in our family. My grandpa was a big son of a gun, but I think Ian has him beat. Hell, he's bigger than me and I'm 6' 3" and over two-hundred pounds." Henry patted his full belly. "Well, I am now. Didn't used to be, but..."

Ian's father was correct. The Blessing-or the curse, as Ian preferred to think of it-had worked along with his physical maturity to mold him into a well-muscled, athletic specimen. He stood over 6' 5" now and his 240 .lbs was evenly distributed over his long limbed frame.

"Shoot, look at the time," Verna said. She popped up from her seat like she was on a spring. "Didn't you say you had to meet your friends at eight?"

"Yeah, but I still have to take care of the dishes."

"Don't worry about the dishes," Henry said. "I can rinse them off and load the dishwasher."

"I don't want to leave them for you, Dad."

"I can take care of them this time. You need to be going."

"I told them I'd meet them at the food court," Ian said. "If I'm early that's no biggie. You sure you don't mind dropping me off, Verna?"

"I go past the mall on my way home," she said. "It's no trouble."

It was 7:15. The sun set at 8:33. Within minutes of that time, Ian would no longer be human. He'd concocted a story about meeting friends at Eastgate Mall to justify his absence from the house for the two hours before his father left for work. It was a tight schedule, but it would get even tighter when the clocks were set back. Verna's offer to drop him off at the mall was too good to pass up. As far as she and his father knew, he'd be going out with these friends for a movie and a late snack then they'd give him a lift home. In reality, he'd be trotting overland and arriving home shortly before his father.

Five minutes later they were on the road. Verna drove a big Ford pickup not unlike his father's but newer. The truck seemed much too large for her, bright red with gospel music radio station bumper stickers plastered over every available inch of the tailgate. Inside, the charcoal gray dash was decorated with further testimonials to her religious zeal. Directly in front of the passenger seat, two stylized fish logos with their bodies forming the word TRUTH flanked a tiny, flattened replica of the same Durer praying hands Ian's mother had been so fond of. A pair of fuzzy dice hung from the rear view mirror, the dots spelling out JESUS on one and SAVES on the other.

Ian smiled at the display and found himself in surprising good humor. He was actually looking forward to the night ahead. They still passed as in a dream, with only the fuzziest of memories making it very far into the next day, but he was no longer confused when he awoke. Instead, he felt refreshed. Famished, but refreshed. The black wolf never failed to return home and most important of all, the wolf hadn't killed anyone. *The wolf. Me.* Ian smirked. *It is me.* He was getting used to the change. The pain didn't seem that bad anymore. *Sometimes, I can even-*

"Casual day?" Verna said.

"Huh?" Ian didn't realize he hadn't spoken since they got in the truck. They were nearing the the highway by the time she interrupted his thoughts.

"You're looking pretty ratty."

"Oh. I didn't feel like getting dressed up. It's only friends."

He had on old clothes and shoes he wouldn't miss. The Mall marked the farthest he'd dared to venture on a full moon night. It was an experiment to see if the wolf would follow the directives of his will. If it worked and the wolf made it back to the forest behind his home, he would leave the old clothes there in the woods. If not, he'd wake up in the woods and at least he'd have something to wear.

"Ian, honey, you know me. I don't like to pry or cajole, but...I'm worried about you."

"I'm OK, Verna."

"Are you? It's been years since you've been to church. I know you don't like to talk about it, but I've got to say it; blaming God for what happened to your friends isn't going to bring you peace."

"I don't blame god, Verna. There just doesn't seem to be much there for me anymore."

"There are people there who love you. At least one, anyway." She smiled sideways at him, her eyes still on the road. "I won't nag. I just want you to know that if you ever do want to go and you need moral support, I'll be there for you."

"I know you will, Verna." Ian smiled back at her and looked out the window at the orange sky. "After mom died, our lives lacked a woman's presence. We're just two big, dumb guys, my dad and me. I appreciate what you do for us and I know Dad does, too. You filled a void in our lives."

"Your mother was a special woman. She was my best friend. You and your father are special to me. I know no one will take her place, least of all me, heaven forbid, but she wanted me to look after you two. She told me so. Did you know that?"

"No," Ian said. "I didn't. I'm glad, though."

"The two of you filled a void in my life, too. I'll never get married or be a parent again."

"Again?"

"Oh, yes." Verna nodded. "I was married once. I had a child, too."

Ian's eyes widened. As far as he knew, Verna was the classic spinster, a sweet lady entering her golden years without a husband or children. He'd never imagined that she might have once been married, not to mention having a child. She'd always just been Verna and that was it.

"Don't look surprised," she said. "Thirty years and a hundred pounds ago, I was quite a looker."

"What happened?"

The corners of her mouth twitched into what could be interpreted as a grin, a wince of pain, or a little of both. "You're mother never told you?"

"Not a word."

"Bless her heart. She knew I left that life behind when The Lord found me."

"Don't leave me hanging," Ian said. "I want to hear it."

"My maiden name is Schmidt. My husband was Jack Cooper. I won't bore you with all the details. Jack and I were flower children, leftover hippies. We only got married to make his folks happy. They owned the house we lived in, you see. Then Benji came along. Benjamin David Cooper.

"Long story short, they died. Benji was only four. It was a fire. They said Jack fell asleep with a lit cigarette. We'd turned that place into a real hippie pad with shag carpet, posters all over the walls, bead curtains, you name it. The place went up fast."

"You weren't there?"

"I was at a friend's house getting high."

"You?"

"Yes. Me."

"What happened?"

"Your mom happened. I was getting a lot of meals from soup kitchens then. I wasn't quite homeless, but I was heading that way. Your mom volunteered at one of the kitchens I went to. She saw something in me that no one else did. Or that no one took the time to see. She reached out to me, demonstrated real love. God's love.

"I know what people say about me and I'm flattered. They say I'm real. I'm not. Now, your mom? She was real. As real as it gets."

Ian stared at Verna, speechless for the moment.

"When your mom met me, I was angry at God. I blamed him for the deaths of the people I loved. The last thing I wanted to do was go to church."

"What changed?" he managed to say.

"Love. That's the only thing that really changes people. Your mom showed me what real love looked like. Not everyone responds to that. Some people just take and take and manipulate. They don't want the real thing, no matter what they say. I responded. Your mom helped me get back on my feet, showed me the way back. That was thirty-two years ago. I've been clean and sober for twenty-nine."

"You own the bakery shop in Stonelick. When did that happen?"

"That was your mom, too. I got on there with her help. She helped me find a place to live. It wasn't much, but I could afford it. I worked at the bakery while I got my life back in order. After fifteen years there, the owners were ready to retire. I took it over from them and the rest is history. They could have gotten a lot more, but they let me have it for a song if I agreed to keep it in town. It was an easy decision.

"It all started with your mom. If it hadn't been for her... One person can change a life, Ian. So now you know." Verna smiled and winked at him.

They were nearing the mall and the light outside was fading fast.

"So don't you give up, hon.

"Thanks, Verna. I won't." He smiled at her, this time as much from amazement as fondness. He'd learned more about her in a few brief moments than he had in all the time he'd known her.

She pulled into the mall parking lot. Ian jumped out and said goodbye. As Verna pulled away, he stood in the lot and watched her go, thinking that beneath the jowls and the putty nose, she was quite a looker still, and that even though his mother was gone, her legacy lived on.

The black wolf padded through the forest. He was more graceful with each full moon, more of the wolf and less of the man to outward appearances. A sharp eye could still detect where he'd stepped, but he was learning more and more each month how to live without drawing unwanted attention to himself. Still, he had to eat and there was nothing to be done about the odd deer carcass here and there,

After the deaths of Chevy and Kelly, there was for a time a general unease among the local hunting community. Both had died months before the hunting season, but the memory lingered as the hunters took to the forests that fall. The trucker's story of a huge black wolf made the rounds, and even though Ian lived a self-imposed hermit's existence, he couldn't help but hear the tales. His father heard them at work, too. The stories became local legend. Things did return more or less to normal as they tend to do. The legend of The Giant Wolf Of Ohio took it's place alongside stories of alien abduction, Bigfoot encounters, and the living Elvis, even meriting an entry into a book on paranormal Ohio. Along the way, it lost its ability to frighten, becoming instead a source of amusement. Other than a few cryptozoologists, no one seriously entertained the idea that an actual werewolf was responsible for the attacks, no one but a sheriff whose suspicions would only grow over time and a reformed punker who no longer lived in the area but couldn't forget the clawed hand that had gripped his throat.

September 1995
Stonelick, Ohio

"Poor Larry." Verna frowned, her eyebrows crinkled in sympathy. "God love him. No matter how many times I see this movie my heart goes out to him."

"You don't have to watch this with me again if you don't want to," Ian said.

"Oh, I love it. More than all that slasher garbage. I just want to give Lon Chaney a big hug."

"Larry Talbot."

"Larry. Lon. Same difference."

"If you say so." Ian grabbed another handful of popcorn from the bowl between them.

"I've been meaning to ask you, hon. How's your dad doing? Don't tell me he's fine. He's not. He gets tired earlier than ever. He doesn't look so good. He acts like nothing's wrong but I can tell."

Ian sighed. "He's been seeing a doctor, but he hasn't told anyone."

"What did the doctor say?"

Ian was certain his father was asleep now, but he looked over his shoulder in the direction of his father's bedroom anyway. "The doc is concerned." Ian kept his voice down just in case. "He's going back next week to talk about his options. They're talking about an angioplasty."

"Angioplasty? My Uncle George went through that."

"How's he doing?"

"He had a bad liver. That was what got him in the end. George passed away in 1990."

"Sounds like he had a lot of problems."

"He did. Your dad is strong, though."

"Yeah." Ian tossed the handful of popcorn into his mouth. He didn't want to talk about his father's health. He felt conflicted. On the one hand, he worried that his father worked too much. 60 hour work weeks weren't unusual for him. On the other hand, that made it easier for Ian to hide his dual nature. His father really should cut back or even think about retiring, but there wasn't much chance of that, regardless of what the doctor said. Work was his life now. *If Mom was still around...* Ian still mourned for her, but he had accepted her absence long ago. He wasn't sure his father ever would.

"Hey, Ian?" Verna's eyes were fixed on the screen. The blue-white glow from the TV was the only light in the room, illuminating her face from a low angle. She looked like someone holding a flashlight under her chin to produce the 'spooky' effect.

"What?"

"The first werewolf. Bela Lugosi. The one that bit Larry. When he changed he looked like an ordinary wolf. How come when Larry changes he's just a hairy guy with a black nose and big teeth?"

Ian paused for a moment before answering. "I guess Bela had been a werewolf for a long time."

"You mean the longer he was a werewolf the more like a wolf he became?"

"Something like that."

They sat in comfortable silence for a few minutes, the only sound other than the TV was the crunch of popcorn and the slurping of root beer. On screen, Larry Talbot recoiled in horror at the sight of the pentagram in the palm of his love interest, Gwen Conliff.

"Wait a minute," Verna said. "What about that funny movie he made with Abbott and Costello? Wasn't that years later? He was still just a big hairy guy."

"Hollywood." Ian shrugged as if that explained it all. There was so much he could never tell Verna. There was still a degree of separation between his wolf self and his humanity, but the two were closer than ever. He could change at will now. It was hard and unpleasant, but it was getting easier. It was strange to think of his transformations in such prosaic terms, but it was true. He was troubled by the thought, though, that he might need some kind of catalyst to close the gap and make the two one. That sounded like asking for a tragedy and he felt he'd already experienced more than his fair share. Tragedy? Geez, how selfish could he get, he thought. What about the Martins? Now there was a couple who-

"Hmmm....I wonder," Verna said, her expression serious.

"What?"

"If someone really could do that, you know, change into a wolf? What if they liked it better that way? Could they just stay a wolf, and run off to join a pack? Seems like they might be happier."

Ian stared at her. He wanted to tell her it wasn't that simple but stopped. *Wasn't it?*

October 1995

The wolf bit down hard and the bone cracked. He sat down, pinned the small end between his massive paws, then searched the head of the femur for the weakest spot. If he bit down in just the right place the bone would split, revealing the rich, delicious marrow within. He would take his time with this bone. The marrow was red, soft, and young. The marrow in older prey tended to be more yellow and spongy. Drier. Less appetizing. He intended to enjoy this rare treat. First one femur then the other, then the hip bones. The hip bones were harder to crack, but in healthy, young prey were full in the centers with the moist, delectable tissue.

He had already stripped the lower half of the carcass of much of its flesh. Fortunately he hadn't had any clothing to deal with. The tough, dry fibers were annoying, especially the unnatural man made fabrics so many wore these days. That had not been a problem with this one. Her death had been sweet and easy, her flesh readily available, tender, and coated with the salty tang of perspiration.

As human beings go, she had been exceedingly lovely. He was surprised at his ability to still appreciate human beauty in his wolf form. Not that her beauty gave him pause. Rather, it added a certain something to the experience, a sensual quality that appealed to both the human and the wolf. He left her upper body alone for just that reason. Her round, full breasts, the large nipples still stiff with arousal, defied his ability to savage them. And her face. Her beautiful, perfect face. He had barely been able to resist admiring her beauty to tear out her throat. For a few brief moments he hadn't been entirely sure which he desired the most; to devour her literally or figuratively.

He found the precise spot he'd been searching for and bit down hard. The head of the femur split with a loud crack and the aroma of fresh marrow filled his nostrils. He used the smaller nipping teeth in the front of his mouth to scrape the glistening red tissue from the center of the bone, delighting in its texture and taste before swallowing it. Not for the first time he wished the wolf possessed the cheeks he had as a human. What would it be like, the wolf wondered, to be able roll the delightful wet tissue around in his mouth the way a human child might with a piece of soft candy or ice cream?

He finished stripping the femur of its precious store of marrow then dropped it and rose to his feet. He took three steps to the carcass and was about to wrap his jaws around the other bloodied femur when the wide open eyes of the corpse's face caught his attention. Her eyes were large and of the deepest brown, the dark pupils surrounded by a rich, nuanced mahogany. He stepped closer and nudged her head with the tip of his snout. A strange feeling welled up within him, a dawning emotion it took him most of a minute to recognize. When it arose in the fullness of its strength it was all he could do not to cry out. A grief beyond any hope of expressing buckled his front legs and he almost pitched forward onto the naked torso lying among the leaf litter at his feet. A single tear pulsed from the front corner of his left eye, then another. They mingled together then traced their way down his long, black snout, threading through the short stiff hairs until they found the flesh of his nostrils. They clung there for one second then another, then dropped as one, landing on the girl's face just below her right eye.

Kelly blinked.

Ian yelled and sat upright in bed. He gasped for breath and groped for the headboard behind him, swung his feet around, and stumbled out of bed toward the hallway. He made it to the bathroom and threw up the toilet seat just in time. For the next minute he wretched almost nonstop, his muscles trembling and weak when he was done. When the last violent wave passed he slumped against the wall beside the toilet and began to sob. In another minute he lie sprawled across the tile floor, his shoulders and back still hitching every few seconds. The cool tile was a slight relief to his burning skin, his sweat pooling around him on the bathroom floor. After another three minutes he was able to pull himself up first to his knees and then, putting far too much of his weight on the sink, to his feet. His legs wobbled and the sink shook but held. He filled the basin with cool water, splashed it onto his face, and stood hunched over, waiting for his body to stop trembling. When he was as ready as he would ever be to look himself in the eye he chanced a glance at the mirror.

A minute later Ian wiped his face on the towel hanging beside the sink, tossed it into the hamper, and limped out to the living room. He wrapped himself in the old blanket kept in the wicker basket beside the couch, reclined in his father's easy chair, and reached for the remote. For the next five minutes he scanned the channels until settling upon some old black and white movie, then he dropped the remote onto the coffee table and settled back into the overstuffed chair. It was only 4:15 AM, but he wouldn't sleep any more. Instead, he stared at the TV and did his best to empty his mind and his heart of the residue of the worst nightmare he'd had in years.

Chapter 13

November 1995

The North American Wolf Studies Center

Eldon, Minnesota

Ian stood inside the outer door, removed the elastic band from his hair, and shook out his pony tail. The forecast called for clear skies later, but a light snow was falling at the moment, coating his shoulders. If he were a wolf, he would give himself a good head to tail shake and that would be that. The niceties of human social life didn't allow for such practicalities.

The Great Lakes Wolf Lodge was the public face of the North American Wolf Studies Center. From the outside it looked like any number of faux rustic lodges built to recall a bygone era where log cabins were the most common structure in the wilderness. He wasn't sure if such an era had ever existed or if that impression was a product of television and the movies. If that was the case, it was clear that the Center embraced the illusion.

The lobby was a postcard-perfect replica of the idealized nineteenth century American inn. Warm, amber light filled the room from floor to beamed ceiling. To Ian's left, a large alcove broke the illusion with a well-stocked gift shop. Plush wolves, books, ceramic figurines, T-shirts, and all manner of *canis lupis*-themed trinkets and tchotchkes filled the room. To his right, another alcove held a cozy little coffee shop, the forest green logo of the shop harmonizing perfectly with the deep red timber décor of the lodge. Straight ahead, a broad desk sat between branching corridors, a sign mounted above the desk reading "Welcome To The Lodge" in the same forest green as the coffee shop logo.

The Center was enjoying a busy day. The light snowfall outside had deposited less than an inch of new snow on the ground. It didn't seem to faze the locals. Back home, an inch of snow would be enough to induce panic, but in Minnesota they took it in stride.

When the family of four gathered around the desk moved away to begin their visit, Ian stepped up and pulled out his wallet.

"Hi!" the girl behind the desk greeted him. She was all smiles and perfume, perhaps twenty at the most and rather pretty. "How are you doing today?"

"I'm good." Ian returned her smile. "I'm here to see the wolves."

"Well, you came to the right place."

"Thirteen dollars, right?" Ian said. He found her accent delightful. It reminded him of Verna.

"Yes. Have you been here before?"

"No, but I signed up for your newsletter, got some fliers in the mail."

"Well, I'm glad you're here." She flashed him a different kind of smile. "We have a lot to offer."

"I'm sure you do," Ian said looking first one way then the other. He handed her a twenty dollar bill and waited for his change.

"Here's your change and your ticket, and here's a visitors guide that will help you find your way around. You came at a great time. Our wolves have been very active. It's warm for this time of year."

"Back home, this wouldn't be considered warm. I'm from Ohio."

"My Aunt lives in Ohio. Lorain."

"I'm from the other end of the state. Near Cincinnati. It's a different world down there."

"Well, enjoy your visit. I'm Sandy. If you have any questions and none of the guides are around, come and see me."

"Thanks. I'm Ian. Nice to meet you, Sandy. Which way to the wolves?"

"Down this corridor to your left. You'll turn the corner and you should see several guides. I'd recommend Richard. He knows his stuff."

"Thanks. I'll look for him."

Ian smiled again and walked down the hallway. He unfolded the visitors guide and gave the map a look. The opposite hallway led to a theater and auditorium but he had little interest in multimedia presentations. He wanted to see the wolves.

The hallway was lined with regularly spaced portraits of wolves, each tastefully matted and framed. Lobo. Cheyenne. Ranger. The names were pure cliché, more PR than anything, Ian thought, his disappointment growing with each step. So far the place was nothing but faux rustic kitsch.

At the end of the hall Ian turned the corner and his dismay lessened. The room was a good sixty feet wide. The wall opposite the entry was twelve feet high and glass from corner to corner. Outside, he counted four...six...no, seven wolves in full view. A dozen people watched the wolves through the glass. The children among them seemed especially enthralled, pointing, smiling, and chattering. A tall teenage girl leaned against the glass, a wistful half smile on her face. Behind her, a kid Ian took for her boyfriend sipped on a coffee and stared straight ahead, his face blank. A couple of young men in matching forest green pullovers stood among the visitors, answering questions and pointing to the wolves outside. Ian figured that one of them must be the knowledgeable Richard.

The enclosure beyond the glass was wider than the room and deeper, the ground sloping upward into a thick stand of pine trees. The fences on either side were plainly visible near the glass but they ran diagonally from each corner, disappearing into the trees fifty or sixty feet away. The entire enclosure seemed to be roughly the size and shape of a baseball diamond. As an exhibit area, it was expansive and impressive. As a living space for active, intelligent animals, it seemed stifling and claustrophobic.

The wolves appeared in good spirits despite the constraints. They were spread out in the open space between the trees and the building, ignoring the crowd of gawking spectators on the other side of the glass. Two of the wolves were playful youngsters, barely half the size of the rest, all big feet and gangly-limbed, chasing each other in circles around the enclosure, snapping at snowflakes. Three larger wolves pushed and jostled among themselves, nipping at each others' ears and snouts, playing the dominance games that would define their social standing in the pack. In the center of the activity two wolves sat, calm and at ease. They were big, sleek, and beautiful. All of the wolves appeared well fed and content, so picture perfect Ian had to wonder if they were regularly groomed.

"They were just fed."

Ian turned at the voice. Beside him a tall, attractive woman stood with folded arms. A bright white streak ran through her lustrous dark hair from above her left temple over the crown of her head. He recognized her instantly from her picture on the web site.

"This is the nicest day we've had in a while," she said. "They're feeling pretty good."

"You're Doctor White, aren't you? You run this place."

"Yes." She smiled. "At least about the Dr. White part. I oversee things here, but I answer to a board of directors. They really run the place. Have we met?"

"No. I've been on the web site. A lot, I guess. I recognized you from your picture." He extended his hand. "Ian Murphy."

"Nice to meet you, Ian." She gave his hand a firm shake. She was wearing heels that brought her to within two or three inches of his six foot five inch height. He guessed that barefoot she had to be close to six feet tall. A physically impressive lady, to be sure.

"I've been meaning to make it up here for a while," he said.

"What do you think of our little place?"

"I've only been here for a few minutes but it's nice. From a visitor's standpoint, at least."

"And from the wolves'?"

Ian sighed. "This enclosure is really big, but it's still an enclosure."

"The wolves can't see us," she said. "It's two way glass. It's a pain to constantly adjust the light in here but it's worth it."

"If they were free, I'm sure they would cover more ground in an hour than this place allows them all their lives."

"Are you a researcher?"

"No. Just an interested amateur. Wolves are a fascination of mine."

"Have you ever observed wolves in the wild?"

"Not yet. I would like to, though."

"It can be dangerous."

"I suppose, but I can take care of myself."

"Really?"

"I'm sorry. I didn't mean to sound cocky. I've read your articles on the web site. I looked up some of your journal papers. You know these animals."

"It's my job. You're a big guy and wolves are naturally shy around humans, but if they ever felt threatened by your presence..." She pointed a manicured nail at the two large wolves reclining among the pack. "Lobo, there-yes, I hate the name, too-is one hundred and twenty-seven pounds. If he were so inclined, he could tear someone your size apart."

"It's good thing wolves rarely attack people."

"True, but you don't want to press your luck. We keep our distance so they don't feel like we're intruding on their territory. And we never approach a pup. Never. I'm careful about how close I get. They tolerate us to an extent, but..." She stopped and shook her head. "It's another world out there, and it's not ours. It's theirs."

Ian nodded. He wanted to say more, but he felt tongue-tied. She was exceptionally beautiful. She was perhaps ten years older than him and clearly more at ease in her own skin than he had ever been. She exuded confidence and he suddenly felt like a teenager with a crush. He hadn't allowed himself to feel anything like that since...

The guilt always followed close behind whenever he felt a flicker of attraction to anyone, the ghost of Kelly looking over his shoulder, at least in his mind. This woman was so far out of his league he almost blushed at the thought of her being attracted to him.

"Enjoy your visit," she said then nodded and took a step away. "If you have any questions about the wolves or our program here-"

"Richard really knows his stuff, I hear," Ian blurted out.

"I see you met Sandy." She smiled again. "She's sweet on Richard but he doesn't seem to know she exists. She's right, though. Richard does know his stuff. Are you from around here?"

"Ohio. Cincinnati area."

"I hope the drive was worth it."

"It was nice to meet you, Doctor White." *Geez, you're an idiot.* It was all he could manage to blurt out. He could feel himself blush. He hoped it didn't show.

"Call me April. Stop by again."

"I will. Thanks."

He stayed there for another half an hour watching the wolves gambol about in the snow, but the entire time he was thinking about the tall, alluring woman with the shock of white in her hair and the piercing grey-blue eyes.

January 1996

"You're back," April White said.

"I am." Ian was pleased she remembered him. He hadn't been able to stop thinking about her since his first visit. He even tried to convince himself that he wasn't there primarily because he hoped to see her again. The difference in their ages was less significant than it otherwise would be since he would outlive her, but that didn't change the fact that she was far out of his league. Then again, sometimes you just have to swing for the fences. *What are you thinking, you dope?*

"I have an hour free." She smiled. "Do you have any questions about the place I can answer?"

"I do. If I'm not imposing."

"You're not."

He had no idea how to go about this. He hadn't felt much for anyone since Kelly, but April had stirred something in him he wasn't sure was even still there. Was it her beauty? He had to admit that was a part of it, but there was something else about her. He didn't know what it was, but it was there.

"Did you drive up again?" she asked.

"Yeah."

"The roads get a little dicey around here in the winter."

"I can deal with it," Ian said.

They strolled around the center, looking through the broad glass he stood before the previous month. The snow was deeper and there wasn't a wolf in sight this time.

"Where are they?"

"Off doing what wolves do. They were here this morning. They might come back this evening."

"They might?"

"No guarantees, I'm afraid."

"Well, in that case, can I get a refund?" Ian smiled. "I'm just joking."

Ian felt like a kid with a crush again. The more time he spent with her, the more time he wanted. He was encouraged that she seemed fine with that. She answered every question he had, and when she did have to step away, he got the impression that she regretted it. *Right.*

"Would you like to see the wolves?" April said when she returned.

"Well, I saw them last month. I'll be back."

"Not in here. Out there. In the forest."

"You're kidding."

She shook her head. "Not at all. You're as interested in wolves as anyone I've ever met. Some of the students who pass through here don't have your enthusiasm. They lost something along the way."

"Why do you think I'm any different?" He knew he couldn't tell her just how different he was.

"A hunch," she said. "I take it you're not just here for the day. You've come a long way."

"I was going to head back tomorrow. I have a job to get back to Monday."

"Tomorrow's Saturday. I'll take the day off. Come out with me. We'll go into the forest."

"You don't have better plans for tomorrow?"

"No. We'll need to keep our distance, but I can find the pack."

"Well..."

"Are you afraid?"

"No." Ian *was* afraid, but of her more than the pack.

"Good. I take it you're staying in a hotel."

"Yeah. About twenty minutes from here."

"Meet me here tomorrow, then."

"OK. What time?"

"We could go early or late, but I'm kind of a night owl. Our wolves tend to be more active late until it gets really cold. Let's say one o'clock. We can grab lunch then be in the woods by four. We should at least see them."

"OK. If you're sure I'm not imposing. How can I thank you?"

"Don't worry about it. Wolves are my life."

"All right, I'll be here."

"Great. It's a date then." She flashed him a smile and walked away.

It's a date then. Geez, man. It's a date.

May 1996

Savannah State Forest, Minnesota

"This it it. My home away from home." April opened the door.

Ian stepped over the threshold into the small cabin.

"I had one in the UP," April said. "A long time ago."

"The UP?"

"Upper Peninsula. Northern Michigan."

They had met the last three months to go into the forest and observe wolves in the wild. The previous month, April told Ian she had a cabin on the edge of the state forest, not far from the Center, that she would show it to him the next time he came up. He felt more nervous than ever in her presence, and he knew it must show, but if April noticed, she didn't let on.

"We could have lunch before we head into the forest. My little fridge is pretty well stocked."

"That would be good," Ian said. Her cabin was one big room with a little couch across from the fireplace and a table with two chairs near a kitchenette that spanned the back half of the wall. A big, four-poster bed dominated the room. Ian sat on the couch.

"I'll do that, but for now I have a better idea."

"OK."

"It's something I've been thinking about for a while now."

April took off her denim jacket and dropped it on the floor next to the couch. She sat next to Ian. "I didn't get where I am by being subtle, Ian. I can tell you've been thinking about it, too."

"I, uh, well..," Ian stuttered.

"Well?"

"I have," he said. "You're very attractive." His heart was pounding and his hands felt sweaty. He fought the urge to swallow hard and looked into her wide open eyes. "There's a lot you don't know about me. Are you sure you want to go there?"

"100% sure." April kissed him and pressed her body against his.

Ian responded. It had been so long since he'd held someone, since he'd allowed himself to be like this with anyone. It felt good. He felt insecure and excited at the same time, but it felt good.

April released him and stood. She seemed to be waiting for something and he hesitated for a moment before he took her hand and walked with her across the room to the bed.

"I have to be honest with you," he began, and he started to tell her it had been several years since he'd done this, since the only time he'd done this, but she silenced him with a finger to his lips.

"I don't care," she said. "You can tell me your life story later." She pushed him gently and he sat on the bed, then she pulled her sweatshirt over her head and dropped it on the floor. "Off with your clothes, young man," she said, then shed her khaki pants as if they were a second skin.

He took off his jacket and his shirt and tossed them aside, then she was in his lap, naked and breathing heavily. Her body was lovely and mature, the body of a woman. Kelly had been as lovely as a girl could be, but she had been just that, a girl, a seventeen year old with years ahead of her before she matured into the woman she would have been...should have been...Ian flinched at the memory.

"Ian." April looked into his eyes. "I'm not sure whatever it is in your past that's making this so difficult, but you can't go through your life like this. You have to let someone in sometime."

"I know. It's...hard to explain."

"Don't worry about it right now. Just let right now be about us. You and me. We're the only ones here. I have a past, too. We can talk about that later, but right now none of that matters. If you let all that go, I will, too."

Be here. With me. Right now.

August 1996
Stonelick, Ohio

"You met this lady on line?" Verna set her plate next to the sink and turned on the water.

"I met her at the Wolf Center up there in Minnesota. I'd read some of her work on the Center's web site. I stopped in and there she was. I had to at least say hi."

"I'd like to meet her sometime."

"She lives up there. I don't think she gets down here often." Ian got up from the table and set his plate and silverware on top of Verna's. "Besides, I think we're still just friends."

"Uh huh."

Right. Friends. We just have sex once a month.

"Does *she* know you're just friends?

"Of course."

"And what about you?" Verna squirted dish washing liquid into the filling basin and stirred it around with her hand. "Are sure you know where you stand?"

"I think so." Ian opened the cabinet, took out a dish towel, and leaned against the counter.

"You think? Honey, look at me."

"What?"

"I just want you to be honest with yourself. It's been how many years?" Verna didn't need to add 'since Kelly' to get her point across. "I know you're afraid."

"Afraid of what?"

"Sweetheart, I've been around the block a time or two. I get the impression you really want something else with her, but you're hedging your bets." She stood with folded arms looking up at him.

Ian sighed and looked at the floor for a moment then back up to meet her gaze. "What if I do want more, but she doesn't?"

"You've been corresponding with this woman for months now. Talking over the computer."

"Chatting. Yeah."

"And you've seen her how many times?"

"Once a month. Since January."

"And she's been calling you?"

"I've been calling, too."

"You two talk most every day, don't you?"

"One way or the other. Phone. Email. Chat."

"And you still think she just wants to be friends?"

"She's older than me. Did I tell you that?"

"You mentioned it. How much older?"

"Not sure. Ten years maybe. It's bad form to ask a lady how old she is. At least that's what I always heard."

Verna smiled. "Well, you're right there. But, Honey, something about this doesn't sit right with me. I'll be blunt. Have you had sex with this woman?"

"Verna!"

"You heard me. Have you?"

"Yes." Ian turned red, but also smiled.

"You sure she's not married and just looking for some young thing to fool around with?"

"No, Verna, she's not married."

"Well, take my advice. Find out where this thing you have with her stands. If you want something she doesn't, you could wind up getting hurt."

"What do you suggest? She lives 800 miles away."

"I think you need to be clear about what's going on." Verna turned around and began washing the dinner dishes. "How long are you going to keep these trips up, anyway?"

"I don't know."

"You're going up this month?" she said.

"Yeah. I'll be up there for two nights, but I'll only see her for one. I'm taking a personal day from work and going up Friday. I'll be on my own the first night."

Ian was relieved that it wouldn't be a full moon Saturday, but he couldn't tell her the thing that ate at him the most. How could he maintain a successful relationship with any woman? *"Sorry, honey, but it's my time of the month. I'll be back tomorrow night."*

"You know, I'm not a kid anymore, Verna."

"I know you're not. And I'm probably just being overprotective. But be careful."

Ian rolled up his dish towel and snapped it at Verna's leg. She laughed and flicked soapy water in his direction. They spent the rest of the evening in much lighter conversation.

He was looking forward to the trip north. He couldn't deny that the sex had something to do with it. April was more intoxicating in the bedroom than he'd ever thought possible. Friday night he really would be on his own, though, running in the forest on all fours.

November 1996

The doorbell rang.

"Your lady friend is here," said Henry. He was sitting at the dining room table, sipping coffee.

Ian knew his excitement was obvious. April was his first love interest since Kelly and he was anxious for her to make a good first impression on the two people that mattered the most to him.

Verna peaked out of the kitchen, wiping her hands on a towel. "Well, let her in," she said.

Ian was glad Verna was here. He and his father knew their way around the kitchen, but they weren't good cooks. Verna was not only a splendid cook, but she loved to prepare a hearty, full meal. It was essentially their Thanksgiving dinner, though the holiday was half a week away. Ian knew the roast chicken and sides she planned would be a damn site better than anything he or his father could whip up.

"Go ahead, Son," his father said. "I won't get up until she's in the house. Don't want to overwhelm the poor lady."

"Don't worry, Dad. She's not the type who is easily overwhelmed."

"Let her in, for Pete's sake."

"Right," Ian said. He opened the door. April White stood holding a bottle of wine in a burgundy sleeve closed with a braided gold cord. She had one hand raised to ring the doorbell again.

"I found you," she said, dropping the hand.

Ian grinned and stepped aside to usher her in.

In contrast to her usual work attire or her outdoor look of jeans and sweatshirt, April was wearing her hair down, the long white streak prominent against her form fitting burgundy dress. Almost six feet tall in her bare feet, she wore heels that brought her eye to eye with his father.

Henry flashed a crooked smile and an arched eyebrow at his son then walked across the room. "Ian didn't tell us you were so tall." He extended his hand. "Henry Murphy. Pleased to meet you."

"My pleasure." April gave his hand a firm shake. "Ian's told me all about you." She stepped past Henry to approach Verna, towering over the diminutive woman. "And you must be Verna."

"I must be," Verna said. "How do you do?"

"Tired but fine. Thank you so much for having me. Dinner smells wonderful."

Verna looked up at April with an expression that was pleasant yet guarded. "We've heard a lot about you but, my goodness, you are a tall one. Ian told us you hate flying. You didn't drive all the way down here from Minnesota in that dress, did you?"

"Oh, no." She still held the wine in front or her, a conspicuous barrier between them. "I stopped to change. I wore sweats and running shoes most of the way. I avoid planes whenever possible. They're so confining. But in my line of work, they sometimes can't be avoided."

"Ian tells us you're a scientist," Henry said. "Let me take that off your hands."

April passed him the wine bottle. "I'm a biologist. I study wolves."

"Let's have a seat," Ian said. He rubbed his hands together, still nervous. Verna was smiling, but he could see she'd taken an instant disliking to April. It was so unlike her that he knew they had to talk about it later.

"Could I help you in the kitchen, Verna?" said April.

Verna waved off her offer. "You're our guest. Everything will be done in a few minutes."

Ian, April, and Henry took their places around the table while Verna disappeared. A radio tuned to a gospel station played low from the kitchen. Ian could hear her moving around in there, busying herself, but muttering under her breath, too low for even him to make out what she was saying. The three of them small talked for a few minutes before Verna appeared with a large wooden bowl of tossed salad in one hand and another bowl of hot rolls in the other.

"Let me help you with-" Henry started, but Verna cut him off.

"Don't be silly," she said. "I love to serve." She was gone for another minute before returning to the dining room with a roast chicken on a big, oval platter.

It seemed to Ian that Verna intended to spend as much time as possible in the kitchen, a suspicion that was confirmed when she left the room several times during the meal, first for butter, than for more coffee, and finally for dessert.

"Sit down and enjoy yourself," Henry said at last. "You're making me dizzy."

Verna looked as if she wanted to say something, but she remained silent, sitting in her chair and fussing with her napkin before filling her plate and taking dainty bites.

The food was outstanding as usual when Verna cooked, but the conversation lagged. There was only so much small talk Ian could endure. It was clear that his father was impressed by April, but it was also clear that he was tiring quickly. Two glasses of wine may have had something to do with that, but Ian knew there was more to it. When they finished Verna's splendid peach cobbler and moved to the living room, he could see that his father's motor was running down by the minute.

Ian and April refilled their drinks before taking a seat. During dinner, Verna had declined to partake of the wine, opting for iced tea. She held up her end of the conversation in the living room, but the undercurrent of her dislike of April was still evident to Ian.

After Verna left for home, Henry excused himself and turned in early. Ian and April sat on the porch swing in front of the house and looked up at the darkening sky.

"Your friend Verna doesn't like me," April said.

A half-moon was already high in the sky above the empty farmhouse and barns that had once been the Patella diary farm. The For Sale sign still stood at the end of the gravel drive, but it was looking worse for the wear.

"She'll come around," Ian said.

"She thinks she's your mother."

"No!" Ian protested. "She was Mom's best friend. She's always been close."

"Did you hear what she said? She said 'You're our guest.' Like the house is hers, too."

"She didn't mean it like that. We're a sort of surrogate family to her," Ian said. "And she is the closest thing to a mother I have now. I think Mom would be all right with that."

"She's very religious. People like that make me uncomfortable."

"Why?"

"It's religious people who are so quick to condemn others."

"Sure, but not Verna. Aside from my mom, she's the most loving person I've ever known."

"That may be, but it was religious people who led the witch hunts, who had people tortured and burned at the stake."

Ian had heard this before. It wasn't much different than what Stubbs said. Of course, they didn't come much more religious than Stubbs, even if his own brand was twisted in such diabolical ways.

Stubbs was the past, though. Ian had resisted his instruction out of sheer spite, aside from his advice about the cycles of the moon. He was glad he didn't have to worry about that for another two weeks. Coming up with an excuse for why April couldn't come down to meet his family on a night close to the full moon would have been difficult. He needed to tell her something soon, though, if their relationship was going to move forward.

"Your father's not well," April said, shifting topics.

"It shows, huh?"

"Yeah. If you know what to listen for."

"Listen?"

"Listen. Look. Just paying attention."

Ian sighed. He'd listened to his father's heartbeat before. It wasn't as strong as it once was and he was trying to think of a tactful way to suggest that he should tell his doctor how poor he was feeling. His father was stubborn, though. Ian knew he couldn't expect him to just act on his advice.

"Let's go to my hotel," April said.

"Huh? We have a room you can stay in."

"I didn't come all this way to leave without jumping your bones, mister, and I'm not about to do that down the hall from your father. You make too much noise."

"Me?"

"OK, I'm the noisy one." She gave him a twisted grin. "I'd feel too self-conscious. What if we woke him up? I doubt he wants to hear us."

They'd spent the night together several times at her cabin, and he'd been taken aback at first by April's uninhibited manner. He knew he was an inexperienced lover, but he doubted most women were as energetic, as ferocious for lack of a better word, as April. His only previous experience had been with Kelly. He was glad he had little memory of their second time. Their first time-his first time-was still a treasured memory. It was clumsy to be sure, but it was also sweet, caring, and loving. Sex with April was different. She was voracious, insatiable. He'd get little sleep until the early morning and while he found himself more and more willing to go wherever she led, there was still something about their marathon couplings that troubled him. It only troubled him afterward, though.

"Where is this room?"

"Milford. Just off the highway."

"All right."

"It'll take us about twenty minutes to get there. Tell you what," she said. "You drive and I'll make sure your motor keeps running until we get there. Just don't take your eyes off the road. "

"I, uh, think I can manage that."

He did, but just barely.

January 1997

"What's that?" Verna said as she looked over Ian's shoulder. She'd dropped by to bring some leftovers for dinner. Her leftovers were better than many fresh meals.

"A map of Minnesota. The NAWSC is there." Ian drew a circle on the screen around the Center. He couldn't help but think about Verna's strange reaction to April over Thanksgiving dinner.

"Hmmm. So that's where it is. Where does your girlfriend April live?"

"Not far from there."

Ian shrugged. As far as Verna knew, his monthly trips to Minnesota were to see April. He couldn't tell her that he was considering testing her off-hand comment about living with a wolf pack. He hadn't told April yet, either, but he was running out of excuses for leaving after a day, only to take off into the woods by himself and observe the pack they'd been following.

"I don't care much for her," Verna said. "I guess that's obvious."

"Yeah. It is. I've been meaning to ask you about that, but the moment never seemed right."

Verna patted his shoulder.

"Why, though? What's wrong with her?"

"I'm not sure I can explain." Verna stepped back and shook her head. "I know it isn't fair to her or to you, but I can't help it."

"She noticed."

"She's older than you, you know."

"A few years. No big deal. I'll be twenty-five next month. She's over thirty, but that white streak makes people think she's older than she is. It's a genetic thing. She's had it since she was a child."

"I think she's older than she's letting on."

Ian rolled back from the desk and swiveled his chair to face Verna. "And this is a problem?"

"There's something else about her."

"What?"

"I'm not sure, but if she's not being honest about her age, she probably isn't being honest about other things."

"Are you sure you're not just being overprotective?"

"Maybe I am. I'm sorry, Ian. Just be careful with her. Be smart."

He nodded and turned back to his desk. He clicked off the map of Minnesota and went back to his work. "I have to finish this."

Verna paused as if she had more to say but walked away. When she reached the door, she looked back at Ian. "Dinner's in the oven. Your father's in the garage. I'll let him know. See you later, sweetie. I love you."

"I love you, too," Ian said, but he didn't turn around. "Thanks for dinner."

Over dinner, Ian had a brief conversation with his father about how his job was going. Ian worked from home as a cartographer for a company that produced maps. The maps were primarily a vehicle for selling ads. GPS was out there, though, and he knew it was only a matter of time before the folding map-and his current job-was obsolete. After that?

Ian headed for the woods as soon as his father left for work. The full moon was a week away. Tonight was another practice night. He was getting better at changing at will, but it still wasn't easy or comfortable. Soon he would have to attempt remaining a wolf for an extended period, at least a full day or two, but that would have to be in Minnesota. There was no way he could attempt that at home. Ian loved his father and couldn't imagine leaving him, but he had to know. If he could really do this, it would open the door to his future. If one or two days was possible, why not a week or even more?

February 1997

A thick blanket of snow covered the ground. The weather that winter had been mild, light snows in December and January with the temperature hovering around the freezing mark, but February came in cold and hard. The first real snowfall of the season left almost five inches on the ground. The temperature warmed enough for a freezing rain to fall that crusted over the snow. The salt trucks and snow plows were busier than they had been in years.

The black wolf's paws broke through the crust and sank into the powder beneath. It was near dawn but he was almost home. One minute he was a wolf, the next minute he was a man, changing as he walked, the pain and popping joints nothing now. He was halfway across the yard when the change was complete and he was once again Ian Murphy. So close were his two natures now that he barely broke stride as he rose from four feet to two.

Ian shivered in the 15° air, goose bumps dotting his naked body. The cold was invigorating, but his human body would soon crave warmth. He was about to remind himself to come back out and obscure the footprints behind him when a movement in the big picture window facing the back yard caught his eye.

His father was staring at him through the glass. A coffee cup dangled from the fingertips of one hand, the steaming liquid dripping from the downturned rim. His other hand moved upward, clutched at his chest, then stopped and curled. Henry's mouth opened to form what might have been a word, but the word never came. His eyes rolled back in his head, his knees buckled, and he fell to the hardwood floor with a heavy thud.

"No!" Ian screamed and bolted for the house. "Oh, Jesus, please! Oh, shit! No!" Even from a hundred feet away he saw what his father looked like before he hit the floor. He nearly tore the door off its hinges as he burst into the house and knelt by his father's still, lifeless body.

Chapter 14

Tap tap.

Ian struggled up through layers of darkness, a stifling blanket of fuzz muffling his perceptions. He felt sick to his stomach and had a splitting headache.

Tap tap.

"Ian?"

A muted voice penetrated the haze.

"Ian?"

He opened first one eye then the other. The hazy half-light of the winter morning was diluted by frosted windows. Ian's cheek rested against cold vinyl. It took him several seconds to realize he was lying across the front seat of his car.

Tap tap! The sound was more forceful now.

Ian's eyes rolled around in his head, searching, trying to make sense of things. Two empty bottles lay on the floorboard. He smacked his lips, the crust on his mouth sticky and thick. He belched. A taste like licorice filled his mouth and he knew he was going to vomit within seconds. Fumbling for the door handle with uncooperative hands, his cold fingers found the latch and popped the door open just in time for him to hang his head out of the old Maverick and spew into the icy gutter.

He heard the soft crunch of crusty snow and looked up, gasping for breath, to see Eve Martin walking around to the passenger side. She was bundled in a huge, blue parka over a floral housecoat. The winter boots on her feet were several sizes too big. It appeared that she'd thrown on whatever was at hand, most likely her husband's coat and boots.

"I'm sorry," Ian whispered. He pulled himself out of the car, avoiding the steaming puddle in the gutter, and leaned against the car. His right arm ached from being trapped under his body for hours.

"Come inside," Gram said. She put her small, soft hand on his shoulder.

Ian nodded but didn't move. He was trying to put together exactly how he wound up in front of the Martin's house. He remembered leaving his own house shortly after Verna left. She was reluctant to leave him alone after his father's funeral, but he convinced her he was all right.

The funeral was a blur, relatives and acquaintances he rarely saw came but left afterward. His father's brother and wife, Uncle Paul and Aunt Marlene, were on their way back to North Carolina. They'd helped with the arrangements and promised to call when they got home, but it wasn't a call Ian was anxious to take. His father was gone and there was nothing to be done about that. He considered changing and running the forest, but he was afraid of what the wolf might do in the dark mindset he was in after the funeral. What he wanted was to forget about it all for a while, so sometime during the night he'd bought two bottles of ouzo. He downed the first one in minutes but hardly felt it, his constitution resisting the numbing effects of the alcohol. The second bottle did the trick. He didn't remember finishing it.

"Well, at least now I know how much it takes to get a werewolf drunk," he muttered.

"Come on," Eve Martin said.

"I'm sorry, Gram," he was able to say ahead of another wave of nausea. He pulled away from her and staggered around behind the car just in time to empty his stomach. "Damn," he gasped. When he was done spitting into the snow, he wiped his mouth on his sleeve and leaned against the car again. The sparkle from the sun off the snow hurt his eyes and aggravated his pounding head.

The small lady moved around the car, choosing each step with great care, and took him by the arm. "Come inside, Ian. You can warm up."

He straightened, took a deep breath, and chanced a look into her eyes. He was afraid of what he might see there. His father's funeral the day before was the first time in several years they had been together in the same room. Ian avoided the Martins as much as possible until Gram finally cornered him and gave him a long, affectionate hug. He stood there after she left him, his eyes welling up, feeling immense gratitude and relief tempered by a horrible guilt. Now, with his head pounding, his hair going in seven different directions, and the acrid smell of bile burning his sensitive nostrils, he looked her full in the face at last.

Eve Martin smiled, a pained grimace of a smile, but a smile nonetheless, and he knew the pain in her eyes wasn't just for her lost grandchild. "Come inside. Please."

His car was parked next to the sidewalk in front of the Martin's house, his front bumper inches from a mound of compacted, snowplowed slush. It was a small miracle that he made it there given that he must have been three sheets to the wind. He wasn't sure. He couldn't remember. Whatever the case, he knew he was fortunate to get there in one piece given his condition and the icy roads.

By the time they reached the front door Ian was no longer listing to the left. Standing at the door, wearing the same terry cloth robe Ian had worn for a while over four years before, was Roy Martin. His face was grim, his broad frame filling the doorway. For a few seconds Ian thought Roy was going to forbid him from entering, but the older man turned and walked into another room.

Gram led him into the kitchen, still clutching his arm. He sat at the small wooden table there, both hands on his forehead, while she put on coffee then left the room.

"Eve, I don't want him in this house!" Roy Martin's tone was emphatic though he was trying to keep his voice down.

Ian could picture Roy stabbing the air with his finger as he spoke. He didn't want to listen, but Ian picked up every word from the living room.

"Roy, the boy lost his father," Eve said. "Where's your Christian charity? For god's sake, he was practically family."

"He was there! He was with Kelly the night she -"

"He loved Kelly. You know he did. I don't know what happened that night and neither do you, but I know one thing; Ian would never have hurt her. Never!"

"I'm not saying he did, but he's the only one who knows anything about that night."

"He doesn't, Roy. He told the sheriff everything he knows and I believe him."

"I don't, and I'm not going to just stand by and-"

Ian cleared his throat. He stood in the archway between the living room and the hallway leading to the kitchen. He wanted to come clean, to tell them what he was, what he knew he had done. He'd been able to tamp down the guilt, to rationalize that he'd had no control over his actions that night. It was true but it didn't matter. He killed Kelly and nothing would ever change that. Roy Martin's words were a hammer blow to his carefully constructed defenses. The man was more right than he knew, and Ian felt the full weight of his guilt again, not just for Kelly but for Chevy. And now for his father.

"I'll, uh, be going now," Ian said. "I'm sorry to bother you. I'm sorry for...I..." He stopped. There was no way to go on without breaking down in front of them. They wouldn't believe him if he told them and telling them wouldn't help. It had to be torture to never know the truth, but he knew that the truth was even worse.

"Are you sure you're all right to drive?" Eve crossed the room and took his hand. "We could give you a ride home."

"That's OK, Gram. I feel better. My head hurts, but I'm all right." He at least wasn't lying about that. His strange, supernatural metabolism worked its own small miracle on his hangover. Other than the headache, he felt as sober as a judge. He didn't welcome the recovery, though. It only meant the grief and guilt were back, undiluted and inescapable.

"Well, at least let me get you some pain reliever and some coffee. You wait here."

Ian stepped aside and she walked down the hall. When he turned back, Grandpa Martin was standing in the middle of the room, silent, unmoving, his hands deep in the pockets of his robe. Ian saw his lips tremble. When Roy tried to speak, his eyebrows knitted together and his face sagged.

"Well, you..." the man finally was able to say, "...be careful out there. The roads are terrible. It's a wonder you made it here safe." He shrugged and his lips trembled again. "Are you sure we can't, uh, give you a ride home?"

"I appreciate that, but I'll be fine. Thank you."

Roy Martin looked past Ian, closed his eyes then opened them and walked to the stairs. He patted Ian on the shoulder as he passed but didn't look at him and went upstairs without another word.

A few minutes later, Ian drove away. Gram stood on the front porch and watched him go, her arms wrapped around her against the cold.

Ian stepped on the brake a bit too hard as he approached the end of Daytripper Road, the wide residential street that led out of the Martin's neighborhood, Strawberry Fields. Apparently, someone was a huge Beatles fan. He had shared many laughs over that with Kelly and Chevy. On his way to the main road through Stonelick, he passed Lennon Street, Penny Lane, and McCartney Terrace. "What, no Ringo?" Ian said right before the car fishtailed. He took his foot off the pedal, brought the car back under control, pumped the brakes, and rolled to a stop at the intersection.

Gram's travel mug of strong, hot coffee was wedged between his legs, the warmth against his thighs welcome. The temperature had dropped even more with the dawn, the cloudless skies letting what heat there was in the air rise up and dissipate. He took three tablets from the bottle of pain reliever Gram had given him and washed them down with coffee. "Shit!" he muttered. "Hot."

He could turn left and go home, but he wasn't ready to go back there yet. The place was empty and cold, lacking the warmth of another human being. If he had one of those cell phones that were becoming popular he could call April or Verna. April was still in California at a conference, though, and Verna would be getting ready for church. She might even be in bed. *No one is out this morning but you, idiot.* The Martin's street wasn't completely awful, just bad. State Route 131 was a mess. He shrugged and turned right to head for the cemetery two miles out of town. Home was two miles in the other direction. He could manage four miles under any conditions if he took it slow. Kelly was up there. So was Chevy. Now his father was, too. He'd drop in and commune with them for a while then be done with the place. After that, he could go home and start getting used to living alone.

Ian crept most of the way, but he knew he needed some momentum to climb the hill sloping up to the cemetery and the intersection of 131 and 727. He gave it a little more gas and made it to the top of the hill. It was there that things went bad.

The cemetery was located across the road from an open field. Overnight, the wind blowing across the unbroken width of 131 polished the surface till it was as smooth as glass. He underestimated how soon he would reach the top and when he did, he was going too fast for the conditions. One moment he was cresting the hill, the next he was sailing without control. Out of reflex, he stepped on the brake a little too hard again. The car spun sideways, the lid flew off the mug, spilling hot coffee in his lap, and the Maverick headed straight for the cemetery gate. Ian tried to turn out of the skid but it was useless. The car slammed into the gate with a loud, metallic crunch.

Ian sat behind the wheel catching his breath, shaken but unhurt. He had to push hard on the door before it would open enough for him to squeeze his big body through. Once out, he was able to appraise the damage. The frame was bent. That was obvious. "Dammit!" The right quarter panel was a crumpled mess. He crouched and looked for gasoline just in case. There was none, but it looked like the entire contents of his radiator was a puddle of steaming neon green. The stone column on the left side of the gate had taken much of the impact, but his grill was a tangle of bent metal. The car had cut a deep trough through the snow, into the grass and soil underneath.

Ian pressed his hands to his forehead. His head hurt worse than ever and his coffee-soaked lap had gone from steaming hot to a wet, frigid cold. "Fuck." He raised his head and looked around, There was no one in sight.

Through the spider-webbed side window, he saw one of the two empty liquor bottles on the floorboard. He walked around to the other side of the crumpled Maverick, wrenched open the door, and located both bottles. The other one had come to rest wedged between the seats. He walked across the slippery street to the ditch and hurled the bottles one at a time at least fifty yards into the open field.

Half an hour later he sat on the frozen ground next to Kelly's grave. His father's grave was a hump of snow-covered soil next to his mother's that had yet to settle. He sat next to the mound for a while then walked over to Chevy's grave. He stood there for a quarter of an hour, silent, wishing again that he remembered something of that night but at the same time thankful that he didn't. From there, he walked to Kelly's grave and settled down. Sooner or later somebody would pass the cemetery and see his crumpled car. He resolved to wait with Kelly until they did.

Ian heard a car pull off the road, but he didn't bother to turn around. Whoever it was couldn't miss seeing his car, and sitting there in the open he was hard to miss, as well.

A few minutes later he heard the crunch of boots on the compacted snow. He didn't have to look up to know who it was.

"Bad morning, Ian?" Sheriff Kearsey said.

He imagined the sheriff doffing his hat as he spoke. *Maybe they only did that in movies or on TV.* When Ian spoke, he kept his head down. "They're all buried here," he said. "Did you know that? Everyone I ever loved. Except Verna, and I bet she has a plot waiting for her, too."

"In its own way, this is a beautiful place," the sheriff said. "People are comforted knowing their loved ones are resting somewhere nice."

"I'm not," muttered Ian. He reached out to the name engraved in script on Kelly's elaborate headstone, tracing the letters with his extra-long index finger. "And I'm not going to another goddamn funeral as long as I live. The next one I go to will be my own."

The sheriff's lined leather jacket creaked as he looked around the cemetery. After a few seconds he sighed and took two more steps that brought him next to Ian. His knees popped in protest as he crouched. "Let's tend to your car, Ian. OK?"

"I don't care."

"You must be cold sitting there on the ground."

He was cold but he didn't care. How many times today were people going to give a damn whether he was cold or not? He was already tired of hearing it. He didn't want their concern.

"It's warm in the cruiser," the sheriff said. "We can wait there. I called a tow truck."

"Did someone call you?"

"I was headed back to town. There was a wreck a little ways up the road." He looked at his watch. "It's only half past nine and it's been a long morning already."

Ian stood up. He didn't care about the cold, but he knew he should be there when the wrecker arrived. He also had some explaining to do.

"So tell me, Ian. What happened here?"

The sun was high in the sky, the temperature climbing toward 20° by the time Ian made it home. Sheriff Kearsey had waited with Ian till the tow truck arrived, then gave him a lift. The culvert in front of the gate had absorbed much of the impact and the damage to the stone column and the gate was minimal, but the car was a lost cause. A bent frame and 234,000 miles on the odometer meant the old beast had seen the last of the road.

The sheriff walked with Ian to his back door, chatting but looking around. He seemed to accept Ian's explanation that he'd simply lost control on the icy road. In Stonelick alone, a dozen drivers found themselves in similar circumstances the last forty-eight hours. If it hadn't been the sheriff making the call, the tow truck would have taken a lot longer to get there.

"Do you have any other means of transportation?" Sheriff Kearsey asked.

"Yeah. Dad's...well, Mom's old car is in the garage."

"I thought he sold it years ago?"

"Still there. I'll be in the market for something else, but it'll get me by for now."

"I'm sorry about your father," the sheriff said. He put his hand on Ian's shoulder. "He was a good man, one of my oldest friends. If there's anything I can do, let me know."

"Thank you, Sheriff. My father thought highly of you, too. Would you like a cup of coffee to go? Only take a few minutes."

"No, but thank you."

Ian fished his keys out of his pocket but didn't unlock the door. He turned and saw the sheriff standing on the bottom step, looking out at the back yard. "What is it?" he said as his mind supplied the answer. *Oh crap. The footprints.*

"You having problems with stray dogs in your yard?" The sheriff walked across the covered porch into the back yard, his head down. He stopped and crouched to study the tracks crossing the middle of the yard. The snow was still crusted over, preserving the prints in perfect detail.

Ian trotted down the steps and joined the sheriff in the yard, stepping on the human tracks, positioning himself between the lawman and the rest of the prints.

"Big dog," the sheriff said. "Helluva big dog."

"Must have been overnight." Ian knew it sounded weak. "I haven't seen any dogs back here during the day. Then again, I've been a little distracted these last few days."

Sheriff Kearsey stood and looked at the tracks for several long seconds, his narrowed eyes betraying something that looked to Ian like either confusion or disbelief. The look passed and the sheriff's features softened. "Take care, Ian. Let me know if there's anything I can do. And drive safely."

The sheriff sat in his cruiser with the heat on full blast. He turned the vents so the hot air would hit him square in the face and thought about the tracks in Ian's yard. One set went from the house to the woods, the other from the woods to the porch. The tracks heading toward the woods were made by someone with big, bare feet. Barefoot in this weather? The tracks leading to the house were made by a dog but a dog with feet as wide as a big dinner plate. They could have melted somewhat, he supposed, giving the impression of a larger animal, but he doubted it. Nothing around his own house had melted the last week. Even the icicles that hung from the corners stopped reaching down last Tuesday. He scratched his head. There was no way around what he saw. The tracks were those of a four-footed animal, then they weren't. The prints were human the rest of the way to the house. The feet that left those prints were big and bare, the toe impressions clear, and the stride was huge, as if whoever left them was sprinting across the yard.

"How the hell am I supposed to make sense of that?" A quiet voice from deep in some neglected corner of his mind whispered an answer. It was the voice of the child he once was, the child who loved comic books, wax candy lips with long white fangs, and ghost stories. It was the voice of a boy who lived for monster movies, model kits, and Halloween records.

Matthew Kearsey-sheriff, father, responsible adult-shuddered from head to toe and shook his head to bring that rebellious, imaginative child to heel. What was that saying? "That way lie madness."

The doorbell rang the next morning.

Ian had to chase away the fog that had settled over him as he sank into the cushions of the lounge chair in the living room. His father's favorite chair. Sometime in the middle of a documentary about prehistoric marine reptiles, he'd fallen asleep. The current feature was about life in the Serengeti.

The doorbell rang again.

"All right," Ian said. He wrenched himself from the depths of the chair and stood. His head still hurt and he was only half awake. "Hold your horses." He squinted at the clock on the wall. 9:51 AM. No one ever used the front door, at least no one who knew him. Verna would be at the bakery by now. April wasn't due to arrive for another full day. They both would have come to the back door, anyway.

Ian swung the door open and his breath caught in his throat. He was fully awake in an instant. Peter Stubbs stood on his front porch.

"Hello, Ian? May I come in?"

Without a word, Ian opened the screen door and stepped aside. As soon as Stubbs stepped over the threshold the atmosphere in the room seemed to change. It felt to Ian as if the air pressure inside the house increased as if Stubbs was made of denser material than the average man. Ian had forgotten the effect Stubbs could have on him. It was like being in his presence the first time, so much so that he was taken aback, speechless, but only for a second before his anger flared.

"It's good to see you again, Ian, even under these circumstances."

As Stubbs turned, Ian closed the door, wheeled, and fired a right hand at the man's face, all the hurt, anger, and frustration of the last few years driving the punch. Had it struck a normal man it would have been a fatal blow.

Stubbs was no ordinary man. He reacted with near-impossible speed, slipping the punch with a sideways twist of his upper body. Before Ian's arm could even complete its circle, Stubbs grabbed the extended arm and using the younger man's momentum against him, hurled him head over heels across the room. Ian landed with a heavy crash, the air expelled from his lungs.

"There is no call for violence," Stubbs said, his voice calm and even.

Ian rolled over onto his knees and sat on all fours, catching his breath. "Fuck you," he rasped.

Stubbs shook his head like a teacher disappointed with the progress of a promising young student. "Your vocabulary has expanded since we last met, and not for the better. I am sorry about your father. I was unable to be here for the funeral. I came as soon as I could, though."

"What, were you busy killing more innocent people?"

Stubbs ignored the remark. "I had a prior commitment. Please, Ian, let's sit down and talk." Stubbs gestured toward the living room, playing the host as if the house was his.

On the television, a pack of African wild dogs tore at the haunches of a desperate wildebeest.

Ian got up rubbing his shoulder and sat in the recliner again.

Stubbs, still standing, regarded the death of the hapless animal. "That is how it ultimately is for those who reject The Lord. 'I will also send the teeth of beasts upon them.' The Word of God."

"You don't say?" Ian snorted in disgust. "Is that supposed to bring me comfort?"

"The Word of The Lord is comfort, Ian. It shows us the way, gives order to our lives. Your purpose and mine is found in its pages." Stubbs sat down on the sofa. "I am truly sorry for your loss."

"How did you know? Are you some kind of psychic, too?"

"Pastor James told me." Stubbs sat on the couch but leaned forward toward Ian. "We were speaking on the phone about another revival. He also told me you haven't been to church in quite some time. He's worried about you. So am I. I've been worried about you for a long time now."

"Why? Are you worried that I haven't turned into a murdering monster like you?"

Stubbs remained calm, even compassionate. "I understand loss, Ian. I lost my own father. My children are lost to me. If being a sounding board for your anger brings you some peace, then so be it."

"It's because of you that he's dead." Ian growled the words through clenched teeth. He felt the tips of his canines lengthen into points pressing against the inside of his lips.

"I was under the impression it was a heart attack."

"He saw me change. I didn't know he was home. He never comes home early but...he wasn't well." Ian looked at Stubbs and his anger burned again. "He was standing at the window when I crossed the yard. He saw a wolf change into his son! His heart..." Ian stopped to wipe tears from his eyes and stood up. "He's dead because of you and what you did to me. Chevy. Kelly. Now my dad! You come here for the first time in years, quoting scripture about beasts, talking about the will of God. You want to hold another revival here? Why? So you can spread more of your disease?"

In the space of a breath, Stubbs sprang from his seat, grasped Ian by the throat, and lifted him, pinning him against the stone fireplace along the wall. "You tread on dangerous ground, young man," he snarled. " 'He that blasphemeth against the Holy Ghost hath never forgiveness but is in danger of eternal damnation.' "

"What do you call this?" Ian growled back at Stubbs. His teeth grew longer over his lips, dark hair sprouted from his face and the backs of his hands, and his fingernails turned black and lengthened.

Stubbs smiled, revealing canines like daggers. His face was elongated, his silver hair more coarse. "You've learned!" He beamed and relaxed his grip on Ian's throat. "You can't run from your calling. The Hand Of God is upon you in a mighty way. There have been few like you, Ian. You have passed a test merely by surviving this long."

"What about the ones who haven't survived?"

"Their fate lies in the hands of God. Your fate has yet to be determined, but there is every reason to be encouraged." Stubbs relaxed further then, his hands no longer gripping Ian but resting on his chest, the tips of claws just touching Ian's throat. "Your father has passed. I am truly sorry for your loss, Ian. Let me step into that gap. Let me be the father that-"

Ian raked a clawed hand across Stubbs' face with all the speed and power he could muster, snapping the man's head back and dropping him to his knees. Drops of blood spattered the wall.

"Don't you dare compare yourself to my father!"

Before Ian could move, Stubbs lashed out, backhanding him with a sweep of his powerful arm. For the second time that morning, Ian thudded against the floor, dazed this time as much by the blow as by the impact.

Stubbs arose and stood over Ian. Blood ran down the side of his face from the four ragged furrows Ian's claws had dug into his flesh. The dark red liquid soaked into the brilliant white of his suit jacket and shirt, a crimson bloom that spread across his chest and throat. "What father do you have now but me, boy?" he said. Anger flashed in his eyes for a moment and he was as much beast as man. "You aren't ready yet, I'm afraid, but one day you will be. On that day, you *will* have to choose."

Stubbs breathed deep, his anger faded, and his face moved beneath the skin, retracting as he stood smiling at Ian like a stern father satisfied with the lesson taught to his wayward son. In seconds he was fully human again. He turned to leave, opened the door, then paused.

Ian pulled himself from the floor and stood on wobbly legs.

"The Lord will not tarry with you forever, Ian." Stubbs was no longer smiling. "I instructed you before to find out who you are. The Lord's patience is great, but it is not limitless. Perhaps the next time we meet you will be ready to take up your cross."

Ian dabbed at his bloody nose as Stubbs closed the door. Footsteps crunched through the crusted snow outside, a car started, then the preacher was gone.

Chapter 15

September 1997

Savannah State Forest, Minnesota

The big male wolf lie in the clearing, his dark gray flank glistening silver in the evening light. His long muzzle rested on his front paws, but his eyes moved back and forth as he watched two juveniles play a canine version of tag. His mate, the biggest female, sat a few feet away, nibbling at a persistent itch in her right hindquarters. The black ruff of fur around her shoulders twitched as she stretched to scrape her teeth across the irritated patch of skin.

Approaching the pair with his tail down and eyes averted, a younger male sat near them. Though he was nearly as large as the leader of the pack, he was still young and inexperienced. The leader raised his head to regard him for a moment, then licked the younger male's muzzle. The young adult's eyes brightened at this sign of approval and his shoulders straightened. He sat proud but not too proud. Not yet.

The pack was relaxed and happy. Times were good. Prey was plentiful and the weather agreeable. The last breeding season hadn't gone well, the pups dying before the Minnesota snows melted. The leader and his mate would have more offspring next season and if all went well, the pack would increase in number.

The younger adult female's head snapped up, her ears twitching. She stood and paced. The others noticed but didn't stand. The pack ruled this part of the forest. Satisfied that no threat was imminent, the female crossed the clearing and settled closer to the two large males and the big female. Their presence quelled any anxiety she felt and her full stomach reassured her that all was right in their world.

Two hundred yards away, Ian lowered his field glasses. "I want to get closer."

"Not safe," said April. She was next to Ian, propped up on her backpack and her elbows.

"Why?"

"They won't tolerate us getting closer. This is as close as we get."

"You've never gotten closer?"

"Once. Never again. I've been studying them for years."

"What happened?"

April ignored him.

"How am I supposed to learn anything about them from this far away?" Ian said.

"Watch. Pay attention. We can collect scat."

"Scat?"

"Droppings."

"Yeah, I know what it is, but...."

"But what?"

Ian hadn't figured out how to tell her what he was. He was sure she wouldn't believe him, so he would have to show her. She'd be terrified at first, but he hoped she didn't reject him, that once she got over the initial shock, she might find his condition fascinating. If anyone in the world would understand, it would be her. He didn't really love her, certainly not in the way he'd loved Kelly, but he wanted April in his life. She was a good companion and he rationalized that in time he might come to love her. The sex was certainly good, but there was something missing. Perhaps it was just

Verna's influence, but more and more he felt that April wasn't being completely honest with him. Of course, he wasn't being honest with her, either, so it worked both ways. She had her reasons just as he had his.

Verna still didn't care for her. That troubled Ian. She wasn't his mother and despite what April said, he knew Verna would never try to be. Her approval was important to him, though.

"I think they've settled down for now," April said.

"Do you think they can hear us?"

"Not from this distance if we keep our voices down."

They couldn't smell them, either, unless the wind shifted. Still, Ian was pretty sure the pack knew someone or something was there. There was nothing to be done about scent. After they were gone, traces of their presence would linger. He could smell the pack all around them on the ground. They'd been there recently and would be there again.

"Let's go back to the cabin," April said.

She was looking forward to another tryst. He could smell the arousal on her. It was getting more difficult for Ian to mask his ambivalence. Once they were undressed, he would rise to the occasion, to be sure. She was beautiful, after all, and exuded a magnetism that was almost animalistic in nature. It was easy to lose himself in the physical act, but afterward...

Ian got up early in the morning. April was still asleep, sprawled facedown next to him, the blanket rolled down to her waist. Her dark hair covered most of her back in a wild tangle. The white streak divided her dark covering, rising and falling with her breaths. He stepped over his discarded underwear, went outside, and stood in the grass.

The moon was nearly full. He had to go home tomorrow to be ahead of the phases and even though he did most of his work from home, he couldn't get away any time he wanted. Despite that, he'd come to a conclusion; he would try what Verna had mused about. Maybe his employer would grant him a leave of absence long enough for him to know if his plan would work. A family emergency, he'd tell them, and worry about the details later. He would have to make arrangements first in case anything kept him from returning, for good or bad. The house would have to be dealt with. Uncle Paul seemed the logical choice, even though he lived in North Carolina. He could sell the place if he wanted. Ian didn't care. He had a savings account, too, and because of his spartan existence the amount was considerable. Verna could have it all. He had no one else.

"What are you doing out here?" April stood in the open doorway, the blanket from the bed wrapped loosely around her naked body.

"Couldn't sleep," Ian said.

April walked outside and stood next to him. She loved being barefoot, feeling the grass between her toes. It was one of the things they had in common.

"Penny for your thoughts." April chuckled at her use of the tired old cliché.

"Do I look like I'm thinking?"

"Something's going on inside that noggin of yours."

"I was thinking about the wolves."

"What about them?"

"They don't have a thing to worry about. They're free."

"We're free."

"Not like they are."

April pulled the blanket closer and rested her head on Ian's shoulder. "They aren't as free as you think. They were hunted before," she said. "Wiped out. Just like the witch hunts."

"That again?"

"It's true. People saw wolves as devils. They didn't understand. Beautiful creatures, all eliminated. We had to reintroduce them to the wild."

"So you're repaying a debt?"

"You could say that."

"There's something I need to tell you," Ian said. "Or show you."

"What?"

Ian sighed and put his arm around her. She snugged up close, their musky scents mingled together in his nose. "When I figure out how, I will."

"You're not secretly married, are you?" April smiled and nudged him with her hip.

"You know I'm not."

"I know. I'm kidding. Is it Kelly? You told me all about her."

"Not exactly," Ian said. "It does have something do with her, but not...like that."

"I get it. She was your first love. That never really leaves."

Ian held her closer. She couldn't understand. She'd might never understand. *Maybe I should just let her go.*

"While you figure that out, I've got something I want to give you."

"What?"

"Keys."

"Keys?"

"To the cabin."

"Are you sure you want to do that?"

"I am. We talked about this. I made you a set. You can come here any time you want."

Shit. If she tells me she loves me again, what am I going to say. She'd already said the L-word a number of times and every time he hadn't been able to say it back. With Kelly, he'd burned with the desire to tell her what he felt. With April, he still held back, even after being in a relationship with her for more than a year. She was patient, but perhaps that was the way out, the way to end things. He did care for her, but in the end she was just one more thing he'd have to leave behind if he was to abandon humanity to join the wolves. If that worked.

"I put them on your key ring already."

"You did? When?"

"Before I came out here."

"I...I don't know what to say."

"Just say 'thank you,' silly."

The cabin would come in handy. It could serve as a jumping off point, a place he could come to and spend weekends letting the pack become used to his presence. *Shit. Now I really am using her.* "Thank you," he managed.

"You're welcome." She kissed his bare shoulder. "Want to come back inside?"

"In a minute."

April kissed his cheek and left him standing there.

Great. More guilt. Am I really just an awful, self-absorbed person?

He felt guilty for using someone who had the best of intentions. On the one hand, if anyone would ever understand it would have to be her. On the other, if he was going to leave humanity forever, it might be better if she never knew. She knew the pack, though. She kept tabs of every wolf in the wilderness around them. He wouldn't go unnoticed. He'd observed the wolves for months now, studied their habits, their interactions, but not like April. Still, there was no way she could know he was the newcomer. If he could make it work, if he could really do it, it would mean freedom forever from Stubbs and his mad vision. There was no way for April to know, but she was giving him more than just the keys to her cabin. She was giving him the keys to his future.

February 1998

The black wolf dipped his nose into the snow and sniffed. Beneath the cold blanket of powder, the ground was covered by moss and pine needles. He snuffled back and forth, taking small steps, covering every square inch of the forest floor. After a minute of searching, he found the scent trail and followed. He found the pack resting in a clearing at the bottom of a tall slope. From a distance of less than two hundred feet, the black wolf could smell the fresh blood still drying on their muzzles. The pack's hunt that evening had been a success.

He knew about the human. He understood that he was both man and beast, his humanity like an especially vivid dream. It had been days now, the longest uninterrupted period of wakefulness he'd ever experienced. During that time, he kept his hunger in check by catching small game and scavenging what was left of the pack's kills. The human was always there, not looking over his shoulder but ready to regain control. The black wolf awakened from slumber several times feeling the urge to change, the need. He was able to resist, but it was becoming more and more difficult.

He'd spent several days moving closer to the pack, advertising his presence with his scent, marking the ground with the glands between his toes, with his urine, and with his scat. He was careful to not give the impression that he was claiming any of their territory as his own. The previous day, he'd allowed them glimpses of himself but only from a distance. He wanted them to know he was there.

They knew.

The larger female was the first to catch his scent. She stood, her ears erect and eyes wide, grumbling deep in her throat. Their leader, sluggish from a bellyful of fresh venison, raised his head and snapped to attention. He stood next to her, his tail high, scanning the trees at the top of the slope.

Nervous and uncertain, the black wolf stayed low. He feared he'd approached too boldly, come too close. He could slink away and wait for another time and place, but when would that be? He would have to return to his human form soon. He couldn't resist the change forever. Would he have to start the process all over again? Would the pack be any more likely to accept him? He was tired of being alone. Perhaps one day he would no longer need to yield to his humanity. Perhaps the acceptance of others would render that unnecessary. If he hoped to ever find a place among these creatures he would have to take a chance some time. If not now, when?

The entire pack was on their feet, but the scrawniest of them was the only one moving. He paced behind the rest of the pack, unsure of whether his manner should be submissive or aggressive.

The black wolf made his decision and stepped out of hiding. He brushed past a low branch and a load of snow dropped onto his shoulders. Shaking off the snow, he stood straight, his tail down and his ears up but pointing away from his head. Torn between wanting to court their acceptance and wanting to impress them, he wagged his tail and pulled his lips back into a canine grin.

When the black beast uphill moved into view, all but their leader startled and stepped back. The others whined and yipped until they were silenced by a growl. The big gray wolf stepped in front of the pack and called upon all his confidence and composure to conceal his own fear. What he saw up the slope was far beyond anything in his sphere of reference.

The sky was clear and the moon, bright and almost full, shone over the interloper's shoulder. The backlighting cast the black wolf as a silhouette, the white of the snow reflecting off his eyes the only break in the dark shape. From their vantage point, the thing on the slope above them appeared as a giant, disembodied shadow emerging from the forest with eyes that sparkled like stars.

The shadow took two steps forward and stopped. Whatever this thing was, the leader decided, it was not one of their kind. It smelled like a wolf but also like a human. Now that it was out from under the trees in plain sight, the thing was revealed to not be a shadow after all. It was no wraith. It was solid and it was twice the size of any of their pack.

The leader's thick shoulder hair stood on end and he paced back and forth, not in the same manner as the cowardly lesser among them, but to send a message; come no closer. He growled a warning to the monstrous interloper, the growl extending into a forceful howl, a call to arms for the rest of the pack. They joined him one by one, each claiming a part in the chorus until the seven wolves sounded like seventy.

The black wolf knew then that this was a mistake. His humanity cut through the bestial and whispered words that were clear in meaning even if the words themselves made no sense; *Get out of here. Now.* He turned, head low, and headed back toward the cabin. To get there he would have to navigate thick forest, cross a frozen creek, and make his way through more than a mile of woodland.

He made it to the creek, covered with new fallen snow, and paused at the edge. The wind picked up, whirling and whistling through the creek bed. Powdery snow stirred, picked up by the wind, and for a moment the world became a vortex of blinding white. The black wolf couldn't see more than a few feet ahead so he kept his nose to the ice, searching for his own scent to guide him back. On his way to the pack he had crossed farther downstream, but he decided to cross now and count on picking up his scent on the opposite bank.

He was halfway over the ice when he heard movement along the bank. He stopped. It was a slight noise, nothing above a rustle, all but drowned out by the whistling wind. He raised his head and strained to see past the swirling snow. To his left, a twig skittered and and bounced down the creek, cartwheeled by the wind over the snow.

The big male burst from cover less than fifteen feet away on the opposite shore. The black wolf barely had time to turn before the gray blur slammed into his shoulder, tumbling him onto his back. He thrashed and snapped, legs flailing until he felt solid ice under his paws.

The leader of the pack attacked again, kicking up snow with all four feet as he accelerated.

The big gray wolf was still half a dozen yards away when the black wolf saw another shape rushing toward him. It seemed the other large male had approached from behind and waited for the leader's signal to initiate the attack. The lesser of the two reached him first, sinking long teeth into his shoulder. The black wolf screamed in pain and bucked the smaller animal over his back where he landed with a loud crack on the ice.

The biggest male was upon him, teeth and claws rending. The black wolf lowered his shoulder and rammed the gray wolf in the chest, plowing him over with ease. Rather than turning to maul his foe, he bolted downstream over the ice. He had no desire to fight with these creatures. Even as they attacked he had marveled at their beauty. He longed for their fellowship and as he ran down the creek, his heart broke with the knowledge that they had rejected him. He was not like them. To them, he was a freak, a monster. There was no place for him in their world.

In an instant he made the choice against running for the forest. The closeness of the trees there might act against him, preventing a full out run while providing them with cover, negating his advantages. He wasn't just bigger and stronger than any of them but faster as well. The clear avenue of the frozen creek seemed to offer the surest route of escape.

A bend loomed ahead, the creek doglegging to the left. He chanced a glance behind. His pursuers were still there but losing ground. In a few more minutes he would out-distance them with ease. He turned into the bend without breaking stride.

A streak of white collided with his right shoulder, the big female tearing his flesh with her teeth. He stumbled and the two of them fell end over end, spinning to a stop on the ice.

The black wolf looked up to see the two males approaching, trotting toward him with their ears pressed against their heads, their shoulder and back hair on end. Behind him, the female found her feet. From the forest to his right, the smaller female stepped onto the ice, her shoulder muscles bunching, gathering energy for the attack. Beyond her, the two juveniles and the scrawny one patrolled the shore. The entire pack had been pressed into service to dispatch the monster.

As they closed around him, the black wolf despaired at what he would have to do to leave the forest alive. For a brief moment, he considered surrendering his life to them, baring his throat and offering no resistance. It would be an honorable death to fall beneath their teeth and claws. It would be fitting. When the attack came, though, it brought an abrupt, painful end to such deliberations.

The big gray wolf hit him like a train. Had he not lowered his head a second earlier, the canines would have fastened on his throat. As it was, they sank deep into his left shoulder, tearing through muscle and scraping bone. With the agony, the black wolf lost all ability to restrain his actions. His survival instincts took over and he flew into a rage.

Twisting sideways, he grabbed the gray wolf's head in his jaws and snapped back clockwise, tearing the wolf's teeth from his shoulder. The gray wolf barely had time to yelp in pain before his violently rotated body spun around his head nearly 180°, snapping his neck with a loud crack.

The black wolf dropped the lifeless body just as the other big male and the larger female hit him from each side. The male savaged his torn left shoulder while the female lunged for his throat. He drove her to the ice with a swat of his paw, dislocating her jaw. Turning back to his left, he sank his teeth into the other's side, crushing ribs with a bite that had more than twice the power of any natural wolf. The smaller female hesitated for a second then attacked, her teeth shearing through the sensitive flesh of his snout. Her grip faltered, though, and he crushed her head with a single, crunching bite.

Within a few moments, the black wolf dispatched the two wounded wolves that lie tangled with him on the ice. He looked toward the shore and saw the juveniles retreat, their tails between their legs. He snarled a warning at them and they fled, yelping and crying. The scrawny one was nowhere in sight.

The black wolf stood on shaky legs and pulled himself from the mutilated bodies around him. The snow was trampled and soaked with the blood of wolves, the pack's and his own, glistening pools and smears of dark red against white, illumined by the moon overhead. His rage drained off, replaced by horror at what he had done. Exhausted and bleeding from half a dozen wounds, his legs buckled and he nearly fell, but he forced himself to remain upright. Drawing frigid air into his lungs, the black wolf poured much of his remaining strength into a ragged howl, a dirge both for those he'd killed and for his own hope that died along with them. His cry reverberated down the creek bed. Somewhere in the forest, the thin, high voices of the juveniles joined the song. When the cry faded, he dragged himself from the ice, dripping blood onto the snow, and staggered a few feet into the forest before he collapsed.

Stumbling, falling, then rising to take a few more steps, the black wolf labored through the forest. He was still in the trees when the first light of morning filtered through the branches. Each step was agony, dark red smears of blood marking his progress. His snout, sides, and both shoulders bore deep, ragged wounds that might end his life if they weren't treated soon. With the dawn the urge to change was more powerful than ever. The black wolf was ready to leave this world of pain behind, but his instincts told him the human would have no chance in such a state, so he fought off the transformation.

He was aware that two creatures were following him. He caught glimpses of them but was too damaged to care who they were, much less defend himself. Was it the two juveniles come to end what their elders had started? He didn't care. If they moved in to finish him off, so be it.

The black wolf dragged himself up a low incline that might as well have been a mountain for all it cost him. The cabin was there, less than a hundred yards away. He could see it through his heavy, half-closed eyes, but he could go no farther. He had to rest. To sleep. He resolved to try again when he awoke. If he awoke. He was beyond caring.

Just before he closed his eyes and drifted away, his bloodied nose picked up a familiar scent.

Ian was on the wheel again. As far as he could tell he'd never left it but had been there ever since that first experience. Was it years ago or only hours? The thick cords that bound him to the rough wood dug into his wrists and ankles. There were more pains now, adding to his misery. His shoulders, his sides, and his face all dripped blood. The blood pooled beneath him on the unfinished wood.

When did he acquire those new wounds? He wasn't sure. He recalled being beaten by men in the field, but their instruments were heavy and dull. He recalled...being a wolf? Fending off a pack, much like the men in the field. Were they the same event, recalled differently by some peculiar trick of his mind, the blows from staffs, poles, and booted feet becoming slashing, lacerating teeth and claws? He recalled the death of a friend, of a lover, of a father, and the grief and guilt that followed. Then there was the young girl in the field. Where did she fit in? None of it made any sense.

The robed man grabbed his face and wrenched it upward, settling the question for now. This was real. The ropes were real. The bright sun beating down on his naked skin was real. The man looked at him long and hard. His face was lined and brown, withered by exposure to the elements. His fingers were rough, his palm cracked. He smelled musty and unwashed. The man spoke to him, but Ian didn't understand a word. He let go of Ian's face, stepped back, and shook his head.

Ian's left eye was swollen shut and his mangled lips were impediments to his attempts at articulate speech. He tried anyway, but the sounds he made were gibberish. If anyone on the podium or in the crowd understood him, they didn't respond. He twisted against the ropes, trying in vain to escape his bonds, but his joints rebelled, aching even worse with the effort. His back was a knot of pain and the ropes dug deeper into his arms and legs. Something rolled down his face into his mouth, the salty tang of sweat mixed with the metallic taste of his own blood.

From his right, Ian caught the smell of burning coals, heard them being stirred. He felt their heat upon his shoulders, his back, and his legs. The sensation had been there all along, but it was only now that he was able to differentiate it from his many other agonies.

The robed man sighed, pointed a bony finger at Ian, then let the hand drop. The corners of the man's mouth twitched and for a moment his gaze went watery and soft. He looked weary, a man worn down by the execution of his dreadful duties. He nodded toward someone beyond Ian's field of view, turned, and descended a wooden staircase at the edge of the platform. The crowd parted before him, reverent but perhaps also fearful, and the man passed from view.

Heavy footsteps approached from Ian's right and a gasp came from the crowd.

Ian turned as much as he was able and saw the hooded man with thick gloved hands holding the red hot tongs. As the man came nearer, Ian arched his back and struggled, desperate to throw off the ropes, but they held fast. He twisted away, but there was no escaping. The red hot metal drove into his side and the pain was far beyond anything he'd ever imagined. He couldn't scream. He could only gasp, unable to comprehend that such pain was even possible. His flesh sizzled, his bodily fluids turned to steam, and he convulsed, his teeth sinking into his own lip. The gloved hand pulled back, tearing flesh from bone, and Ian explored new frontiers of anguish.

"I told you this was a bad idea, Peter. We should have helped him."

Ian heard April White's voice as he emerged from the awful...dream?...vision?

"He had to learn," said Peter Stubbs, "to experience first hand that there was no place for him among the wolves. You had to learn that yourself."

"He almost died."

"He was rather impressive, though, wasn't he?"

"You act like you're proud, Peter."

"I am. Very. He is everything I hoped he would be."

"Peter, he was almost killed and an entire pack was destroyed."

"Four of them."

"The most important four! We've been studying that pack for years. Now they're gone. Those juveniles don't stand a chance. The other one is out there somewhere. They'll all be dead by spring. How am I supposed to account for that? I'm not like you, Peter. I have people to answer to."

"You'll think of something," Stubbs said. "Don't forget that you have blood on your own hands. You're in this, too. The Lord has-"

"Oh, knock off that crap! I've had about all of that I can take."

"Where else will you go, April? You know The Lord isn't finished with you."

Why the hell is Peter Stubbs here? What is April talking about?

Ian opened his eyes and thought about sitting up, but his head was spinning. He was in the cabin, in the bed with a blanket up to his waist. He managed to raise his head enough to see that his wounds had been bandaged, probably cleaned as well. He felt a bandage secured against his face by a tight gauze wrap. It hurt too much to move so he just lie there and listened.

"I had a hard enough time covering up for you a few years back," April said.

"We've been over that," said Stubbs. "It couldn't be avoided."

"Yes, it could have. You didn't have to bring that man here."

"This wilderness was the perfect place to dispatch someone who wasn't working out."

"Perfect for you. A nightmare for me. My own traces can be mistaken for a big male, but yours are just too big. That man you got rid of up here was too big, and then there's your friend Ted."

"He's your friend, too. He's part of our family. You know that."

"I had to ruin a young man's career to cover up your little mission!"

April was getting angrier by the minute. Ian knew her well enough to know when she was getting pissed off but trying to tamp it down. But...her own traces...what did she mean?

"Tim was a good researcher," she said.

"You did what you had to do," said Peter.

"He went to the fucking tabloids!"

"Where the story was taken as seriously as accounts of Bigfoot and alien abductions."

"We had paranormal nut jobs showing up here for six months."

"And they were the only ones who put any stock in those stories," Peter said. "Anyone whose opinion matters thinks it's all hogwash. That serves The Lord's purpose."

"It serves your purpose," April said. "Not mine."

Ian wanted to speak up, but he was too groggy and weak. A moment later he was unconscious again. This time there was no wheel.

It was dark when he awoke again. His bandages had been changed. An empty plasma bag hung on a stand beside his bed. A square adhesive bandage adhered to the inside of his left forearm. He sat up though the effort proved painful, and looked around. April White was on the other side of the cabin, her back to him as she stared at the bright screen of her laptop.

"Where is he?" Ian said.

April turned around and smiled. "You're awake."

"Where is Peter?"

"We weren't sure you were going to make it at first. You were in bad shape. I wanted to get you to a hospital, but-"

"You're with him."

April sighed. "I'm not *with* Peter." She left her chair and sat on the bed. She touched Ian's face. "He has his agenda. I have mine."

"Are you a..."

"Yes," April said, "I'm like you. We followed you, made sure you were safe."

"Oh, Jesus," Ian said. He remembered his experience with the pack, the most vivid memory he'd brought back yet. "I killed them, didn't I?"

"You had no choice," she said. "They would have killed you. They almost did. I wanted to help you, but Peter wouldn't let me."

Ian sat all the way up. He batted her hand away. "Oh, my god," he mumbled. "I was wondering how to explain what I was to you."

"You don't have to now." She put her hand over his.

"Don't touch me!" He pulled back.

"Ian? You know me." April glanced over her shoulder toward the door. She leaned in close to him and spoke in a whisper. "Keep your voice down. Peter is outside. He'll hear you. I'm on your side. You should know that by now."

"You're with him!" Ian hissed.

"No, I'm not," she said again. "I know all about his 'wolves of God' bullshit, but there aren't many of us. There were more once, but he's killed anyone who opposed him. Only one person has ever gotten away from him."

"Yeah? Where are they now?"

April shook her head. "It's better that you don't know. Good riddance to bad rubbish."

"I want to know. They can't be that bad if they're against him."

"I-," she stopped before going further. "He's coming."

A second later the cabin door opened and Stubbs entered. Ian felt none of the charisma he'd experienced before in the man's presence. All he felt now was anger.

"You're awake,'" Peter said. He was wearing pressed jeans and a light gray sweatshirt.

Even dressed casually, Peter still looked like he'd just come from a modeling shoot. "We were afraid for a while that you weren't going to make it, but April is a skilled nurse. Did she tell you that her background was in medicine before she became a biologist?"

"No," Ian said. "There's a lot she didn't tell me."

"Ian, please," April said.

"Don't be too hard on her," Stubbs said. "You had a rough time out there. You aren't the first to make such an attempt. It's understandable, but the wolves don't accept us. We're bigger, stronger than they are, and different. They can smell the human in us. We belong to the Kingdom Of God and they are only dumb beasts."

"Do dumb beasts dream about the wheel? I'd trade my life for theirs any day."

"We all spend time on the wheel. We all share in the fate of my unfortunate ancestor. You still have much to learn, Ian. April can help you. She's experienced the wheel herself."

"You?" Ian looked at her.

"Yes." April nodded.

"Does it ever stop?"

"Not entirely," she said. "It's been years for me, but I don't think I'm done with it yet."

"How long have you been a werewolf?" Ian said to her.

"April is one of my oldest confidants," Peter said.

"One of your oldest?" Ian looked at April. "Verna was right about you."

"Your friend Verna doesn't have any idea what she's talking about," April said.

"She knew enough not to trust you."

"Ian," April began, but Stubbs cut her off.

"April is beautiful, Ian, tantalizing I am sure. I do not approve of her hedonistic methods, but if it brings you closer to accepting God's will for your life, so be it."

"Peter," she said, "you're not helping."

Ian shook his head. "I've heard enough." He leaned over, opened the drawer next to the bed, and took out the change of clothes he'd brought.

"You're in no shape to travel," April said.

"I'm not staying here." Ian winced as he pulled a shirt over his head.

"Let him go," Peter said. "He learned a valuable lesson this week."

"This week?" Ian said. "What day is it?"

"Saturday," said April.

"Saturday? How long was I out?"

"Two days," April answered.

"Two days?"

"You woke enough to eat, but that was all."

"I have job! I took a week, but that was all the time I had. I need to be back home." He threw the blanket aside and pulled on his pants.

"I knew you were here," April said.

"We both knew," Stubbs said.

"If the pack had accepted me, I would have stayed," Ian put on his shoes while he spoke.

"You would have left me?" said April.

"I would have left everything." He sat up and looked at her. "That shouldn't matter to you. I mean, you were only using me, right? Reeling me in for your master?"

"That's not true, Ian. You matter to me."

"Let him go," Peter said again. "Give him the space he needs. He'll join us in the end. Where else will he go? 'It's hard to kick against the goads.' Our prodigal son will return."

Ian stood, his shoes still untied, and shoved his wallet into his back pocket. He grabbed his jacket and his keys off their hooks next to the door but stopped in the doorway to remove the cabin key from his key ring. He threw it at April and left the cabin. He was getting into his 4X4 when April came out and caught the drivers side door before he could close it.

"Please, Ian," she said. "Don't listen to him."

"And I should listen to you? You're one of his...his pack."

"No." She was whispering again. "His agenda isn't mine."

"What is your agenda, April?"

"I love you, Ian. That's my agenda."

"You almost sound sincere."

"Together, we can make a break with him. We can leave Peter. I can't do it alone."

"There it is," Ian said. "I don't trust you, April. I can't. I don't want any part of anyone's agenda. I'll have to figure this out on my own." He wrenched the door from her grasp and started the engine.

Chapter 16

December 1998

Miami University, Oxford, Ohio

Carmilla Andersen held the phone to her ear and rolled her eyes. Finals were in full swing. She was besieged by frantic students in need of a last minute pep talk and she was facing a deadline for the final draft of her second book. Now there was this business with her Jeep.

"It'll come to about $950 or so, plus tax, Professor." The voice on the other end of the phone belonged to Joe Bushup. Joe was the most reliable, honest mechanic she'd found. Most of the work his shop handled was done by underlings, but he always saw to Milla's needs himself. "I wish I had better news, but that's what you're looking at. A Dealer would charge you twice that."

"I know, Joe," Milla grumbled. "I trust you." At least he hadn't asked her out again...yet. He was an attractive guy. His ex-wives must have thought so at some point, but she wasn't the least bit interested. "Go ahead, Joe. Do what needs to be done. When will it be ready?"

"I'll have it by Friday. If it's any earlier I'll give you a call."

"Thanks, Joe. I'll hold you to that."

"I know you will, Doc." He paused for a second then continued. "I've got an extra ticket to see The Boss in Columbus this Saturday. You don't get too many chances to see him anymore. Interested?"

"I'm afraid not. This week is going to be murder and I need Saturday to decompress before I head north next week. Besides, I hate Springsteen. Thanks for thinking of me, though."

"Hey, you can't blame a guy for trying, huh?"

"I guess not, Joe." *But if he asks me out again...*"I'll see you Friday when I pick up the Jeep."

"You got it, Doc. It'll be ready to roll."

Thirty seconds later her hand still stung from slamming down the receiver. She hated it when he called her Doc. She could cope with being referred to as Dr. Andersen wherever she went. She'd worked hard for her degrees and she had the respect of a small circle of academics. It was another thing, though, when a twice-divorced mechanic who couldn't grasp that she wasn't interest in him adopted "Doc" as his pet name for her. Not to mention that she had better things to do with $950.

She stood and was reaching for her jacket when the phone rang. Milla stared at it as it rang three more times, considering letting her voicemail take it, but on the fifth ring she picked it up."Yes?"

"Doctor Andersen? Could I have a moment of your time?"

Stonelick, Ohio
February 1998

Verna gasped when Ian came through the door. "Oh, my lord, what happened to you?"

"I had an accident."

"I'll say."

Ian tried not to flinch when she wrapped her arms around him and gave him a hug. His facial wounds were still obvious but the deeper wounds to his shoulders and side were concealed.

"What happened?"

"Well...I went to Minnesota. You know that."

"OK. You went to see April."

That was his cover story, at least. He hadn't intended for April to even know he was there, but the way things turned out was worse than he could have imagined.

"You were right about her." Ian walked past Verna into his house. The place was cleaner than it had been in years. Before he left he'd tried to persuade her that housesitting didn't mean housecleaning.

"Did you two have a falling out?

"That's putting it mildly. It's over."

"How are you doing? You know I never cared for her, but I don't like to see you in pain."

"I'm all right. It just wasn't to be. That's all."

"OK. So, what about this accident?"

"It's pretty stupid, really. I was hiking up there and I walked right over a ledge. Didn't see it. I didn't break anything, but I tumbled face first into this huge thorn bush. Scratched the hell out of me."

"Looks like more than just scratches."

"I'm lucky I didn't lose an eye."

"I'll say."

Ian could tell she didn't buy his story, but she didn't push it any farther. She didn't even remark on his lack of luggage. He was glad for that so he offered nothing more.

Verna brought dinner over every night for the rest of the week, casting him a concerned glance when he grimaced now and then. The trouble he was having with his left shoulder was hard to hide. After four days Ian insisted she take a break. It wasn't that her mothering was getting old. It was kind of nice, he had to admit, but he needed time to himself. There were things to figure out.

April called over and over. He let it go to voicemail every time. He had nothing more to say to her. Still, it was hard not to respond. He might not have loved her like he had Kelly, but she was an important part of his life. He felt betrayed. Used. *But that isn't entirely fair, is it?*

Within two weeks of returning home, the wounds on his face had faded. He changed almost every night and with each transformation the gashes healed further, but it became clear he would always have scars, and in the right light they were obvious. *Maybe it's time to grow that beard I always wanted when I was a kid.*

His shoulders and side were slower to heal. The scars there were even more visible, but the muscles were knitting, and every day his range of motion improved. He'd never be as good as new, but he could settle for good enough.

December 1998

"Sure. That would be great." Ian stood at the dining room window looking out at a frosty lawn. The temperature was hovering around 33°, but the forecast called for more typical temperatures in the 40s the rest of the week. Snow was in the forecast, but Ian his doubts. It was southern Ohio after all.

Ian liked snow. Winter had always been his favorite season. With each passing year he felt more and more at home when the weather turned cold. He wasn't sure if that was because of the wolf in him or because winter was the farthest removed from the summer deaths of Kelly and Chevy. Whatever the reason, he was beginning to consider a permanent move north. One day, perhaps.

"You're kidding me?" Ian said. On the other end of the line was Jeff Boudreaux, his classmate from high school, the single link with his teen years he'd maintained. "Congratulations!...So when's the big day?...I'll be there...I've never been to Boston...It'll be a fun drive...Naw, I hate flying...."

As they talked, Ian moved away from the window and stepped over to his drafting table. He had a guest room that would make a reasonable work space, but he preferred the dining room with its big picture window and wide view of the back yard. He didn't stay by his table for long, though. Pacing while talking on the phone was a habit he'd picked up from his mother. His father used to say that watching her talk on the phone was like watching a tennis match. With the cordless phone, his range now extended to anywhere in the house.

"I'm happy for you...I'll look for the invite."

As they talked, Ian went to the front door to check the mail. Not that he was expecting anything important. It was just a daily habit. He found a box wrapped in brown paper leaning against the side of the house. He glanced at the mailbox near the road and decided to go there later, his curiosity aroused by the package. He looked at the return address and scowled. It was from a PO box in Minnesota. He knew only two people from Minnesota and he wanted nothing from either of them.

Ian closed the door and set the package down on his drafting table while he half-listened to Jeff extolling the virtues of his fiancée. He almost dumped the thing in the trash but opened it instead as he talked. Inside the box was a hardcover book. The dust jacket showed a wolf in silhouette, howling, backlit by an oversized full moon breaking over the crest of a mountain. The title was printed in stark white against the dark purple/blue background:

In The Likeness Of A Wolf:
The Werewolf in History, Folklore, And Fiction
Carmilla Andersen, Ph. D.

A note accompanied the book. It was from Peter Stubbs.

Ian,

This author knows her subject well. Her book may answer some of your questions. Please accept this as my gift and as a peace offering. There is much here for you to enjoy, as well as some things you need to know. I hope you find it useful. I look forward to seeing you again in the future.

Peter

"Great. Just great," Ian mumbled. "No, Jeff. I'm sorry. It's just...Naw, man....Go on."

Ian almost threw the book into the garbage again but instead flipped it open and read the copy on the inside flap. It was fairly standard prose extolling the virtues of the book and its author. He followed the blurb onto the inside back cover. A picture of the author was there, a studio portrait of an attractive lady, rough-edged but pretty, with straight blonde hair streaked with brown. Her large, expressive eyes were serious, intense. The impression it gave Ian was of someone not especially happy about posing for the photo. According to the paragraph beneath, Dr. Andersen was a specialist in folklore and taught at Miami University in Oxford, Ohio.

Opening the book to the title page, Ian saw a black and white line drawing of the cover image. He flipped to the contents page, his tongue tucked into his cheek. He again felt the impulse to pitch the thing into the trash. If it came from Peter Stubbs, he didn't want-

Ian stopped. The title of Chapter Seven caught his eye;

Stubbe Peeter; The Werewolf Of Bedburg

Ian's knees went weak and he sat on his chair at the drafting table so heavily it almost overbalanced. His friend's voice on the phone seemed distant. "Jeff, I, uh, I'm gonna have to call you back," he stammered. "Something, uh, just came up and I have to deal with it...Yeah...I'll call you back...Congratulations again."

Ian ended the call but sat holding the phone in one hand. "Shit," he said. "It can't be..."

The chapter told the story of Stubbe Peeter, known as Peter Stumpf, Peter Stubbe, and other variants. He was born in 1525 near the town of Bedburg in Germany. In 1590, he was executed for a series of terrible crimes including murder, rape, and cannibalism. Quoting at length from existing documents, Andersen detailed the story of how Stubbe acquired a girdle from Satan himself, "...which, being put around him, he was transformed into the likeness of a wolf, strong and mighty, with eyes great and large, which in the night sparkled like brands of fire; a mouth great and wide, with most sharp and cruel teeth; a huge body and mighty paws."

Stubbe was accused in the murder of sixteen people, including two pregnant women, the documents claiming he tore "the children out of their wombs, in most bloody and savage sort, and after ate their hearts panting hot and raw..." Adding to his horrific activities, Stubbe was also accused of incest and the murder and cannibalism of his own young son.

In the end, Stubbe was convicted and executed along with two female accomplices. His execution was particularly gruesome. Ian's eyes grew wider as he read of the werewolf being "laid on a wheel, and with red hot burning pincers in ten places to have flesh pulled off from the bones." Afterward, his four limbs were broken and he was beheaded. His mutilated body was burned, but the wheel and his head were affixed to a pole and mounted in the town, sixteen lengths of wood hanging from the horrific effigy to represent his victims. The two women who were convicted as his accomplices were burned alive along with his body.

Ian read the awful account once, barely able to breath, then read it again. Stubbs had spoken of his misguided ancestor. Andersen addressed the possibility that Stubbe Peeter was perhaps a serial killer or even an innocent dupe caught up in a hysteria akin to the witch hunts that plagued Europe, but she does not waver from the claim that the executions were real in all their graphic brutality. Ian needed no convincing of this. He had done too much time on the wheel himself. Where he had once considered it a possible shared nightmare or hypnosis among their kind, induced by some unfathomable suggestion, the story of Stubbe Peeter's execution was far too on point to be ignored.

After his second reading of the chapter, the pain of the red hot pincers rending his flesh more vivid than ever outside of his dreams, Ian took the book and moved to the more comfortable chair in the living room where he turned back to the first page and began reading.

Miami University, Oxford, Ohio

"Yes, this is Carmilla Andersen." She cradled the receiver between her chin and collar bone while she slipped into her jacket. "How can I help you?"

"I read your book." Ian tried not to let his unease show. "I need...I would really like to talk with you about it if you can spare the time. I have a few questions."

"Do you have a name?" Milla knew she sounded frosty but didn't care.

"Ian. Ian Murphy."

"Well, Mr. Murphy, what do you want to know? And please be brief. I'm on my way out."

"It's difficult to explain. Could I meet with you up there? I live about an hour away from the college. If you have the time I'd really appreciate it."

Oh, god. Just what I need. "I'm afraid it's going to be difficult to carve out the time. Finals are underway and I'll be out of town next week. Why don't you give me a call the week after that?"

"Doctor Andersen." The man on the phone drew in his breath then continued. "I can't explain it over the phone. I...I'm not some kind of stalker or crazy person. I just need some answers."

"What makes you think I'll have those answers, Mr. Murphy?"

"Maybe you won't. Maybe no one does. But please, let me back up a little. Someone gave me your book. They thought it might, I don't know, point me in the right direction."

"My book on folklore?"

"Werewolves."

"I see."

"If I told you everything right now, you'd hang up on me."

"And you think if we met in person it would go over better? No offense, Mr. Murphy, but I don't know you from Adam. Why would I meet with you?"

"I understand your reluctance. I just want to talk about your book. You name the place. Make it public. Make it broad daylight in the middle of a crowd. Give me a few minutes and I'll be gone."

Milla sighed. The note of urgency in the man's voice was as genuine as it was alarming. "Have you ever been to Oxford, Mr. Murphy?" She shook her head and tried to ignore the voice inside her screaming that this was a bad idea.

"I haven't, but I can look it up."

Milla gave him directions to Miami University and to the King Library on campus. "Meet me there Friday afternoon at three. I'll have a few minutes before I leave for break."

"Thank you, Doctor. I can't tell you how much I appreciate this."

"You don't have to. And you don't have to call me Doctor. Ms. Andersen will do." She paused for a moment then said "How will I know you?"

"Well, I'm tall," he said, "and...don't worry. Your photo is on your book jacket. I'll find you."

"Yes, that." *I hate that photo.* She sighed again. "Be there at three. I won't wait."

"You won't have to. Thank you so much. I'll see you Friday."

Milla hung up the phone and left her office. She walked out of the building and crossed the parking lot, the wind stirring the light snow, sending what brown leaves remained on the lawn swirling across her path. She reached her rental car, unlocked the door, and reflected upon the appointment she'd just made. She wasn't in the habit of granting such requests, but she would meet with the man. She didn't think he was a stalker or a psychotic, but he sounded shaken. She just hoped it wasn't a mistake.

Milla sat at the table with her laptop in front of her. She'd been in the library since 1:30, polishing the final draft of her second book, "Altered

States; The Shapeshifter In World Mythology." It was proving to be more of an ordeal than her first book, but she was done with the changes her editor suggested. All that was left was the lingering grammatical errors.

The clock over the front desk read 2:48. She hoped Ian Murphy was the punctual sort. Finals were done, she'd picked up the Jeep at Joe's garage, ditched the rental car, and packed. All she had to do was head north and she'd be free of academia for three blissful weeks. If he wasn't here at 3:00, she wasn't inclined to wait.

Outside, the sun was shining, the temperature hovering near 45°. Clumps of snow clung to the shadows, the rest of the season's first covering already reduced to puddles. It would be a perfect early spring day even though it was the middle of December.

Milla hated it. She loved winter weather with its cold temperatures and abundant snowfall. Her childhood home was in northern Michigan, the blustery winter nights there her favorite memory. Things went sideways, as they say, in her teen years. You can never go home again. In her case, that was the literal truth.

She sat at the table, tired of looking at her screen, and stared out the window at nothing in particular. The campus was still buzzing with activity. Some students still had finals left. She could tell who they were, their brows furrowed, their steps fast and purposeful as they crossed her field of vision.

A large man walked through the crowd, looking up to check his location. A long ponytail reached halfway down his back. A brown beard, darker than the hair on his head, covered his cheeks and chin. With his broad shoulders and powerful build, he would have been intimidating if he didn't have such an open, friendly air about him. As she watched, the man entered the library and scanned the bottom floor till he found her and waved. She wasn't sure what she was expecting of Ian Murphy, but it certainly wasn't the grinning colossus threading his way through the desks toward her.

"Ms. Anderson?" he said in a deep but soft voice when he reached her.

"That's me." She stood and offered her hand, giving his large hand a vigorous shake she could see took him by surprise. She was used to that reaction. Her strength took everyone by surprise. They saw a lean woman and expected her to be dainty. She wasn't dainty at all and she always smiled when she saw that dawn on them. "Have a seat," Milla said. "Did you have any trouble finding the library?"

"Not much." He settled into the wooden chair across from her. "This campus, this town, is beautiful. I love the cobblestone streets. I went to a little community college. It was nothing like this."

"Oxford is beautiful, especially in the fall. You should see this place when the leaves change."

"I bet."

Milla had always thought of herself as a good judge of character. Despite his size, he showed no signs of being dangerous in any overt way. He was friendly and eager to please, as shy as he was large. She was glad she'd decided to meet in a public place, though. She wasn't worried in any way about her personal safety. She could take care of herself, more so than people expected, but she still didn't know him and it never hurt to err on the side of caution. "So tell me what brings you here, Mr. Murphy?"

"I hope this doesn't sound weird or spooky or anything but..."

He paused. He was nervous, Milla noticed, and he made a point of keeping both hands in his lap. They moved under the table though. He was in the habit of gesturing with them.

"The subject of werewolves is of special interest to me," he said.

"That's not weird at all. At least not to me. Some of my fellow professors don't understand my passion for the subject, especially those outside of the Humanities Department. It's a rather esoteric specialty, but it's what makes me tick." She closed her laptop with a click. "I've spent most of my adult life compiling legends, myths, folklore, anything having to do with lycanthropy, so your interest doesn't strike me as strange at all."

He relaxed a little more at that, Milla noticed.

"It's refreshing to talk with someone who doesn't think it's weird," said Ian. "Not just werewolves but wolves in general. They're beautiful creatures."

His smile faltered a little. Milla wondered what he'd been through that could make him so transparently melancholy. She was warming up to this man in a way she hadn't expected. If she wasn't mistaken, he was warming up to her as well, and not just because he found her attractive, which she could tell he did. Most people thought of her as cold until they knew her for six or seven years, with the exception of Joe Bushup, but he was a horndog so that didn't count. Most people were right. She was cold and she knew it. She had no intention of getting close to people. She sensed that in Ian Murphy as well, but she also sensed he wasn't happy about it.

"I know your time is precious so I'll get right to the point." He put his hands on the table but kept them closed into loose fists. "Peter...uh...Stubbe Peeter."

Milla nodded. "What do you want to know about him, other than what I wrote?"

"The account in your book, it's from an actual trial transcript? From 1590 Germany?"

"It's from a pamphlet that was distributed throughout Europe in the 1590s. There are copies in existence today. The Lambeth Palace Library in London has one. I've seen it myself."

"Did he really exist, though, or was it all just some kind of cautionary tale like Perault's Little Red Riding Hood?"

"You have been reading. Yes, he did exist."

"Did he do what they said he did? Murder, cannibalism, rape?"

"Maybe. When his trial took place, the church was the ultimate authority. If you were accused you were guilty. The inquisitor acted with the full authority of the church. To be found innocent was to find the inquisitor guilty of sin and since he was standing in for God, that wasn't going to happen."

"So he had no choice?"

"People will say anything, even admit to fantastic things if they think it will put an end to their torture. He was tortured. There's no doubt of that."

"It's hard to imagine a worse death."

"He didn't die easily, that's for sure."

"So what about the witnesses? People testified that they saw him change from a wolf to a man."

"During the Salem witch trials, people pointed the finger at others and came up with all sorts of wild accounts. Sometimes people say what they think the powers that be want to hear then rationalize it later. Eyewitness accounts aren't as reliable as people think. That's as true today as it was in 1590."

"So you don't think he did what he was accused of?"

"I don't know. Maybe he did. Maybe he didn't. Or maybe only some of it is true."

Ian stared out the window, through the same area he'd passed moments before, and chewed on his lower lip. His hands were back in his lap but he fidgeted in his seat.

"Say what you came here to say, Mr. Murphy."

"Do you believe," he started, still looking out the window. He looked back at Milla and tried again. "Do you believe a man can really change into a wolf?"

"Do I think Stubbe Peeter was an actual werewolf?" Milla took a deep breath. She wasn't sure how to answer that question. "What about you? What do you think?"

"I think you must think I'm crazy to even ask that question."

"I don't think you're crazy at all, Ian? Can I call you Ian?"

"Sure. Ian is fine."

"Good. You can drop the Ms. Anderson. Call me Milla." She made a decision and hoped she wouldn't regret it. She liked the man. He was troubled, to be sure, but for all she knew he had reason to be. "Come over to my office. I'm leaving soon, but I have some materials you might be interested in."

The breeze outside the library felt good on Ian's face. His meeting with Milla was going better than he hoped. Nightfall was still hours away and it wasn't a full moon night. He had no need to hurry.

Students were milling around the campus much as they had several years before at Clermont College. The community college campus was nestled on a wooded hillside outside Batavia, Ohio. It was a nice setting, but it couldn't compare with the more spread out Miami campus and the charming town of Oxford. Still, the faces were much the same, mostly bright and full of cheer. The students seemed energized by the coming Christmas break. Some were dressed for travel and loading car trunks in the dorm parking lots. Some were seeing off departing friends. Others were tossing football in the open areas. Splashing through puddles and slipping on the wet grass was all part of the fun.

Ian walked next to Carmilla Andersen. She was as pretty as her photo. Though she was around 5' 6", she had to weigh no more than 110 .lbs, her build muscular but lean, almost completely devoid of body fat. Her posture was straight, her shoulders back, and she took long, confident strides. More than a few guys and some girls stole glances her way. A few even said hello or waved. There were those who noticed him, to be sure, but the looks they gave him were less appreciative, more of the 'who is that guy and what the hell is he doing with her' variety.

"Milla?"

"Yes?"

"What's with the girdle stuff? According to the account, Stubbe had to wear it to transform?"

"The word girdle is misleading. Think of it more as a belt. In some traditions a salve is applied. Sometimes they work together. Do you remember the story of Jean Grenier?"

"Yeah. The Man Of The Forest gave him salve and a belt. I presume that was the devil. Satan."

"Yep."

They reached a large red brick building, more utilitarian than the library but still attractive in an old school way, as if the architect was consciously mimicking the east coast Ivy League schools. Milla opened a door and led Ian down a long hall to her office. She unlocked the door and ushered him into a small room lined with shelves full of volumes, many weathered with age. A big window interrupted the shelves along the west wall, allowing what light made it past the trees to filter into the office.

Ian took a seat across the cluttered desk from Milla and continued their conversation. "So how does one become a werewolf?" he said.

"It varied, usually conforming to local beliefs, attitudes, customs.

Sometimes people would seek it out for themselves."

"Like Stubbe Peeter."

"Him again, huh? Yes, according to the story he brought it on himself."

"None of those stories seem to include a bite, or pentagrams, or any of that stuff."

"Hollywood nonsense," Milla said, her lip curling. "Silver bullets, too, but there's a grain of truth there. Silver was considered pure, whatever that means, so it made some sense it could be used against creatures people thought were satanic in origin."

"It's interesting how many of those stories intersect with religion," Ian said. "Until I read your book, I'd never heard of someone becoming a werewolf by being cursed by a priest." *But I do know of at least one case of someone being condemned to lycanthropy by a Pentecostal evangelist.* "I love the story of Saint Patrick. Everyone knows about him driving the snakes out of Ireland, but I doubt that many know the story of him turning a hostile chieftain into a werewolf. I wonder how many Catholics are familiar with that little gem?"

"You'd make an excellent student, Ian. Half of them don't absorb this stuff like you do."

"I guess I'm just motivated."

"Tell me about that." Milla sat back in her chair, one leg crossed over the other. She rested her elbows on the arms of her chair and steepled her long fingers. Her eyebrows, darker than the streaky blond hair on her head, knitted together.

"About what motivates me?" Ian ran his tongue across his teeth and sighed. He looked away from her for a moment then sat forward and looked her straight in the eye. "I'm a werewolf."

Milla didn't flinch or show any reaction whatsoever other than a smile. "Well, you don't meet one of those every day."

Ian had been holding his breath. *She doesn't think I'm serious.* Still, it felt good to say it.

"Tell me, though," she said. "You seem especially fascinated by Stubbe Peeter. Why him?"

"He..." *How do I put this?* "He reminds me of someone I know."

"Must be a pleasant fellow."

"You said you had some materials for me?" Ian said, changing the subject.

"Yes." Milla turned her chair around and rummaged through a box on the floor. After a moment, she turned back and laid a thick softcover book on her desk. The book was dog eared, dozens of colorful sticky notes protruding from the pages. "This is an uncorrected galley of my second book. It's pretty rough. You'll have to put up with my notes and a shit ton of grammatical errors. It recycles material from my first book, but my publisher tells me this one will be more widely distributed so it supersedes it. I think you might enjoy this."

"Wow. I wasn't expecting..."

"I've made all the changes highlighted in there so I don't need it any more. I'd appreciate your feedback. It won't be published till next year. Just don't show it around, please."

"Are you sure you want to trust me with this?"

"I'm sure. I think I can trust you. For one thing, you're a terrible liar. I like that."

Ian smiled but he was confused. "What..?" *What did she mean by that?*

"You're different, Ian." Her big eyes narrowed as she said it, but the smile remained. She seemed ready to add more but decided that would do for now.

"I'm honored." He picked up the book and leafed through it. Nearly every page was marked with red ink. The pages with sticky notes were the most marked, almost as much red ink as print. "I'll get it back to you as soon as I can."

"No hurry. I'll be gone for three weeks. Take your time."

"Well, I've taken up enough of yours." He meant it, but he also had the impression she would have continued the conversation as long as he wanted. "Thank you so much, Doct...Milla."

"My pleasure, Ian. I'm glad we met." She held out her hand. "I hope you enjoy the book. Let me know what you think."

Ian shook her hand. "Certainly. Thank you for your time. I appreciate it. It was a pleasure meeting you."

"Likewise," Milla said. "Can you find your way out?"

"Yeah. No problem. Have a good vacation."

Milla stood in the doorway and watched him stroll down the hall. When the door closed behind him, she went back into her office to gather her things. On the edge of her desk next to her laptop bag, the light blinked on her answering machine. She'd seen the light blinking when she walked in the door after Ian but ignored it. Instead of listening to the message, she picked up her laptop bag and left.

Chapter 17

May 1999
Wisconsin

The white wolf hurtled the log at full speed. His eyes were intent on the panicked man ahead, but he was aware of the two wolves keeping pace behind him. The man fell, landing hard on his face, scrambled to his feet, and continued running.

He'd gotten off a single shot, grazing the troublesome novice Stubbs had determined must be dealt with. Bert Callet, his second oldest disciple after April White, knew they weren't invincible, that a well placed bullet could kill them. The novice didn't seem aware of that fact. Joshua Brown showed promise at first, his human and wolf natures merging quickly. Sometimes that was a good sign but not in Brown's case. Rather than seeing himself as a servant of The Lord, he enjoyed killing for the sake of killing. He was a loose cannon that could not be trusted. The unfortunate man the three of them chased was nothing more than a tool. He was simply in the wrong place at the wrong time from his perspective, guilty of nothing more than rifle hunting out of season, not a crime worthy of death. He would be collateral damage. Stubbs could live with that.

They dogged him for over half an hour, driving him deeper into the forest. After the one shot that sent Joshua spinning into the brush and whining in surprise, Stubbs rushed the man and batted the gun away. Instead of crushing him right there, Stubbs seized upon the opportunity to take Brown farther into the forest, using the unfortunate man as a ruse. In a sense, the man would be furthering The Lord's work. Perhaps that was the plan after all, Stubbs surmised.

It took some prodding to make the man comply. He'd been incredulous at first. When Stubbs batted away his gun, the man stumbled and fell, blubbering and holding his hands up in a feeble effort at defense. Stubbs set him to running, if not broke the man's sanity outright, by stomping and nodding until the poor wretch understand he was being told to run.

When Stubbs judged they'd gone far enough, he easily overtook his exhausted quarry, swatting him to the ground. He stood over the hysterical, slobbering man and looked back at his companions. He nodded toward the wolf that was known as Joshua Brown when he was a man.

While Brown made quick, messy work of the unfortunate hunter, Stubbs approached Bert Callet and nodded in a different way. They had discussed the matter beforehand and prayed. They'd been patient with Brown, even tolerating that "Beast Of Bray Road" nonsense the fool had taken part in. Many are called, but few are chosen. Stubbs was disappointed, but it was part of the process. Some proved true to the calling. Some did not.

"Praise the Lord!"

"Glory!"

"Hallelujah!"

The little building that housed the Full Gospel Pentecostal Church was full to the last pew, 210 men, women, and children pushing the limits of the fire code. As the last chords from the worship band reverberated throughout the sanctuary, dozens of people either exclaiming in English or speaking in tongues, their hands raised, palms open. A thin lady and her rotund friend in the second row twitched and swayed. The thin lady held one hand closed against her chest while tears rolled down her wrinkled cheeks. Her friend smiled and waved both hands in the air.

"Brothers and sisters," Peter Stubbs boomed over the din. "There is indeed power in the blood. The Lord himself is in our midst tonight! Can you feel His presence?"

"Amen!"

"Jesus said He came to give you an abundant, joyful life." Stubbs spoke softly now, his rich voice exuding warmth and compassion. "He is here now to minister to your every need, to heal your hurts, to bring a little bit of heaven into our lives tonight." He stepped down from the small stage and stood in the middle of the narrow space between the podium and the first row. From the vest pocket of his white suit he produced a handkerchief and a small bottle.

"For centuries it has been customary of believers to anoint each other with oil. This oil is from the Holy Land, from olive trees growing in the very soil upon which Jesus walked." Stubbs paused to open the bottle and moisten the handkerchief with the oil he had purchased in Israel the previous year. "As a servant of that same Jesus, I am humbled to carry on that sacred tradition."

Behind him stood a tall, dark haired man with a long, friendly face. Bert Callet's eyes were open, but his hands were raised toward heaven, fine dark hairs distributed across his palms. His acoustic guitar hung from his shoulders and he was praying under his breath. To Stubbs's left, a portly man with a trimmed beard and thick glasses stood with his hands together. Pastor Brian Lowe had never met Stubbs personally, but he knew of him by reputation. He was impressed with what he'd seen, so much so that his conviction was firm that Peter Stubbs was every bit the man of God he had expected.

"Anyone here with a special need, a burden that has grown too heavy to bear, is invited to come forward and receive the encouragement of The

Lord. Do not doubt that He is here to meet that need. Doubt is our enemy. The Lord is our friend, a friend who sticks closer than a brother. Form a line down this center aisle and lay your burden before Him."

Stubbs extended his hand in invitation, the handkerchief dangling from his fingers like a flag. Men and women began moving across the rows of seats toward the center aisle. Somber faces and smiling faces, tear-streaked and joyous alike, filled the aisle, a column of believers awaiting their turn.

For the next hour Stubbs anointed foreheads, grasped hands, and prayed. His voice was by turns commanding or soothing as the circumstances required. He was in no hurry to leave, intending that every need be meet, that everyone was encouraged that God cared for them enough to send him personally as a conduit for His unfathomable love.

Miles away outside in the dark Wisconsin forest, insects crawled over the dismembered body of the wolf that had been Joshua Brown.

October 1999
Oxford, Ohio

"Rye bread, huh?" said Ian. "That's bizarre."

"Not like this rye." Milla nodded toward the sandwich on her plate. "But if the grain were infected under certain conditions, the alkaloids generated by the fungus could mutate into ergonovine, which is pretty much the same thing as LSD as far as the effects go."

From their seat next to the window at Dino's, a small cafe a quarter mile from the Miami University campus, they had a perfect view of the Oxford business district, a compact, picturesque section with cobblestone streets and red brick buildings. The sun was breaking through the dark clouds that had dropped a cold rain on the town that morning, the glow framing the window seat in gold, reflecting off the sidewalks slick with wet, fallen leaves.

They'd been discussing Milla's second book, in particular the eleventh chapter wherein she critically examined everything modern investigators have offered as explanations for the persistence of werewolf legends throughout history. Ergot poisoning, rabies, porphyria, and other explanations failed her analysis. In each case, the victims displayed significant loss of vitality and often an early death, not consistent with the concept of transforming into an imposing, ravenous beast.

"Trippin' on rye bread." Ian smirked and pushed his empty plate aside. "You're right. It's a lousy explanation." He'd read the review copy of her book twice. It was already dogeared and marked.

Milla smiled and took another bite of her pastrami on rye.

They talked on the phone at least once a week now. They met in person twice during the spring semester and three times over the summer. Now that the fall semester was in full swing, her schedule was an obstacle but they worked around it.

Ian enjoyed being able to talk openly about these things. Despite Milla's knowledge on the subject, though, Ian knew she would never believe him. Her interest was in the mythology, the folklore. It was too much to ask for her to believe it was real, but being able to at least talk about it was invigorating. For the first time since April and before his horrible experience with the pack, he felt hope. Now as they sat in the cafe, Milla's hair golden brown in the autumn sun, he knew that wasn't the only reason he looked forward to seeing her again. *Don't be a fool, Ian.* He thought of Kelly and his heart ached, then he thought of April and his face fell.

"Are you OK, Ian?" Milla looked at him with equal parts curiosity and concern.

"Uh, yeah. Something went down the wrong way." Ian took a sip of cream soda and composed himself before speaking again. "There is one thing missing from your book."

"Oh?" Milla feigned annoyance. "Enlighten me, sir, if you please."

"You debunked pretty much every explanation proposed for the origins and persistence of werewolf mythology. What you didn't do was offer any ideas of your own."

Milla nodded. "My editor said the same thing. So how do I think the legends originated?" Milla looked at Ian, her thick left eyebrow arched. "Simple. Werewolves." She shrugged her shoulders then downed the last of her Guinness.

"You believe it's possible that a person can turn into a wolf?" *Careful, Ian.*

"Look, I..." Milla stopped and looked out the window. A young man passing by on the sidewalk smiled and waved. "One of my students." She returned his wave. "Hell, Ian, if I wrote that in a book I wouldn't have a job anymore. Or a career. It's just that there are more things we don't understand than things we do. I think everyone should keep that in mind."

Ian hesitated for few seconds, unsure of what to say next. She seemed open to possibilities many wouldn't consider, but there was open and then there was open. He didn't want to push it any farther so he opted to lighten the tone.

"Why Carmilla? Don't get me wrong, I love the name, but..."

"My father's idea. He read a lot." She shook her head. "He loved old books, like 19th century, mind you. One of his favorites was Carmilla by J. Sheridan LaFanu. It was written in 1872. The title character was a vampire. My mother wanted to give me a biblical name like Esther. I should count my blessings, I guess."

"Your father passed away?"

"No." She shook her head.

"You used the past tense when you referred to him so I assumed...I'm sorry."

"We're not close. He's my father, but he's not part of my life now. I prefer it that way."

"I didn't mean to bring up something painful for you."

"You didn't know. What about your folks. What are they like?"

"They passed away. Mom died when I was seventeen. Cancer." Ian pushed the crumbs around on his empty plate. "My dad died a few years later. Heart attack."

Milla shook her head and offered an apologetic smile. "Some date I turned out to be."

"A date?" Ian's heart beat a little faster.

"Close enough. I haven't had an actual date in quite a while. They tend not to end well."

"This one is going pretty well."

Milla smiled. "I think we're done here," she said. "Let's walk to the ice cream parlor. I feel like some comfort food."

They left enough money on the table for their meals plus a tip then stepped out into the autumn air. They'd only gone a few feet when Milla slipped on the slick sidewalk and gripped Ian's arm to steady herself. "Damn leaves" she said.

To Ian, it seemed she left her hand there a bit longer than necessary. That might have been his imagination, but he certainly didn't imagine what he felt at her touch. He walked close beside her, their footsteps clicking on the cobblestones. *No, this one isn't going too bad at all.*

March 2000
Stonelick, Ohio

"So when do I meet this 'mystery woman' you've been seeing?"

"Verna, I haven't exactly been 'seeing' her. She's..," Ian waved his hands in the air, searching for the right word. "...a friend. We talk."

It was Wednesday night. The remains of a large meat-lovers pizza sat on the table in front of them. Verna wiped her mouth with a napkin and smiled at Ian.

"What are you grinning about?" he said.

"You, sweetie. You've taken a liking to this woman. I recognize it when I see it." Her smile faded. "As long as she's not another April."

"She's not." Ian took another slice from the box. "Is it that obvious?"

"Ian, honey, when you talk about her, it's in your voice, it's in your eyes. I haven't seen that in your eyes for a long time."

"Since Kelly?"

"Well, it sure wasn't there for that April woman."

"I told you you were right about her, OK?" Ian looked down at the slice in his hand. The moon was full tonight and he'd need all the calories he could consume. Verna remarked now and then about his prodigious appetite but it had never dawned on her that his appetite was especially huge when the moon would be full.

"Does your Milla know how you feel?"

"I think she feels a little of the same thing. What do I do, Verna?"

"Try telling her."

Ian bit off half of the slice at once and thought things over while he chewed. Verna paid more attention to her salad than to her second slice.

"The thing is," Ian said around the remainder of his bite. He swallowed and set the other half of the slice on his plate. "I didn't feel this with April and it's kind of confusing."

"What?"

"I feel like I'm being unfaithful. To Kelly. Is that stupid?"

Verna sighed. "Honey, it's been what? Ten years? Eleven? You're allowed to move on."

"I know it's been a long time. I know it down to the day. It just feels kind of strange. With April, it wasn't about love. It was about not being alone. I feel like the stakes are higher with Milla."

"Honey, where is this book your Milla wrote?"

"Which one? There are two."

"Whichever."

"They're on my desk."

"Let me see one. The one with the best picture of her."

Ian was out of the room for a minute. When he returned, Verna was pushing away from the table, her salad bowl empty. Her second slice of pizza sat on her plate, untouched.

"Here ya go. Her picture is on the inside of the dust jacket." Ian placed the book on the table. He picked up his half-eaten slice and popped it into his mouth.

" 'In The Likeness Of A Wolf; The Werewolf In History, Folklore, And Fiction.' " Verna looked up at Ian and scowled. "More of that werewolf stuff." She looked at the book again. "Carmilla Andersen, Ph. D. Hmmm." She flipped it over and opened the back cover. "Look at those eyebrows! She looks a little rough around the edges, but some guys like that. Is her hair frosted or is that natural?"

Ian swallowed and smiled. "It's just a picture," he said. "There's more to her than that."

While Verna studied the photograph, Ian took the last slice of pizza from the box.

Verna closed the book and wiped her mouth again before she spoke. "Honey, I'm no psychologist or psychiatrist or anything like that, but I think what you need to do is to give yourself permission to move on. Now, I know you still go out to Kelly's grave."

"Verna, I..." Ian shook his head. *How did she know that?*

"You do and I think that's kind of sweet. I think it might be time to stop, though. I'm not saying you should never go there again, but you need to give yourself a break. Go one more time. Maybe even take this book with you. Introduce them to each other."

"You don't think she's..."

"Of course not. I don't think Kelly's there. She's with Jesus now, but that place is special to you. I think it would be a good thing for you to take some kind of symbolic action so you can move on with your life." Verna reached across the table and placed her hand atop Ian's. "It's OK to move on with your life, sweetheart."

"What if Milla doesn't feel the same? What if it is April all over again?"

"It won't be."

"How can you tell? You don't even know her."

"I know you. Does Milla know about Kelly?"

"Some. Not the whole story, though." *No one does but me.*

"Well, hon, maybe you can start by letting Kelly know about her."

May 2000

The black wolf padded through the forest until he was as close as he could get to his destination without breaking cover. The sky was clear. The full moon shown bright enough to cast sharp-edged shadows across the ground. He didn't fully comprehend why he was here, but he knew one thing for sure; the female he'd left in the middle of the road years before was buried up there.

He looked up the steep hill before him. The dark grey path that passed the cemetery dipped and wound before climbing again and straightening toward town. The wolf knew the area by heart, where to go and where not to go. There was no cover between the edge of the forest and the high fence enclosing the cemetery. He waited until there were none of the loud, smelly vehicles. When the coast was clear, he bolted, tearing up divots of soft earth as he went. He reached the top of the hill and hurtled the fence without breaking stride. In the cemetery, he trotted then slowed to a walk.

There were many stones here and the wolf understood that they marked other resting places. They were all important to someone, but none gave him pause. There were three others that held meaning for him, one in particular, but there was something tragic about the young female's place, some note of unfulfilled promise, that the black wolf did not understand but couldn't deny. He looked at the other stones as he passed them but didn't stop. When he found the female's big stone, he nuzzled the engraved markings. They were as indecipherable as ever, but he knew they were important. Had this female been the human's mate? If he and the human were the same did that make her his mate as well? He was confused, unsure how to make sense of it, but he mourned the young girl's death all the same.

He settled down in front of the stone. The grass he pressed down there would have ample time to spring up if he was gone before dawn, but he decided not to worry about leaving signs of his presence. The ground was soft and his footprints would be there to be seen. No matter. He understood he needed to reach some kind of resolution tonight. After that, he might never return.

The big black wolf had no experience of the human's prospective new mate, but he was aware of her existence. He knew her smell and the emotions the man felt for her passed through the barrier separating his two natures without losing their potency. The wolf knew the seeds of hopeful love had taken root in the man's heart and somehow in his own as well.

The black wolf lowered his head to his paws and sat still in the warm spring air, attempting to make his silent peace with the spirit of a girl he would always love, regardless of whether he would ever understand why. He closed his eyes and let himself drift on the memory of her soft, sweet skin, her dark, fragrant hair, and the scent that would always belong to her alone.

Sheriff Kearsey hated nights like this. Weeknights were usually peaceful around Stonelick. Any trouble tended to be on the weekends, especially in the summer and early fall when the local farm boys were blowing off steam after a week of fieldwork. Sometimes there was a fight to deal with, fueled by too much cheap beer. Once in a while someone called about a party getting out of hand, sometimes because of noise or because of the cloud of pot wafting into their yard. None of that troubled the sheriff. He'd handled those situations many times. They were nothing new to him, but domestic violence was another thing and it always left him with a sick feeling in the pit of his stomach.

He was technically off duty, but he knew sleep wasn't going to happen so he'd headed back to the office after a late dinner to catch up on a little paperwork. Better there than at home. Since school was still in session, Mel and the girls would be in bed. Why not get something done?

The call came in a little past midnight. According to the night dispatch, there was a commotion, lots of shouting, and the possibility of physical violence. Junior Barker and his wife Lucy were at it tonight. The new deputy Ricky Thorogood was near the Barker's house and already on the way, but the sheriff knew Junior and Lucy well enough to assume Ricky might need help. He was a tough guy, but the Barkers were a handful, so Matthew headed out the door.

Sheriff Kearsey was still amazed at the maturing of Ricky Thorogood. Whatever had happened to that boy must have been powerful. Ricky was a constant thorn in his side during the boy's teen years. It was heartening to see the man he had become. It proved to the sheriff that people could indeed change. He was sure the death of the Shepherd girl had something to do with it, but Ricky wouldn't talk about it. He did say that he'd dated her for a while before she dumped him for the Murphy kid who still lived out on Stonelick Road. Then she wound up dead. Ricky had taken her death hard. He said it shook him up and made him think about his life. It was as good an explanation as any for the change in Ricky. Still, the sheriff could never shake the feeling that there was more to the story.

Sheriff Kearsey was sipping on his coffee when he passed the cemetery on his way to the Hickory Glenn Mobile Home Park on State Route 131. Had he been looking to his left, he would have seen the dark shape huddled on a grave in clear sight, its long bushy tail and pointed ears traced in silver light by the glowing white moon.

The black wolf lapsed into semi-consciousness as he lie upon the grave, his mind playing back disjointed images of the female buried beneath him. The night breeze rustled his thick fur. The mingled odors of grass, earth, stone, and nocturnal creatures large and small played across his nostrils, but his focus narrowed inward, following the image of the girl.

As he followed, he passed through a veil of some kind and all became clear. More than clear. Color. Rich, full color. The sudden experience of a new spectrum of visual sensation made the wolf's eyes water. The girl made a sound, a delightful, husky noise the man in him recognized as a giggle. He stopped and closed his eyes, wiping a paw across them, then opened his eyes again.

She stood in a rectangle of light, her hair soft and flowing, her smile warm, eyes dazzling. He lifted a paw to her, but it wasn't a paw anymore. She took his offered hand and pulled him closer, embracing him. He buried his face in her hair and breathed deep, drawing in her sweet fragrance. He ran his hands across her shoulders and down her smooth back to her waist. She kissed the nape of his neck and he tightened his embrace. She responded, pressing her curving, warm body against his.

He tried to speak, but there were no words, no vocabulary to express the depths of his sorrow, his guilt. He had no words because he was still somehow a wolf even though he knew he was also a man. He began to sob and folded before her, his forehead almost touching the toes of her bare feet.

The girl knelt, ran her fingers through his hair and kissed the top of his head. She cupped his chin in her hand and lifted his face, then traced a line with her lips from his forehead down to his mouth. She kissed the scars on his face, on his muzzle, then fixed her eyes on his. Her mouth moved and he knew she was speaking, but he didn't understand. She kissed him again and he blinked once, twice. Her mouth moved again and this time he understood. "I love you," said Kelly. "I always will. I forgive you. So does Chevy."

She pointed over his shoulder. He turned, fully human now, and his jaw dropped at the sight of the lanky, red haired teen walking toward him.

Chevy wore the same black Van Halen T-shirt he wore the last time they'd been together.

Ian let out a cry of joy and embraced his friend in a hug so tight it took his own breath away. When they released each other, Ian kept one hand on Chevy's right arm, reluctant to fully part.

They were in the woods behind Ian's house. The night was warm, insects buzzing and chirping around them. A million scents tingled Ian's nostrils, borne to him on the slightest of breezes. Overwhelming them all was the wonderful, sweet scent that belonged to Kelly alone.

Ian turned back to her and realized she was standing in the doorway of the little shack he and Chevy had called their cabin. Kelly smiled and nodded, an all-wise gesture that seemed at odds with her youthful appearance. She took two steps back and he saw a raised platform beneath a single, broken window, his old sleeping bag spread there on the very spot where...

Ian swallowed hard. His eyes clouded with tears again, but he blinked them away. Unable to stop himself, he searched the walls and floor for stains, for spatters of blood. There were none.

"Listen to me, Ian," Kelly said. "Maybe your mother wasn't right about the God thing. Maybe she was. I can't say, but there is something you can do, perhaps something only you *can* do."

"What?" Ian choked out the single word. It was all he could do not to weep as he looked at her. She hadn't aged a single day.

"Don't cry for us anymore, Ian. Go on with your life. It's right that you should love again. She can help you."

"She?"

"Milla," Kelly said. "Listen to me. Your father was right when he said you make your own meaning, but our choices, our actions, come at a cost. It's up to you."

Chevy tapped him on the shoulder. "Dude."

Ian looked at his friend. Chevy gestured over his shoulder. A second later, Ian was blinded by a bright, white light and he heard the click of metal against metal.

The situation at the Barkers wasn't as bad as the sheriff feared. It was mostly shouting. The only real damage was to Junior Barker's ego. It seemed he had forgotten Lucy's birthday and gone bowling with the boys from work. Lucy gave him hell when he got home. Ricky was already there when the sheriff arrived and Junior was offering sheepish apologies to his wife, promising to take her out tomorrow for a proper birthday dinner. Matthew stood back, shaking his head, and let Ricky handle it. Lucy was a loose cannon. She always had been, even back in high school. Now she was three times her high school size and not at all happy about life. There was a good person still in there, but her volcanic nature kept that person down. Junior was big, a real hoss of a man, but he wasn't the type to hit a woman. The sheriff was glad for that. There would be no charges, but Ricky gave them a stern warning. After all, when they made enough noise for a neighbor to be concerned, it couldn't be ignored.

Thirty minutes later Matthew Kearsey was back in his car. It was late, he was tired, and the last thing he wanted to do was to finish paperwork that could wait until tomorrow. Still, he was too wound up to go home yet so he decided to have a nightcap, just one, at Bingo Bob's. *Maybe that guy who plays blues guitar will be on stage tonight.*

The sheriff veered right at the fork, following 131 back toward town. Before passing the cemetery, the road veered to the right, looping around the hilltop. For a few seconds he had a diagonal view across the field of tombstones and monuments.

"What the?"

There was something there among the graves. A dog? "Shit." *That's all I need. Some pooch digs holes in the cemetery and I'm the one they'll call. How the hell did it get in?*

Sheriff Kearsey pulled the car off on the shoulder, turned on his hazard lights, grabbed his big flashlight, and got out.

He could see the shape from outside the gate. He stopped by one of the reinforced columns that were erected after Ian Murphy plowed into the gate years before. He had no trouble making out the outline of the animal in the bright moonlight, even with his flashlight off. It was about 100 feet or so back among the graves, a hulking black mass that looked like a dog. The profile was certainly canine, but it was bigger than any dog he'd ever seen, closer to the size of a small bear.

The gate was closed but not locked. He opened it with the greatest care, trying not to alert the creature, and inched forward one slow step at a time. His hands were sweating, the rubber grip of the flashlight sticking to his palm. Though the light from the full moon was bright enough to cast shadows, he would have to turn on the light to get a good look at the thing. He didn't want to be right on top of it before he was sure of what it was. *It's a dog, dammit! A big dog.* The closer he got, the less likely that seemed. It had to be ten feet long, nose to tail. No dog got that big. No wolf, even.

Wolf? What was it, ten, eleven years now since that trucker's cockamamie story about a giant black wolf that stood up like a man?

The sheriff unsnapped his holster, drew his service revolver, and thumbed off the safety. His other thumb rubbed the flashlight switch, but he didn't press it yet. He was going to turn on the light, but he needed to be ready to shoot in case the beast charged him. Chances are it would bark, growl, or make some kind of threat display before it either charged or ran. He'd have a few seconds to get off a shot if need be, and even if he missed the noise would spook the beast. His hands were shaking as he braced himself, swallowed, took a deep breath, and switched on the light.

His sight overwhelmed by the light, Ian had to depend upon his other senses to evaluate the situation. His nose told him two things; first, on the other end of the light was Sheriff Kearsey. Second, he had a weapon, the scent of gunpowder and steel almost as strong as the man's smell. No sooner did he process this information than he heard the click of the gun's hammer drawing back.

Ian bunched his powerful muscles and leaped. The gun roared as he hurtled Kelly's headstone and a hot pain shot through his left leg. He landed in a heap, but he was up and he bolted just as the gun roared again. This time the shot missed, the earth exploding where his left foot had been a second before. He took evasive action as he ran, darting in and out among the headstones. Twice more the gun fired, one shot spraying Ian with chips of marble. His left leg burned as he neared the fence and jumped. He cleared the iron tips with room to spare and turned on the speed when he landed. Within a few more seconds he made it to the cover of the trees. Still, he ran until reaching the creek at the bottom of the slope, out of range of the man and his gun.

At the stream, he took a long drink and settled down to examine his leg. It burned, the hair there singed, a shallow gash on his thigh bleeding, but he knew he was fortunate. The bullet had only grazed him. It hurt, but he had survived worse.

How could I have been so careless, he chided himself? He'd been so intent on the vision or whatever it was that...Ian stopped. He had reacted so quickly he hadn't taken a moment to reflect upon this new state. He was still a wolf yet he was thinking like a man. He had the wolf's memories, the wolf's instincts and reactions, yet...Something happened up there. He had crossed a threshold, some kind of barrier, and now he and the wolf truly were one.

Was Kelly still out there somewhere? Chevy, too? How about his mother and father? Had he been granted a moment on some other plane of existence or had they come to him? He'd seen the cabin, the little building he'd pounded into rubble years ago. Did it still exist somewhere? He knew they were questions that would probably never be answered. What was important was that Kelly had given him permission to move on. Of course, it might have been nothing more than his conscience finally coming to terms with their deaths. Whatever the truth was, Ian felt a weight lift from his shoulders. He rose from the edge of the stream and trotted off toward home. All the way there, his thoughts were dominated by two people; a chestnut-haired young beauty with deep chocolate eyes and a fair-haired woman he hoped might hold the key to his future. There were others looming over them like ghosts; a tall, white-haired monster dressed like a man and a broad-shouldered woman with a light streak running through her dark hair. Their specters faded with each step, though. By the time he reached his house, only the two he loved remained, standing side by side.

Sheriff Kearsey lowered the gun. He gulped in air while sweat ran down his face and soaked through his shirt. He holstered the revolver, lifted his hat, and ran his hands through his wet, gray hair.

"My god." He traced the animal's path backward from the fence, past the tombstone he chipped with a shot-*Jesus, how am I going to explain that*-to the spot were the beast had been. There was some blood there, so he'd grazed it at least, but it didn't slow the thing down at all. He hadn't intended on pulling the trigger unless the thing charged him, but when he turned on the light and got a clear look at it...It was a wolf and yet it wasn't. It looked like some kind of awful chimera, an amalgamation of beast and man. That was what spooked him so, what pulled the trigger for him. The way it looked at him, the way it moved, the way it used the headstones as obstacles instead of running for the fence in a straight line. It understood guns. It understood bullets. "Dammit, animals don't do that!" he said.

What if it hadn't run? What if it had come for him instead? Would a single shot have brought it down before it got him? The sheriff decided not to think about that now. The monster was gone. He decided instead to look at the grave, to try to understand where the beast had been and why.

Sheriff Kearsey settled his hat back on his head and walked up to the grave. He crouched, his knees popping, and read the inscription;

Kelly Shepherd. 1972-1989. Beloved daughter and granddaughter.

He shook his head. "Hell, no. That's insane." *Of course it is.* It made no sense in a logical, rational world. The Shepherd girl had been killed by something huge and powerful, something that could tear her throat out in a single motion. Buddy Hargiss saw what he described as an enormous wolf carrying her body across the road near Stonelick Lake. He claimed it stood up like a man. Then there were the footprints in the snow in Ian Murphy's back yard. They changed from the footprints of an animal to the prints of a man. Now this thing was lounging on Kelly Shepherd's grave. No. Not lounging. Keeping some sort of vigil? Communing with the dead? Mourning?

He stood, walked back to his car, and sat behind the wheel, pondering the elements of a story so strange he dared not tell a soul. If he told anyone they'd think he was crazy, but he had to do something.

Kelly Shepherd and the Patella kid were Ian Murphy's two closest friends, his girl and his best buddy. The trucker's story, the footprints, and now this beast visiting the Shepherd girl's grave...

Sheriff Kearsey headed down the hill but turned before he reached the center of town. Bingo Bob's could wait. Everything could wait. With that thing out there it made the most sense to go home, load every gun in the house, and check all the windows and doors.

July 2000
Indianapolis, Indiana

Ian grimaced.

"Your leg still troubling you?" Milla asked.

"Every now and then."

"How about the sheriff? Is he still bothering you?"

"I'll tell you later."

Ian didn't want to talk about the conversations he'd had with the sheriff. The man suspected something but wouldn't come right out and say it. That alone told Ian everything he needed to know. Sheriff Kearsey was not one to play it close to the vest, but he was afraid to say what he suspected. Ian put that aside for now. He'd looked forward to this trip for weeks. If all went well, it would mark the true beginning of his new life with Milla.

The occasion was the 1999 HorrorFest Expo in Indianapolis. Milla was scheduled to speak on werewolf folklore. Every summer, thousands of enthusiasts descended on the Excelsior Inn to take in the sights, the celebrity guests, and wander through the dealer room where dozens of booths hawked everything from hard to find independent films, classic horror film posters, model kits, magazines, autographed photos, and countless other items. Going in, Milla couldn't have cared less about that, but after walking the through dealer room, she agreed with Ian that there was a kitschy kind life to the place. *If only you knew what was walking among you right now*, Ian thought.

On their way to the room where Milla would be speaking, they passed three vampires, two mummies, and a dozen generic ghouls. Ian shook his head and smiled as they passed a rubber-masked werewolf.

"This is an interesting crowd," he said. "Do you do this often?"

"My publisher's idea," Milla said. "They thought it would boost sales." She didn't often wear dresses, but on this occasion she decided on a simple black one. "I have to admit, I feel a little overdressed."

The organizer of the fest met them at the door to the smaller auditorium and twenty minutes later Milla stepped up to the podium. Ian would have preferred to watch from the back of the room, but she insisted he sit with her in front of the crowd. Over the next hour, Milla guided the eighty people present through a highly condensed version of her second book, accompanied by a prearranged slide show illustrating the major points. Starting with the second century B.C. Akkadian Epic Of Gilgamesh, she guided the audience through a whirlwind tour of lycanthropic literature and folklore.

Ian had read her book several times, but he found the presentation enthralling. In particular he was impressed by the 2000 year old story of Niceros, a Roman ex-slave turned wealthy free man. At the urging of his host, Trimalchio, Niceros entertained a crowd at a banquet with the tale of his encounter with a young soldier, a guest of the house who accompanied Niceros on a moonlit journey. The soldier was a werewolf (a versipellum or "turn-skin" in the Latin) and Niceros witnesses a fantastic transformation. He is later informed that his flocks have been attacked by a wolf, but not before one of his servants wounded the creature. Troubled by these events, Niceros discovered the young soldier being tended by a doctor, his wound corresponding to the wound the wolf received the night before.

All the classic elements are there, Milla pointed out. The transformation occurs beneath a full moon. The soldier removed his clothes first in a symbolic shedding of his human skin. The transformation is effected via the use of magic. Lastly, there is the 'sympathetic wound,' the presence in the human body of the wound received as a wolf.

It was this last part of the tale that had Ian squirming in his seat. His left thigh still troubled him from the incident in the cemetery. Even transforming several times hadn't totally healed the wound. It knitted fine enough on the outside even if he would have a permanent scar. The damage to the muscle was more severe than he first thought, though. It would be some time before he felt no pain in the limb.

He told Milla he'd pulled a hamstring and she accepted the explanation. Sheriff Kearsey was not so easily satisfied. He stopped by several times to question Ian and go over the deaths of Kelly and Chevy though those cases were now officially closed. Ian recalled clearly his encounter with the sheriff in the cemetery. The observant lawman commented upon Ian's favoring of the leg. Ian respected the sheriff, even liked him, but the man wasn't going to let this go. He would have to be dealt with. *Dealt with? God, what am I thinking? I'm not Stubbs.*

He shook free of his dark thoughts and looked at Milla. Sitting behind her, appreciating the way her smooth, black dress complimented her golden hair, he felt once more the stirrings of something he had been experiencing more and more with her; hope. In her writings and even more through her presence in his life, he'd begun to believe he might have found a place in this world at last.

Did Stubbs suspect she would have this effect on him? Was that why he'd sent Ian her book? The thought made him uneasy. It tainted his hopefulness. He wanted to believe he really was onto something good. He didn't want to believe he was being played by a master manipulator. He hadn't seen Stubbs for years now. If the man was working out some kind of plan, a strategy to bring Ian under the thrall of his twisted vision, he was in no hurry. Of course, what was a decade when your life span is measured in centuries?

"You ready to go?"

"Yeah." They were in the dealer room. Ian was admiring a vinyl model of a wolf. The details were tremendous. The beast's black lips were pulled back into a snarl, its left front paw in mid-strike. The animal looked graceful and powerfully muscled, its black and brown pelt rendered with precise, beautiful artistry.

"Dire wolf," said the man behind the table. "They lived in North America during the ice ages. They were bigger than modern wolves. Some of them might have reached two hundred pounds. Can you imagine that? A two hundred pound wolf?"

"Impressive," Ian said. The figure was indeed impressive, more so than the bipedal movie monsters for sale throughout the room. Next to the menagerie of prehistoric animals on the table were stacks of magazines. On the cover of each issue was a colorful painting of some ancient animal, most often a dinosaur. "Are there any articles about these wolves?"

"Sure." The man flipped through one of the stacks and pulled out an issue with a mastodon on the cover. The poor beast was caught in a tar pit, several wolves surrounding it but yielding to a huge saber toothed cat. Enormous birds resembling condors circled overhead. "This one's all about prehistoric mammals. There's a feature article on the dire wolf."

"How much?"

"Ten bucks. If you like what you see there's subscription information on the contents page."

Ian pulled out his wallet and handed the man one of the four ten dollar bills he had with him. He turned around to Milla, who was standing a few feet back from the table, patient but ready to go.

"How much time do we have?"

"The movie starts in half an hour," she said.

"Sorry," Ian said. "I just couldn't tear myself away."

Half an hour later they sat in the theater where festival guests congregated each night to watch classic horror films. Tonight's feature was The Wolf Man starring Lon Chaney. *Junior, that is.* Even if Milla hadn't followed her publisher's advice, this year's theme celebrating the classic Universal monster movies would have held a powerful fascination for Ian. It was one thing to watch them on TV. It was another to see them on the big screen in a theater packed with appreciative fans.

Ian nestled into his seat. Milla threaded her arm through his and grasped his hand.

Over the next eighty minutes, while the crowd oohed, aahed, gasped, and chuckled, Ian sat wide-eyed and silent. Most seemed to know the movie well enough to anticipate the major scenes and they reacted on cue. He doubted any related to the film on his level. He'd seen every werewolf movie in existence, from the 1925 silent Wolfblood to the most recent. He thought most were awful and none had the cultural impact of Universal's 1941 classic. He loved Universal's iconic Frankenstein and Dracula films, but though they sprang from the world of literature while The Wolf Man was a purely cinematic creation, neither held anything personal for him. In Larry

Talbot, Ian found something of an avatar, an onscreen representation of his own struggles. Chaney's performance was clumsy and ham-fisted, but it somehow made the character more relatable. Ian loved the guy. Verna was right. Poor Larry, indeed.

As the movie approached its conclusion, Milla rested her head on his shoulder. Was it really possible that he could have a life that was in most respects normal? To love, to not envy what others had? He was happier now than he'd been in years. He was learning to embrace the wolf and he no longer feared he might kill someone again. Something changed that night in the cemetery. Kelly had forgiven him, urged him to move on. The words of his mother and father came back to him. God has a special plan for your life. A man makes his own meaning. Kelly had acknowledged both. It might have been nothing more than his subconscious, a mere dream, but what if it wasn't?

Of course, there was still the matter of Peter Stubbs. He was a monster but not because he was a werewolf. He was a monster because he used religion as a justification to kill. The blood of Kelly and Chevy and that poor girl in Missouri might be on Ian's own hands, but his teeth and claws had been Stubbs' tools. Then there was the question of God and where he fit into all this. Ian was more certain than ever that God didn't exist, but if he didn't, from where did Stubbs draw his power?

On screen, Claude Rains was clutching the silver headed cane, trudging through the misty forest toward a fateful meeting with his son.

After the movie, they went cruising for somewhere to eat, settling on a faux-Italian place two blocks from the Excelsior Inn. The food was passable and the servings large.

When they'd planned their excursion they debated whether to book two rooms or one. They both knew where their relationship was headed. Ian was as reluctant as he was hopeful and he sensed the same reluctance in Milla, though it must be for less unusual reasons than his own. In the end, they opted for adjoining rooms. When they reached the hotel, they lingered in the car and talked.

"I'm not sure if this is something a man should ask a woman," Ian said. "I don't know the rules."

"Rules?'

"You know what I mean. I-"

Milla put a finger against his lips. "Let's forget about the second room."

"OK." Ian felt himself blush. *Great. I'm blushing. Now-*

"What is it?" Milla said.

Ian looked over her shoulder. *No. Not here. Not now.*

Milla turned and looked. There was nothing there.

"We have to leave," Ian said.

"Now? Why?"

"It's not safe here anymore."

"Why not?"

"I can't explain. Just trust me."

"I can take care of myself, Ian. And you're with me."

"Doesn't matter. We have to leave. Now."

Milla sighed. She reached for the door. Ian put his hand over hers.

"Is there anything in your room you can't live without?" he said.

"Well, no, but-"

"Leave it then."

"We have to check out. We still have our room keys."

"Mail them. We can call them from the road, tell them an emergency came up."

"Ian, what did you see?"

"Please! We have to go. Now!"

"Ian...." She shook her head but started the jeep and pulled out of the parking lot.

Ian scanned the trees along the side of the lot until the curve of the road made it impossible to see past the edge of the hotel. At the last second he saw the figure again, standing in the shadows, the eyes reflecting the street lamps and headlights, bright coins burning in the darkness. The white wolf.

Part 3

Chapter 18

October 2000

Oxford. Ohio

Milla dropped into her favorite chair, her bag and briefcase thudding onto the floor beside her. It was only 6:30 PM, but she was beat.

Things had been testy between her and Ian since the HorrorFest Expo. They'd come close to spending the night together at last, a bigger step for her to take than Ian realized, but their hasty drive back home put an end to that. Milla accepted that. She knew she couldn't force things. They hadn't seen each other since, but they talked over the phone several times a week, Ian insisting it wasn't safe for her to be around him. Now that the semester was back in full swing, she had little time anyway. There were lessons to plan and students knocking on her office door all day. She left the house in a hurry that morning and forgot her cell phone, but decided it would do her good to be without it for one day. Now that she was home, turning in early sounded good.

Milla dragged herself from the chair after a few minutes and started the bathwater. A good soaking then one of those old movies Ian was always talking about while she drifted off sounded like the ticket. With the water started, she walked into the kitchen and popped open a cold stout. Her phone was on the counter. Next to it was her old answering machine, the light blinking. More and more, she thought about ditching the old thing and relying on nothing but her cell's voicemail, but the machine still served its purpose. She hit the play button and took a drink.

"You have twelve messages," the mannered synthetic voice declared.

She endured the messages of little importance to her: sales people, auto service plans she didn't want or need, a faculty meeting she was already aware of. The usual crap. After that were several messages from students who were already overwhelmed and wanted a moment of her time. She didn't give them her cell number for a reason.

Milla walked to the doorway and stood there, her head against the doorframe. She drank, listened to the machine, and to the water filling her tub. "Yeah, yeah," she said, rolling her eyes and her free hand, impatient to run the gauntlet of messages.

"Hi, Milla. My name is Verna Cooper. Ian may have mentioned me."

She stood up straight. Ian had told her all about Verna. Milla looked forward to meeting her when she and Ian got things straightened out, but the tone of Verna's voice told her this wasn't a pleasant call.

"I got your number from Ian's address book. He's been hurt. It's bad."

Milla lost her grip on the beer. The bottle slipped from her fingers and hit the floor with a heavy crack. It tottered, spun a half circle, then tipped over. The puddle of dark brown liquid spread across the polished wood but Milla ignored it.

"He's in the hospital in Batavia. I know you two have had your troubles lately, but Ian cares a lot for you. Milla, he's in a bad way. I called your cell phone, too. My number is..."

Milla stepped over the puddle and jotted the number down on the sticky pad next to the answering machine. She stood there looking down at the machine as the rest of the message played.

"It makes no sense," Verna said. "I don't know what to think. They found him in the woods near the body of another man. The other man was all torn up. Ian...he had an arrow through his chest."

"What did you do, Ian?" said Milla. She bit her bottom lip and reached for the jacket she'd discarded moments before. She turned off the bath water and headed for the door.

Milla was speeding south on Route 27 when she finally got through to Verna.

"Hello?"

"Verna? It's Milla Andersen."

"I'm so glad to hear from you. My line has been busy. I've been talking to, well, to everyone."

"How is Ian?"

"I just spoke with the doctor. It's not good, but Ian is a strong young man, and God is good."

"Let's hope so. Where is the hospital?" Verna gave her the directions and Milla jotted them down with one hand while she kept the other on the wheel. "Thanks, Verna. I'm on my way."

Ian opened his eyes. It took will to keep from closing them, but he was determined, his eyelids fluttering with effort. The room around him was a blur of pastel colors, the shapes fuzzy and indistinct.

As his awareness increased, so too did the pain. It felt as if someone had punched a hole in his chest and filled it with jagged glass. He shifted in the bed and the pain flared. The smells of dried blood, antiseptic, and perspiration mingled. A clear plastic bag filled with fluid hung from an IV stand. A line ran from the bag to his forearm, a broad strip of tape over the entry into his arm.

"Again?" Ian mumbled. Familiar scents in the room cut through the hospital odors.

"Easy," Milla said. "Don't try to talk."

"Praise Jesus!" Verna said. She was standing next to Milla. "I'll go find the doctor."

Ian started to protest but didn't have the strength. Milla touched his forehead, brushing back strands of sweaty hair. Her own hair was still bleached in streaks by the summer sun. Her eyebrows were so furrowed with concern they almost touched over her small nose. She leaned over the bed, careful not to put any weight on Ian, and kissed him on the lips.

"Welcome back."

Milla smiled, broad and warm, and Ian thought the reflected light in her green eyes seemed to dance. "You're beautiful," he managed to croak but paid for it with a fresh burst of pain.

"Thank you. You've looked better, but you're alive."

You should see the other guy, Ian wanted to respond, but he remembered what he'd done to the other guy. He gulped hard, fighting the urge to vomit. The effort caused his entire upper body to throb.

"Easy," Milla whispered. "Don't try to say anything right now."

He took a deep, careful breath and closed his eyes. The nausea passed. The smell of lilac hand lotion announced the presence of Verna Cooper again. The strong smell of expensive cologne applied with too much enthusiasm followed her into the room. Ian's eyes watered when he opened them. A heavy set man with black hair and and a neat mustache stood beside her. "Mr. Murphy," he said in accented English. "I'm Doctor Oland. I've been looking after you. Your friends have been very concerned, but I told them you seem to be very strong. We'll talk later, but I wanted to say hello."

"Sweetie, we've been praying for you," Verna said as the doctor looked over his chart. The whole church, people you haven't seen in years." She patted his arm and smiled. "Milla and I have been getting to know each other these last few days."

Days? Ian glanced at Milla. If he'd had the energy, he would have asked her how many. As it was, it was all he could do to manage a smile.

"Here ya go, hon." Verna sat next to Ian's bed and took out the VHS tapes one at a time. "*The Wolf Man.* I like that one," she said. "*The Company Of Wolves. An American Werewolf In London.* It's a good thing you kept these after you got that VDD player or whatever it's called."

"Yeah. The hospital only has the VCR. Did you bring the books?"

"I brought them." She produced from the depths of her shoulder bag two hardcover books and a paperback. "*The Wolf's Tale. The Wolf's Hour.*" She recited each title as if it were something foul. "*The Bloody Chamber?*"

"Thanks, Verna. What would I do without you?"

Ian had been in the hospital for four days. The rate of his recovery confounded his doctors. He felt well enough to go home, but the doctor insisted he stay two more days. Ian heard part of a conversation while he drifted in and out, the sheriff wanting to question him about the death of Lester Booth, Doctor Oland insisting he wasn't well enough.

"I know you love this werewolf stuff, Ian," Verna said. "I won't pretend to understand and you're a grown man, but...do you think this is healthy?"

"What do you mean?"

"Honey," Verna grimaced and paused for second. Ian could see that she was choosing her words with care. "I know life's been tough on you the last ten years or so, but before this...this accident...things had been going pretty well. I mean, you and Milla have something good, right?"

"Yeah. We do."

"I know Rose used to tell you God had a special plan for your life."

"She did."

"Well, maybe this was a wake up call. Maybe the Lord wants you to put all this werewolf stuff away."

" 'When I became a man, I put away childish things.' eh?"

"It's not that it's childish. It's that it might be dangerous."

He was at a loss for words. There was no way to explain this to her.

"Ian, honey?" she said, her voice dropping to a whisper. "What where you doing out in the woods before dawn? Naked?"

He looked away. "I don't remember much." He hoped the lie didn't sound as obvious as he feared. He remembered the look on Lester Booth's face before he died. He could still taste the man's blood. *Oh, god. His blood.*

"I'm worried that all this werewolf stuff has gotten into your head. The movies, the books...I almost didn't bring them. When they found you out there I wondered if you were beginning to think you were-" She stopped and looked away from him.

"A werewolf?" Ian said.

Verna nodded and her lips trembled. Ian could tell her composure was barely intact.

"Verna? Look at me." He took a deep breath. It was his turn to choose his words with care. "I do not think I am a werewolf."

"I know it's crazy for me to even think that," she said. "I also know you have a lot of questions about the Lord. I've been there myself. It's just that there are other forces out there, forces that would like to claim your soul. I believe demons are real."

"They are, Verna," Ian said just above a whisper.

"When can I go home, Doc?"

"Soon." Doctor Oland sighed. He leaned in close to Ian. "A county sheriff wants to have a word with you."

"Matthew Kearsey? It's all right. I knew I would have to talk with him sooner or later."

The doctor left the room but stopped outside the door to speak with the sheriff. Ian felt better than he had since before the hunter ran him through. *Then I tore the other guy apart*. He tried not to dwell on that. It was kill or be killed, he told himself. Still, it was a grisly reminder that it wasn't safe for him to be around people, especially near the full moon. Fortunately, it wouldn't be full again for a couple of weeks.

"Five minutes," the doctor said. "As we agreed."

"Agreed." The sheriff took off his hat and entered the room. "How are you feeling, Ian?"

"Better."

The sheriff was attempting to look casual and non-threatening, but it was obvious that he was anxious. Ian was certain he detected something else there. Anger? Fear?

"Glad to hear it." Sheriff Kearsey walked over to the window, hat in hand. Normally confident and decisive, he appeared unsure how to proceed.

"The doctor thinks I'll be able to go home soon," Ian said. "I have a feeling my insurance company told him as much, anyway."

"Hmmph," the sheriff snorted. "Gotta love the HMOs."

Ian nodded and forced a smile onto his face. "What can I do for you, Sheriff?"

"I've been doing some thinking." The sheriff paused again and looked out the window.

"And?"

"I've been thinking about things that are hard to believe. Things I never thought were real. They simmered there in the back of my mind. One way or the other, they all seem to come back to you."

"Me?"

"Yeah." The sheriff gestured at Ian with his hat. "You." He left the window, turned around the padded chair next to Ian's bed, and sat down straddling the seat. "Let's start with this most recent event. Now, there's no law against a man being outside at night naked on his own property, so long as he's out of public view. I'd call that strange behavior but not illegal. And believe me, I've seen stranger."

Reasoning the less he said, the better, Ian put on his best poker face and said nothing.

"That poor bastard." Sheriff Kearsey shook his head. "They were crossing a corner of your property, taking a short cut to Turner's uncle's house. They claimed they had been out deer hunting. Didn't get a thing. No surprises there. I figure they were out there to drink beer and forget their troubles. Hunting and drinking don't mix, but neither of them were ever the sharpest knife in the drawer.

"Anyway, Turner Jenkins put an arrow through you. I locked him up for it, but he made bail so I can't do anything more right now. There's a court date coming up. You'll be hearing about that."

"It was an accident," Ian said. "I don't want there to be any charges."

"He almost killed you. Turner's kind of an idiot, frankly, but he's no troublemaker. I've known him for years. He's big and rough looking, but he's never hurt anyone."

Ian almost said something then but closed his half-open mouth.

"Now, why would he put an arrow through you? Let me tell you what he said. Turner swears that he and Les were charged by a giant, black wolf. Turner says he shot an arrow straight through its chest, but it got up and tore Lester's throat out. Damn near decapitated him. I saw the body. Terrible."

Ian remained silent.

"Turner ran. He was scared shitless. He's still scared. Won't set foot out of his yard after dark."

Ian swallowed hard and looked down.

"That's quite a story," said the sheriff. "A killer wolf in southwest Ohio. Of course, it could have been just a big dog. Maybe Turner had too much to drink. Some people see purple elephants. He saw a monster wolf. That may be, but I don't think so."

Sheriff Kearsey got up and walked back to the window. Outside, the leaves were beginning to turn, orange, red, and burnt sienna sparkling among the green in the late afternoon sun.

"I remember standing in your back yard, Ian, after your father passed away. God rest his soul. Footprints in the snow. You remember that?"

Ian nodded but still said nothing.

"Eleven years ago your best friend and your girl were killed a month apart. I'm sorry to bring up painful memories, but I'm sure you recall that the circumstances surrounding their deaths were unusual, for lack of a better word. And you were the last person to see either of them alive. I gotta tell you, Ian, only the fact that they were obviously attacked by an animal kept you out of serious hot water."

"You mean only the fact that there was no evidence linking me to their deaths!" Ian snarled. He had to restrain himself to keep from spitting out the words. *Will I ever get past that? Just when I thought...And now this Lester Booth...*

"Nothing that would hold up in court, anyway." said the sheriff.

If the sheriff meant to draw him out, Ian thought, to raise his ire so that he'd speak and give away something, it wasn't working. Or maybe it was. "Where are you going with this, Sheriff?"

"Just trying to put things together. I've been working this out for a while, even when I didn't know I was. It was there on a back burner in my mind, but it was there. I'm just following the clues where they lead."

"Which is where?"

"You know my deputy, don't you? He's been with the force for a while now. Ricky Thorogood? You and Ricky go way back, from what I understand."

"We were never what I would call friends," said Ian.

"No, you weren't. Ricky tells me he used to date Kelly Shepherd. He told me about the three of you." The sheriff sat down straddling the chair again as if it was a saddle. "Ricky used to be quite a punk. A real troublemaker. He's grown up a lot since those days. He's a good man, Ian. He really is."

"Good for him," Ian said.

"I asked him what changed him, what turned his life around? You know what he said?"

"I have a feeling you're going to tell me."

"He said it was Kelly Shepherd's death. He told me he loved her. He also told me he didn't treat her right. She told him she loved you, said you treated her like she was special, like she was worth something more. She dumped him and went with you. A month later, she was dead."

Ian kept his voice down, but his anger was rising. "That was the darkest time of my life. Why are you dredging all that up now?"

"Ricky told me about a little altercation between you two. Apparently, you put the fear of God in him. He won't tell me exactly how, but you really rattled him. Now, you're a big guy, Ian. Hell, just lying there in bed you look strong as an ox, and you were at death's door just a few days ago. Regardless of your size, it's hard to imagine a mild-mannered guy like you intimidating a tough guy like Ricky Thorogood. Do you remember the incident he was talking about?"

"Yeah. I remember. Ricky followed me home one night. He accused me of having something to do with Kelly's death and he took a swing at me. I put him in his place."

"That you did."

"What does that have to do with anything?"

"Just one piece in the puzzle. Let me give you another; last summer I was on my way home from a night call. I had an encounter with some kind of animal. It was sitting on Kelly Shepherd's grave. I took a shot at it, winged it, but it got away. I'd call it a wolf because I'm not sure what else to call it. I've never seen anything like it. Whatever it was, it wasn't just an animal. I'll tell you something else, Ian. I spoke with that trucker who found Kelly Shepherd's body. You know what he says?"

"Everybody around here knows his story," said Ian. "It's local legend. He saw the wolf man. He saw Lon Chaney, Jr. standing over her body."

"Something like that."

"And you believe him? What's next? Bigfoot? The Loch Ness Monster in Stonelick Lake?"

"No." Sheriff Kearsey shook his head. "No, but after what I saw myself-"

Ian cut him off. He raised his voice even though he knew he should keep his cool. "Sheriff, I'm tired. What did you come here to say?"

"He thinks you're a werewolf," boomed a baritone voice from the doorway. Peter Stubbs stepped into the room, immaculate in his white suit, every hair in place, a grin crossing his handsome face. "He's afraid to say so, but he believes it. Don't you, Sheriff?"

Ian was so intent on the sheriff's interrogation that he hadn't noticed the preacher's scent enter the hallway. At first he was almost glad for Stubbs' timing, but a moment later he wondered if his troubles hadn't gone up another notch.

"Who are you?" Sheriff Kearsey stood up, his chest out.

"Peter Stubbs, evangelist and servant of The Lord Jesus Christ." Stubbs offered his hand. "Pleased to make your acquaintance, Sheriff."

Sheriff Kearsey shook his hand but scowled at the preacher.

"People seem to have a high opinion of you," Stubbs said.

"I do my best. What brings you here, Reverend?"

"Ian and I have known each other for a long time."

"Is that so?"

The sheriff turned to Ian and they exchanged glances Ian knew told the sheriff that Stubbs was not a friend.

"Do you know The Lord, Sheriff?"

"I'm not what you would call religious. I do believe in a higher power, though, and I expect I"ll have to answer for myself some day."

"Thus the conviction with which you carry out your duties. So..." Stubbs let the unfinished sentence hang in the air.

"So?"

"So," Stubbs continued, "what would your constituents make of this werewolf theory of yours?"

"Where did you get the idea that I believe such a thing?"

"Come now, Sheriff. I heard every word. You were dancing around the subject and I'm sure you are usually more direct. Tell me, did you realize that the deaths of those unfortunate youths years ago occurred on full moon nights, just as this recent incident did? I'm sure that hasn't escaped your notice."

Sheriff Kearsey fumed, his jaw clenching.

"I am also sure that if word got out that the local sheriff believed this town was haunted by a werewolf, it would do damage to his sterling reputation. Is that why you haven't told anyone?"

Ian breathed deep and remained silent. Stubbs appearance had put an end to the interrogation for now, but was Sheriff Kearsey the kind of man who would take matters into his own hands regardless of the consequences?

"Are you threatening me, Reverend?" Sheriff Kearsey straightened up and did his best to look Stubbs in the eye. He was clearly unnerved, but his anger was beginning to override his fear.

Stubbs' grin grew wider, his lips pulling back to reveal perfect white teeth. "Goodness, no, Sheriff. On the contrary, I only speak the truth to serve the will of The Lord."

The two stood facing each other. Moments ago Ian feared that the sheriff had realized what he was. Matthew Kearsey was a friend of his father's, a good man. If he knew Ian's secret it would complicate things, but Ian had always figured if that were so, he would just move away. He had no intention of harming the man. He feared Stubbs would have no such qualms. The sheriff had no idea who he was dealing with now.

"Sheriff?"

Doctor Oland walked into the room, a wary expression on his face. His eyes were on Stubbs even as he addressed the sheriff.

"Yeah, Doc. I was just leaving." Sheriff Kearsey put his hat on and stepped over to Ian's bed. "I'll send Ricky by tomorrow to get your statement."

"Does it have to be Ricky?"

"Yes. It does. We're a small department. He's my deputy."

"All right. If it gets antagonistic, though-"

"It won't." He doffed his cap at Ian, glared at Stubbs, and left without saying another word.

"Until we meet again," Stubbs called after him.

The doctor turned to Stubbs, craning his neck to look Stubbs in the face. "And you are?"

"Peter Stubbs. I'm a minister. I came to offer encouragement to Ian then I'll be on my way."

"See that you are. My patient needs his rest." He looked at Ian, his expression somber, his tone brooking no nonsense. "I'll be back in another minute. I expect you'll be alone and resting by then."

Ian nodded.

The little man cast a glance at Stubbs then left.

"Why are you here?" Ian snarled at Stubbs. "Don't you have some other poor shit to curse?"

Stubbs shook his head and smirked. "It appears I arrived in the nick of time. April wanted to come, but I convinced her to stay home."

"I have nothing to say to her."

"Be that as it may, I wanted to leave this with you." Stubbs reached into the pocket of his suit jacket and withdrew a dark orange envelope. "I came to extend an invitation. It is time to decide if you will spend the rest of your life in the service of The Lord or running from Him."

"An invitation?"

He laid the envelope on the bedside table. "Read it after I'm gone. Give it some thought."

"If I don't?"

"Do." Stubbs left it at that but paused at the door. "In the meantime, I'm off to do you a favor."

"What?"

"It's something that must be done, I'm afraid. Read the invitation. I'l see you soon."

Ian stared at the doorway as Stubbs left. *An invitation? To where? Hell?*

Matthew Kearsey yawned. He pushed against the corner of the booth, scratching an annoying itch in his left shoulder. Bingo Bob's was the only place for miles around where he could get any peace. It was dark, the music was loud, and the customers left him alone. They might nod or say hello, but they seemed to understand that he was here to unwind. He could come when he was off duty, have a beer or four, and clear his mind of the week's mental debris. He was carrying a lot of debris these days.

Melinda didn't care for Bob's. She preferred the brighter atmosphere of Cartwright's Diner on 131. She enjoyed the family friendly eatery and liked it when they couldn't get through dinner without half a dozen people engaging them in conversation. He loved the people of Stonelick. He was one of their own, born and raised there, but unlike his wife, he wasn't a people person. Still, when he retired in a few more years he intended to stay in Stonelick despite Melinda's ideas about moving to Florida.

"Can I get you anything else, Matt?" Bob Longstreet said. The huge proprietor never sent anyone to serve the sheriff. All of Bob's employees knew he preferred to get Matt's food and drinks himself and they were always on the house. "Bowl of chili? Some chips?"

"No thanks, Bob. I think I'll be heading out."

"Going home?"

"Eventually. I've got some things to sort out."

Bob shook his big head. "Nasty business with poor old Les last week. Was it as bad as I hear?"

Matt's eyes narrowed. He tilted his head to look up at Bob. "You been talking to Turner?"

"He's been in here. After Lester's funeral, he sat at the end of the bar drinkin' one shot after another till I told him to slow down. I could tell he needed to unload, so I listened. He was shakin' all over, scared to death. He didn't want to go home by himself and he didn't want Bonnie to come get him. Said he didn't want her out after dark. I wound up taking him home."

"What did he say?"

"He said he shot an animal, but it got up and damn near tore Lester's head off. He swore it was some kind of wolf but big as a bear. Said he took you back out there and you found that Murphy kid just about dead, with an arrow through him."

"What do you think of his story?"

The big man shook his shaggy head. "I don't know. Lester was killed by something and you did find the Murphy kid."

Matt nodded and slid out of the booth. "Bob, I might be a day late and a dollar short on this, but keep that talk to yourself. I don't know what happened yet, but as for Turner, I'm not sure how much stock I'd put in his story. You know what I mean?"

"I do."

"What do I owe you, big guy?"

"Same as always." Bob waved a hand and smiled.

"I always ask, don't I?'

"And it's always on the house."

"Thank you, Bob." He patted the man's massive shoulder and left.

Matt paused under the awning outside. He didn't feel like going home. He got into his pickup, took off, turning right at the four way onto Stonelick Road and heading toward the lake. He passed Ian Murphy's house and the old dairy farm. Both were dark, the farm deserted and unsellable, it seemed. A mile and half later, he reached the former location of Sim's Bait 'N Tackle. The gravel lot was one his favorite places to sit and think. He turned off the ignition and sat outside the rundown building.

Across the road, dark green water from Stonelick Lake trickled over the curved concrete spillway, once smooth and light grey, but now dark and discolored. *What was that damn movie I saw when I was a kid? Some poor bastard was infected with some kind of virus or serum, a guinea pig for one of those mad scientists who always popped up in those movies. The serum turned him into a werewolf and the movie ended with the poor schmuck being shot on top of a dam or levee.*

After sitting there for half an hour, he decided it was time to go home. He started to turn on the radio but decided to drive home in silence and hold Melinda close. She'd wake up, but she wouldn't mind. She never did.

Turning right out of the lot, Matt headed back up Stonelick Road. It would take him past Ian Murphy's house again, but it was the shortest route home. The rain had started falling while he was sitting across from the spillway. It was coming down in big drops now, bouncing off the waxed finish of his truck and pattering on the asphalt. He stopped at the four-way then continued, but with a big S-curve a quarter of a mile ahead and the roads already slick, he kept his speed down. He'd gone through a pack of smokes back at Bob's and even though he'd promised Melinda he would quit, he still kept some in reserve in his glove compartment. He was reaching to push in his cigarette lighter when a large white shape shot out of the long grass to his right, darting across the road a few feet from his front bumper.

Acting on reflex, Matt hit the brakes and the truck fishtailed on the narrow road. The right rear tire slipped off into the deep ditch and the right front followed, pulled into the ditch by the truck's forward momentum. The vehicle jerked to a stop as the front bumper dug into the soft earth.

"Damn it!" The sheriff knew without getting out that he was stuck good. The left side was still on the road, but the truck was canted at an angle. Even with the four wheel drive, he knew there was no way of getting out of the ditch without a tow.

Matt reached for the cell phone clipped onto his belt but stopped. *What the hell?* He cut off the engine-the truck wasn't going anywhere-and listened. At first he thought he was imagining it, but there it was. Something was out there, maybe the thing that caused him to skid into the ditch, and it was howling. The deep, undulating call was loud now that the engine was off. It couldn't be more than a few hundred feet away. There was a pause then the thing howled again. It was closer. Much closer.

His palms were sweating as he reached across the tilted cab and opened the glove compartment. Matt's fingers pushed the cigarettes aside and closed around a .38 caliber revolver. He withdrew the handgun and opened the chamber. He knew what was in there, but he found the sight comforting. "My god," he said as the thing howled a third time, closer than ever. He never thought he would need the six silver bullets he'd been able to get ahold of. It wasn't easy, but he was glad he had them now. He couldn't load his service revolver with silver, so he couldn't go through normal channels. "This is insane," he said, but he closed the chamber and sat clutching an unregistered gun, loaded for werewolf.

Come on Matthew. Get it together. His breathing had just returned to normal when he saw something moving through the trees across the road. He couldn't see it very well in the dark and through his rain streaked window, but it was there.

Matt weighed his options, talking to himself under his breath in clipped half sentences. *Call for help? Probably the smart thing...what if that thing out there...go ahead and say it...what if it's...but he's still in the hospital...isn't even a full moon...Matthew, what the hell are you saying? If it is him, and let's just say it is, I'd be doing him a favor...who wants to live that way?...God, I'm sorry, Henry...I'll do this then retire. Move to Florida after all. Melinda will be happy.*

Not at all sure that what he was doing was sane, Matt reached under the seat for his big flashlight. Reluctant to let go of the gun, he sat the flashlight in his lap and reached up with his other hand to flip the switch so the cab wouldn't light up when he opened the door. That done, he opened it, stepped out onto the wet shoulder, and shut the door behind him.

The rain had picked up, the drops dancing on the asphalt, thousands of minute splashes between Matt and the opposite side of the road. If he turned on the flashlight he wouldn't be able to see a thing outside the beam. Too much contrast. The thing could blindside him. He kept it off while his eyes adjusted and strained to see in the darkness. He could make out the rough shapes of the bushes at the edge of the forest. The raindrops pirouetted on the slick blacktop and tinkled off the shiny red finish of his truck. The sheriff's heartbeat throbbed in his ears, almost as loud as the rain.

A low grumble betrayed the presence of something just inside the tree line. The grumble turned into a snuffling, chuffing noise.

Matthew flipped off the safety and gripped the .38 tighter. His jacket was already soaked through with rain and his shirt was wet with a mixture of rain and sweat. He straightened up, shoulders back and chin out. "OK, you son of a bitch! I'm on to you." He walked across the road a slow step at a time, his eyes scanning the dark line of the forest. His breathing was heavy in his own ears, almost asthmatic, and he had to stop at the edge of the road and remind himself to take more measured breaths.

The noise stopped. No grumble. No shuffling of heavy feet.

He was about to switch on the flashlight when the creature howled again. The sound was deafening. It couldn't be more than a few feet away. He resisted the urge to cover his ears as the howl rose in volume. If he did, he would have to drop his gun and flashlight. He wasn't about to do either, so he hunched over and tucked his head into his shoulders, covering his ears as best as he could. It didn't help. The howl rose in strength until at the very end it twisted, morphing into something else altogether; a laugh. A delirious, perverse chuckle.

"Jesus," Matt whispered under his breath. *That can't be Ian Murphy.* Gritting his teeth, he renewed his grip on his gun and flashlight. He wanted to turn on the light, to see the creature but also to be relieved from his near-blindness. If it was a full moon and there wasn't all this damn cloud cover...

"Sheriff," a deep voice boomed. "As a wise man once said, 'Come let us reason together.' "

"Who...who are you?" Matt winced at how frightened he sounded.

"What you really want to ask is *what* am I. I think you know."

"I'm not in the mood for games. If you know what's good for you, you'll show yourself. You want to reason together? OK, let's do that."

"Repent, Sheriff. Make peace with your Creator."

"That sounds like a threat." He had heard that voice before, that hint of a southern twang. *The preacher from the hospital?*

"Turn on your light, Sheriff. I'm right in front of you."

His left hand slick with rain, Matt loosened his grip on the light and thumbed the switch to ON. He raised the beam and pointed it at the forest. Just inside the treeline less than twenty feet away stood the preacher, his hands at his sides. He was smiling, every hair in place though it was slick with rain. He was naked from head to toe.

"Come out of the trees. Now!" Matthew gestured with the gun, not taking the light off the man.

"You've discerned the truth, Sheriff, but not by revelation. The Enemy would use you to hinder The Lord's work."

"I have no idea what you're talking about."

"It is as you suspected. I have no doubt you don't want to believe it even now. You may even fear you are losing your mind. You are not. It is true and it is glorious!"

The man smiled and his eyes seemed to change shape in their sockets. His face moved under the skin and his teeth lengthened. Matt was sure of what he saw, but when he squinted and looked again, the preacher's face was normal except for that awful grin.

"Ian Murphy is indeed what you believe him to be, as am I. He is my disciple, Sheriff. He follows me as I follow Christ."

"You're insane."

"Perhaps you should call for help. I can smell the beer on your breath. You are off duty, but you are never really off duty, are you? The phone on your belt. Use it, Sheriff."

How the hell could he see that in the dark with a flashlight in his face. Matthew stared through the rain at the preacher. *What was his name? Stubbs?* He gritted his teeth, unsure of what to do next and hating the feeling. *Peter Stubbs. That was it.* The preacher smiled again, then he was gone.

"What the?" Matthew took a step back, unable to accept that anyone could move so fast. He tucked the flashlight under one arm and whipped the cell phone off his hip. He went to memory, chose #2, and hit send, all in a matter of seconds.

'Stonelick Sheriff's office. How may I-"

"Junie. Where's Ricky?"

"Oh, hi, Sheriff. He finished his rounds and went to Bob's for a late snack. It's been real slow-"

"Listen! Get him out here now. I'm on Stonelick Road just up from the spillway, headed toward town. My truck's in the ditch and I've got a...a madman on my hands."

"A what?"

"Now, Junie! Call Ricky. I need him now!"

He put the phone back on the clip and held the flashlight in his left hand. He braced it against the gun in his right and stepped off the road. Shuffling to the edge of the trees, he swept the light around in a tight, fast arc. Nothing.

The rain was coming down harder than ever, smacking the autumn leaves, running off, and puddling on the ground. In the distance, a slow roll of thunder played out, fading as Matt blinked the rain out of his eyes. He wished he had his damn hat on, but it was in the truck, on the...

"Boo!"

A white face was before him, eyes wild, teeth long and gleaming. The preacher gripped Matt's right wrist, twisted before he could get off a shot, then backhanded him. A second later he felt the smack of mud against his back. When he looked up, the preacher loomed over him.

"What do we have here?" Stubbs held the .38 in his left hand, opened the cylinder, and shook the bullets out into the palm of his right hand. "This will be of no use to you anymore," he said before flinging the gun over his shoulder.

Matt strained to make out the man's face. He'd lost his grip on the flashlight when the preacher backhanded him. It lay on the ground behind the preacher now, backlighting him, rendering his body in silhouette. The preacher's body had a halo of sorts, Matt thought, then he realized it was hair. Short, fine hairs lined the figure, glistening in the rain and the beam from the flashlight.

Stubbs laughed. He held one of the bullets up, the casing reflecting the white of the flashlight beam. "My, Sheriff," he said. "You have seen too many movies. Didn't you notice Ian's silver earring? A bullet is a bullet if you are a good enough shot." He stopped smiling and his voice lost any trace of amusement. "My dear, departed father can attest to that."

Matt began crawling backwards, unable to take his eyes off the man.

"You're a good man, Sheriff. I don't doubt that, but good isn't enough. 'There is none righteous, not even one.' You are a pawn of our Enemy. He seeks to disrupt, to hinder, to claim as many souls as he can. He cannot win, though, and he knows this."

Stubbs took one step then another toward Matthew. He opened his right hand and let the bullets fall one by one. They smacked the ground like the heaviest of raindrops.

"For centuries, the evil one has driven men such as you to persecute my kind." Stubbs advanced one step at a time, matching the sheriff's slow, desperate scramble. "We have been imprisoned, hounded. We have been crucified, burned at the stake, dismembered. Shot. Yet the commission given five centuries ago to my wretched ancestor has survived. The day of judgement is now upon you. I advised you earlier to settle up with your Maker, Sheriff. I advise you once more to do so."

Finding his feet at last, Matt stumbled backward before righting himself and breaking into a full-out run. He had no direction, no goal other than to escape the thing that stalked him. He ran blindly, barely able to see in the darkness of the forest.

After a minute of running, dodging the trees he could see and bouncing off those he could not, the ground sloped beneath him. Before he could stop himself, his feet skidded on the wet leaves and his momentum sent him tumbling downhill. He landed with a thud at the bottom of a slope, rolling over three times before he came to a stop. Coughing and sputtering, he pulled himself up.

" 'Behold! I stand at the door and knock.' "

The voice was loud but distant, at least a hundred yards away.

Matt started to run again but stopped, his knee throbbing and his back aching. He slumped against a tree to catch his breath, then heard a loping, rhythmic padding of four feet on the forest floor. He couldn't outrun the beast. The preacher. It was true. Monsters did exist and he was about to die. He stood up to his full height, thought of Melinda and the girls, then prayed, getting himself right with whatever God tolerated the presence of such a creature.

The monstrous white wolf crested the slope. Matt could see little in the dark, but he could see enough. The beast stood there and licked its lips.

"Come on, motherfucker," Matt said. "Let's do this."

Chapter 19

October 2000

"Ahhhh." Ian stretched, twisting to his left then back to his right before pulling the old Cincinnati Reds sweatshirt over his head. The stretch felt good, but he couldn't overdo it. He still had stitches in his upper back and his chest. He could feel them when he moved, but there was little pain. His doctor was amazed at his recovery. He would have been even more amazed to come into Ian's room at night and find a huge wolf in his bed. Ian had learned to anticipate the nurses' rounds and changed three times during his stay. With each change his wounds were more knitted.

"Is that everything?" Milla said.

"Yep." He'd filled his duffle bag with the books and tapes Verna brought for him. "It feels great to be in jeans and a shirt again. I can turn around now without exposing myself."

"I liked that gown," she said. "You sure you don't want to bring one home?"

Ian smiled and shook his head. "Thanks for coming today."

"No problem."

"It's a long drive from Oxford. What about your classes?"

"I made arrangements. I can be gone for a week. I told them it was a family emergency."

"Family?"

"I've missed you. After Indianapolis, I was afraid-"

Before she could finish, an orderly with a wheelchair appeared along with Doctor Oland. The doctor expressed his amazement again at Ian's recovery. He had explained that judging from the entry and exit of the arrow, it should have destroyed Ian's aorta, but the shaft of the arrow literally bent around his heart. Ian couldn't help but smile. He'd been a quadruped as a wolf, the shaft of the arrow bending as he transformed. The doctor summed it up with a shrug of the shoulders and referred to Ian as an anomaly.

Good word, Doc. Damn good word.

The doctor did insist that Ian sit in the wheelchair so he let the orderly push him onto the elevator and out the front door. He walked to Milla's Jeep, though, and belted himself in. He was glad she had the canvas top rolled up. The rain from the last two days was gone, and after spending the better part of a week in the hospital, the outside air felt wonderful.

"Verna is a nice lady." Milla started the engine but didn't pull out yet. "We had some pretty good talks the last few days."

"Do tell?"

"Yeah. It was almost like meeting the folks. She wanted to know all kinds of things about me. She's very protective of you."

"Tell me about it. She's been my surrogate mother ever since Mom died."

"She was close to your mother."

"Her best friend," Ian said. "So what did you tell her?"

"Everything. Almost." Milla laughed. They were miles from the hospital on the way to Ian's house before she spoke again.

"She didn't care for April."

"You talked about her?"

"We did."

"April was a mistake."

"You don't say?"

"You sound jealous," Ian said.

"I am. A little."

Ian leaned back and enjoyed the breeze on his skin. He undid his pony tail and let his hair go where it would. When he got home, he smelled bacon before they walked in the door.

"In here," Verna called from the kitchen. Her voice was flat, not cheerful as Ian expected. She was at the stove, sliding a sunny side up egg onto a plate piled high with bacon and biscuits.

"Are you OK?" he asked.

"I'm glad you're home, Honey. It's just that I'm a little out of sorts."

"Why? What's up?"

"You haven't heard the news?"

"No," said Milla. "Nothing."

"It's terrible." Verna sat the plate on the counter.

"What happened?" Ian said.

"It was just up the road from here." Verna shook her head.

"What was?" Milla said.

"It was on the news a little while ago. Sheriff Kearsey is dead."

The sheriff's death was the lead story on every AM talk radio station. According to the reports, Deputy Richard Thorogood found the sheriff's truck half in the ditch on Stonelick Road. There was no sign of foul play near the truck, but the sheriff's body was found in the woods half a mile away. It seemed he died in similar fashion to Lester Booth, though there were hints that the sheriff's death was even more grisly.

Ian didn't touch his food as they listened to the report on first one station then another. After a while, Verna had to leave the room. Like most people around town, she liked Sheriff Kearsey. By the time Ian got home, she'd already heard the story several times. That was enough for her.

Milla managed to eat, though she was as discreet as possible out of respect for Ian and Verna. She hadn't grown up here like Ian and she wasn't a part of the local community like Verna. It couldn't strike her as personally as it did them. She didn't want to mention that the sheriff had died so soon after this Lester Booth fellow, a death Ian was too closely associated with for her comfort. They would need to talk about that, and soon.

At noon, Ian turned on the TV to catch the story on the local news. He didn't have to wait long.

"A small rural community in Clermont County is in shock today," a blond anchorwoman spoke into the camera. "Our own Rachel Caldwell reports live on the shocking death that has many recalling events from a decade ago."

Ian flinched. *Great. Bring that up again. Someone has done their homework. They needed an angle for the story.* This is worse than Milla or Verna could know, he thought.

"Before we proceed," added the square-jawed coanchor, "I must advise you that the details are gruesome. Rachel?"

"Yes, Troy and Tina. Behind me is where this terrible event took place sometime in the overnight hours. The body of Clermont County Sheriff Matthew Kearsey, a beloved life-long resident of the town of Stonelick, was found in this forest."

Verna stepped into the living room, her eyes fixed on the screen.

"The sheriff was apparently mauled by some kind of animal. His death occurred just over a week since the death of Lester Booth, a deer hunter killed within a few miles of here. For many, the incidents have a disturbing resemblance to the deaths of a pair of teenagers in these same woods eleven years ago.

"I've spoken with local law enforcement and with citizens. While the sheriff's department has made no official statement, the locals have been more forthcoming. Bow hunter Lester Booth's brother-in-law declined to comment on camera, but he is adamant that the animal that killed Mr. Booth was a huge wolf-like creature."

Next came a taped interview with Ricky Thorogood. "I can't comment on Matt's...on the Sheriff's death right now. I can't comment on Lester Booth, either. It's possible the FBI may become involved. Right now we have no one of material interest, but that may change."

"As I understand it," the reporter said, "a man was found injured near the body of Lester Booth. Is he involved in any way? Is there a connection between these tragedies?"

"Oh, shit," Ian said under his breath.

"I don't know," Ricky said. "Sheriff Kearsey was my mentor, my friend." He stopped and looked at the ground. When he raised his head again, his face was red. "That's all I have right now."

The reporter signed off and the broadcast from the studio resumed. A cheery face filled the screen, promising your "frosty fall forecast" after the commercial break.

Ian turned off the television. *I'm off to do you a favor. Jesus.*

The black wolf sniffed the ground, the trees, the air. He placed his paw in one of the dozens of prints adjacent to the spot where the sheriff's body was found. It was large enough to accommodate his own oversized foot. Stubbs' scent was everywhere.

The coppery tang of Sheriff Kearsey's spilled blood mingled with the smell of earth, leaves, and the musk of the white wolf. It appeared that the sheriff ran at first, falling several times, but after the last fall, he stood and faced his pursuer, faced certain death, in a last defiant stand. He stood no chance. The white wolf slaughtered him. Ian had feared the sheriff's discovery, but he didn't want another innocent person dead. His anger at the monstrous injustice-

At the edge of his vision, Ian detected movement in the forest, a white shape in the dark. It was hundreds of yards away and downwind, but it was there. Stubbs? Who else could it be? Ian kept his head turned away from the interloper even as he prepared to rush him. If he could get closer before he realized Ian's intent, he might be able to run him down. If it was Stubbs, they would settle the matter right here, right now.

Ian bolted uphill toward where he'd seen the white shape. Before he reached the crest of the rise, he stopped. The white creature was gone. If it was Stubbs, he had moved with a silence and speed Ian never dreamed was possible. He thought about tracking the beast by smell but decided against it. He knew where he could find Stubbs. They'd settle up soon.

The monster wouldn't be alone. He would have to face them all, however many there might be. He didn't look forward to seeing April again, but he knew she'd be there. She claimed she had her own agenda, that her relationship with Stubbs was only one of necessity. That may be true, but he didn't care. If Stubbs died, perhaps his mission would die with him, but could he trust April to go her own way? He had his doubts.

Ian was no longer the black wolf when he slipped in the back door. Verna was gone, but Milla had stayed the night, taking the guest bedroom. There had been some awkward moments. He wanted her, wanted to be with her all night, and he was sure she wanted the same thing. If their stay in Indianapolis hadn't been cut short they would have already crossed that bridge. He wanted to let her into his world, into his heart. Milla wasn't April.

He was sure she wasn't at all like that deceptive she-wolf, in league with Stubbs while he thought she might actually care for him.

What about you? Are you so righteous? You were using April yourself. You didn't love her. You just didn't want to be alone.

It felt different with Milla. Meeting her had been a spark to his heart, jump-starting a part of him that had been dormant for a decade. He couldn't deny any longer that he was in love with her, but would he wind up with her blood on his hands as well? Was it worth the chance?

However it worked out between them, it wasn't going to happen that night. He needed to visit the site of Sheriff Kearsey's death. It had to be Stubbs. After their tense confrontation at the hospital, who else could it be? He needed to investigate the scene so he used his still aching chest and shoulder as an excuse for turning in early. When there was no more noise in the house, he slipped out the window and headed for the trees.

Sometime after the sun came up, Milla knocked on Ian's door.

"Yeah?" Ian said.

"How about some breakfast?"

"Sounds good," he said.

Milla opened the door, but she stayed in the hallway. She was dressed and brushing out wet hair. "Grab a shower while I fix something."

"Do you need any help out there?"

"I'll be fine. I've been in a kitchen before, you know."

"Sure. I...I'm glad you're here."

"So am I. Now hurry up. I've got plans."

"That was...," Ian pushed back from the table, searching for the right word, "...heavenly."

"Don't get used to it."

"You don't often cook?"

"I can, but I usually let others do it for me. Wait. That didn't sound like I meant it to sound. What I mean is I eat out a lot."

"I'll cook next time."

"Deal."

"I'm not a great cook, but I do all right," Ian said. "You'll find out."

"My mom was a better cook than I could ever be," Milla said. "She could make anything taste special." A sad, wistful smile crinkled the tiny crows feet in the corner of her big eyes. "She wasn't too adventurous outside the kitchen, but she was fearless inside it."

"You don't talk much about your mother," Ian said.

"My mother..." Milla's smile faded. "Ian, there are things you need to know about me." She reached across the dining room table and squeezed his hand. "I know a lot about you. I want you to know about me."

You don't know everything. Jesus. You don't know everything.

She let go of his hand. "My mother had a breakdown. I was thirteen. My parents had separated years before. Raising two kids alone was hard, especially when one of them was me."

"Wait. Two kids?"

"I have a brother. William. We'll talk about him later."

"OK."

Milla shrugged. She looked down and examined her nails. Ian was unused to seeing such an obvious sign of self-consciousness from her. She was the most self-assured person he'd ever met with the exception of Peter Stubbs, and since he was probably insane he didn't count.

"The Cliff's Notes version is this; my folks split up. My mother left him and took us with her. My father didn't try to stop her."

"That must have been hard on both of you."

"It was."

"Who is older? You or William?"

"Me. There's a lot more to it than this, but when I was almost twelve my father wanted to be part of our lives again. He'd had some kind of spiritual awakening or some shit. My mom didn't want to have anything to do with him and she sure didn't want me or Will to have anything to do with him, but he had a lawyer and he got visitation rights. For the sake of my brother I went along without causing much of a fuss."

"Where's William now?"

"I'll get to that." Milla looked away. When she spoke again, her voice was choked with emotion. "To make a long story short, my mother lost her mind. Her cheese slid off its cracker, so to speak. She's been in an institution for years. She'll die there."

"I'm sorry, Milla."

"It's all right. I want you to know." Milla cleared her throat and took a long drink of orange juice before continuing. "Anyway, after they put Mom away, Dad got full custody. There was nowhere else for us to go. I ran away, but I always came back. I couldn't leave Will there alone."

"Was your father abusive?"

"No. Not at all, at least not physically. Emotionally, that's another story." Milla poured the last of the juice into her glass. "He took us to church," she said, peering into the empty carton for a few seconds. "The same kind of holy roller churches you grew up in. We butted heads a lot as I grew older. He had my life all figured out for me, but I didn't want any part of it. When I turned eighteen I couldn't handle it anymore. I left."

"What about your brother?"

"Will left home soon after I did. He was on the streets. I had to track him down. He lived with me for a while then one day he was gone. He's out there somewhere."

"Did you ever see him again?"

"I tried to find him. I even went overseas."

"Overseas?"

"He left the country. He sent me postcards from France. Germany. England."

"Do you ever visit your mother?"

"I can't." Tears welled up in Milla's eyes, spilling over her cheeks. She didn't bother to wipe them away. "She gets hysterical if she sees me. Her doctors would rather I stay away. The more I do, the better off she is. She's terrified of me."

"Why?"

Milla shrugged and wiped her eyes. "Like I said, she lost her mind. So that's my cheery life story in a nutshell. Part of it, at least."

"I'd like to know the rest."

"Another time." She pushed Ian's chair back from the table so she could swing her leg over and sit on his lap facing him. "I want to finish what we started in Indianapolis. You have any plans for today?"

"Uh, nothing that can't wait."

Milla brushed her lips across his, then repeated it with more pressure. Ian moved his lips against hers, trying not to tremble from a combination of fear and excitement. Her tongue parted his lips, pushing past his teeth and circling his tongue, inviting him to respond. He did and they shared a long, slow kiss, savoring each other's taste, breathing through their noses in deep, noisy breaths. When their lips parted, Ian pulled back. "It's...uh...been a long time since I..."

"You don't want to know how long it's been for me."

Ian was thrilled but terrified at the same time, his eyes betraying his conflicted state of mind.

"What's wrong?"

"I'm sorry," he said. "I just had a flashback."

"To April?" Milla's lips twisted into a snarl.

"God, no! Not her."

"Kelly?"

"I..," Ian searched for the right words, but he feared that no matter what he said it would come out wrong. "I've lived for so long thinking I'd never love anyone else again that when I realized I was falling in love with you, I felt like I was being..."

"Unfaithful?"

Ian nodded. "Yeah. Silly, huh?"

Milla bit her lip. "Only the most romantic fucking thing I've ever heard in my life. So I'm competing with a ghost?"

Ian blinked and shook his head. "No." He wrapped his arms around Milla. "No, you're not competing with anyone."

"OK," Milla said. This time it was she who pulled back. She looked into Ian's eyes, her expression stern. "I love you too, for the record. Life has been pretty rough on you, but I've taken my own lumps. Just to be here with you is more than I could have hoped for a few years ago."

Ian started to ask her why, but she stopped him with a kiss. She pulled back again, but this time with a smile and scooted up onto the table for more room. She pulled Ian's sweatshirt over his head and dropped it onto the floor.

"I need this," she said. "I think you need this, too."

Ian was glad the full moon was still almost a week away, on Halloween, as it tuned out. His upper body was no hairier than usual. He hadn't had to shave between his eyes, though his beard was beginning to roughen. The wounds on his left chest and shoulder bore ugly pink-edged scars that looked months old instead of less than two weeks.

"You heal fast." Milla said.

"High metabolism." He knew it was lame, but it was all he could think of at the time.

"I bet," she said then reached down to take the edge of her Miami Redhawks jersey and pulled it over her head. Her shoulders and arms were lean and muscular, her breasts full and high, a trickle of sweat running between them down to her rippled abdomen.

"You're stunning," Ian said as he marveled at her physique.

"Good genes," Milla said, grinning.

"Yeah."

"Tell you what; how about we get your high metabolism and my good genes together and see what happens?"

Ian opened his eyes enough to let a little of the dull light in. The room was dim. He rolled onto his side and opened his eyes wider. Milla was sitting up in bed, her naked back to him. He could see the clock beyond her on the nightstand. 5:32 PM. They'd been asleep for almost three hours. He sat up, ran his fingers through his tangled hair, and looked over her shoulder. She was holding the envelope Stubbs gave him in the hospital.

"That...uh..." Ian had to clear his throat before continuing. "That's from the preacher I told you about, the one who came to see me in the hospital. It's, uh, an invitation."

"Are you going?"

"Well...wait...what?"

"Are you taking him up on his invitation?"

"Milla?"

"I know who it's from." Her voice was just above a whisper. She turned around to face Ian. "He's my father."

"Your...?" Ian's voice failed him. His mouth hung open, his eyes searching her face for a sign that this was some kind of bizarre joke.

"I was going to tell you. I just had to figure out how."

"You're one of his, too?"

"No!"

"Oh, shit." Ian breathed out hard. "You know what I am."

"Yes." Milla nodded. "I know."

Ian's heart raced.

"Ian? Last night, the wolf you saw was me."

"You?"

"I kept my distance. I wanted to know if it was my father who killed the sheriff. I got close enough to tell. I didn't think you'd see me, but your senses are sharp, very developed. You've only been a wolf for a little over ten years. You're still young. For most, it takes twice that long to master the-"

"The Blessing." Ian snarled. "That's what your daddy calls it."

"He's not my daddy, Ian. He's just my father. There's a difference."

"So I'm young?" He looked away from her. "I'm twenty-nine, Milla. How old are you?"

"Well, my birthday is December 11th. You know that much. I was born in 1951."

"You're forty-nine?"

Her thick eyebrows were knitted almost painfully, an expression somewhere between embarrassment and shame etched on her fine features.

Ian smirked, swung around the bed away from her, and stood. He walked to his dresser and fished out a fresh pair of underwear. After he pulled them on he turned to face her again. "I knew you were older, but I figured you were maybe thirty-five."

"Ian, there's twenty years between us. We'll live to be at least two-hundred. Maybe even three-hundred. All things considered-"

"Stop! There's a lot more than years between us, Milla." He sat down on the bed with his back to her. "How long have you known what I am?"

"Since the day we met."

"What? How?"

"For one thing, your fingers. The way your middle and index fingers are the same length. All the old legends get that wrong. It's not the third finger. And I could tell you shave the spot where your eyebrows meet. I do, too, by the way."

"But you," Ian sputtered. He was angry and curious at the same time."Your fingers..."

"It's a secondary sexual characteristic. Only males have that feature. It's the same with the palms. I'd trade my unibrow for hairy palms any day."

"Right." Ian stood and paced in front of the bed. "Was this all planned? How many other werewolves have you known?"

"How many of them did I fuck? That's what you really mean, isn't it? One. Years ago. I've had other lovers, if you want to call them that." She pulled the crumpled bedspread around her like a security blanket. "You had April and I had Thomas."

"Milla, I didn't mean...," Ian started then stopped. He knew it wasn't a fair thing to say. He'd meant to hurt her because she hadn't been honest with him. Then again, he hadn't been honest with her, but he had his reasons. That made it different. *Sure. Just like it did with April.*

"Yes, you did," Milla sighed. She looked away from Ian, but her voice softened. "It was twenty years ago. Thomas...well, let's just say he didn't meet with my father's approval. Thomas tried to stop him. My father killed him. My father and your precious April."

"She's not-"

"I'm sorry. That wasn't fair of me." Milla wiped her eyes. "April has never bought into my father's shit, but she goes along with him because...hell, I guess because she doesn't want to be alone. Wolves are pack animals after all." She smirked. "I read the invitation. I know what you're thinking."

"Your father is responsible for the deaths of my best friend and the first girl I ever loved. I killed because of him. I killed that hunter and some poor girl in Missouri. Now he's killed the sheriff."

"He's a monster. You don't have to tell me that."

"He gave me your book."

"He meant for you to contact me. He's a manipulator. He creates situations, isolates people, makes them think they need him."

"Why didn't you tell me?"

Milla shook her head and looked away but didn't say anything.

"What, did he think he could use you to draw me in or something?"

"Goddammit, Ian, stop! I'm not April. Stop talking like I'm some kind of fucking double agent." Milla exhaled through her nose, her jaw clenched. She shook her head again and went on. "I don't know what's going through his mind. He might think he can draw us both in. He's been calling me the last few years, sending me letters, trying to 'reconnect' or some shit. I do know this; he thinks you're chosen by God to be his protege. His heir."

"Why would he think that? Why me?" Ian felt like everything was falling apart. The last several years when he felt he was finally learning to live with himself, to embrace what he was...*I'm right back to where I started. Right back to square-fucking-one. Back to being a monster.*

"He wants you to think you need him." Milla scooted across the bed and put a hand on his shoulder. "He wants you to believe you can't survive on your own, that without him you'll become a monster. He did the same thing to me and I'm his daughter, for Christ's sake. He waits for people to either self-destruct or come crawling to him."

"I'm not going to crawl," Ian said. He tried not to sneer at her. "So where did Andersen come from?"

"It's my mother's maiden name. I started using her name when I left home. In 1982 I made it legal. I buried Carmilla Stubbs."

"What did your father think about that?"

"I don't give a shit. I didn't then and I don't now. After the death of Thomas I told him to stay the hell out of my life. I've told him to go to hell, to fuck off, you name it. He's hard to shake, though." She laughed but it was a bitter laugh. "He says he's proud of me, says I'm the family historian."

"Because of your books?"

"My studies are a coping mechanism. They give me a sense of place in the world."

"Hmmph," Ian snorted. "What do you think of my coping mechanisms?"

"Watching horror movies and listening to that fucked up alt country? Whatever it takes."

Milla scooted up close to Ian and put her arms around him.

Ian wanted to return her embrace but couldn't bring himself to do so.

"I'm sorry I didn't tell you sooner," she said. "I was frightened."

"Frightened?"

"When you came into my life I wanted to help you. I said I've known other werewolves in my life. Most of them are dead now. I wanted it to be different with you. At first it was just because you were kind and decent."

Ian sighed, relented, and put his arms around her. He loved her. He couldn't deny that.

"If I had told you I was his daughter any time before the last few months you would have run from me. You don't even know whether or not you can trust me now. Admit it."

"You could have told me," Ian said. It was weak, but it was all he had left.

"I did. Just now. Is there any good way to say it?"

Ian took a deep breath. "I need to sort all this out." He could see around the edge of the drawn curtains that daylight was fading fast. "I need to think. I need to run. Leave me alone for now."

"All right," Milla said. "But when you're out there running, watch out for people, please, and remember this; I'm not like my father and I'm not April. I love you."

Ian broke the embrace and stood up. Milla was beautiful, exciting, everything he could want. She was right. She wasn't April. He'd never loved April. Milla was Peter Stubbs' daughter, though. Whatever that meant to him he had to figure out.

"You, uh, can let yourself out when you're ready." He moved toward the door but paused before leaving the room. "I love you, too."

"Well, that could have gone better." Milla stood looking down at Kelly Sheperd's grave. It took her a while to find it, but the cemetery wasn't all that big, not compared to a place like Spring Grove. She only had to cover a few acres instead of hundreds. Milla was less than halfway through her survey of tombstones when she found what she was looking for.

"I'm sorry for what my father did to you," she said. "You were ripped off. I know that doesn't cover it but..." She shook her head. "Your cousin is here somewhere too, I understand." She wasn't here for Kelly or Ian or anyone else. She was here for herself, contemplating the awful things her father had done, wondering if she could have stopped him somewhere along the line.

For the first time in years, Milla craved a cigarette. Health concerns were meaningless to her kind. She didn't even have to work out the way she did. The cigs were pure stress relief, but she gave them up on principle. She wasn't about to give up the workouts. She ran ten miles a day, listening to music all the while and barely breaking a sweat, and she trained three days a week at a boxing gym, sticking to the machines, the weights, and the heavy bag. She had no intention of sparring with anyone. She'd done that before. What would be the point? No one there had any idea what she was. What she'd done. She didn't want to kill anyone ever again. *Well, maybe April. I might make an exception for her. Or another of my father's cronies.*

"Listen," she said to Kelly's grave. "I know I'm just talking to myself here, but it helps to pretend I'm talking to you. Do you know what it's like to have your mother lock herself in the bathroom while you lie on the floor sprouting hair? I wish I could explain what it's like, but something tells me it wouldn't be too hard for you to understand. From what Ian told me, not a lot of people took you seriously. The boys only saw you as a toy, a trophy.

"I have to say, I've seen photos of you. Ian still has a few. He didn't want to show me, but I insisted. God, you were beautiful! I'm sorry your life ended just when you were figuring out you had so much more to offer than just your looks. I know Ian saw more in you. I'm sure that in time a lot of people would have. There will always be those who don't, though. Hell. I don't have your looks by a long stretch, but there are still guys who just see me as a piece of tail. I wish you and me could show them together that there's more to us than that."

Milla shuffled her feet. She felt a little silly, but it also felt good to pour out her heart, even if it was to a seventeen year old girl who wasn't alive anymore.

"I'll tell you what; I'll do my best to show 'em. Ian talks about making his own meaning. I like that. It's a pretty good idea. And I'll love him the best I can. Right now things are a little tense between us, but we'll figure it out. Anyway, I just wanted to tell you I'm sorry. Somebody owes you an apology, someone other than Ian. It wasn't his fault. Of course, you know that or at least you would. It's my father's fault. And he's going to pay."

Chapter 20

October 30th, 2000

The snow flakes were large and glistening. They fell mere centimeters apart, a blanket of white riddled with thousands of holes. The low cloud cover was unbroken save for a gap through which Ian could see the round, white orb of the moon against a black velvet sky. The moon wore a halo of diffused light that reminded him of the ring of bone around the eye of a huge fossil reptile he'd seen in a museum. An enormous eye. He wished there was someone up there, looking down on him, looking out for him, but he couldn't believe that anymore.

The snow compacted under his boots with a muffled crunch as he walked on the frozen creek. Somewhere on the bank to his left was the cabin. Around the bend ahead was where he and Chevy used to swing out over the creek. Chevy had climbed up the big tree on the bank and shinnied out on a stout limb twenty feet above the water, a feat Ian would have never done, and secured the bailing twine rope. It was Chevy who also hung their sleeping bags in the tree half a mile downstream. This was somehow also the creek in Minnesota where he'd slaughtered most of a wolf pack. Had they always been the same?

A fallen tree protruded from the high bank to his right. The log had been taken over by the eroding bank at some point, its branches below the frozen surface of the creek, its tangled mass of roots like gnarled, arthritic fingers reaching ten feet above the ice. A great drift of snow was piled against the roots, a twin drift along the bank nearly meeting in the center of the creek. Ian had to turn sideways to walk through the narrow gap.

The wind picked up as he passed through, churning the snow into a storm of white. He saw a tangled mass in the middle of the creek ahead, but he couldn't tell what it was through the blizzard. The driving snow felt like tiny needles against his cheeks. He tried to shield his eyes with his left hand held low across his brow. As he drew closer, Ian could make out the shape. It was the wolf pack he'd slaughtered, their corpses piled like kindling one atop the other. The broken bodies were frozen, contorted into grotesques that vaguely resembled the majestic creatures they once were.

As a man, he'd never seen the black wolf's handiwork up close. He thought of Kelly and Chevy, and bent over, head between his knees, gasping for breath. He felt ill. *This is what I am capable of?*

The wind died as he knelt and the snowfall lessened to a light drifting of flakes. His breathing slowed as his nausea faded, and he half-stood with his hands still on his knees.

A stream of blood flowed from the piled carcasses in a single dark rivulet that cut a steaming path through the snow and spread across the creek. In its wake, he could see through the ice. Ian whined from high in his throat, a nasal, canine sound. Kelly stared back at him through the ice. She looked warm and soft as if it were only a pane of glass separating them. Her beauty took his breath away. She put a palm flat against the ice, her fingers spread. Ian placed a trembling hand against his side of the ice, matching hers, and she smiled. He saw the faces of others emerging from the depths behind her; first Chevy, then his father, then another man he didn't recognize but knew must be Lester Booth. There were others beyond them; two young women, Sheriff Kearsey, and countless others, the multiplied victims of Peter Stubbs and his mad vision.

He looked back at Kelly and she was no longer smiling. Her lips were moving and though he could not hear her words, Ian understood it was a warning just as he detected the familiar unwelcome scent. He spun and saw Peter Stubbs less than ten feet away. Behind Stubbs, a pack of wolves was approaching, their growls low and threatening.

Ian snarled in return and dropped to all fours as his form shifted.

Stonelick, Ohio

Ian groped for the alarm clock and pushed the round button on top to stop the shrill buzz. He rubbed his eyes with the heels of both hands. He'd promised to help Verna get some things from her barn. The last time he'd helped her with "some things" it turned into a five hour ordeal, so he decided to get an early start. He'd looked forward to getting up early again. Appreciating the morning sun was now a rare experience. He could sleep in tomorrow morning. Tomorrow night would be a long one.

He dozed until the alarm went off again. The damn snooze. Ian turned it off and sat up. Now where is that remote? After fishing around for a moment he finally found it. It had slipped off the nightstand and landed between two stacks of books on the floor. He intended on rereading them soon. *Boy's Life* by Robert McCammon topped one stack. Dan Simmons's *Summer Of Night* was atop the other.

Ian turned on the TV and found a morning news show. He got clean underwear and socks from his dresser. He'd shower after helping Verna, when he was a sweaty mess. His reflection in the mirror showed a thick, pink line across the left side of his chest, a remnant of the arrow and the subsequent surgery. He found it hard to believe that barely a month ago there was a hole there big enough to put two fingers through. His palms were coated in fine, dark hair, his teeth felt sharp, and his gums ached. The space between his eyebrows itched from stiff, new-grown hairs. *Shit. I'll need to shave.* He couldn't do anything about the scars visible under his beard. They were permanent.

"Fair skies and above average temperatures will stay with us throughout the week." The statuesque brunette on screen went on to explain this run of meteorological good fortune. "Halloween night looks very pleasant. You won't need to bundle up your little ghosts and goblins."

Ian flipped the channel to a nature program. An excitable man with shaggy blond hair crouched behind a bush, waxing poetic about the beauty of the black mamba. That was more like it. Ian didn't want to think about Halloween. If that night didn't go well it would be his last Halloween. And if it did?

Ian was tying his shoes when the doorbell rang. *At least it's the back door this time.* He was still several feet from the door when he knew who it was. The silhouette was unmistakable, as was the scent. He stopped and considered shouting for her to go away, but shook his head, shrugged, then stepped forward and opened the door.

April White stood on the other side of the screen. "Are you going?" she said.

"Why do you want to know?"

"Peter will kill you. He decided you've had enough time."

"I figured. Shouldn't you be with him?"

"I care about you, Ian. I loved you. I still do." She sniffed the air wafting out of the house.

"So you say."

April sniffed. "She's been here, hasn't she?"

"Who?"

"You know who I mean. His filthy little daughter. Carmilla."

"Yeah, I knew who you meant. I just wanted to hear you say it."

"He will kill you, Ian. He'd rather you join him, but he'll kill you if you don't."

"And you've come to warn me?"

"I'm here to ask you not to come."

"If I don't, he'll show up here sooner or later."

April looked away. He could tell she knew he was right. "What if I stand with you?"

"I don't need you to stand with me. You made your choice already."

"I told you-"

"I know. You have your own agenda. Well, I have mine."

"You can't kill him, Ian. Please listen to me."

"We'll see. Maybe I can. Maybe I can't. If I can't, I'll die trying."

"That sounds a lot like-"

"Thomas?"

"Carmilla told you about him, I suppose."

"She said you killed him. You and your master."

"It's not that simple. She makes it sound like it is, but it isn't."

"Isn't it, though? You're either with him or against him."

"I'm not with anyone!"

"You're not?"

"I could be with you. We could go away together."

"And I could be part of your agenda? Tell me, April, does your agenda involve killing innocent people?"

April brushed the white streak in her long, dark hair out of her eyes. "You have no idea what it's like out there. I've been at this for a long time. You do what's necessary."

"That's the difference between us, April. I don't think it's necessary."

"Oh? How about that bow hunter?"

Ian took a deep breath. "That was different."

"Was it? You're a werewolf, Ian. No matter how much you want to think otherwise, you will always be a danger to people. And they will always see you as a monster. Always."

"Milla doesn't."

"That's because she's one, too."

"Go away, April." Ian slammed the door in her face.

Batavia, Ohio

"Have you talked with Milla recently?" Verna Cooper mopped her brow as she spoke.

"We talked a couple of days ago."

"Did you two have a fight?"

"Not a fight. We just needed to sort some stuff out. I'll see her later this week." *If I'm still alive.*

It was almost noon. The day was getting warm. Ian's t-shirt was sticking to his back. What many considered pleasant, he considered hot.

Verna's barn was the size of a two-car garage, full of miscellaneous items belonging to the church. Getting a few things out involved reorganizing and condensing an array of seasonal items. Verna told him the staff at the Lighthouse had discussed building onto the church or getting their own shed for storage, but nothing had come of it yet. Until then, she was happy to allow them to use her little barn.

"What do you want to do with the Harvest Festival stuff?" Ian said. He wiped the sweat from his brow. He'd shaved between his eyes, but with the full moon two days away, the stubble there was coarse and stiff. He wore work gloves so he didn't worry about the hair on his hands.

"Oh, that stuff?" Verna said over her shoulder. "Put it over there." She indicated a spot on the lawn that wasn't occupied by stacks of boxes.

"What about this?" Ian nodded at the five foot high wooden cross leaning against the barn door.

"We're giving it to a church up in Xenia that was damaged a few weeks ago by all that wind. Some folks up there insist it was another tornado. It sent a tree through their roof and collapsed a wall. Snapped their cross in two. Pastor James figured it would lift their spirits."

Ian took a drink of the lemonade Verna had brought out earlier. He lowered the glass but couldn't take his eyes off the cross.

"That's the cross that hung over the baptistry at the Lighthouse before they remodeled, isn't it?"

"Huh?" Verna walked over to Ian. "You know, I believe it is."

"I got baptized under that cross. It looked bigger up on the wall."

"Honey, why don't you come back? Just for a visit."

Ian drained the glass. "I don't think I'd feel at home there anymore."

Verna shook her head. "There are still lots of people there who care for you."

"Maybe, but it's mostly because of Mom."

"God rest her soul. She used to tell you God had a special plan for your life. Remember?"

"Yeah." Between his memories and Verna's constant reminders, he couldn't forget it if he'd wanted. "I do believe there's something I can do and I'm going to do it. I'm going to try, at least."

"Care to tell me about it?"

"I can't. It's complicated." *Yes, Verna, it's complicated. You see, I am going to kill an evil man who thinks he's a man of god. Oh, and he's a werewolf. Did I mention that I'm one too?*

"Does this have anything to do with you and Milla?"

Ian looked at Verna and thought for a moment before going on. "Did I tell you I love her?"

"She loves you. I'm sure of it." She put her arms around Ian and hugged him. "So do I."

"I love you, too. Now what do you want me to do with that cross?"

Verna stepped back and put her hands on her hips. "Hmmm. Just put it right inside the door. They're picking it up next week."

Ian nodded and picked up the rough, wooden cross. It was lighter than he expected. He took it inside the barn and leaned it against the wall.

"You hungry?" Verna called from outside.

"Am I hungry? What do you think?"

"Silly question. Let's go inside. I'll rustle up some lunch."

Ian left the cross there and followed Verna into her house.

Chapter 21

Halloween 2000

Duck Creek, Indiana

Ian sat on a bench throwing handfuls of birdseed to the resident mallards. Every few minutes, one of the braver birds waddled closer, quacked for another handful, then scrambled back to the edge of the canal. None of the birds appeared to sense anything unusual about him. No animals ever did. Ian added that to the list of fictions movies advanced about his kind.

His kind. Ian was comfortable with that now. He was a werewolf, but whether or not he would be a monster was up to him. Stubbs might wear a human disguise most of the time, but he was still a monster. Mom might have been wrong about God having a plan for my life, Ian thought, but she was right about what makes a person good or bad.

The last time he was in Duck Creek, he sat waiting on the same bench with his father. His mother was never in a hurry to leave, even after riding the canal boat and the train, and visiting every shop in town. Rose Murphy insisted they make their yearly visit despite her diagnosis, her first round of chemotherapy just a week away. Her energy level increased with each of the fifty miles they traveled. By the time they arrived, she was glowing and full of life. It was their last outing as a family.

The center of town was bisected by what remained of the Duck Creek Canal, a once-busy waterway rendered obsolete by the railroads. The highways rendered the railroads obsolete. After Duck Creek was designated a state historical site in 1965 the horse-drawn boats returned, but instead of pulling loads of goods to towns along the way, they pulled tourists along two miles of restored canal. Merchants and artisans followed, opening various 'olde time' stores. By 1980, over thirty shops, inns, and restaurants lined the banks. A stretch of the existing railroad was put to use as well, the steam powered train taking people on an eighteen mile round trip out of town and back.

From where he sat, Ian had a view of the entire business district. Merchants were readying for the influx of trick or treaters expected to descend upon the town that evening. Halloween decorations were everywhere. Ghosts, goblins, and witches loomed over doorways and jutted around corners. Some shop owners had already taken up positions outside their doors, buckets of treats on the sidewalk next to their lawn chairs. The air was warm. The sun wouldn't set for another two hours. It was shaping up to be a pleasant evening.

Across the narrow strip of water, the Canal Express awaited its passengers. The vintage locomotive was set to make one more trip. Soon the train would be filled with costumed men, women, and children who paid twelve dollars apiece to take part in the annual "Halloween On The Rails," a sort of rolling haunted house for all ages.

A hundred yards away, a slender man in a worn, leather jacket and jeans was walking toward the canal boat, leading a large, muscular horse along the towpath. The boat was still empty save for a lone figure with his back to Ian. He was sitting on the last bench on the left, hunched over a guitar, plucking each string, tuning, then plucking again.

Ian reached into the pocket of his denim jacket and pulled out the dark orange envelope Stubbs had given him. He ran his fingers over the embossed image of a church steeple and removed the letter inside. The paper was a brighter orange with 'Stubbs Ministries' across the top. Below the black line separating the letterhead from the body of the letter was a handwritten message;

The harvest is plentiful but the workers are few. Ask The Lord of the harvest, therefore, to send out workers into His harvest field.

Matthew 9:37-38

The time is upon us, Ian. These truly are the last days and time is short as men measure time. Will we spurn God's gift and turn from His face?

The Lord is patient, but he will not tarry forever. I fear for your remaining loved ones if you do not heed His call. That may sound harsh, but you should know by now that you are more dangerous than you once believed.

Join us, Ian. There is safety with us. There is community, fellowship, and love. Our kind were not meant to live alone.

On October 31ˢᵗ I will be presiding over a special service in Duck Creek, Indiana as the culmination of a week of services hosted by the Duck Creek Full Gospel Fellowship. It seems appropriate that we worship The Lord on the devil's night. We will take the boat up the canal and back, praise God, and thank Him for his goodness. There will be others of our kind in attendance. I believe you have misjudged April White, by the way. Her care for you is sincere and it's not too late to reconcile with her.

After the service, those of us with our special gift will meet and serve The Lord as only we can. Please join us at 6PM that night. It is time to choose, Ian. Together, we can explore your future in The Lord.

In His Name,

Peter Stubbs

Ian folded the letter and tucked it back into his pocket. He would throw it away later. *Yeah, I'm here, Peter. I'm here and I'm going to tear your goddamn throat-*

"Quack!"

Less than two feet away a bold little mallard stood rocking from foot to foot, impatient for another handful. "You again," Ian said. He reached into the bag beside him and took out another handful of birdseed. "Why aren't you migrating south or something?" He tossed the seed onto the ground and the duck gobbled it up in seconds.

"Why should he?" Milla stood at the end of the bench. "He's got everything he wants here."

"How did you...?" Ian said. "I didn't hear you. Or smell you."

"The breeze is going this way." She hitched her thumb over her shoulder. "And I can be quiet." She sat on the bench beside him. "You didn't think I'd let you do this alone, did you?"

"Do what?"

"Where's your car?"

"I took a cab. You wouldn't believe the fair."

"So we're both on foot, then. Dammit, Ian, I thought you'd drive."

Ian smiled a little, but the smile turned down in an instant. "I left my car at home in case I die tonight. If I do, they'll find my body and-"

"You don't have to worry. No Hollywood lap dissolve. If we die as a wolf, we stay a wolf."

"Comforting." Ian took her hand. "I didn't want you here. You have a life."

"I have a career. You're my life."

The smile returned to Ian's face. "You're mine. You gave me hope that I could live with this."

"I called you yesterday. Texted you. You ignored me."

"I was afraid you'd try to talk me out of this."

"Ian, I know how my father operates. The others here tonight will follow his lead all the way."

"Even April?"

"Especially April. She's ruthless, Ian. She's out for herself."

"She came to my house."

"When?"

"Yesterday. She wanted me to go away with her."

"Oh."

"I told her to fuck off."

"Even if you had gone with her, Peter would come after you both. She knows that. She just doesn't want to face him alone."

"She was wasting her time. I would never go away with her. With you, but not with her."

Milla kissed him on the cheek.

"What about you?" he said. "Would you be here if it wasn't for me?"

"I'm here tonight because I love you. Like I said, the others will follow his lead."

"I'm not going to wait for him to do any leading. I'll kill him in front of a boatload of people if I have to. He has to be stopped. I don't care who's with him."

"You're underestimating him. The congregation on the boat will be in danger, too. They're just human shields to him. He won't hesitate, but you're not like him. You aren't a killer."

"Tell that to Lester Booth."

"That was different. That was self-defense. You've read enough to know that wolves rarely attack people. They aren't monsters. Peter is a monster. He kills without remorse and justifies it after the fact. He tells himself it was the will of god. You know better and I do, too, but that gives him an edge. Can you kill as easily as he does? Can you commit premeditated murder?"

The clock in the tower chimed, marking the bottom of the hour. Ian looked over the town and saw some early arriving trick or treaters milling about, straightening their masks, fidgeting with their costumes. Daylight was fading, the sun low above the treetops. It was still warm, but Ian felt a chill run through him, goosebumps rising on his skin.

"Maybe you're underestimating me, Milla. Because of him, three people I loved are dead. And Sheriff Kearsey. I was afraid of what he had figured out, but the sheriff was a good man. He was my father's friend and Peter tore him apart. Two innocent girls in Missouri are dead. Peter manipulated me into killing one of them. Then there's Lester Booth. I have blood on my hands that wouldn't be there if it wasn't for your father. I hate him. Sometimes I hate myself, too, but it's because of him."

"Ian, there's no-"

"Listen to me! I told you about my mother, how she insisted I was chosen for some great task. I wasn't. There is no such thing as a chosen one. Mom was wrong. Dad said we make our own destiny, our own meaning. I think he was right. I have a purpose and I chose it myself. I live to kill your father."

"And after that?" Milla said.

"I'll worry about after when the time comes. If it comes."

Milla looked down and swallowed hard. When she looked back up, her face was so full of pain and dread that for a moment Ian feared she was going to leave him there. Instead, she gritted her teeth, nodded, and breathed out through her nose, her mouth a hard, firm line. "I'm not going to let this happen again," she said. "I'm not going to let him do to you what he did to Thomas."

"Can you stand against him? I wouldn't blame you if you couldn't. He is your father, after all."

Milla smirked. "You and I have different images of what a father is. To you, a father is someone who tossed ball with you and tucked you in at night. To me, a father is someone who waved the Bible around and talked about the love of god, but tore out people's throats when he felt 'led' to do so. He taught me how to kill and get away with it. I've got blood on my hands too, a lot of it." She shook her head. "I don't know if we'll live through this night, but if you die, I'll die with you."

Ian put his arms around her and held her close. He buried his face in her hair and breathed deeply of her scent. He was encouraged by her presence, by her touch, but he was also troubled. She was right. He had never deliberately set out to kill someone. She told him he wasn't a killer, that he wasn't a monster, and he wanted to believe it. Her father insisted he was in danger of becoming exactly that. If he succeeded in killing Peter Stubbs, who would be right?

The boat was beginning to fill. Stubbs was there now, chatting with the man with the guitar, whom Milla identified as Bert Callet.

"He's a Wisconsin dairy farmer," said Milla. "He's bought into the whole 'wolves of god' thing. He looks like some 'aw shucks' country boy, but don't let that fool you."

"What about him?" Ian indicated a broad-backed man with a buzz cut. His muscular physique strained at the seams of his suit.

"Ted Bell. He used to be April White's boy toy. She didn't tell you about him?"

"No."

"She took up with him after Thomas rejected her."

"Your father let them carry on?"

"I doubt he liked it, but they're useful. He's already here so it doesn't seem that she went back to Ted after you, unless they're trying to be discrete."

"Speak of the devil," Ian said. April White arrived. In her black dress and high heels, she was an impressive sight. Ian noticed men stealing glances at her. Two men even stared open-mouthed. She locked eyes with Ian for a few seconds, but her expression gave away nothing, then she glanced at Milla and sneered.

"You know a lot about his little pack," Ian said.

"There were more at one time. Counting myself and Thomas, there were ten. Peter was aiming for thirteen." Milla shook her head. "Twelve disciples with Peter at the center, of course, but it was already falling apart. I had one foot out the door. When they killed Thomas it was the final straw for me. That was a long time ago. Most people would think it was, anyway. It's been twenty years, but it still feels like yesterday."

"So why hasn't he..." Ian wasn't quite sure how to put the question.

"Why hasn't he killed me yet? I suppose being his daughter counts for something. He wouldn't cut me any slack if I openly opposed him, though. He'd have one of his disciples do the deed, but he would approve."

"April?"

"She would love to get the chance. She's a jealous bitch."

"Could you take her?"

"I don't know. I don't look forward to trying, but I don't think I'll have any choice tonight."

"It's not too late," Ian said. "You could leave."

"No. My place is with you."

They stood and walked hand in hand toward the boat. A pair of children maybe four or five years old each tottered in their direction on the sidewalk, an already-flustered adult close behind. One of the children wore a Darth Vader mask and a black robe. The other wore a Frankenstein costume. As they passed, Vader raised a plastic light saber. The monster raised one hand like a claw, and growled. The lady behind them smiled and sighed.

"I feel like I'm walking into a Ray Bradbury story," Milla said.

Ian coudn't help himself. " 'By the pricking of my thumbs, something wicked this way comes,' " he said.

"Shakespeare," said Milla. "and Bradbury too. When I was a kid that story scared the shit out of me."

"Especially since your father is Mister Dark, huh?"

"Knock it off."

"Sorry. Gallows humor."

"Appropriate," she said. "You know, we really could die tonight."

"I know, but I don't plan on it."

"What exactly is your plan?" Milla stopped walking. They stood under a tree a short walk from the boat, talking in hushed tones. "You said you would kill Peter but..."

"I will when I get close enough," Ian snarled.

Milla slumped against the tree, her free hand on her forehead. "It won't be that easy. What about all the other people on the boat? That's a local congregation. Do you really want them drawn into this?"

"I don't care. I already told you, I'll kill him front of everyone if I have to."

"Don't be stupid, Ian!" Milla let go of his hand and stepped away from the tree. "If we start something on that boat people could get killed. Our first order of business will be to get them away from those people. Then we have to take care of the others, but it won't be easy. They'll protect Peter. You saw the look April gave me. She intends to kill me tonight."

"I won't let that happen."

"You'll have other things to worry about."

Ian rocked back on his heels and looked up through the branches of the tree. The moon was on the rise. Stubbs' timing was impeccable. One night before the full moon the urge to change was strong. "If we wait, we lose the element of surprise."

"There is no surprise. He knows what you're here for. We go to the service. We get through it. The boat goes up the canal then back. Everyone goes home but the six of us."

"We're outnumbered."

"The numbers we can handle, at least Bert and Ted. Don't underestimate me, Ian. They always have. This will come down to me and April, and you and Peter. After that, there are no guarantees. We live or we die. Do you understand?"

Ian sighed, kissed the top of Milla's head, and held her close.

"Well, praise God!"

Peter Stubbs crossed the narrow street to greet Ian and Milla. On the way, he patted a kindergarten Spiderman on the head and waited for a little vampire and her father to pass. "It's good to see you both. I was afraid you wouldn't be coming, Ian. And my darling Carmilla, it does my heart good to see you here." He put both hands on her shoulders.

There was a genuine, fatherly affection in his touch, Ian noted. The thought made him shiver. Milla didn't flinch but she did squeeze Ian's hand harder.

"You know, Ian, she's the very image of her mother. So beautiful it takes your breath away. But what father doesn't feel that way about his daughter?" Stubbs leaned in close to Ian. "I have always been very protective of her," he whispered. "I haven't always thought highly of the men she kept company with, but you I wholeheartedly approve of." He put a hand on Ian's shoulder. "I am certain I can trust you with her."

Ian wasn't quite sure how to respond. He glanced at Milla, but her face was unreadable. "I love her, Peter," he said.

"I believe you do." Stubbs nodded, his eyes on his daughter now. "I trust the feeling is mutual?"

"Yes, Peter," she said. "It is."

"Well, I am glad you decided to join us. Shall we?"

Ian knew that Peter's use of the word 'join' was deliberate. The message was clear; they were in or they were out.

After waiting for a dozen trick or treaters to pass on their way to the shops, Ian and Milla crossed the sidewalk and stepped on board. Stubbs followed close behind.

The crowd on the boat ranged in age from the twenties to more than seventy. There were no teenagers or younger children with the exception of half a dozen babies and toddlers. Ian guessed that the older children were at some alternative-to-Halloween party like the ones he attended in his youth at The Lighthouse. Otherwise, it was a cross-section of conservative middle America. Most of the older people were wearing well-kept but old fashioned suits or dresses, their habit of wearing their Sunday best still holding sway despite the unconventional setting. The younger adults favored jeans and light sweaters. Altogether, there were about fifty people on the boat.

"I believe there are still a few seats near the front," Stubbs said from behind them.

Ian held onto Milla's hand up the narrow center aisle until they reached the second row and sat on the bench next to a small, bespectacled lady. She smiled at them and said hello, an enormous black Bible in her lap. Milla was right, he thought. He couldn't make a move on the boat. There were too many people who could get hurt.

Bert Callet stood in the front and smiled. "Good evenin'," he drawled. From this close, Ian could see that Callet was smaller than he had thought, perhaps six feet tall but thin, and narrow in the shoulders. The man's skin was tanned like leather, rough from exposure to the elements. Ian knew that look well. His father had had the same look and Leon Patella had it in the extreme. Bert Callet looked no older than either of them. Then again, he was a werewolf. He might be a hundred for all Ian knew.

"Greetings, everyone," Stubbs said when he reached the front of the boat. His resonant voice carried easily in the boat. He removed his jacket and laid it over a folding chair behind him. His tie remained in place and his white hair was as magnificent as ever. "It's good to be here tonight. I want to thank you all for joining us. It has been a rare pleasure to be with you this week." He turned to a paunchy, dark-haired man seated behind him. "Thank you, Pastor Rodanthe for inviting me. Would you like to lead us in prayer?"

The chubby man rose from his chair and stepped to the wooden podium. This Rodanthe was probably a decent man unaware of the evil next to him. Ian hoped they were well clear of the pastor and his congregation before things went the way they must.

"...We ask this in the name of Your one and only Son, our risen savior, The Lord Jesus Christ." the pastor said, concluding his opening prayer. "Amen."

"Thank you, Tony." Stubbs shook the pastor's hand then nodded to the man on shore with the massive horse. The man patted the horse on the neck and began to walk. The horse followed. A few seconds later the boat shuddered and started moving.

In his youth, Ian loved looking over the side of the boat. There was something about the water running past, the big horses and the grassy shore a few feet away, that fascinated him. The nostalgia for an innocent time before werewolves and monster evangelists almost brought tears to his eyes. It was followed close by anger. He shouldn't have to do this. Milla seemed to sense his state of mind. She took his hand in one of hers and rubbed his arm with the other.

When he was a child, the boat only ran in the daylight. For this special evening run it had been outfitted with battery operated lights of the sort Ian and Chevy had used when camping. The lights hung from each corner, front and back. The man leading the horse carried a larger lantern in his free hand but he hadn't turned it on yet. Apparently, it was still light enough to negotiate the worn path.

"Brothers and sisters," Stubbs began, "as we look around us tonight we are confronted with the symbols of darkness. Goblins, ghosts, devils. October 31st is for many the devil's night. It is a sad state of affairs that our modern American culture embraces this darkness more each year, but does not The Word of God tell us that it will be so in the last days?"

Several people in the congregation muttered amen.

"But we do not serve the lord of this world. Look at these lights, friends. They are here so we can see each other, but they are also reminders of the task before each and every one of us, to be lights in the darkness."

"Amen!" There was more gusto in the responses this time.

"We serve the Creator of Heaven and earth, the Alpha and Omega. Our task is to light the way until He sweeps away the darkness and establishes his Kingdom for all time. Can I get another amen?"

The little lady seated next to Ian and Milla nodded and said "Yes, Lord" in a small voice. She was drowned out by the louder shouts from the crowd around them.

"Turn with me to the Gospel of Matthew, Chapter seven, verses sixteen through twenty."

To Ian's surprise, Milla produced a small New Testament from the pocket of her jacket. The leather-bound book was dog-eared and worn. It took her only seconds to reach the scripture her father indicated. Ian looked at her and she smiled and shrugged. The little lady on the other side of her was waiting with her Bible open in her lap to the appropriate page.

" 'Ye shall know them by their fruits," Stubbs said. Just as at the fateful tent revival years before, he recited from memory. " 'Do men gather groups of thorns or figs of thistles? Even so every good tree bringeth forth fruit; but a corrupt tree bringeth forth evil fruit. A good tree cannot bring forth evil fruit, neither can a corrupt tree bring forth good fruit. Every tree that bringeth not forth good fruit is hewn down and cast into the fire. Wherefore by their fruits ye shall know them.'

"Bless The Lord and His Word."

Stubbs stepped aside, his head almost touching the roof of the boat. Bert Callet took his place front and center, his lacquered acoustic guitar gleaming. "Let's worship, shall we?" he said.

As the congregation stood, Ian looked at Milla and shrugged. They stood a moment later, Ian feeling conspicuous. He towered over those near him. It took him a few seconds to place the song Bert Callett was playing. Halfway through the first verse, Ian recognized "In The Garden." Ian recalled most of the lyrics-something about dew on the roses and God walking and talking-but he couldn't bring himself to sing. He liked the melody, though, so he hummed along. From several rows behind he heard one of the few children in attendance say something about 'that big man's hair.' Ian turned enough to make eye contact with the little boy. The child's eyes went wide, surprised that the 'big man' could hear him over the music. Ian smiled at the boy and sighed. *I wish you weren't here, little guy.*

Bert Callett finished "In the Garden" and upped the tempo with "I've Found A Better Way." The congregation clapped and sang louder. The small lady next to Milla brought her hands together with gusto. Outside the boat, the enormous horse clopped along the path, it's hooves striking the ground in counterpoint to the 4/4 beat of the music.

They were outside the town now, approaching a covered wooden bridge. A man on the outside of the boat leaned into view. The covered bridge was one of the last wooden aqueducts in existence. The man riding outside the boat would detach the stout rope and toss it to the man on shore. The boat's forward momentum would carry it over the Whitewater River where it crossed beneath the canal. Once through the aqueduct, the rope would be passed back to the man on the boat, who would reattach the rope. On the way back, the process would be repeated.

The sky was darkening as they neared the aqueduct, a thin band of gold lining the treetops to the west the last vestige of daylight. The moon was brighter against the deep purple sky. Ian could feel it calling to him, his arm hairs standing on end, his muscles tingling. Milla squeezed his hand. She felt it, too. *Don't underestimate me, Ian.* Despite all he'd been through, her words from earlier chilled him.

They were entering the aqueduct when Ian looked to the front of the boat again. Stubbs was singing but staring back at him. There was no malice in his gaze, but something passed between them. Understanding. Awareness. Stubbs pursed his lips and sighed, the corners of his mouth turning down. He shook his head in what Ian took to be genuine sorrow, then looked away.

As the boat glided under the aqueduct's wooden roof, the lanterns cast everything in a golden glow. The singing and clapping echoed inside, bouncing off the slatted walls on each side. Small shapes fluttered under the peaked roof then darted into the night sky in a nervous rush of membranous wings. Milla craned her neck to watch the fleeing creatures and squeezed Ian's hand even tighter. Her palm was sweaty in his grip.

They emerged from the aqueduct as the song ended. There was loud, fervent praise all around Ian. It seemed darker now, the moon brighter. Ian released Milla's hand to put his arm around her shoulders. She looked up at him and her eyebrows, always strong and full, now looked even heavier, and her lips were a straight line. She might be nervous, but she was determined.

Bert Callet led the congregation into the next song, "Just A Closer Walk With Thee." Hands were raised in worship, eyes lifted heavenward or closed to gaze with some inner spiritual eye to realms beyond the pale. Ian knew the experience well, and he regretted that it was poisoned by the monster leading the service. The people around him knew nothing of the man's true nature. They sang with honest, open hearts. It was a regular Old Time Gospel Hour. With werewolves. He recalled Stubbs' warning from the Bible on that awful night in the tent. *Grievous wolves, indeed.*

"Glory to God," Stubbs declared as Bert Callet strummed the final chords of the song. The majority of the crowd were lost in worship, some swaying with their hands upraised, others standing with the heads down, lips moving in quiet supplication. Several were speaking in tongues, their bodies twitching with spiritual electricity. The diminutive lady next to Milla clutched a handkerchief to her chest, a radiant smile on her wrinkled face.

The boat slowed. The man leading the horse on the bank unhitched the animal and led it away from the canal toward a small barn. The barnyard was lit by a bright light mounted under the eaves near the peak. Inside the barn, two more horses of similar mass munched from troughs while a pair of women in denim and sweatshirts stroked their sides with large, round brushes.

It was full dark now, the sky beyond the lights an inky blue-black. The night had turned cool, the breeze spinning fallen leaves across the grass, signaling the change of seasons. The moon was a glowing white circle in the sky, only a little lopsided, all but the brightest celestial objects swamped by its brilliance.

The boat came to a gentle stop against the end of the canal.

"Brothers, sisters," Stubbs rumbled in his deep baritone. "Let us remember The Lord tonight. Let us honor Him with Holy Communion."

"Great," Ian mumbled under his breath. Milla patted his arm and gave his hand a quick squeeze.

" 'Jesus took bread, gave thanks and broke it, and gave it to his disciples, saying 'take it; this is my body.' Then he took the cup, gave thanks and offered it to them, and they all drank from it. 'This is my blood of the covenant, which is poured out for many,' he said to them."

Bert Callet handed Stubbs a large metal goblet and a round loaf of bread, then picked his guitar up again and began to pick at the strings.

"I can't do this," Ian whispered to Milla.

"You have to."

"Milla, this is...obscene," Ian hissed. He glanced at the woman on Milla's right. She was still glowing with contentment, her eyes shut. If she heard Ian she showed no sign. The people in front and behind them likewise appeared too deeply into the worship to have heard.

"The aisle is narrow," Stubbs said, "so instead of having you form a line to come forward, I will bring the sacraments to each of you starting in the back."

Stubbs walked down the center of the boat, his head down in apparent prayer. Ian thought Stubbs might pause or at least glance at him, but the preacher did neither. As he passed, Ian felt none of the power Stubbs had exuded before. He wondered if he had grown immune. Did the power reside in his own attitude, in his reaction to the man? Tonight Stubbs appeared to be no more than an ordinary man. He didn't even seem as large as before. Ian watched him all the way to the back of the boat and all he saw was a tall, country preacher tending to a flock.

When Ian turned back he saw April White staring at him. She was as striking as ever, but her expression was hard. The shock of white in her long black hair shone like lightening.

Milla pressed closer and held his arm. "No matter what happened between you two, don't turn your back on her tonight. She wants to kill me, but don't put anything past her."

Ian put his arm around Milla and kissed her forehead. April smirked and looked away.

On shore, a slender young man was hitching a fresh horse to the boat for the return trip. A lit camp lantern sat on the ground near his feet, illuminating his features from below. Ian guessed he was no more than twenty. His face was smooth, unlined, but his eyebrows were thick and his beard heavy.

A knot took hold in Ian's gut. He had to admit that he wasn't so sure of his chances, even with Milla at his side. He felt a twinge of shame. He didn't want to die. He wanted to run, to leave this awful task to someone else. But who? There was no one else. If he turned from his dreadful appointment, Stubbs would go on killing and the blood of future victims would be on his own hands. Besides, the implications of Stubbs' letter were clear. The time to choose had come.

The boat began to move again, a massive black and white horse pulling it back toward town. The lantern in the young man's hand bobbed as he walked beside the animal. The trees lining the side of the bank opposite the tow path were alive with the chirps, clicks, and buzz of insects. Somewhere far in the distance, one owl hooted and another answered. Farther away still, a dog barked.

"God bless you, brother and sister."

Stubbs was behind them now. Ian could smell the liquid in the goblet. It was non-alcoholic, perhaps sparkling grape juice, but certainly not wine.

"Join us, Ian," Stubbs moved forward and said when the couple behind was finished. "And you, as well, my daughter. Join us in commemorating the covenant Christ has made with His people."

Ian looked at the torn loaf in Stubbs' left hand and the goblet in his right. The bread was fresh and soft, like the loaves Verna brought from her bakery twice a week. The juice in the goblet was sweet and dark. The communion elements were fine in themselves, but he found their association with the man foul. He looked at Milla again and she shook her head and flashed a warning with her eyes.

Gritting his teeth and gulping hard, Ian raised his hand to tear off some of the bread but stopped short. His heart was pounding, sweat pasting his shirt to his back despite the cool night air. He reached again for the bread, trying to will himself to go through with the vile pantomime.

" 'A man ought to examine himself before he eats of the bread and drinks of the cup,' " Stubbs said. " 'Whoever eats the bread or drinks the cup of The Lord in an unworthy manner will be guilty of sinning against the body and blood of The Lord.' Are you worthy, Ian?"

Ian's hand stopped short again. "Are you?" he said through clenched teeth.

"Ian, no," Milla pleaded.

Ian heard Milla but couldn't contain himself any longer. He dashed the cup and the bread from Stubbs' hand with a sweep of his arm. The grape juice sprayed across the aisle, spattering half a dozen people with fat, purple-red splotches of color. One man who had been standing with his eyes closed in prayer was hit full in the face by the goblet and staggered backward. The loaf of bread tumbled over the side of the boat, hitting the water with a muted plunk. There were gasps and exclamations from around Ian and a ripple of murmurs spread to the back of the boat.

"Young man, what has gotten into you?" Pastor Rodanthe said, his face flushing red.

"Are *you* worthy, Peter!" Ian shouted.

Bert Callet stopped playing the guitar. Ted Bell stepped around April White with his hands clenched into fists. April stayed where she was and smirked.

"Ian! Please." Milla tugged at his arm and reached up to his face but he pulled away from her.

"I won't," Ian said to Peter then he turned to look over the crowd. "You don't know what he is!" he yelled. "You have no idea what he's done! He's no man of God! He's a monster!"

Ian felt a hand on his elbow, a small hand with a gentle touch. He looked down and saw the little lady reaching around Milla. Her face shown with compassion. The pastor's hand gripped his shoulder. "Let us pray for you, son," he said. "Let the Lord help you."

"Ian, look at me. Me!" Milla pulled him to her by the collar of his shirt. "Don't let him do this to you," she whispered.

"Praise God, brothers and sisters," Stubbs boomed over the murmuring congregation. Behind him, the man who was struck by the goblet sat on the bench, holding a handkerchief to his bleeding nose while he was tended to by several others. "Let us pray for our troubled brother." Stubbs put his hand on Ian's other shoulder and squeezed. "Let us join together to cover him with the love of Christ."

"No!" Ian screamed. "What he's offering isn't love!" He looked at the people closing around him. Some where confused, a few angry, but most were as compassionate as the little lady. "You don't understand!" Ian was near tears now, all of his anger, frustration, and sorrow boiling together. It was too much to handle. Stubbs stood an arm's length away, with his hand still on Ian's shoulder.

Milla felt Ian's muscles bunch in her grip, intuited his intention from the twist of his hips. She saw for a second the fingernails of his right hand begin to lengthen just before he struck at her father.

Stubbs released Ian's shoulder and caught his right hand by the wrist, stopping it in mid strike. With his free hand he pushed against Ian's forehead and drove him to his knees.

At Stubbs' touch, the same strange power Ian felt on that first night years before traced a lightning path through his veins to his outermost extremities then rebounded back through him to Stubbs' hand. Ian convulsed under the assault and nearly lost consciousness. He saw the wheel, felt the ropes dig into his wrists and ankles, and experienced the rending of his flesh with the white-hot tongs. The smell of his own burning flesh filled his nostrils and he screamed.

"Peter!" Milla yelled. "Don't do this to him!"

The vision passed. More hands reached for Ian. The people around him were praying, invoking Jesus' name, weeping for his deliverance. He felt the familiar cold ripple that presaged transformation. The prayers turned to gasps then to cries of alarm as he felt himself begin to change.

"Good Lord!"

"Dear Jesus!"

Ian twisted and writhed, trembling from head to toe as his joints popped and his body reoriented itself. He fought against the transformation, but he was losing and he knew it. It had gone too far. Dark hair burst through his skin as Stubbs bore down even harder. Ian's face burned as it lengthened and his teeth throbbed in their sockets. It wasn't supposed to happen like this, Ian thought, but he was powerless to stop it.

"It's a demon," one of the men around him shouted and pulled back.

"Peter, how could you?" Milla yelled.

"He's made his choice, daughter," Stubbs said. "Have you as well?"

The circle around Ian had broken apart. All but Pastor Rodanthe remained with his hand on his shoulder. The chubby man was sweating profusely, dark, wet circles under each arm. His eyes bulged in their sockets, his face red with excitement, and spittle flew from his mouth as he beseeched God. Everyone else had moved away, unsure of what to do. The little lady next to Milla stepped back against the side of the boat, her Bible clutched to her chest like a shield, but she still had one hand extended toward Ian, and she was praying out loud.

On the shore, the lanky young man stopped the horse and stood transfixed by the commotion on the boat. The horse snorted and stamped its hooves in place, unsettled. The boat drifted forward until the line tethering it to the horse grew taught and it stopped with a jerk, the corner of the vessel bumping against the side of the canal.

"In Jesus' name, you foul demon," the pastor cried, "release your grip on this young man! By the power of the risen savior, I command-"

Ian arched his back and howled. Stubbs still held him in place, but the transformation was half-complete, resistance useless now.

The congregation retreated to the back of the boat, condensing into a tight knot of terrified souls. Several were crying and looking for a way off the boat. One father took his toddler in his arms and jumped. They just made the bank, landing with heavy thud. The man's wife followed but didn't clear the water, landing in the canal like a cannonball. She went under for a few seconds then resurfaced, coughing and sputtering. The water was only up to her chin and she made the shore in three slippery, labored steps. As her husband helped her from the water, others followed. A young couple jumped hand in hand and tumbled down the bank in a tangle of limbs, splashing into the canal. A woman in a long, heavy dress clutched her baby to her chest and leaped. She hit the water with a sharp smack, lost her footing, and slipped under the churning brown water. A pair of men jumped in after her and emerged with the flailing pair, the baby sputtering and crying but otherwise unharmed.

Milla looked past her father to Bert Callet. The man had set his guitar down and his eyes were closed. He appeared to be praying, but coarse brown hair was spreading across the backs of his hands. Beyond him, April White slipped off her shoes and her light jacket, revealing her lean, powerful shoulders and arms. She caught Milla's eye and winked. Ted Bell calmly took off his ill-fitting suit jacket and sat down to unlace his shoes. This is getting bad, Milla thought, very bad.

"Choose this day whom you will serve," Stubbs roared as he bore down on Ian with both hands.

Ian tore at his clothes, reducing them to tattered shreds.

Pastor Rodanthe pulled back, stumbling to remain on his feet. "Lord Jesus!" he gasped.

The little lady feinted, slumped on the bench behind her, and rolled onto the floor.

Milla drove into her father, ramming him in the chest with her shoulder, catching him off guard. He fell backward, arms flailing for balance, one of his hands striking the lamp suspended from the ceiling. Both Stubbs and the lamp crashed to the floor and the front of the boat was thrown into half shadow. A second later, Milla sprang over her prone father and took Bert Callet to the floor. Her canines elongated as they fell and she clamped her jaws on his throat. He clawed at Milla, but it was too late. She bit through his carotid artery and her face was drenched by his fountaining blood. She wiped the hot crimson from her eyes and turned just as Ian leaped over the side of the boat, a partly human, near-wolf trailing tattered clothes. He hit the bank running and darted for the trees beyond the footpath.

The rear of the boat was in chaos now, more people jumping for the shore. Some made the leap, but others did not, splashing into the canal like stones. Some went under and surfaced sputtering and gasping, only making the shore with difficulty. The elderly were not up to the task. Three men took it upon themselves to help the seniors off the boat. Still, at least half of the congregation remained on board, a frightened, confused mass of people pressing together in the rear. Their view blocked by the struggling figures of April, Milla, and Ted, they were unaware that the man who lead them in worship was now bleeding out in the shadows at the front of the boat.

Stubbs had regained his feet and was helping Pastor Rodanthe with the little lady on the floor. She was awake again but glassy-eyed and disoriented.

"What's happening?" the pastor said.

"That troubled young man.," Stubbs said. "He is in the grip of powerful demonic forces."

Behind them, Ted and April pulled at Milla, attempting to drag her off of Bert Callett. She sank her teeth into Ted Bell's arm, his pained gasp cut off as she reached between his legs and squeezed. He released Milla and doubled over. She raked a clawed hand across April's cheek and leaped onto the boat's railing, then scrambled across the roof and jumped onto shore. The big horse bucked and reared as she ran past, jerking the man who still held the lead off his feet. The animal bolted, but it only managed a few feet before the slack ran out. The boat jerked and ground into the side of the canal, then the lead tore free and the horse took off along the tow path toward town.

"Tony" Stubbs said to the pastor. He gripped the man's cheeks in both hands to redirect his attention. "You must lead the congregation back to town. Help those who are still on the boat to shore, than follow the path."

"But your friend Bert?"

"April and Ted are with him. We are dealing with deadly spiritual forces here, Tony."

"That woman...is she-"

"She is under the same influence as the young man."

"But he...they...I saw-"

"Leave them to us. Your flock needs their shepherd. They're in your care. Do you understand?"

"Yes, uh, I do." The man looked only half aware of his surroundings, but he nodded and moved to the back of the boat.

Stubbs walked to the opposite end. "How is Bert?" he said to April.

"Dead." She was snarling, hair sprouting from her skin, her teeth lengthening. Her cheek was bleeding from the deep tracks of three claws. Her dress lie crumpled on the floor behind her.

"You're little girl is a handful," Ted Bell said. He was on one knee but couldn't stand yet.

"You knew that before tonight," Stubbs said. "I trust you won't take her lightly again."

"I'm going to kill that little demon," April said.

"It seems we have no choice. As much as it pains me to say it, she has chosen to stand against us and therefore against God."

"Whatever," said April. "We should have killed her years ago along with Thomas. If she wasn't your precious daughter-"

"And perhaps if you'd been less interested in fornicating with Ian than in persuading him to join us, we wouldn't have to kill either of them."

"You sent him the little bitch's book, Peter. They're together because of you, not me."

Stubbs backhanded April and she crumbled to the floor. "I've had enough of your insubordination. You will do as I say."

April crouched on the wooden floor, blood from her nose mingling with the blood from her cheek. She snarled with rage but wouldn't strike back at Peter.

"Take your fury out on my traitorous daughter," Peter said, "Then we'll talk about your future."

The boat was emptying fast. Tony Rodanthe had enlisted others to help the elderly off the boat. No one was looking back.

"What about this mess?" Ted Bell said. "All this blood? If someone calls the police..."

"Take Bert into the woods and bury him." Stubbs took off his tie and began unbuttoning his shirt. There will be questions to answer, but as far as anyone knows he left the boat with us, alive."

"Peter, one of them will talk." April tore off a piece of her discarded dress to hold to her bleeding cheek and nose. "One of them must have seen something."

"What do you suggest, that we kill them?" Peter pointed to the last of the congregation climbing off the boat. The rest were already on shore where Pastor Rodanthe appeared to be conducting a head count. "Look at them. They're innocents. When they're all off the boat, dispose of Bert's body."

"Those two will be miles away by then." Ted Bell said. He was still grimacing but he was standing upright now.

Stubbs shook his head. "They came here with a purpose. They won't leave. I'll track them. Join me when you are finished."

Ian sat in the forest and tore off what remained of his clothes. He was still caught between wolf and man, but now that he was away from Peter the imperative to change was lessening. He could probably arrest the process and reverse it altogether, but what then?

Dammit, how could it have gone so wrong? You know how, asshole. Stubbs took control as you lost it. And you ran. You left Milla there-

"Ian?"

Milla was discarding her clothing as she walked, glistening with sweat and covered in fine, white fur, but her body was still that of a woman. When she came closer he saw that her face was smeared with blood.

"I'm sorry, Milla. I didn't mean for it to go this way."

"My father made it happen. He forced you."

"When he put his hands on me I just...How did he do that? He made me change."

"I don't know." Milla shook her head. "There are still things I don't know about him."

"I left you there!"

"I'm glad you did. We needed to get Peter away from the boat. None of those people were hurt."

"They'll come after us."

"They will."

"There are four of them and two of us."

"Three."

"Three?"

"Bert Callet," Milla licked her lips. "He won't be joining us. Or anyone. Ever again."

Her voice went icy in a way that chilled Ian but excited him at the same time.

"We don't have much time," she said.

A howl rose into the night from the direction of the canal. Ian recognized the powerful animal voice of Peter Stubbs. Two more voices answered. The hunt was on.

Ted Bell dug his claws through the carpet of pine needles to grip the soil beneath. His forearm still throbbed from Milla's bite. The transformation knitted the wound well enough to stop the bleeding, but it did little for the pain. It hadn't done much for the ache in his crotch, either. Wolf or man, balls were balls. The nausea had passed, but it would be some time before he recovered from her vice grip.

Peter and April were out there, driving the two renegades in his direction. Ted heard their howls and could tell approximately where they were. If the wind was blowing in his direction he might be able to pinpoint their exact location but it wasn't. That also meant he couldn't rely on smell to alert him to their quarry's approach, either, so he thought it better to stay in hiding until he saw the infidels.

The snap of a twig made Ted's ears stand on end. He heard the tread of a heavy paw not twenty feet away. It had to be that Murphy kid. Another few steps and he would be within striking distance. *He had a lot to learn about stealth.* Stubbs wanted him to just head them off, to occupy them until he and April closed in from behind, but this opportunity was too good to pass up. The boy was alone. Perhaps Milla had struck out to lure her father and April away. Ted didn't care. He only cared that the boy was by himself. This could be over sooner than they'd hoped.

Ten feet from where Ted hid, Ian emerged from a dense thicket. He made far too much noise as he stepped into the narrow clearing. When he fully emerged from the underbrush, Ted saw why. The black wolf was huge, bigger even than Peter Stubbs. So what did you expect? He was a big kid. As a wolf, he was an intimidating sight, but he was still just a pup, too young in the ways of the wolf to be a real threat. Ted had seen his kind come and go, even helped Peter send a few of them to their final reward. They all looked the part, but when it came down to it, they lacked what it took to serve the Lord. He was surprised the pup hadn't turned tail and run, for all the good that would do him.

The black wolf came closer, head down and sniffing. Ted was glad he'd approached the underbrush from the opposite direction. There was no scent on the ground for the big pup to detect.

He had to admit, the way Stubbs' little girl took out Bert was impressive. He'd never seen anyone move with such speed and precision, not even her father. He was sure he could handle this big, black bruiser, but the two of them together? He wouldn't want-

The pup lunged forward and closed his massive jaws on Ted's snout. He tried to cry out, to alert Stubbs and April, but all he could manage was a strangled whine before the black wolf's teeth punched through his palate and clamped his jaws shut.

He knew I was there all along! He's strong. Good Lord, he's strong!

He batted at the black wolf, gouging deep grooves into Ian's muzzle, but the pup kept his grip. Ted dug his claws deeper into the earth, but it did no good. His snout felt like it was on fire. With a great jerk of his powerful neck and shoulder muscles, the black wolf pulled him from his hiding place and flung him to the ground in the clearing. Ted landed on his back, breathless from the impact, but the beast had released his grip. Ted scrambled to his feet, his mouth full of his own blood, his anger rising again. He was frightened and in terrible pain, but he wasn't about to concede defeat to this pup. He started to howl to let Stubbs know where they were, but the agony in his torn mouth wouldn't allow it. All he could do was prepare for the fight of his life.

Milla hit him from the side. He'd seen the white blur from the corner of his eye, but before he could turn his head she closed her jaws on his throat. She was fast, but she was also much smaller. If he could take her down...

He didn't get the chance. Her jaws closed on his throat and she jerked back, tearing a gaping hole in his neck. He had the strange sensation of breathing not through his nose or mouth but through his exposed windpipe. A second later his breath was cut off by his own blood. He coughed and hitched, but there was no taking in another breath. He slumped to the ground and before his mind went blank, he prayed. *Lord, if this is your will then so be it. Be with Peter and April. Deliver your enemies into their hands. I must say though, Lord, she really is beautiful. So beautiful...*

The smells of grease and steel filled the nostrils of the white wolf as he sat concealed in the brush on the slope high above the train trestle. The arch of the crosshatched girders gave the impression of an enormous steel insect spanning the Whitewater River from bank to bank. The tracks were black with grime and age but slick with oil. The shimmering circle of light in the cloudless sky above was reflected on the surface of the water beneath the trestle. The two figures on the bridge moved as quickly as they could while being mindful of their footing. A misstep could send either of them plummeting into the river thirty feet below.

Their plan wasn't a bad one, Stubbs had to give them that, but their intentions were clear. Milla and Ian would cross the river where it narrowed upstream then double back, drawing himself and April farther from town in the process. Staying away from populated areas was a lesson Milla had learned well in her adolescence. The less their kind were seen the better. The Lord knows people had seen enough tonight as it was. So now Milla and Ian were downwind of them, a fact they no doubt considered to be in their favor. Of course, now that they were within eyesight it no longer mattered.

The silver and black wolf waited for Peter's signal. With Bert Callet and, he presumed, Ted Bell gone, she was his oldest disciple. He didn't trust her as he had Bert, but she would be his ally for a time tonight. She'd always loathed his daughter and now that Ian had spurned her and was with Milla, he knew she would relish the opportunity to dispatch her rival. Stubbs felt regret for his daughter. He felt betrayed even more so than when she demanded he no longer be a part of her life. She had chosen once and for all, though, and the will of The Lord would not be denied. If April was unable to kill her, he would do so himself after dispatching Ian. If April lived, he would kill her too and start over. He'd started over before. He had another century to live. There was time.

Ian and Milla were off the trestle now but still on the tracks. Peter knew they would have to leave the tracks for higher ground soon. The railroad passed through a narrow cut in the hill a few hundred yards ahead. There was nowhere to walk on either side. The Halloween Express hadn't made its final return trip to Duck Creek tonight and the cut in the hill was no place to be when it did. The opposite side was sheer rock. There was nowhere for Milla and Ian to go but up the very hill were he sat hidden among the branches of a tree with April in the bushes below. He would have to be quick and April would have to be ruthless. A little good fortune would help as well, but with The Lord on their side, how could they fail?

Ian and Milla were nearing the top of the hill when the attack came. April's impatience got the better of her and she struck without waiting for Peter's signal, a black and silver bolt that shot from the underbrush and bowled Milla over before she could react. The two wolves tumbled downhill toward the tracks, snapping and clawing at each other as they rolled.

The ill-timed attack saved Ian's life. He scanned left and right then looked up just as Stubbs launched himself from the trees overhead. He twisted sideways just in time to avoid the jaws that snapped shut on empty air inches from his throat. Stubbs landed on all fours in front of Ian but rose onto his back legs, a half-man, half-wolf monstrosity. Ian was astonished to see that Stubbs had been able to assume a form intermediate between the two, allowing him to climb trees and launch his attack from above. It was a mastery over the dual nature he'd never dreamed was possible.

Ian hesitated and it was all the opening Stubbs needed. The bipedal wolf man pounced, his left hand closing on the black wolf's right forelimb. He lifted Ian off the ground and forced his head back to expose the underside of his throat. Ian writhed in his grasp and kicked upward with his back legs, driving one hind paw between his own throat and Stubbs' snapping jaws. His black nails raked the nose and lips of the white monster. Stubbs cried out in pain and dropped him. No sooner had Ian hit the ground than he sprung back up, biting and tearing at his adversary.

Milla and April tumbled downhill until they hit a hump in the slope and bounced together onto the tracks. Milla was beneath her larger foe when they hit the steel rails. She would have yelped in pain had the impact not knocked the breath out of her.

April fared better on impact, the smaller white wolf cushioning her landing. Her momentum carried her over Milla, though, and her left leg folded under her as she hit the tracks. She stifled a whimper when she rose and tried to put weight on the limb. It was at least sprained, perhaps even broken. Growling low and mean, she steadied herself on three legs and prepared to continue the assault.

Milla stood but with difficulty. It hurt to breath, her right side burning with hot flashes of agony whenever she moved. Broken ribs, perhaps three or more.

The two damaged creatures faced each other from a dozen feet apart, heads low, their bodies shuddering. When April surged forward on her three good legs, Milla met the charge and they once again joined together into a savage, writhing mass of teeth, claws, and hair.

Ian struck Stubbs across the snout with a sideways swipe of his paw, gaining a momentary advantage when the wolf man fell and landed hard on his back. The black wolf pounced, his teeth driving for the creature's throat. Stubbs jerked sideways and Ian's jaws snapped shut on the thick fur of his shoulder instead of his neck. Ian ripped the mouthful of fur from the wolf man's ruff and spat it out, but the advantage was lost as Stubbs rolled from under him.

They had been fighting for ten minutes without a second's pause. The intense struggle was showing on both. Stubbs' once-lustrous white fur was red with blood from a dozen savage wounds. Three times he had dodged a lethal strike, his left ear was shredded, and his neck and face were lacerated in half a dozen places.

The black wolf was in even worse shape, his wounds not as deep, but they were more numerous. He'd surprised Stubbs with his sheer strength, so the wolf man had adjusted his strategy. He was now intent on bleeding Ian with precision strikes instead of attempting to dispose of him in one brutish rush, relying on his speed and experience instead of going strength against strength with the younger beast.

Stubbs backed up while considering his next move. They'd fought up and down the slope then along the peak. They were above the cut in the hill now, the tracks twenty-five feet below. He dropped to all fours, the better to keep his footing so near the edge. He weighed his options, doing his best to block out the throbbing pain from his multiple wounds. Behind him, the Halloween Express turned into the cut and gathered speed on the downgrade toward the trestle.

The black wolf heard the train, but his attention was fixed on the ghastly white thing in front of him. He couldn't let his focus waver for an instant, not even to consider Milla's possible fate. He only knew she was fighting for her life down there. As for himself, he was nearing the end of his resources. If he didn't deliver the lethal strike soon he would die and all would be lost.

The wolf man feinted left, then right, but Ian wasn't fooled. He launched himself forward and hit the monster with jaws wide open, just missing his opponent's throat as his momentum carried them both over the edge.

The vintage locomotive had been transformed into a haunted house on wheels. Orange and black streamers crossed from corner to corner in the two passenger cars, and plastic skeletons hung from the ceiling. The windows featured vinyl decorations of black cats, tombstones, and other traditional Halloween images.

The theme for this year's festivities was The Wizard Of Oz. The conductor made a satisfying scarecrow with his long-limbed body and tattered straw hat. A cardboard witch leered from one corner of the forward car, hovering over an enormous crystal ball, while a bulbous-headed Oz The Magnificent peered around the curtains in the back of the rear car. In the cab, the engineer sat with his eyes on the track ahead. His elaborate, homemade Tin Man costume was complete with an enormous red plastic heart dangling over his silver chest from an oversized chain. One gloved hand gripped the throttle, the other resting on his lap, inches from the air brake lever.

There were several Dorothys on board. By far the most adorable, a little girl of no more than six sat next to her mother, clutching a large wicker basket containing a stuffed, black Scottie. The conductor had just dropped a mini-bag of jelly beans into her basket when Stubbs and Ian crashed through the roof, a combined five hundred pounds of wolf and wolf man popping the rivets on a section of the overhead sheet metal.

The little Dorothy jumped onto her mothers lap and her eyes went wide. "Werewoofs!" she cried. Several passengers, not all of them children, screamed and scrambled to get as far away from the beasts as possible. The scarecrow, who had come within inches of being flattened, stumbled and fell, striking his head on the floor.

The black wolf rolled over, moaning. He tried to get up, but his legs failed him and he slumped against a seat, breathing hard, a man and his terrified mummy child huddled against the window less than three feet away.

The white wolf man pulled himself first to his knees, bracing himself against another seat, then swayed back and forth as he stood. He spat a broken tooth and a mouthful of blood onto the floor.

"Oh, my god!" A green-haired fairy huddled beneath the faux crystal ball. Her prim little ballerina daughter burrowed into the fairy's chest. "Mommy, I'm scared!"

A man started toward the engineer's cabin in the locomotive but realized he would have to go past the bloodied wolf man to get there and thought better of it. "This can't be real," he muttered.

Over the wolf man's shoulder, the engineer's silver face peered through the glass. His mouth hung open as if he was waiting for Dorothy to oil the hinges in his jaw so he could tell her how everything would be all right if he only had a heart. He reached for the brake, but Ian had regained his feet and barreled into Stubbs, driving them both into the door between the cars. The locomotive door popped off its hinges and slammed into the Tin Man, cracking his plastic heart and knocking him unconscious. The engineer slumped to the floor and the train picked up speed down the long grade.

The two battered female wolves were on the trestle, panting, each marshaling their remaining strength for another assault. The bright white beam of the locomotive washed over them as the train accelerated down the cut. They cast about for a means of escape, but there was none. Their only hope was to make it across the trestle and off the track. They ran, but halfway across it was clear that they weren't going to make it.

The train roared onto the trestle going far too fast. It almost derailed right there but held to the track, the vibration passing under the paws of the fleeing wolves. Milla cast a glance over her shoulder, saw a dark, bulky shape looking down at her from the train, and leaped.

Stubbs attempted to rise, but the black wolf swatted him down with a heavy blow from his forepaw. The wolf man raked Ian with taloned fingers then sank his teeth into the black wolf's side. Ian howled, rearing up in agony and rage in time to see Milla look up at him before she jumped. April was slower to react and Ian felt the jolt of her body against the locomotive's steel.

The wolf man clawed at him with both paws. Ian swatted him down and plunged his snout into the monster's neck. He missed by inches but sank his teeth into Stubbs' collarbone, bit down, and snapped the bone in two. He pinned his weakening foe's head to the floor with his left paw and bunched his shoulder muscles for the final strike just as the train jumped, lurching sideways as it hit the tracks on the other side of the trestle. A second later the cabin tilted and he was thrown off Stubbs as it rolled. He bounced off one wall, the roof, then the other wall. He saw alternating flashes of indigo sky and dark earth, then hit something unyielding and blacked out.

Chapter 22

Batavia, Ohio

Verna tapped her foot in time to the music as she rolled up her long, gravel driveway. Some of the new country was OK with her. Not that Garth Brooks with his rock show theatrics, but this Dwight Yoakum she liked. She could do without some of his lyrics, but she liked his twang.

She stopped the truck at the top of the loop outside her front door. She had groceries to unload and she wanted to be as close as she could get. She waited until the Dwight Yoakum song ended before she took the keys out of the ignition. Just in time, too. As Yoakum faded, the new single by Shania Twain started up. Verna couldn't stand the woman. *The hussy.*

Monday was grocery day for Verna. Both her bakery and the church office were closed so she had the entire day to herself. Thanksgiving was around the corner and she had a full house every year despite having no extended family to speak of. This year she was hosting some friends from the church, and she hoped Ian and his lady friend Milla would be there too. With the spread she'd be putting on the table, there was no such thing as getting started too soon.

She decided she could handle the milk and her keys at the same time without dropping either so she walked to the porch with a gallon. She sat the milk down and was about to insert her key into the lock when she noticed that the doorknob looked strange. She looked closer. *Broken?* Who would break into her house and why? Nothing like that ever happened out here in the sticks, she thought. *Oh, no, Verna? Look at what happened to the sheriff and that Lester Booth fellow. Look at everything that has happened to Ian.*

"Verna."

She jumped at the voice coming from behind the door. Whoever broke the door was in her house. For a moment, she was as frightened as she'd ever been despite the bright sunshine and the warm country air. The voice called to her again, but this time she recognized it and her fear turned on a dime to concern.

"Ian?"

"I'm sorry about the door," he said. He opened it enough for her to hear him more clearly. It was Ian, but he sounded different. He didn't sound well. "I...couldn't go home...not yet."

"Ian, honey, what's wrong?" She pushed at the door, but he was blocking it with his body.

"Promise me. No hospitals. No doctors. No...no police."

"Honey, I don't understand. What are you talking about?"

"I need you to prepare yourself, Verna."

"What?"

"Before I let you in, I need you to prepare yourself. I don't look good."

"You're worrying me, Hon."

"Please, Verna."

"OK. I'm prepared." *Prepared for what?*

She could hear Ian breathing heavily as if their brief conversation had taken a lot out of him. The door opened wider and Verna stepped inside. She was afraid and confused, but she loved Ian like a son. The blinds were closed and the curtains were drawn, but it was almost 1 PM and there was enough light to see by.

Ian closed the door but remained in the corner, half in shadow. He was wrapped in a blue plaid blanket, the pattern partially masking the blood that seeped through the material in places. There was no concealing the lacerations on his face.

"Oh, dear Jesus," Verna gasped. "What happened to you?"

"I've, uh, had better days," Ian said.

"Well, good Lord, sweetie, let's get you...Ian honey, you need a doctor." Verna reached into the pocket of her purple windbreaker and pulled out her phone.

"No!" Ian shuffled forward and put his hand over hers. His hand was matted with dirt and blood. "No doctors. No hospitals. No police. Remember?"

"I...I don't understand."

"Please. I just need to clean up and rest a little." He dropped his hand and pulled the blanket closer around him.

Verna sighed. "Come into the bathroom." They were halfway across the living room when Verna stopped. "Ian? Why is my extra shower curtain on the couch?"

"I didn't want to get anything on the couch. I was going to clean up, but I heard you coming."

Verna led the way to the bathroom and gestured for Ian to sit down. The room was dark, the only window small and covered. She reached for the light and Ian stopped her again.

"I'm sorry, Verna. I really am."

"For what? You're scaring me."

Ian sighed this time. "Turn on the light."

Verna flipped the light switch. When she turned around she jumped back a full foot and gripped the door frame to steady herself. "Oh, Jesus!" Her eyes teared up and her bottom lip quivered. "You've got to tell me. What happened."

"I...I can't. You wouldn't believe me." *And you'd never look at me the same way again.*

Verna stepped closer and lifted Ian's chin, examining his wounds. "Try me." She opened the cabinet and took out a big tube of antibiotic ointment and a box of gauze bandages. She rummaged in the closet for a few seconds and produced more first aid supplies. "Always be prepared."

"Thank you," Ian said.

She took a deep breath and began dabbing at his face with a damp washcloth. "If I didn't know better, I'd swear some of these gashes are a week old, but I saw you two days ago. Some of them are already scabbed over."

"I heal fast."

"You need a doctor." She said it in a firm manner that brooked no disagreement.

Ian tried to sound just as firm. "No. No doctor."

Verna shook her head then began applying ointment and covering the still open wounds with gauze and first-aid tape. One laceration ran from under his left eye past the corner of his mouth. Another ran from the bridge of his nose across his top lip and continued over his bottom lip to his chin. A third wound was shorter but deeper, a ragged gash through the beard along his left jawline. The hair in his beard was crusted with blood and the gash oozed thick and dark. His beard prevented her from covering the gash so she had to be satisfied with cleaning and treating it. Verna tended to all his visible wounds while Ian wondered what, if anything, he could tell her.

"Well now," Verna said as she stepped back. "Let's see what's under that blanket."

"Verna, I...it isn't pretty."

"It can't be worse than your face. You'd be-"

Ian lowered the blanket from his shoulders. His body was a mass of bruises, welts, scrapes, and cuts. His bruised skin was crisscrossed by deep furrows. The furrows were in groups of four parallel lines, some of them covering more than half the width of his body. On his left side a different kind of wound bled freely from deep punctures.

Verna had to cover her mouth to stifle a gasp. Her eyes watered and she reached out to take Ian's hand. "Ian, honey, you've got to go to a hospital," Verna pleaded, tears rolling down her round cheeks. "You're hurt, sweetheart. Bad hurt."

"I know, but I'll be all right." *As soon as I turn into a wolf and back a few more times.* "I've had enough of doctors. They can't help me. I just need you to help me as much as you can."

"This is over my head," Verna said. She wiped her eyes with a towel.

"Please, Verna." Ian tried to smile. "It's not as bad as it looks."

"Yeah. Right. You can't tell me anything and you don't want a doctor. What am I supposed to do? You need more help than I can give you."

Ian started to say something then stopped when a possible explanation for his condition occurred to him. It wasn't a very good explanation, but it was something. "Have you heard any news this morning? Anything about Duck Creek?"

"The train? Good lord, Ian. Were-"

"I was on that train."

"Did you see anything?"

"No."

"How did you get here? Your car isn't outside."

Ian looked down and bit his bottom lip. The pain was considerable, but it was insignificant compared to the ache in his heart. He'd seen Milla go over the side of the trestle. She was dead. She had to be. April was probably dead, too. She'd actually been hit by the train. He made it to Verna's, but the overland journey took him all night even as a wolf. Every step was agony. He was afraid to go home. If Stubbs was still alive he'd go there first. Where else would he expect Ian to go?

"I...I can't explain it."

"We're back to that."

"Yeah. I guess so."

"On the news they said the car with the engine-the locomotive, I guess it's called-detached from the other cars and rolled downhill. The coupling or something or other snapped. The other two cars had a bumpy ride, but they coasted back into town."

"Was anyone killed?"

"No. Some people were pretty banged up, though. They're lucky to be alive."

Ian breathed out and relaxed a little.

"They said there was some kind of commotion on the canal." Verna thought for a moment then appeared to reach a conclusion. "I'll be right back."

"You're not going to-"

'I'm going to get a chair," she said. "This is gonna take a while."

Verna left the bathroom and came back with one of the chairs from her kitchen table. She sat down, but before she resumed tending to Ian, she took another deep breath and wiped her eyes on the towel again. "How about Milla? Was she with you?"

"No." He looked away so the lie wouldn't show in his eyes.

For the next twenty minutes Verna cleaned and dressed Ian's torso and legs in silence but for an occasional comment about the severity of this or that wound. "Well, that's all I can do," she said when she was done. "You really need to-"

"I know. I need to see a doctor." Ian stood, still holding the blanket around his hips. His midsection felt stiff, constrained. Then again, it was almost completely covered by gauze. "Maybe I'll do that," he said, but he doubted she believed him.

"Not only should you see a doctor, but you need to talk to the police about the train. I'm sure they have questions."

"Verna, I-"

"Tell them you wandered here in a daze."

"All the way from Duck Creek?"

"Well, you won't tell me anything."

"I can't."

"I know. I know." Verna sat back. "So were you planning on spending the rest of the day wrapped in a blanket? Where are your clothes, anyway?"

"I, uh..."

"You can't tell me. OK. Come into the living room and rest on the couch. We can put away the shower curtain unless you've got more bloody wounds under that blanket you aren't telling me about."

"No. That's it."

"Thank God for small miracles. I'll run over to your house for some clothes."

"No! I mean, you don't have to do that." He didn't want her anywhere near his house in case Stubbs showed up.

"Don't be silly." Verna led him by the arm into the living room and took the shower curtain off the couch. "Lie down," she said. She left him there for a minute then returned with another blanket and spread it over him. "Take this, at least." She dropped a bottle of ibuprofen into his lap.

"Verna, my house is half an hour away," Ian said as she poured him a glass of water from the kitchen sink. "There's a Meijer and a Walmart right up the road. Just get me some sweats and a t-shirt. Maybe some flip flops. I'll pay you back."

"Ian, you-oh, my goodness!"

"What?"

"My groceries. I left my milk on the porch and my truck is full. Wait here."

In the time it took Verna to bring in the groceries, the pace of the last twenty four hours began to overtake Ian. He was almost asleep by the time she left to buy him some clothes. "Verna?" he said, so groggy he could barely lift his head.

"Yeah, hon?"

"No doctors, remember. Promise?"

She stood in the doorway and sighed. "All right. Promise."

Before falling into an exhausted sleep he hoped it was a promise she would keep.

Ian was sitting next to Kelly in the doorway of the cabin. She was wearing the plaid shirt and jeans he'd last seen her in. The last time he'd seen her clothed, at least. A faint voice in his head asked a question; *Do you wear the clothes you die in forever?*

She was as beautiful as he remembered, perhaps even more so. Everything about her was perfect. Had that ever been true or did she only exist that way in his memory? Surely there had been imperfections, a tooth that was not quite straight, a subtle acne scar on the side of her nose that was only visible from a certain angle. Anything. He searched her face. It was flawless.

He still loved Kelly. He'd left a part of his heart with her that he'd never get back.

He loved Milla, too. She was also gone now. Was it always going to be that way for him, that the women he truly loved would never survive? Did good things never last?

Kelly embraced him. Her fingers stroked the thick black fur around his shoulders. She kissed his scarred face and whispered into his ear.

"He's coming."

Ian sat up. He was still on Verna's couch, but he could smell Kelly's sweet scent. He wanted to be with her, especially now that Milla was also gone. Perhaps in whatever visionary world he sometimes found himself in there was a place for both. And for Chevy. His mother and father, too.

He started to drift off again to that place of rest. *Wake up! It was a dream, nothing more. It was just your mind engaging in some wishful thinking. It was just a great, big, fucking 'if only.'*

"He's coming."

He could still hear her whispering into his ear.

Ian grimaced and rolled his head around on his shoulders. He had a kink in his neck and no idea how long he'd been asleep. He couldn't stay much longer. Tonight was a full moon. His hunger flared at the same time he noticed the smell of food.

"It's about time you woke up." Verna came into the living room carrying a tray and sat it on the coffee table in front of the couch. "I fixed dinner. I've been home for a few hours. You sat up and mumbled then went right back to sleep."

"I don't remember."

"I'm not surprised. You were really out of it."

"What time is it?"

"I checked on you a couple of times." The tray was loaded with pan fried chicken, mashed potatoes with gravy, and green beans. "Eat up."

"What time is it, Verna?"

"Clock's right up there." She pointed at the wall behind the couch. "It's a little after five."

"Where are the clothes?" He tried not to sound like it was urgent, but it came out that way.

"Right there." Verna indicated a plastic bag at the foot of the couch. "I bought the biggest flip flops I could find. I don't know how you ever find shoes in your size at the store."

"I'll pay you back." Ian reached for the bag.

"Don't worry about it."

"I need to get dressed, Verna. Can you give me a few minutes."

"Why are you in such a hurry? Eat something first, for cryin' out loud."

"I have to meet someone." *He's coming.*

"Meet someone? Honey, I've been thinking. Don't worry. I didn't call a doctor but...you took an arrow to the chest a month ago. You're doing pretty well for someone as banged up as you are, but..."

"But what?" Ian took a black T-shirt and a pair of gray sweatpants out of the bag.

"You have a scar on your chest, but it looks like it's a year old. You're all cut up, too, but it doesn't look like that happened yesterday. Most of those wounds look days old, at least. Some of them look a week old. What's happening?"

"I don't have time to explain. I think you're right about the doctor. If it'll put your mind at ease, you can take me to the ER after I eat. I need to get dressed first, though."

"Uh, huh." Verna clearly didn't buy his sudden change of heart, but she didn't push it. "I've got some tea in the fridge. I'll get you a glass."

When she was out of the room, Ian gave some thought to bolting out the door. The urge was building in his body. He itched all over and his joints ached, but he didn't want to run out on Verna like that. He still had an hour before sundown and he needed to eat. He was weak from hunger and he needed the calories. If Stubbs was coming, he would need all the strength he could get. He had no intention of letting Verna take him to the hospital. He would dress, eat, then get as far away from her house as he could.

The black T-shirt had a bright green baby T-rex emerging from a beige egg silkscreened on the front. The sweatpants were too big in the waist, but the drawstring would hold them on for as long as he intended to wear them.

"I'm decent," he called to Verna. By the time she came into the room with a tall glass of iced tea, he was halfway through one of the two chicken breasts on the plate. She sat the glass on the coffee table and picked up the blanket Ian had laid on the end of the couch. She started down the hallway toward the stairs to her laundry room in the basement but stopped, frowning and picking at the fabric.

"There are black hairs all over this blanket."

"What?' Ian said, but she didn't hear him. *Had I changed while I was asleep? Was Verna here when it happened?* His body must have been healing itself by transforming without him even willing it to happen, he thought. Ian looked down at his midsection. The bandages were looser. *Oh, God. If she'd seen me...*

Ian could hear Verna's feet on the basement steps. She was back in another minute and she sat across from Ian with her own plate in her lap. They ate in silence, but Ian was aware that she was looking at him between bites. He was afraid of what he would see in her face if he looked up.

"You were making noises," Verna said. "While you were asleep. I could hear you from the kitchen. It sounded like you were having a nightmare."

"What...what kind of noises?"

Verna started to answer but stopped when a deep, powerful howl came from somewhere outside the house.

"Good Lord," she said. "What is that?"

Ian swallowed hard. "He's here." He pulled off the T-shirt and kicked off the flip flops.

"What are you doing?" she said.

Ian put his hands on her shoulders. His pulse was racing in addition to the ache in his joints. "Verna, you have to leave."

"Leave? What-"

"Where's your truck?"

"It's at the top of the loop near the door. I thought we were going to the emergency room after dinner. Your bandages..," Verna said.

"It'll have to wait. Verna, please listen to me. There are things you don't-"

The howl sounded again. Ian thought it lacked the vigor and volume this time, but it was closer. *He's calling me out. He's in bad shape, but he's calling me out.* "I thought he would go to my house, but he tracked me here." Ian was looking over Verna's head as he spoke.

"What? Who tracked you? What are you talking about?"

"I don't have time to explain. You have to listen to me." He squeezed her shoulders harder than he intended then relaxed his grip when her eyes grew wide. "You're not safe here. You have to leave!"

"What about you?"

"I have to go out there. It's me that he wants."

"He? Honey, that's an animal out there. You can't go out there half naked and..."

Ian took Verna's hand and led her to the kitchen door. He opened it enough to look outside just as Stubbs howled a third time. The howl was short, impatient, angry. And closer still.

"The barn," Ian said. "He's in the barn." Stubbs didn't want to reveal himself to Verna, he thought. He didn't want her involved, most likely had no intention of killing her if he didn't have to. The man's mind was a twisted maze Ian would never comprehend, but at least that meant it was safe for Verna to go to her truck and leave.

"I'm calling the sheriff," Verna said then winced and tried again. "I'll call the station."

"Hell, drive straight there! It doesn't matter as long as you leave."

"I can't just leave you!" Verna said. She spoke out loud, doing her best to sound logical, reasonable. "I'll call Ricky. He'll know what to do."

"No! You have to leave." Ian glanced out the door at the sky. The sun was lowering fast. He should have already left. He'd have to change to deal with Peter. "I'm going out there. When I do, you run for your truck and get away from here. Go to the sheriff's office, the church, wherever. Just-"

Verna reached up and touched Ian's bandaged cheek. "I can't leave you. We can leave together."

Ian took a deep breath, put his hand over Verna's, and looked into her eyes. "Verna, there are things you don't want to know. Things I don't *want* you to know. Out there in the barn, it's not what you think it is. Please. Go."

"Dear Jesus-"

"Jesus isn't going to help!" Ian spat the words out, his anger flaring. "He hasn't been around. I don't expect him to show up now."

Verna wiped a tear from his cheek.

"I'm sorry, Verna." He stepped out of the door, away from her outstretched hand. "Please. Leave now." He turned away from her and walked toward the barn.

By the time Ian reached the barn door his nails were sharp and black, his canines jutting over his lower lip. The wounds on his face tingled and burned while his torso throbbed. The barn door was half open and the sharp smell of the rusted metal runners mingled with the tang of congealed blood and half-healed wounds. Underlying it all was the musky scent of the white wolf.

Ian glanced back at the house. The kitchen door was still open. Verna was nowhere in sight and her truck sat empty at the top of the drive. He turned back to the barn, stepped out of his sweats, and walked through the door.

A blinding pain struck Ian behind his left ear, his knees buckled, and he fell forward onto his face. For a moment he could see nothing but white as the pounding in his skull overwhelmed all his senses. He tried to rise and managed to get to his knees when he was struck again, a loud crack echoing in the barn. He landed facedown in the dirt, wondering for a second if it was something in his back that had cracked. He groaned and rolled over, the taste of his own blood in his mouth.

"Well, I'd say this has served its purpose."

Ian forced himself to focus past the pain and look up at the face. Peter Stubbs stood over him holding the wooden cross in his right hand. One of the crossbars had split on the second blow, a long sliver of wood on the ground a few feet away.

"I'd use this to finish my work," Stubbs snarled through bloodied, black lips, "but it would dishonor my Savior to kill you with the symbol of His sacrifice." He dropped the broken cross on the ground.

Ian's head pulsed with pain and his entire body ached. Dark, wet streaks bloomed through the gauze still clinging to his abdomen.

Stubbs was a mass of dried blood and filthy, matted fur. He was caught between wolf and man, too damaged to complete the transformation one way or the other. The fur and skin on one side of his head had been peeled back, a glimpse of blood-smeared skull visible. The left side of his ribcage was swollen and black, a wide gash showing deep red muscle. His left arm was folded against his chest, the broken collarbone above it pushing against the skin.

"I may not look like much at the moment," Stubbs snarled, "But time heals all wounds, as they say. Time and The Lord. I am more than capable of finishing His work tonight."

Ian braced himself, searching for the strength to fight a little longer, when a deafening explosion filled the barn. Blood and singed fur spattered Ian's chest. Stubbs staggered forward, almost falling.

Verna Cooper stood in the doorway, a double barreled shotgun gripped in her pudgy hands. "You get away from him, you demon, or I'll send you back to Hell! I still know how to use this thing." She reached for the wall beside the door and flipped the light switch. Yellow light from the single bulb suspended overhead filled the barn and Verna almost dropped the gun, gasping in disbelief and horror.

Stubbs wobbled then looked at her. His face was smeared with blood, but his gaze was strong.

Confused and shocked, Verna's grip on the shotgun loosened. It was all the chance Stubbs needed. He bolted at Verna and before she could raise the gun, he yanked it from her hands, threw it against the wall, and backhanded her. She crumbled at his feet but rolled over and looked at him, blood flowing from her busted nose.

"I had no intention of killing you, Ms. Cooper, but if it is God's will, so be it."

Ian made it to all fours. His arms and legs were shaking, but he was about to launch himself at Stubbs when he glimpsed the broken cross lying on the floor. His hands closed around the long, unbroken beam and he stood, disregarding the pounding in his head and the racking pain in his shoulders, back, and sides. "No!" Ian screamed and he swung the cross like a hammer as Stubbs bunched his muscles to pounce on the stunned woman.

Stubbs turned instead and the cross struck him square in the chest. The point of the splintered crossbar drove through flesh, bone, organ, bone, and more flesh, erupting from his back in a spray of gore and gristle. He dropped to his knees, the long end of the cross digging into the dirt floor, stopping his fall. Stubbs remained propped upright and he looked up at Ian, his red eyes wide. He opened his mouth to speak, but only coughed, spraying blood over the wood. He looked at the cross, his hands gripping then caressing the rough surface. After a few seconds his hands dropped, his head lolled against the cross, and his body went slack.

Ian knelt before Stubbs and looked into his eyes. For a few seconds the preacher focused on Ian then his eyes went blank and a final gurgling breath left his body.

The sky was darker, the day all but gone. Ian was exhausted, but he could still feel the change coming over him.

Verna regained her feet and staggered over to Ian. She knelt and started to wrap her arms around him but stopped. "Oh, dear Jesus!" She pulled back, her lips trembling. She saw the thin, dark hair covering him, his sharp, black nails, and pointed ears. And his teeth.

There was a noise behind her, a soft exhalation followed by the scraping sound of something being dragged through the dirt. Verna turned and nearly fell backward. Inside the doorway stood a slender white wolf. The animal was dirty, wet, and bloodied. Its left rear leg hung awkwardly from its hip, dragging on the ground.

"Verna!" Ian's eyes went wide at the sight. "It's all right!"

"No! No! This is not all right!" She stumbled, fell, then made it to the shotgun. When she picked it up and turned, the white wolf was licking Ian's bloodied face.

"It's OK, Verna." Ian wrapped his arms around the white wolf. The wolf flinched and yelped then nuzzled against Ian. "It's Milla."

"Milla?" Verna sagged then appeared to recall Stubbs' assault on her in a moment of weakness. She stood up as strong and straight as she was able and raised the gun again.

"There was no way to tell you, to explain about..," *about The Blessing*, he wanted to say, but he couldn't. "It's all right," were the last words he could manage before the full change came over him.

Verna stared, her mouth hanging open as the man she'd known since he was a boy transformed. His body lengthened, lowered, darkened, and changed until a huge black wolf sat in his place. "Jesus," she whispered.

The wolf took slow, deliberate steps toward her. Verna raised the gun again for a moment then lowered it. She was breathing heavily through her mouth, her shattered nose too full of blood to draw in air. The wolf came closer with the smaller white wolf behind. The gauze on his torso strained against his barrel-like ribs, the bandages on his face hanging loose. Another three steps and he was upon her.

Verna looked into the wolf's eyes. She saw no malice, no anger, none of the boiling madness she'd seen in the eyes of the thing that had been Peter Stubbs. "Dear Jesus," she whispered and dropped to her knees. She set the gun down and reached with a trembling hand to touch the wolf's head. She peeled the sagging gauze from his snout. "Ian?" The black wolf licked her hand.

Verna was aware of the white wolf standing back, unwilling to interrupt. She beckoned and Milla joined them for a few seconds then pulled back, looking over her shoulder, her ears erect at the sound of approaching sirens.

"Oh," Verna said, her eyes full of wonder. "Ricky. And an ambulance. When you...when you went outside I called him. I'm sorry." A few seconds later, bright lights turned into her long driveway. "Can you understand me?"

The black wolf glanced toward the light, then at the white wolf and back to Verna. He licked her face. All three of them regarded the limp, mangled body of Peter Stubbs.

"You have to leave," Verna said. "I'll think of something."

The black wolf looked at her then at his smaller companion. They both gave Stubbs' mangled body a last look, the white wolf lingering a moment longer, then they were gone.

Chapter 23

June 2003
Stonelick, Ohio

The black wolf rose to his feet in the moonlit cemetery. He was reluctant to go. The smaller white wolf sat near him as he spent half an hour at the side by side graves of his parents. After that it was Chevy. His grave was the length of a football field from Rose and Henry Murphy's. Ian touched his teenage friend's marker with a paw and whined.

Verna fielded multitudes of questions about the mess in her barn. She doubted Ricky bought her answers, but she didn't care. The deputies were at a loss to account for the surreal tableau. The scene that greeted them when they arrived was beyond any rational explanation; a bloodied, sixty-ish woman, the obvious signs of struggle, and in the center of the barn like some macabre idol or sacrifice, a thing that was neither fully man nor animal impaled on a broken, bloody cross. No answer Verna gave to their questions was satisfactory, but in a time the questions ceased, their will to pursue the matter not strong enough to make the difficult swim upstream against the preconceptions about reality most people, law enforcement included, use to make sense out of life.

Ricky Thorogood was officially elected sheriff the next year. He was open about his dislike of Ian, a fact that didn't score any points with Verna, but despite that, she liked the new sheriff. He was a good man who didn't need to know the truth. Not that he would believe it. While she was sad to see Ian sell his house and move, she understood. He hadn't lived there for much of the last three years, anyway.

Some of the passengers on the Halloween Express in 2000-the last Halloween Express ever-turned a profit selling their stories to the tabloids. Two were even interviewed on TV, their faces hidden by carefully controlled lighting. Few believed their stories of "animal men" fighting aboard the train except the cryptozoology crowd. And Verna. She believed.

Milla took a position on the faculty of a small private college near Duluth, Minnesota. She published a third book, a novel that was far less fiction than her publisher imagined. The sales were modest, but she was happy. Her second book was standard fare among college courses now. That brought her the most satisfaction.

It was over a year before she was able to walk without the aid of a cane. Her doctors were amazed that she walked again at all. To them, her recovery was nothing short of miraculous. Eighteen months after she went off the bridge in Duck Creek, she walked down the aisle without help, and she and Ian became husband and wife.

Things didn't go smoothly for Ian. Ricky stopped asking Verna about the horror show in her barn, but he was determined to uncover the truth about Matthew Kearsey's death, and he insisted that Ian knew more than he'd let on. The stories on the local and national news comparing the deaths of Lester Booth and Sheriff Kearsey with those of Kelly Shepherd and Charles Patella only added fuel to Ricky's fire. The conversations Ian had with Ricky felt more like interrogations and they both knew the most important factor driving the questions was the long-ago confrontation between them in Ian's driveway. Eventually, though, Ricky had to admit that there was simply no concrete evidence linking Ian with the sheriff's death. The only physical evidence at the site were animal tracks and coarse, white hairs of canine affinity. Like the three previous deaths, the cause was listed simply as "animal attack"

Peter Stubbs left no outstanding debts. DNA evidence, still a new science at the time, established that the monstrous corpse in Verna Cooper's barn was indeed what remained of the minister. He left behind a will that named Milla Andersen as the only beneficiary. She inherited a not-insubstantial amount of money as well as a small house on five acres of wooded land in a remote area of Minnesota. Milla sold the property and set up a fund to pay for her mother's care in perpetuity, keeping only enough to make a down payment on a house near Duluth, seven miles from the college.

The decomposed body of Bert Callet was found by some hikers in a shallow grave outside Duck Creek. Ted Bell was presumed missing along with April White.

June 2003
Stonelick, Ohio

The black wolf nuzzled the words engraved on Kelly Shepherd's marble tombstone. He had hoped to see her again, to hear something other than the warning she'd whispered to him at Verna's house. He wanted to tell her one last time that he was sorry. It wasn't to be.

The sale of his house was complete. Ian didn't care who owned it or what became of the house. There was nothing there for him now but memories and too many of them were bad.

He turned to his white companion and licked her muzzle. It was time to go. They trotted together to the fence and cleared it with a powerful leap. The pair hit the ground running and sped downhill toward the woods. Once under its cover they slowed and moved together toward their future.

Across the road from the cemetery, Ricky Thorogood sipped on a coffee gone cold and nodded. He'd watched the wolves the entire time they were there. The big black one was Ian Murphy. He had no doubt about that even though he had no idea how that could be. The smaller white one? He didn't know, but he was sure of one thing; werewolves were real. What's more, Matthew Kearsey had known it, too, and it cost him his life. Ricky was still convinced Ian had something to do with Matt's death. He at least knew something about it. Ian's white friend? She knew something, too, he concluded. She had to. Ricky didn't believe in coincidences. He did believe in mercy, though. Matt had taught him the value of that when he saw more to Ricky than just another worthless, small-town punk. He watched Ian grieve at the graves of his parents, his friend, and last of all, at Kelly's.

Ricky started his car, turned on his headlights, and pulled out of his spot among the bushes. It was almost 2 AM, but Bob Longstreet would still be at the bar. He would be closing by now, but Bob always opened the door for him, and a tall, cold one sounded like just the ticket.

Thank Yous and All That Jazz

This beast has been a long time coming. Distilling life experiences, perspectives on religion, ethics, morality, and finding one's place in the world into 120,000-some odd words, all the while keeping in mind the narrative thrust of the story, has been a challenge.

I would like to encourage those interested to look into some real-life events and places that colored this story. The Werewolf of Bedburg really did exist. His strange, grisly story should be familiar to many of those interested in werewolf folklore, but is worth looking into. Duck Creek is inspired by the real town of Metamora in Indiana, a charming village where you can take a boat along the canal and ride in a vintage locomotive. The North American Wolf Studies Center was inspired by The International Wolf Center in Ely, Minnesota, a fantastic place with a worthy mission. Likewise for the Wolf Creek Habitat And Rescue in Brookville, Indiana. Magic awaits you there.

My heartfelt thanks to those who read this manuscript in its many forms over the years, from the initial behemoth to its current form. (Do you really want to know the history of the Stubbs family lineage from 16th century Germany to the present day? It's in there, as well as thorough backgrounding of both Milla Andersen and Verna Cooper. Trust me, it was good for me to know but...) Huge thanks to my nephew David Burris and editor extraordinaire Jill Ripley Hughes (both of whom saw the pearl at the heart of this mess), the Cincinnati Fiction Writers for encouragement (shoutouts to Nik and Wendi for being truth tellers), David Washburn for friendship and comments, and the coffee shops that fueled this project with innumerable mochas, chief among them Forager and the late great Main Cup both in Milford, Ohio (not to forget the recently lamented Coffee Please in Madeira, Ohio.). Thanks to Mark Sund for digital assistance. Huge thanks to my kind and wonderful son Evan and my creative, inspiring daughter Gillian. A huge thank you also to the fine family of folks at Trader Joe's in Kenwood, Ohio for understanding and encouragement (I have a book signing next Saturday...). I could and no doubt should name many others, but a big blanket thank you to those not specifically named will have to suffice.

Support your local independent bookstore. They deserve it so much. Here in the Greater Cincinnati Area that includes but is by no means limited to The Bookmatters in Milford, The Cincy Bookrack in Anderson, The Tome in Mount Washington, Joseph Beth Booksellers in Norwood, and The Hidden Chapter in Fort Thomas, Kentucky.

Lastly, a long list of books, movies, and music inspired and accompanied me on this journey. I mentioned several within these pages, movies like *The Wolf Man* (1941, please) and books such as *Murcheston: The Wolf's Tale* by David Hollandd and *The Wolf's Hour* by Robert McCammon. Many other books and movies could be called out, but I'll leave them to you to discover. (You may even find some treasures I have missed.) I have listed a soundtrack of sorts on the next page. It is unapologetically 90's in nature and some of the bands are rather obscure (a couple being local to Cincinnati) but all are well worth a listen. I was told that taken as a whole it was "dark as a storm cloud" but so be it. (R.I.P., Mark Linkous. We are fortunate to have your music.)

A soundtrack of sorts to enhance your experience.

"It's A Wonderful Life" by Sparklehorse

"Ball And Chain" by Social Distortion

"Sack Of Religion" by 16 Horsepower

"Bloodstained Glassman" by Hogscraper

"That Is All" by Slobberbone

"Heart Of Darkness" by Sparklehorse

"Happy Man" (Memphis version) by Sparklehorse

"Grim" by Ass Ponys

"People Who Died" by The Jim Carroll Band

"How To Get To Heaven" by The Willard Grant Conspiracy

"Wild Flower" by The Cult

"Big Brown Eyes" by Old 97s

"Your Church Is Red" by The Black Heart Procession

"True Believer" by Superdrag

"I See The Light" by Cracker

"Brimstone Rock" by 16 Horsepower